Lincoln 9
A Tale of Serial Homicide

by

Dave Freedland

Aakenbaaken & Kent

Lincoln 9
A Tale of Serial Homicide

Aakenbaakeneditor@gmail.com

ISBN: 978-1-938436-49-9

Dedication:

This book is dedicated to Linda, whose continued support has made a career in law enforcement possible.

Chapter 1

April 1979

When she failed to show for Sunday brunch, concern arose in his gut that something was seriously wrong. Bethany was meticulous in her habits and punctuality was never an issue for a daughter whose job it was to maintain the schedules of others. As a secretary at one of the county's largest aerospace firms, John Crutchfield's daughter was over an hour late for their regular monthly brunch at El Torito Grill, and her apartment phone provided no response beyond the cheerful recorded greeting. The call for service was broadcast routinely, "39-Bravo 31 with Bravo 42 to follow, handle a welfare check at number 23 Serenade, female, white, 26, Bethany Crutchfield failed to show for appointment, no response by 10-21 (telephone)."

Officer Jim MacNeal put his Ford cruiser into drive and headed toward the Stonecliff Meadows Apartment complex, portions of which, he recalled, were still in their final phases of construction. Having spent the first three years of his police career in Los Angeles County, Jim was still adjusting to the slower pace of handling these rather mundane calls, instead of the customary Sunday domestic brawls following football half-times. His follow-up officer, Terry Nemeth, had transferred from neighboring Costa Mesa, and actually welcomed the interruption of radio silence with an opportunity to stretch his legs.

The ground level apartment was dark with the shades drawn and porch light on. There was no response to the doorbell, heavy knock, or the usual police announcements. MacNeal and Nemeth walked to the rear and found the elevated window ajar enough to slide it fully open. Not wide enough for Nemeth due to his Sam Browne gun belt and his fondness for bagels.

MacNeal, on the other hand, epitomized compactness. With a quick lift from Nemeth, MacNeal disappeared through the drawn curtains.

He stood in the darkened master bedroom straining for night vision. Scanning for threats, MacNeal's head snapped right, catching a nude feminine silhouette lying on her back on the queen sized-bed, legs canted outward 45 degrees and separated the width of a yardstick. Her head was propped with a pillow and wrapped in a water soaked bath towel that covered all facial features.

MacNeal sprinted to the front door, threw the deadbolt, and darted back to the bedroom yelling "927" to his partner, signaling "unknown trouble, or possible dead body." He threw the light switch up, taking a mental note to remind detectives that the switch was off upon his initial entry into the room. Nemeth lumbered across the threshold, hearing MacNeal's tone change from urgency to resignation, with his pronouncement of "927-D," indicating a dead body. Nemeth found MacNeal leaning over the bed, holding the now unraveled towel in his left hand, revealing the battered face, fixed eyes gazing at the ceiling, and matted blonde hair cascading to the shoulders.

Nemeth glanced at the pooling blood, marking the bottom side of her extremities and commented, "Post mortem lividity."

MacNeal retorted, "Don't need lividity to show she's dead, man. Check out the strangle marks around her neck, and the trauma to her skull."

Nemeth knelt down to peer at the small, framed photo on the nightstand, depicting the victim with a brunette of equal beauty clothed in bridesmaid's attire. "She was a looker, Jim," Nemeth said flatly as MacNeal keyed his pack-set radio calling for a supervisor.

Quickly surveying the scene for evidence, the officers thought the apartment's rooms displayed troves of clues, but detectives would ultimately determine what was relevant. For the moment, however, MacNeal and Nemeth's job was to lock down the scene and canvass neighbors.

~

Number 23 was located in the last building in the complex, with eight units left to be completed. The Stonecliff Meadows were to be the final phase of six apartment projects in the Village of Stoneridge, an enclave in the City of Irvine, a community with a population just under 100,000. unlike the rest of Orange County, Irvine was destined to be a master planned community with a diverse group of inhabitants. Officers in Irvine had to be able to converse intelligently on a car stop with a corporate CEO and ten minutes later form sentences which could be translated only by hard-core gangbangers who just happened to be passing through.

As Nemeth wrapped the requisite yellow tape around the ficus tree near the front walkway, Patrol Sergeant Billy Briscoe briefed Detective Sergeant George Hoskins on the general details concerning the crime scene. Briscoe was old school and had come to the organization years prior when the Department was formed by absorbing a core group of Costa Mesa officers who patrolled the few residential tracts that were interspersed between the orange groves. He wanted to get his officers cleared as soon as possible, and have the scene turned over to detectives because the calls were starting to stack up.

Hoskins also came over from Costa Mesa. He was a forty-something goal-oriented and no nonsense guy with a reputation for finding parolees at large.

"Whattaya got Billy?"

"Well, we gotta welfare check, George, and found a female homicide victim inside. She was a no-show for Sunday brunch.

Nemeth and MacNeal made entry through a rear, unlocked window and found her on the bed."

"You guys call the coroner?"

"No, waited for you to make that call. We did call the grief counselors to meet with Officer Jackson, who was with the father making the death notification."

~

MacNeal ascended the stairs to Number 25, located directly above the victim's apartment, and rang the doorbell. An elderly man in his 70s peered through the drapes on the side window and then opened the door upon recognizing the uniform. Following the obligatory greetings, Mr. Vern Perkins invited MacNeal in and recounted his observations from the previous 24 hours.

"Do you live here alone?" MacNeal opened.

"Yes, my wife passed on about two years ago, and I sold our house before moving in here last month," Perkins responded as he put a coffee pot into the coffeemaker.

"Sorry for your loss. Do you know how long Miss Crutchfield lived here?"

"Not really. She was here when I moved in, nice gal, pretty as one of those magazine models selling makeup. Of course, many young lads came a courting, but her place was always quiet – none of that loud partying stuff like those guys across the way."

"Did you hear anything unusual last night?" MacNeal thought, as he asked the question, that the body looked deceased no more than 12 hours.

"Well yeah, now that you mention it, there was a commotion around midnight. Sounded like an argument but lasted only about five minutes."

"Were there voices, objects being thrown, or both?"

"Couldn't make out more than loud voices and maybe a thud or two against the wall."

"Did you consider calling the police?"

"Not really. My hearing's not the best, and I wasn't certain that it wasn't the TV mixed with other noises."

MacNeal thought to himself, *People call us if their neighbor's garbage cans are left out a couple hours after trash pickup, and this guy doesn't call when a murder's happening under his nose.*

Across the greenbelt separating the buildings, the first set of investigators on scene, Detectives Nancy Ballesteros and Phil Rasmussen, were completing a canvass of adjacent apartments and received a response at the door to Number 35. Ballesteros looked younger than her 41 years but had enough experience in the Bureau to maintain a modicum of respect from her male peers. Rasmussen, however, looked older and appeared to have long since abandoned frequenting fitness centers.

Greeting them at the door stood a tall, lanky college-aged kid clad in baggie swim trunks and flip-flops, somewhat dismayed at the presentation of credentialed wallets, golden shields, and the hammers and fixed sights of semi-auto pistols protruding beyond the edges of suit coats. Blake Gruden, a third-year biology major from the University of California, Irvine, had stayed behind from a day at the beach with his roommates to swim a few laps in the pool before studying for his mid-terms.

Following a sanitized summary of the crime involving his attractive neighbor, now turned corpse, Gruden's eyes widened and jaw descended, leaving both detectives with an idea how professors must feel when they talk over the heads of their students.

"Did you know the gal in Number 23?" Ballesteros began, sizing him up.

"Well, I didn't know much about her, but we all kind of looked forward to sunny weekends, when she sometimes went down to the pool in a swimsuit or bikini, 'cause she made quite an entrance."

"Did you or your roommates hear any noises from her apartment last night?" Rasmussen asked.

"No, we were studying pretty late into the evening, but the stereo was going really loud, and those of us who didn't care for the Hendrix album that kept playing put headsets on to listen to our own stuff."

"Did you ever see Ms. Crutchfield date anyone?" Ballesteros continued.

"Oh yeah, she dated a lot of different guys, but she had a boyfriend who she seemed to break up with, and make up with, in between the other dudes that she would see."

"Do you know the boyfriend's name?"

"No, but he would come around the complex when they weren't dating, I think just checking up."

"How did you know when they had broken up?" inquired Rasmussen, suddenly alerted by a potential motive.

"The volume in his voice tended to be louder than normal, and he would leave the apartment looking pissed off. After that, you would see her leave in the evenings with different guys – usually executive types, early 30's."

"Did you ever observe her boyfriend abuse her or display any indication of force against her?"

"No, you could tell the guy was frustrated with the relationship – my roommates thought he was an asshole, but I thought he was kind of a nerd."

Rasmussen and Ballesteros left to meet with Hoskins, and provide their supervisor with an update for his checklist. Ballesteros quipped to Rasmussen, "Don't you find it interesting that the college kid in #35 had that kind of detail on the victim's relationship with her boyfriend and her other male suitors?"

"Not really. When you're a college aged guy living across from a gal that looks that good, you pay attention. You fantasize what your chances are."

Ballesteros looked at her partner's physique, thinking that he clearly lived that scenario, but remained at the fantasy stage. She jotted notebook apartment numbers to check that evening for residents missed, as well as the security guard who might have been on site to patrol the areas still under construction.

~

Crime Scene Investigator Andrew Norbett snapped 35 mm shots from his Zeiss camera, capturing overall shots of the bedroom before focusing in on specific pieces of evidence. Two chairs in the front living room were overturned, and three drops of blood stained the carpet below the archway at the head of the hallway leading to the two back bedrooms. The one bedroom was undisturbed, devoid of any personal effects, and clearly not inhabited by a roommate. The larger bedroom where the victim's body still rested showed signs of a struggle. The bedspread, soaked in several spots with blood, was draped over one corner of the mattress with the remainder wrapped around a bedpost at the foot of the bed.

Curiously, the sheets were water soaked around the body, with a trail of water spots across the carpet leading to the shower in the bathroom. Interspersed along the water trail were droplets of blood, whose obvious origin could be attributed to the five inch gash in the side of the victim's head. Of particular interest was the partial bloody palm print on the bathroom doorjamb five feet up from the floor. The opaque shower glass bore moisture along the bottom edges, and traces of blood lined the grates of the drain. Neither the windows nor doors showed signs of forced entry, but were nonetheless dusted scrupulously for fingerprints.

Norbett turned toward Crutchfield's lifeless body, grotesque and hauntingly still, having undergone a most violent conclusion to her 26 years of existence. Snapping the shutter quickly, he covered every angle, making certain that nothing would be lost when the body was moved. Norbett then focused on the plasma-like milky liquid appearing to have oozed from between her legs. Taking a cotton swab, he swabbed the material that remained on the sheets, waiting for the arrival of the coroner for the collection of portions remaining on the body.

Norbett's head turned toward a shadow in the doorway, recognizing Orange County Sheriff Crime Scene Technician Randy Calloway who had arrived at the request of Sergeant Hoskins. Under an agreement with the County, Irvine detectives would summon County investigative resources to assist in the collection and analysis of evidence at major crime scenes. Calloway had been a familiar face for several years and was within striking distance of his magic date for retirement. After being briefed by Norbett, they both looked at the bloody doorjamb with puzzlement. Since the palm print's impression had been left in blood, it could not be dusted and collected onto a print card.

"How about a one to one photo of the print, and have a copy sent to the County for comparisons?"

"We can saw a section of the doorjamb off, and I'll book it into evidence," Norbett said.

"Sounds good. Anyone in particular that we will be comparing it with?" Calloway asked.

"Not yet."

~

As Sgt. Hoskins entered the bedroom to assess the progress of the evidence collection, he was followed by Deputy Coroner Rhonda Cunningham, who had arrived on scene following her first call of the day, a hanging suicide in a garage in Garden Grove. Cunningham was a 43 year old, 5'2" bundle of energy with a blonde ponytail, who ran marathons and processed dead bodies with dispassion. After she had taken thermometer readings, fingernail scrapings, and cataloging of injuries, Hoskins turned to her and asked, "Well, whattaya think?"

"Preliminarily, I think the time of death was between 11:00 pm to 2:00 am. The petichial hemorrhaging in the eyes indicates strangulation, and I've seen the wrapping of the head once before involving post-mortem sex," Cunningham stated clinically.

"Wonderful, this should result in some interesting interrogations," Hoskins said.

"We'll shoot for early Monday afternoon for the autopsy."

Hoskins gathered the detectives and patrol officers on the front walkway of the apartment to recap preliminary findings and begin the task of assigning responsibilities for back-grounding the victim and identifying potential suspects. The victim's family, employer, boyfriend, girlfriends, security guard, remaining neighbors, and leasing staff were identified for follow up and assigned to additional detectives arriving on scene. Although Rasmussen's primary responsibility was robbery-homicide, clearly a crime of this magnitude required reassigning personnel from various specialties and placing their caseloads on hold until the homicide became more manageable.

"Any early theories?" Hoskins asked.

"Well, she had a boyfriend who may have had jealous motives, but I'm waiting for a report on what her father has to say."

"Okay. Officer Karie Jackson interviewed the father at El Torito. Call her and get the lowdown. Then you and Ballesteros track the boyfriend down and get a statement."

"10-4, a news van just pulled up. Any plans on what you're going to tell the press?"

"A homicide occurred in Irvine, and we generally frown upon that kind of activity," Hoskins responded flatly.

"Nicely done – I'm sure that'll work."

16 Dave Freedland

Chapter 2

"Crutchfield's father was devastated," said Officer Karie Jackson, who had arrived on scene at the victim's apartment to provide Detective Rasmussen with her interview notes.

"She had two older brothers, but Bethany was Mr. Crutchfield's only daughter."

Jackson stood towering over Rasmussen. At 6'2", she had played forward on her basketball team at San Diego State University, and it was apparent that she had maintained her workout regimen since graduating from the Sheriff's Academy.

"Crutchfield said his daughter had been dating a Paul Hendrickson for a little over six months, and felt that he was becoming overly possessive and controlling. He said she began to date others, and it was only recently that Hendrickson had become aware of the change in her dating arrangements."

During their information exchange, Rasmussen also learned that Hendrickson worked as a stock broker. He had an arrest record for drunk driving and a simple assault incident at a night club arising from a drunken argument over flirtations. The charge had been plea bargained to disturbing the peace.

"Where's he live?" Rasmussen inquired.

"Newport Beach."

"Does Crutchfield know if Hendrickson dated his daughter last night?" asked Ballesteros.

"He thinks they went to dinner, but he's not sure."

~

Officer Brig Maxwell had a half hour left in his shift which ended at midnight. He pulled his police cruiser onto the freeway on-ramp at

Culver Drive and headed southbound on Interstate 5 for a final check at the Auto Center. Within a few seconds, he saw a Chevy station wagon rhythmically weaving from side to side between the number three and four lanes. As they passed the Jeffrey Road off-ramp, he could see three subjects seated in the front.

The weaving became more pronounced, and Maxwell activated his overhead red lights and radioed his attempt to initiate a stop on the freeway. The vehicle yielded and rolled to a stop in the emergency lane adjacent to the ice plants separating the freeway from the orange groves. As he walked toward the driver's side of the station wagon, Maxwell saw that the back seats were in the down position, and noticed that the interior was cluttered with numerous car batteries. Having taken scores of petty theft reports in recent weeks involving batteries, he made a mental note to pursue questioning related to their ownership, following his intoxication checklist. As he approached closer to the door drew closer, his right hand rested on the butt of his .357 magnum while his left hand adjusted the collar on his jacket to mitigate the chill that had run down his back.

"Good evening," Maxwell greeted, while scanning for threats within the passenger compartment. The driver, a male white, 25, dressed in a leather jacket, exuded the familiar odor of beer, and presented a first impression of a biker. Sitting next to him was a white female of similar age, slender, with hair so straight, it appeared ironed. She gazed directly ahead, while the passenger on her right, approximately 250 pounds, bearded, with dark straggling hair, sat shotgun looking toward the open driver's window. "The reason I stopped you was due to your weaving in and out of the traffic lanes. May I please see your driver's license and registration?"

The driver produced his license, and upon opening the glove compartment, the male passenger fumbled through the papers and a hash pipe in his quest for the vehicle registration. Upon obtaining the requested documents, Maxwell asked the standard series of intoxication questions before returning to the safety of his patrol car to await the arrival of the back-up which he had requested.

Within minutes Officers Rex Campbell and Scott Hunter's LTD coasted into position behind Maxwell's unit. Campbell dimmed the headlights, turned off the overheads, and activated the four-way emergency flashers. Campbell, a veteran of ten years, was serving as a training officer for Hunter, who was experiencing his first night as an Irvine officer after making a lateral transfer from the Los Angeles Police Department.

Both officers approached Maxwell, who stood in the open passenger door of his patrol car, and briefed them on the circumstances of his car stop. Maxwell handed Campbell a small piece of notepad paper with the names of the station wagon's occupants.

"Rex, can you run these guys, while I check the driver on some sobriety tests? Your partner can cover me." Campbell nodded, and walked back to the passenger door of his own patrol unit, keyed the mic, and began reading names and dates of birth.

Maxwell returned to the passengers, and asked that they stand near the front passenger side of his patrol car while he conducted some tests on the driver. He then faced the driver and advised him that he would be administering a series of balance tests to determine his ability to drive. Maxwell held his flashlight under his left armpit, and held the three drivers' licenses in his left hand. Officer Hunter walked a few steps toward an elevated slope and looked down on the entire scene, scanning and observing.

As Maxwell began to demonstrate the first test, Campbell received a radio transmission that the first subject he had submitted had a bench warrant of arrest for traffic related offenses. As Campbell acknowledged the transmission, suddenly he heard a loud crash.

Andre Washington sat in the driver seat of the Ford box truck as it lumbered southbound on the Interstate 5 freeway. Having been raised in the ghetto of South Central Los Angeles, he found that grand theft auto was a lucrative means of supporting his avid habit for heroin.

Unfortunately, mixing it with alcohol this evening had resulted in a dangerous combination. As his eyelids drooped to half mast, his eyes fixated on the flashing lights of the patrol cars stopped along the right shoulder of the freeway. Forgetting that he had so easily stolen the truck only an hour ago, Washington could only focus on the repetitive flashing that drew him to the scene like a moth to a flame.

At the sound of the collision, all Maxwell could think was, "We're getting hit – good thing we're standing on the freeway shoulder."

With an ear-splitting screech, the box truck hit the driver's side of Campbell's car, peeling the sheet metal off, disintegrating the overhead light bar, and sending shards of plastic into Campbell's scalp. The truck then continued diagonally, striking Maxwell's bumper, sending the trunk to the dashboard.

As though it were all happening in slow motion, Maxwell watched the driver and passengers from his car-stop fly in different directions like bowling pins. His own body spun counterclockwise as the push bars to his patrol unit struck his thigh, knocking him to the ground. As his legs disappeared under the vehicle's front bumper, Maxwell, a former collegiate gymnast, grabbed the push bar with his right hand and held on while feeling his left knee snap. The speed of his body being dragged along the ice plants slowed as the momentum from the patrol car dissipated.

As the truck flipped onto its side, the sound was deafening, and acrid smoke clouded the scene of twisted metal and scattered bodies. Maxwell's unit slowly came to a rest, and he awkwardly crawled from beneath the undercarriage. He could still hear Campbell's elevated voice on his pack-set radio.

As he looked up he could see a male, black subject muscle out the window of the truck, and start running toward the orange groves south of the freeway. Maxwell pushed himself to his feet, only to collapse from the pain from the broken kneecap and torn ligaments. His peripheral vision picked up Hunter taking off in full sprint pursuing Washington. Maxwell then reached for his holster, but felt a sinking sensation in his stomach as he realized that the impact of the collision had launched his Smith & Wesson somewhere into the ice plants.

As Washington reached the barbed wire fence separating the freeway from the orange groves, Hunter took him to the ground. Washington screamed that he was simply a pedestrian. However, Hunter's martial arts training kicked in and the suspect was quickly in handcuffs being escorted back to the crash scene.

Fire department and additional police personnel soon arrived, and Maxwell was on his way to the closest hospital, along with the three subjects from the Chevy station wagon. Upon arrival at Tustin Community Hospital, Maxwell asked for a phone to call his wife. As the ER nurse cut his uniform trousers off, Maxwell looked down at a knee that had grown to the size of a soccer ball. Trying not to alarm his wife, Tara, he spoke in third person regarding an on-duty crash that evening, and by the way, the victim was her husband and could she pick him up?

~

Following orthopedic surgery, Maxwell sat on the couch in his den watching military movies and wondering when he would return to making arrests, shooting at the range, and having Code 7 meals with his patrol buddies. The captain, other members of the brass, and his beat partner had all visited, but the routine of law enforcement had taken over, and for now, Maxwell was a vacancy on the Patrol roster that needed to be filled with overtime.

The new guy on the block, Hunter, had now been thrust into the role of the crime fighter from LA County who had "taken care of business" that night on the freeway. The troops scrutinized him carefully with admiration, as well as some jealousy for having performed well during a rare moment of crisis. Hallway humor usually centered upon such banter as, "Hey Hunter, you put the hooks on a bank robber yet?"

"I've got two hours left before EOW (End of Watch) – give me some time," he would retort.

Despite the jocularity, Hunter was a contender for advancement. Having water polo skills sufficiently significant to earn him a scholarship to USC, his educational resume surpassed Associate's Degree, a minimum requirement exceeding that of most policing organizations. He parlayed his water talents into additional accolades in the triathlon world until ligament issues began to increase his 10 kilometer times. Seeking to continue his quest for athletic challenges, Hunter revisited and resumed the martial arts training to which his father had introduced him, and he then immersed himself in the Japanese systems.

Hunter's goal were detective and SWAT. His father having retired from the Los Angeles Police Department's 77th Division, he was raised with cop stories and firearms. Although graduating first in his LAPD Academy class afforded him his choice of patrol divisions, he was fixated upon the notion of investigating major crimes and exercising his detective skills. However, the moment of clarity arrived in 1974 when the Symbionese Liberation Army chose to engage the LAPD in armed warfare. The SLA domestic terrorist group had kidnapped newspaper heiress Patricia Hearst and were suspected of hiding out in a ramshackle house in South Central Los Angeles. LAPD's previously unknown Special Weapons and Tactics Team became the nation's premiere "special forces" of urban law enforcement following their dramatic resolution to the gun battle.

Hunter was faced with a career dilemma. The size of the Los Angeles Police Department and volume of calls for service required SWAT team members to be assigned on a full-time basis to the Metropolitan Division. Hunter could not work both SWAT and detectives at the same time. He would have to choose one or the other and hope for an opportunity to diversify his resume later. Upon seeking counsel from his father, a unique option came to light – work for an intermediate size department in which SWAT was a collateral assignment to detectives. Irvine's frequent participation in SWAT competitions had garnered their team a reputation of excellence, and provided Hunter with an opportunity to be assigned criminal investigations *and* work challenging missions involving barricaded suspects, hostage situations, and high risk warrant service. Hunter's reservations over the possible lack of Irvine's criminal activity had evaporated the last hour of his first shift following up Maxwell on the Interstate 5 freeway.

~

"Coroner's Office, Deputy Coroner Cunningham."

"Hello, Rhonda, this is Sergeant George Hoskins, Irvine PD. Have you got a minute?"

"Sure George, what's up?"

"When we last spoke at the Crutchfield homicide scene, we were all kind of busy, but I didn't stop to ask you regarding the previous homicide case that you had mentioned in which post-mortem sex was involved. Can you tell me a little more about how that was determined?"

"Sure, without going into the forensics on the semen, you can explain it from the psychological pathology more succinctly. The suspect in our previous case was a psychopath who was sexually fixated on the victim and had a fantasy that she held similar feelings. When she rejected his advances, he exploded in a rage, battering and strangling the victim. Our victim, who prior to the assault was an attractive brunette, was now a bloodied corpse. To continue his fantasy, the suspect carried the victim into the shower to "clean her off," as he stated during his interrogation, and then dragged her body to the bed. To avoid any distractions created by his violent actions, and to preserve his memory of how she looked, he wrapped towels around her head before having sex."

"Boy, that sure captures the essence of our crime scene," Hoskins responded, devoid of emotion, but visualizing the horror.

"Yeah, quite a shame. I saw your victim's nightstand photo. Looked like a very sweet girl. It would be nice if you could arrest that monster so that he could be sentenced to a cyanide cocktail. Any leads?"

"Nothing solid, but we should have an interesting interview coming up soon with her jealous boyfriend."

Chapter 3

"How long had you been dating Miss Crutchfield?" Detective Rasmussen inquired, after having been informed by Paul Hendrickson that he had already been notified by Crutchfield's father that she had been murdered.

"About six months," his voice trailing off as he sat on the sofa in the living room of his condominium.

It was late afternoon and Hendrickson's bloodshot eyes announced his either being overcome with emotion, too much alcohol, or insomnia. All three symptoms could be responsible, but it was apparent to both investigators that he had been drinking and his blood alcohol level was rising. The artificially bleached blond hair atop his six foot frame was mussed and appeared unkempt to the crew-cut Rasmussen, but gave Ballesteros the impression of a sloppy attempt at style for a typical Newport bar-hopper.

"When did you last see her?" Detective Ballesteros asked.

"Friday night. We went out to dinner."

"Where did you go?"

"McCormick and Schmick's," Hendrickson responded, his eyes narrowing slightly in irritation.

"Did you go anywhere after dinner?" Rasmussen interjected.

"No, I took her home."

"Why?"

"Bethany was tired," Hendrickson shot back, showing annoyance to Rasmussen's persistence.

"So when I contact your waitress at McCormick and Schmick's, she's going to tell me that you both departed the restaurant amicably?"

"Okay, look, we had a disagreement, and decided that after we finished eating, she wanted to go home."

"What was the argument about?"

"It was a disagreement, and it was concerning her dating other people." Hendrickson's neck veins began to expand.

"Was she trying to break off your relationship?"

"She said she wanted to date other people."

"Did she give you a reason as to why she did not want to date you exclusively?"

"She said that she thought I was too possessive."

"Did she provide you with any examples?"

"Hey, am I being questioned as a suspect?"

"No, we're simply trying to piece together the last days before your girlfriend's death, and if you could be forthright in your answers it would be helpful," said Rasmussen attempting to dampen down the tone of the interview.

"Have you been arrested before?" Ballesteros continued.

"Yes, drunk driving."

"Are you on probation now?"

"No," Hendrickson responded curtly.

"What did you do Saturday night?"

"Okay, now I feel like you think that I'm a suspect. I was here all night, and I think it's time for you to leave."

"No problem. When can you drop by the station for some prints?"

"Look, she was my girlfriend, I frequented her apartment. My fingerprints would naturally be present there."

"Understand that. We need to establish what prints to eliminate."

"Let me check with my attorney, and I'll call you. Can I have your business card?"

"Sure."

~

Monday morning at Paragon Aerospace began in crisis mode. Word had spread that Bethany Crutchfield had been murdered, and to

26 Dave Freedland

her co-workers the loss was nearly unbearable. To her employer, the event presented potential public relations which could become major negative publicity if a suspect was associated with the organization. Communications Director Peter Corcoran convened a staff meeting to discuss options for anticipated inquiries by the media.

Concurrently, Detective Russell Horvath arrived at the reception desk with a list consisting co-workers and Crutchfield's supervisor. Horvath's normal responsibilities focused on crimes against property, which included commercial and residential burglary. A journeyman investigator with ten years of experience, his interviewing resume included parolees as well as juvenile hoodlums who ripped off their neighbors. Horvath was one of the grandfathered detectives who were exempt from the four year rotation back to Patrol, due to an agreement made under previous contract negotiations. He stayed in the Investigations Bureau for as long as he wanted, with the only requirement that he perform competently. Like the cartoon character with a true appreciation for hamburgers, Horvath frequented the various burger joints in town and paid the physical consequences for his appetites.

"Good morning, I'm Detective Horvath with the Irvine Police Department. I am conducting a homicide investigation, and I would like to speak with the individuals on this list of your employees." Horvath presented his typed list to the young brunette sitting behind the counter on which rested a vase of fresh flowers and a card addressed to "Natalie" displayed on the arrangement. She smiled and directed him to the Human Resources department on the second floor.

Horvath repeated his introduction and was escorted to a conference room where he patiently awaited the arrival of Kimberly Goodman, a secretary from Crutchfield's section. Peter Corcoran entered the room accompanied by a distinguished looking gentleman in a three piece suit, whose mannerisms and bearing announced his occupation as a lawyer.

"Good morning, Detective. I'm Peter Corcoran, Communications Director for Paragon Aerospace Systems. Let me introduce Mitch Feinberg, our corporate attorney."

"Pleased to meet you sirs," Horvath replied respectfully.

"I understand you are investigating the death of one of our employees, and we would like to provide you with whatever assistance that we can afford you."

"Well, I have this list of Miss Crutchfield's co-workers and her supervisor, and if you would allow me to speak with them, it would be appreciated."

"Certainly, I would only ask that Mr. Feinberg be present during your questioning."

"I'm afraid that won't be possible, sir. This is a homicide investigation, and the evidence in this matter must be kept stricty confidential. If your organization is uncomfortable with me interviewing your employees on your premises, we will simply make contact with them at home. Of course I would have to notify my lieutenant, who is also the Department's Press Information Officer, and advise him that officials at Paragon were not cooperative and delayed our pursuit of the murderer in this case."

"Would you excuse us for a moment please?" Corcoran inquired politely.

Corcoran and Feinberg left the conference room momentarily, and then entered with an attractive female in her mid-twenties.

"This is Kimberly Goodman, a secretary familiar with Miss Crutchfield. She is open to answering whatever questions you may have regarding her co-worker. We will be down the hallway if you need us. Please contact the Human Resources specialist outside the conference room when you are finished, and she will summon your next person to be interviewed."

"I appreciate Paragon's accommodation."

~

Kimberly Goodman sat nervously across the table, hands folded in her lap holding a damp tissue. Horvath opened his briefcase, pulled out a notepad and began reading off a list of prepared questions.

"How long have you known Bethany?"

"Almost two years. We worked together as secretaries for managers in the Product Testing and Development Department."

"Did you socialize with Bethany after work hours?"

"We would frequently have lunch together, and would have cocktails on Fridays when we weren't going out on dates with someone."

"Was there anyone within her circle of friends or acquaintances that you felt might be capable of causing her harm?"

"I don't know anyone who could possibly kill her. She was trying to break off her relationship with her boyfriend, Paul, but I can't see him resorting to violence to keep her."

"Did you ever see him violent toward her?"

"No, but she did complain to me after she had had a few drinks that he grabbed her arm and pulled her off a bar stool when he saw her talking to some guy who had struck up a conversation with her."

"Was he jealous, or was the guy being rude to her?"

"Oh, as I recall it was some security guard that she knew who had been working at her apartment complex, and Paul got territorial, raising his voice toward the guy before yanking her arm."

"Did she indicate any other incidents?"

"Not that I am aware of."

"Do you know if she went out with anyone last Saturday night or what she had planned for that evening?"

"Actually, Bethany and I went to dinner together that evening."

"Where did you go?"

"The Rusty Pelican in Newport Beach. We had dinner, hit a few bars, and then called it a night."

"What bars did you visit?"

"Oh, I think we stuck our heads in Blackie's, and then went to the Ritz."

"What time did you leave to go home?"

"We were tired. I think we left around 10:30 or 11:00."

"Did you drive her home, or did Bethany drive?"

"We both drove and met at the restaurant."

"You had mentioned that Bethany was trying to break off her relationship with Paul. How was she trying to do that?"

"She told him that she thought it would be best for both of them to start dating other people."

"How did Paul respond to that?"

"She said that he was not at all receptive to the idea."

"Did you know any of the other men that she had begun dating?"

"Not really. She would mention guys by their first names, and would share summaries of their occupations, sometimes hobbies, but there wasn't much time separating her from her boyfriend, Paul, to indicate that she was on the market for dating. She was careful about providing her phone number to other guys when we were hopping nightclubs. Quite frankly, I only know one by name, her supervisor, Glen Smollar."

"How many times did she go out with him?"

"I only know of one date. He's not her type, and she did it more out of courtesy."

"You had mentioned a security guard that had been involved in the argument involving Paul Hendrickson. Do you happen to recall his name?"

"No, sorry, it was several months ago. How was Bethany killed, was she, well, sexually assaulted?"

"The coroner is still working on the cause of death, and the autopsy results have not yet been finalized. I don't think your friend suffered."

Horvath wrapped up his questioning of Goodman, thinking that Hendrickson might require some surveillance work, as his behavior was becoming suspect. He would need to discuss his observations with Hoskins as soon as he finished with Paragon.

~

As Glen Smollar entered the conference room, Horvath guessed that the 5'9" Paragon manager appeared to be one who would be quite comfortable around computers. After having interviewed several employees, it was time for Horvath to complete his work at the aerospace firm with his last interview – Crutchfield's supervisor. Following introductory courtesies, Horvath opened questioning to a quite obviously nervous Glen Smollar.

"How long have you supervised Ms. Crutchfield?"

"About nine months. I was transferred from our Texas campus."

"What kind of employee was she?"

"Oh, Bethany was very conscientious, detail oriented, and personable."

"Were you aware of any problems that she may have been encountering in her personal life?"

"Other than her on and off relationship with her boyfriend, I was not aware of any."

"Were you aware of any violent acts that her boyfriend may have exhibited during their time together?"

"Well, there were rumors regarding his hot temper and his jealous outbursts, but I cannot recall a specific incident where he demonstrated any violent tendencies."

"Did you experience any confrontations with him?"

"No, he did become somewhat rude with our receptionist when he wanted to speak to Bethany, and she was recording the minutes to a staff meeting which couldn't be interrupted."

"When was that?"

"That was a couple weeks ago, which I assume was when she had resumed seeing him again."

"Didn't you also date her?"

"Who told you that?"

"Well, workplace relationships are the substance of gossip, and I have been talking to people here for a couple hours."

"Yes, we dated on one occasion. I asked her to accompany me to a meet and greet social event sponsored by one of our suppliers."

"That was the extent of your social contact with Ms. Crutchfield?"

"Well yes, quite frankly I didn't want to deal with the possibility of having that hot head boyfriend of hers showing up unannounced."

Horvath wrapped up his final Paragon interview with a better understanding of the professional and personal life of his young murder victim, but his efforts had resulted in some perplexing questions as to who might have been responsible for her early demise.

Did her boyfriend's jealously rise to the level of a motive for murder? Was her supervisor truthful in his account regarding their one-time social event, or did he possess a dark side that hid a deeper obsession for his beautiful subordinate? Or was this tragic homicide simply an interrupted residential burglary? Clearly, more discussions and analysis of the evidence were needed, but his next step was to meet with Detective Sgt. Hoskins to determine the direction of the investigative compass.

Chapter 4

Sergeant George Hoskins sat transfixed at his desk scrutinizing every sentence on the report that lay in front of his bloodshot eyes. It was 10:30 pm, and he was desperately trying to catch up on reading the supplemental investigative reports submitted by the detectives who had been methodically gathering evidence, and documenting their observations.

He glanced over to his in-basket and noticed a report slightly protruding from beneath several documents bearing the Irvine PD logo and recognized the seal of the County of Orange. Hoskins pulled it from the stack and identified it as Crutchfield's autopsy report. He quickly scanned each page, skipping unfamiliar medical jargon, and focused upon cause of death and evidence useful in determining modus operandi.

"Death by asphyxia" jumped from the page, "as evidenced by visceral petechial hemorrhaging," served as an indicator that she had been alive when the strangulation bruising was inflicted upon her neck. "Blunt trauma by solid object" explained the well-defined bruises on her body and the laceration delivered to her head.

Hoskins read further, "analysis of seminal fluid indicates vaginal sexual assault, post mortem." His thoughts drifted back to Deputy Coroner Rhonda Cunningham's assessment, "she was already dead, and he raped her." Hoskins' reading of the text now slowed to every word and detail on this most bizarre account of the young woman's death. Time of death was estimated at approximately 11:00 pm - 2:00 am. His mind again wandered, "What kind of monster are we dealing with?" He needed to remain alert, stay attentive to facts interspersed among the reams of paper, and pull together information leading to a suspect and a motive. Hoskins walked to the break room for coffee.

Upon arrival, he discovered Horvath was also struggling to remain awake as he stirred the creamer into his cup of coffee.

"You look as tired as I feel," Hoskins muttered to Horvath.

"I had to drag my ass in here for some coffee, or I would have planted my nose on my keyboard."

"How'd your interviews go at Paragon?"

"Well, their admin people were wrapped pretty tight, but I was able to get what I needed."

"You know our victim's boyfriend has a motive. I think we need to set up on him quickly."

"I just finished Rasmussen's interview of him and he acts guilty."

"We're maxed out on detectives assigned to this case. You want to put the Narcs on him for a while?" Horvath suggested.

"Not a bad idea. I'll give Keith Miller a call and get them moving. Hey, I know you're beat, but can you run out to the apartment complex and get a quick interview with the security guard?"

"All right. Can I write the report tomorrow?"

"Sure, but call me immediately if he gives you anything useful. I've got to find someone to go with me to Crutchfield's funeral this week."

"How about the guy who was in the crash on the freeway? I heard he's riding a desk in the Training Bureau."

"That would be Maxwell, but he's in a leg cast."

"Well, he's walking, and you're not going to go in foot pursuit at a funeral."

~

At 11:50 pm, Detective Horvath pulled his detective fleet Ford LTD into the apartment parking lot next to the Renaissance Builders' construction trailer where an old Datsun B210 was parked, occupied, with its lights out. Inside the vehicle he observed a male, uniformed figure sitting behind the steering wheel. As he exited the Ford and walked toward the Datsun he found the security guard asleep with the dashboard radio tuned to an oldies station playing the Rolling Stones. Horvath tapped the window, presented his badge, and signaled to the startled occupant to step outside.

As the driver's door slowly opened, a stocky 5'9" stump of a man with Elvis sideburns in a security uniform emerged from the vehicle. He wore the traditional law enforcement Sam Browne basket weave utility belt displaying a handcuff case, 24" baton, and Mace canister. James Bascomb was the classic caricature of a security guard.

"Were you working here Saturday night?"

"Yes sir, I was."

"Well, we're investigating a homicide that occurred here Saturday evening in number 23. Were you advised or aware that that had taken place?"

"Yeah, I just heard about it from my boss."

"What hours did you work last night?" Horvath requested as he retrieved a small notebook from his pants pocket.

"I worked from 8:00 pm 'til midnight, then I went down to Mission Viejo to another construction site."

"And your name is?" Horvath inquired as his voice trailed off in volume.

"Bascomb, sir, James Bascomb."

The guard closed the car door slowly and studied the detective momentarily, before gazing onto his notebook entries.

"Did you happen to see anything out of the ordinary during your shift last night?"

"No, it was a pretty quiet night."

"Did you know, or ever see the victim?"

"Well, I knew who she was, but didn't really know her personally. She was an attractive gal, quite a shame. Any leads on who might have done her in?"

"We're looking into a number of possibilities."

"Do you recall ever seeing her boyfriend around here?" Horvath inquired, probing toward Hendrickson as a possible stalker.

"Well, there was one guy that was pretty regular, but she seemed to have other guys come by to visit."

"How long have you worked this site?" Horvath's eyes rose from his notes toward the guard.

"A couple months - the builder was getting lumber ripped off at night." Bascomb added, shining his flashlight on a stack of 2 x 6's.

"Did you ever have contact or any conversations with Ms. Crutchfield's boyfriend?" Horvath asked, beginning to feel fatigue setting in.

"No, he would come to visit, knock on the door, and she would either let him in, or they would both leave together."

"How many times did you see him at the apartment complex?"

"Hard to say, a few, five or six."

"Ever see them argue?"

"Not that I recall. He sometimes looked impatient, like they were late for something."

"When you left the site last night, were you relieved by another security guard?"

"Yeah, a Mexican guy named Jorge, but I don't know his last name."

"Is he relieving you this evening?"

"No, he's off tonight."

"Have you ever seen anyone suspicious hanging around the complex, or showing a particular interest in Ms. Crutchfield or her apartment?"

No, not much going on here. Irvine's kind of flat-line compared to the other places I've worked," Bascomb boasted, trying his best to look like a veteran cop from South Central Los Angeles.

"Can I take a look at your guard's license, and do you have a business card so that I can call your company to get some information on Jorge?"

"Sure, by the way, are you guys accepting applications? I'm taking the written test for LAPD next week, but I'd prefer working in Orange County."

Horvath departed the parking lot taking mental notes to contact International Protection Service so that they could get an interview with "Jorge," and to obtain both his and Bascomb's fingerprints on file with the Department of Consumer Affairs for comparison or elimination. His only hope, for now, was to remain awake long enough to drive home.

Chapter 5

As midnight approached, it was the third hour of Officer Scott Hunter's patrol shift, and the evening had been uneventful. He had followed up on a few alarm calls and domestic disturbances, but for the last thirty minutes the radio had been silent and there had been relatively few vehicles passing through his beat. Driving southbound on Jeffrey Road he obsessively checked his rearview mirror, a habit he picked up after the spectacular accident he had witnessed on the freeway. As he glanced to his right he caught the image of two boys carrying large objects through the path leading from Stoneridge Village onto the sidewalk adjacent to Irvine Center Drive. Hunter swung his driver's side spotlight across the hood of his patrol car and illuminated the back side of two boys, approximately ten years old, as they carried plywood sheets and wooden studs westbound away from the intersection. Hunter turned right, radioed his location, and then accelerated up next to them, as they stopped on the spot trembling at being caught.

"What are you guys doing?"

"Building a skateboard ramp," replied the taller of the two.

"Where did you get the lumber?"

"My house – we're taking it to his house," replied the taller pointing to the shorter.

Hunter looked over his shoulder, and caught the headlights of Officer Phil Brannigan's patrol unit that had pulled in behind his cruiser. Seeing the apparent theft in progress, Brannigan signaled to Hunter, and they separated the two boys for interviewing.

"What's your name?"

"Sean Melroy," the taller boy responded.

"Where do you live?"

"The Ranch."

"Where does your friend live?"

"Oh, he's my cousin and he lives in Stoneridge," Melroy replied sheepishly.

"You want to tell me where you really got the wood?" .

"I told you, from my cousin's house," Melroy responded averting his eyes.

"What's your name?" Brannigan inquired of the shorter boy.

"Jeff Skinner."

"Where do you live?"

"Stoneridge," Skinner replied, pointing behind him.

"Where did you get the lumber?"

"From the apartments on Barranca Parkway. We needed some wood to build a skateboard ramp because we ran out, and I saw some lying by a trailer, so we grabbed a few pieces to take to my cousin's house."

"Have you borrowed any wood from that location before?"

"No, we've never done this before,"

"Didn't you see any security guards on the property?"

"Not tonight."

"You mean 'not tonight' you didn't see a guard, but you had when you tried to steal before?"

"No, we didn't see any guard, and we've never tried to do this before."

Officer Hunter left the scene with both Melroy and Skinner sitting in the back of his patrol car, and several pieces of lumber protruding from the trunk, destined to be photographed when Crime Scene Investigators arrived for work at 7:00 am.

Upon arrival at the station and contact with Melroy's' parents, it was discovered that his father was employed as a deputy with the Los Angeles County Sheriff's Department. Hunter last saw the two boys exiting the front door to the station, with Melroy's butt on the receiving end of a front kick planted from his father's shoe.

~

Detective Horvath awakened at 5:00 am with a sinus headache so powerful that his vision blurred, and his ears were muffled to the sound of the morning newspaper truck lumbering down his street. He staggered to the medicine cabinet to retrieve an old prescription decongestant, which he washed down his throat quickly, before falling back to his bed thinking that he had two hours more sleep before determining if he would call in sick. His alarm rang at 7:00, and he grabbed his phone from the nightstand and dialed Sgt. Hoskins' number.

"Hello George?"

"Yeah."

"This is Russell. I'm really sick and need to sleep in this morning to see if I can get rid of this sinus headache. I might need to see the doctor to get some antibiotics."

"Do you have interviews scheduled today?"

"Nothing scheduled, but I need to get an interview with the other security guard who worked the night that Crutchfield was murdered. Can I call Ballesteros to see if she can locate the guy for a statement today?"

" Okay, do you think you might make it in this afternoon?"

"Maybe. I'll call you at noon."

Horvath dialed Detective Nancy Ballesteros' number and waited until the recorded greeting initiated. The recording interrupted, and a female's voice acknowledged in a somewhat agitated tone.

"Hello."

"Nancy, this is Russell. I'm sick this morning. Can you do me a favor and see if you can locate one of the security guards that was working the site of the Crutchfield homicide?"

"I thought you interviewed him?"

"I interviewed the guard that worked 'til midnight, but I need you to locate the guard that relieved him, and see if you can get a statement. His name is Jorge and he works for International Protection Service. Can you handle that for me? I owe you a lunch."

"Okay, I'll take care of it. Anything specific you want asked?"

"Just get the hours of the guards covering the site, and find out if he saw anything suspicious, or can he provide any additional background."

"Will do," Ballesteros replied, trying to count the number of lunches he owed her.

~

It didn't take long for Ballesteros to track down Jorge Quintanar's supervisor and the schedules for the guards assigned to the Stoneridge Meadows contract. Quintanar worked nights, so Ballesteros drove to his Santa Ana apartment with her partner Phil Rasmussen in tow.

Following several door knocks, and manic barks from the neighbor's dog, a groggy Jorge Quintanar squinted from sunlight beaming through the widening gap between the doorjamb and the door he gradually pulled open. He gazed at the attractive Hispanic detective officially presenting her badge and inquired as to how he could assist her.

"Mr. Quintanar, I am Detective Ballesteros with the Irvine Police Department, and this is my partner, Detective Rasmussen. We are investigating the homicide that occurred at the Stoneridge Meadows Apartments and understand that you worked that site the evening that that crime occurred. We would like to ask a few questions regarding what you may have observed. May we come in?"

"Sure, come on in. Pardon my appearance, but I work nights, and I finished this morning at 6:00." Quintanar motioned towards the sofa, as he picked up children's toys from the floor.

"We understand that you worked the Saturday night, Sunday morning that the Crutchfield homicide occurred, and that you relieved

James Bascomb, who provided security services earlier that evening. Is that correct?"

"Yeah, a dreadful event," Quintanar replied with a thick Spanish accent. "James works Saturday nights, and I relieve his shift at 1:00 am."

"What hours specifically did you work that night?" Rasmussen prodded for more detail.

"I worked my normal shift from 1:00 to 6:00 am, as I recall."

"Is there any official recording or documenting of the times that you guys log in, and out?" Ballesteros followed.

"Oh yes, we have cards that we time stamp at the construction trailer, and turn in to our headquarters in Costa Mesa."

"Is it normal procedure for you to meet with the guard that you're relieving, to exchange information regarding any activities that may have occurred during the previous shift?"

"Well it's supposed to work that way, but some sites I've worked, the guy I'm relieving has already left. But it's not what the rules say."

"Did you see Bascomb that evening when you relieved him?" Ballesteros inquired, lifting her eyes from her notepad and looking directly at Quintanar.

"Yes, I remember he was out of breath and sweating and said that he had just chased some kids stealing lumber from the stack of beams near the trailer."

"Did he ask you to help him look for them, or do you recall if he called the police?" Rasmussen interjected.

"No, he said they dropped the wood when they saw him and took off running. James just asked me to tell the patrol officer that works this beat when he stops by to see if we're awake."

"And did you speak to the officer?"

"Well yes. I snuck over to Winchell's Donuts at 4:00 like I usually do, and I happened to see the officer. I mentioned it to him." Quintanar responded sheepishly.

"Did Bascomb indicate to you that he had observed anything unusual during his shift that night?" Ballesteros continued.

"Not that I recall."

"Did you see anything out of the ordinary that night?"

"No, other than kids occasionally ripping off wood, this site is pretty quiet compared to the other places I've worked."

"Did you ever see the victim during your shift?" Rasmussen resumed.

"No, but I heard she was a pretty lady."

"Who told you that?"

"Well, James works earlier, and he said that he's seen her coming and going, and he said she's pretty hot – dated a lot of guys."

"Did James mention anything else about her?" Ballesteros inquired with interest.

"I remember him saying that there was one guy that she went out with kind of regular, and said that I should be careful around him, 'cause he's a hot head."

"Do you know his name, or what he looked like?" Rasmussen followed.

"James said his name was Paul, and he was about six foot, 200 pounds, and had blond hair."

"Did you ever see him?" Ballesteros continued.

"No, I guess I work too late, but James said he was a real asshole."

"Did James indicate that he had ever had a negative contact with him?"

"Not really, but James said that he treated her poorly, and that if, I think her name is Bethany, if she was his girlfriend, he would treat her like a lady."

"Did James say that he ever saw Paul do anything violent toward her?"

"No, I don't remember him ever mentioning it."

"Do you recall anyone hanging around or showing any particular interest in Miss Cromwell's apartment?" Rasmussen redirected attention to the crime scene.

"No, it's such a shame. I just wish we could have done something to prevent this. I hope I don't lose my job – this doesn't look good on a resume, if you know what I mean."

Ballesteros and Rasmussen departed, and remained silent for a few blocks as their unmarked Ford coasted to a red light where Rasmussen broke the uncomfortable silence.

"I find it interesting that a number of witnesses keep pointing toward Crutchfield's boyfriend."

"I think it's interesting that security guards working the night shift pay that much attention to details."

46 Dave Freedland

Chapter 6

Brig Maxwell sat at his desk, casted leg propped on a chair, staring at the announcement for a rarely advertised opening on SWAT. His gaze slowly traveled to the cast that had entombed his leg since being nearly run over by his patrol car. Like many of the young hard-charging new officers, he coveted a spot on the Team and knew that this opportunity would pass with his inability to perform the physical fitness testing.

The Team's commander, Lieutenant Jim Bosworth, had been a no-nonsense sergeant assigned to the Los Angeles County Sheriff's Department's Firestone Station prior to being hired as one of Irvine's first lieutenants. Firestone was notorious for being a magnet for LASD's tri-athletes, weight lifters, and boxers, all of whom welcomed the challenges presented by parolees, gang bangers, and crazies. As the founder of IPD SWAT, Bosworth established the team structure based upon the LA Sheriff's Special Enforcement Bureau, or S.E.B. Rather than naming Irvine's Team using the same initials, at the chief's behest, Bosworth chose the title, Special Operations Unit, or S.O.U., much to the chagrin of many team members who felt that the name softened their image in the interests of political correctness. To some extent, the politics of the city council and portions of the community dictated such manipulations.

Maxwell's attention abruptly snapped toward the thick document that broke the silence of the Training Bureau office as it dropped unceremoniously onto his desk. Above him stood Lieutenant Bosworth, and on top of Maxwell's paperwork rested a copy of the Department's SWAT manual.

"I understand you're interested in becoming a member of the Special Operations Unit."

"Yes sir, I definitely am, but I am not in any condition to participate in the selection process."

"Well, we also have an opening for an alternate hostage negotiator, and I'm assigning you to the Team as a negotiator until you can test for a tactical position," Bosworth announced with a half smile, then exited the office.

Maxwell sat in his chair, mouth gaping in amazement, as he slowly opened the manual's cover page. His near tragedy at the hands of a drunken grand theft auto suspect had provided him with an inside track to the assignment of his dreams.

~

Maxwell lumbered down the hallway toward the restrooms as he struggled to master his new walking cast. Upon reaching the door, he was intercepted by Detective Sergeant Hoskins.

"Maxwell, I've got a shitty assignment for you. I need you to go with me to the Crutchfield funeral tomorrow. We need to see who shows up and monitor the actions in particular of the victim's boyfriend."

"No problem, Sir. What time are we going?"

"10:00 am. Can you stand on that leg for an hour or so?"

"Yes Sir. I'll put on my dark suit and tie," Maxwell blurted out, wondering if the pant leg would fit over his cast.

~

Maxwell sat in the back row of the 6:00 am patrol shift briefing, listening to the sergeant read the logs off the board. He made an effort to stay current on the pulse of events in the field while working in the Training Bureau during his orthopedic rehabilitation. At the concluding roundtable discussion when the floor was opened for anyone to contribute, one detective provided a brief summary on the progress of the Crutchfield case which, while interesting, furnished no significant insight as to who the suspect might be.

48 Dave Freedland

Typical of the territorial gulf between patrol and detectives, communication generally flowed upstairs to the Investigations Bureau, and only morsels of information were shared below to Patrol. Maxwell surmised from Hoskins' comments the day before that he was privileged to have been shared some inside information that detectives were focusing upon the victim's boyfriend.

Maxwell slowly climbed the stairs to his workstation, dressed in a dark blue blazer and khaki pants, after having discovered that his plaster cast couldn't quite make it through his suit's pant leg. Passing the hallway outside the Investigations Bureau, he could hear a heated discussion between Hoskins and his boss, Lieutenant Ben Sullivan. Sullivan, a tall, slender individual with a propensity toward orderliness, was suggesting that a psychic be employed to assist in the homicide investigation, while Hoskins adamantly objected to the use of "voodoo investigative methods."

Maxwell continued on toward his desk assignment, alarmed that the case didn't appear to be proceeding well. He had idealistically viewed the aces in Detectives as professionally following up leads, and combining their findings with sound scientific evidence. But the thought of using psychics was totally foreign to him, and a sign that they were giving up.

At 10:00, Hoskins arrived at Maxwell's workstation, and they both descended the stairs leading to the secure parking lot. As their staff car went out the gate, Hoskins turned left and headed toward Newport Beach. Upon reaching the red light at Jamboree Road, Hoskins broke the silence.

"All I really need you to do is to observe, and let me know if you see anything out of the ordinary."

"Do you think the victim's boyfriend was responsible?" Maxwell responded, pushing for insight into the progress of the case.

"Well, he'd been acting like the jealous boyfriend, trying to control the relationship and has a possible motive, but we have not been able to establish solid evidence to list him as a suspect."

"I heard a rumor that the suspect left a bloody palm print in the bathroom. So I assume that you haven't matched that with anyone."

"Who told you that? That was a keeper. We didn't want that to get out. But no, the Sheriff's Department Crime Lab reported no matches with anyone on file, or anyone we've identified as having access to the apartment."

"There're a lot of rumors floating around the Department regarding the case as well as frustration that more information hasn't been forthcoming," Maxwell responded defensively.

"There's been a communication problem for years, but we've been burned before when we share information with Patrol, and the next day it shows up in the newspapers."

"I heard another rumor concerning psychics."

"Unbelievable! People need to keep their mouths shut!" Hoskins exploded.

"The lieutenant plans to employ the services of a psychic in the event that we haven't identified a suspect in the next few weeks – but that stays in this car."

But for the sound of the police radio, the staff car remained silent for the remainder of the trip to the cemetery.

"I'll point out the victim's boyfriend to you. He's a real hothead. I hope he doesn't recognize us or make a scene. All I need is a complaint to the chief from someone offended by our presence. We're taking enough heat for having no one in custody yet."

~

The detective staff car coasted into the mortuary parking lot, which, situated a few blocks from the beach, captured the ocean breeze of the Newport Coast. A few family member vehicles had already arrived, with several somber mourners carrying trays of food for the reception following the internment ceremony.

Hoskins and Maxwell got out of the car and walked toward the small chapel, with Maxwell struggling to keep Hoskins' pace while swinging a stiff leg held in place by the full length cast. Hoskins glanced at Maxwell shaking his head, worrying that the limp would draw attention to them then reconsidered that it might mask their obvious law enforcement stereotypes.

Hoskins gestured toward the back row of pews, and they both slid into place, maintaining a clear view of all mourners entering the chapel's main door as well as a nearby window that provided oversight of the parking lot. As a familiar van lumbered into the lot, Hoskins whispered to Maxwell to save his seat, then exited the chapel heading toward his car, as if on a mission to retrieve some forgotten article. He locked eyes with the driver of the dark colored van, and gave a subtle head nod to Narcotics Bureau Sergeant Keith Miller, as Miller's team of detectives terminated their surveillance of Hendrickson's Porsche at the cemetery.

As Hendrickson got out of the Porsche, Hoskins quickly turned and shook hands with an unknown elderly gentleman, so as not to burn the surveillance team that had followed the decedent's ex-boyfriend from his home in Newport Beach. He merged with a crowd of family members as they made their way through the chapel door, and sidestepped into the pew toward the empty space held by Maxwell. Hoskins whispered that the Narcs had delivered their "package" following their Code 5 (surveillance). Maxwell nodded, and looked to the entrance as Hendrickson crossed the threshold into the sanctuary. Hendrickson glanced toward Hoskins, turned away, and then snapped his head back, flashing rage as veins swelled from his neck. Hoskins elbowed Maxwell, and Maxwell inquired, "Was it the buzz cuts or the moustaches that tipped him off?"

"Probably both, and possibly a guilty conscience," Hoskins responded.

Hendrickson selected a seat in the third row from the small pulpit near the casket, displaying an expression filled more with anger than sadness at the loss of his girlfriend. Maxwell continued to focus attention on him, while Hoskins, having more experience in homicide investigations, scanned the entire audience of mourners, looking for expressions out of place or familiar faces from his near photographic memory of suspects and their crimes.

Chapter 7

Day One of SWAT try-outs was the worst for most applicants. The dreaded obstacle course was deceptive in appearance, but most officers knew that it was a gut-check as to how well one was conditioned to meet the demands of a call-out. Those passing the physical trial were shuttled off to the firing range for a challenging course of pistol skills while struggling to recover from muscles still burning from dragging heavy weights and scaling walls. Those failing to score the coveted "pass" on the pistol range departed, leaving the remaining officers to participate in the mental gymnastics presented in two scenarios staffed by actors playing out critical incidents requiring mature judgment and sound tactics.

The survivors of Day One met the second day with anticipation as to what problem solving questions would be asked by a panel of SWAT Command Staff. A subsequent review of their performance evaluations, a peer assessment, and approval by the chief completed the process for Team selection, followed by a two-week SWAT Academy.

Scott Hunter stood at the Public Works yard perched atop a hillside supporting two large water tanks, awaiting the commencement of the obstacle course. Attired in a tee shirt, fatigue pants, and boots, he walked through each obstacle with the Red Team's Tactical Leader, Sergeant Rex Hanniford, as he demonstrated to Hunter and the nine other applicants the proper technique for completing each station. Hunter looked at his competition shivering in the unusually cool 45 degrees of November, each possessing at least three years more experience than he. For some, that amount can be significant, for others, ten years' experience is one year times ten – no growth.

Graveyard shift officers were given the first opportunity to start, having worked all night and were obviously at a disadvantage to those having worked shifts enabling them to rest. Hunter wasn't much better off, leaving work at 11:00 pm, and sleeping only four hours before traveling to the site for the 7:00 am muster time. Officers commenced the test having staggered start times, with safety rules allowing only two on the course at one time. Officer Jack Pascall passed the finish line first with a time of seven minutes, 44 seconds, making the cut by only one second. He was last seen walking between the parked patrol units, bent over throwing up the breakfast that should have been the protein bar that he had foregone in favor of the ham and eggs special at the all-night diner.

One by one, the list worked its way down to Hunter, who felt the butterflies start to activate as he donned the requisite flak vest. Hanniford yelled Go! and the sprint was on toward the first obstacle, a six-foot block wall awaiting him at the end of 75 yards of gravel. Hunter went airborne five feet from the wall, tapping the top cap of bricks with his left hand and right boot, as he floated over the top in stride, while heading toward the monkey bars. He grabbed the first wrung then swung to the next, skipping one wrung between the span of his arms as he advanced toward the last. Exiting the bars, he attacked the double windows, flipping head first through the top window, continuing head first through the bottom window, while snapping his legs to the ground and pulling the rest of his body through the opening until fully clearing the obstacle. He next grabbed the heavy rope attached to the 165 pound sled, and ran backwards dragging the dead weight until reaching the chalk line that released him for the next six-foot block wall to engage. He flew over the masonry in form, and scaled the chain link fence to the top, then dropped eight feet to the ground, landing in stride.

Hunter then realized why he had been warned to refrain from sprinting between obstacles. His legs were so pumped with blood that he felt as if his shoes were coated with molasses. A moment of panic flashed through his mind as the prospect of having to run a quarter of a mile around the water tank and then engage each obstacle again, loomed ominously. Hunter no longer felt the sting of the morning chill, but sensed that his tee shirt was soaked through with perspiration as the body armor sanded his skin with every swing of his arms. As he reached the halfway point, the timer shouted 2:12, signaling to Hunter that his pace might be too fast to leave him enough strength to clear every obstacle during the second encounter.

He decelerated his gait on the backside of the water tank, thinking that a SWAT operation could not possibly be this physically demanding. He discarded the thought, realizing that he'd never participated in a call-out other than standing on a perimeter; nor had he cleared rooms holding an M4 Carbine in a shooting platform, after having jumped fences and kicked doors while controlling his breathing to make that critical shot.

Hunter felt the proverbial "bear on his back" as he rounded the water tank and headed toward the first obstacle for the second time. He hit the wall, scrambled over the top, and addressed each successive challenge with significantly less finesse, but with greater tenacity. With his last burst of energy, Hunter sprinted to the final punishment, a two foot high cinder block wall, ten feet long, that required the candidate to run end-to-end balancing all the way, fighting complete exhaustion.

"Six zero three!" shouted Hanniford. Six minutes and three seconds, though not the record, would prove to be the fastest time of the day.

~

"When you clear the funeral, meet at Winchell's Donuts at Walnut and Jeffrey," the text read across Hoskins' pager – sender: Keith Miller. Hoskins gave a head nod to Maxwell signaling it was time to leave after having seen nothing remarkable regarding Crutchfield's funeral other than the menacing glances thrown by Hendrickson. Upon arriving at their staff car, Hoskins reached into the glove box and retrieved the bulky mobile phone from its charger, dialed Miller's pager, and cryptically entered, "N Route Winchell's."

During the drive back along Jamboree Road, little was said, as the police radio crackled with transmissions involving a perimeter forming around a bank whose alarm signaled an in-progress robbery.

"Those are never righteous ones," Hoskins commented sarcastically. "If they are, they're always long gone before we get there."

The sergeant issuing radio commands was newly promoted, but was as pompous as they come and seemed to be experiencing difficulty in responding to the scene. The lunch hour traffic was particularly gridlocked, and frustration was increasing with every transmission emanating from the sergeant's microphone.

A sudden change in tone indicated that officers in position were encountering the rare occurrence of an authentic event with the suspect still on-scene. "He's exiting the bank! Male, white, possibly a black wig. He's gotta gun in his waistband! He's shouting something…"

"Hold your fire 'til I get there," interrupted the sergeant, now identified with the call sign, Bravo 20.

"What an idiot," Hoskins barked at the windshield of his car, as Maxwell turned, somewhat startled.

As their vehicle accelerated onto the freeway, Hoskins continued, "The guy's not even on-scene, he has no situational awareness, and he's just ordered all the officers dealing with this mess that lethal force is not an option until "he" arrives?"

"Bravo 12, he's drawing the weapon!"

"914-S."

"Suicide," the final code broadcast in the last transmission announced to all that the crisis had ended with the suspect taking his own life. Further radio traffic re-constructed the scenario in which a suspect had entered the bank branch, displayed a pistol in his waistband to the teller, received a bag of cash, and exited the building. Discovering that a perimeter of uniforms with barrels of .45 caliber pistols and 12 gauge shotguns was leveled at him, the suspect withdrew his own 9mm pistol and pulled the trigger as soon as the front sight made contact with his temple.

Apparently the suspect's wig had fallen from his head. This necessitated a quick photograph and retrieval of evidence to prevent further incidents of bank patrons passing out as had happened with one woman who believed that the wig was scalp and brain matter which had separated from the bank robber following the weapon's discharge.

~

"We'll have to swing by the bank scene on the way back from Winchell's, they'll need a detective sergeant to close out that bucket of crap," Hoskins said as he and Maxwell pulled into the strip mall containing the donut house. "Don't worry, I'll drop you off at the station. I think you've stood long enough on that casted leg."

Narcotics Sergeant Keith Miller was seated outside the shop at a circular table under a brightly colored umbrella. Sporting a ball cap and a tight Oakland Raiders' tee shirt, Miller's biceps reflected disciplined weight training, and his close cropped beard fooled only the naïve that he wasn't law enforcement.

As Hoskins and Maxwell pulled up chairs from an adjacent table, Miller said, "We tracked that guy like bloodhounds, and discovered that he spends most of his leisure time with a new girlfriend who lives about two miles away from our victim in Irvine."

"I guess Hendrickson's period of mourning has ended," Hoskins replied sarcastically.

"An interesting bonus was the construction work on the building next door to his apartment complex," Miller added.

"How so?"

"The condo under construction had been getting hit for lumber and tool thefts, so the contractor hired a security firm to place a pole camera on-site to record and deter crime. The camera had a wide angle lens that captured the parking place for Hendrickson's Porsche in his carport."

"How much historical data?"

"Back beyond the date of the homicide and the Saturday evening to Sunday morning that Crutchfield was killed. Hendrickson's car didn't move from his parking spot."

"Wow. That tends to corroborate his statement that he stayed home all night. He could have been picked up by somebody, but we don't have any evidence to establish that. Does he hang out with anyone besides his new squeeze?" Hoskins asked, thinking that an accomplice to the murder could be possible, but rare.

"In a ten day period he played racquetball twice with his brother, who's a firefighter for the City of Santa Ana. His brother's schedule indicated that he was on duty the night of the homicide. We didn't observe him associate with anyone else during his time away from work. Interestingly, he started dating his new girlfriend, Tiffany Binghamton, two weeks before Crutchfield was murdered. We interviewed her outside her place of employment, the same brokerage firm in Newport Beach where Hendrickson works and she said they were introduced at a company party. "Here's the kicker, she reluctantly gave up that Hendrickson spent the night at her apartment the night of the homicide."

"That's odd. Hendrickson said that he spent the entire night at home the evening of the murder. What gives? She just gave him an alibi and he didn't use it to keep us off his ass. We'll need to have another chat with him, but I would assume that this time we will have the pleasure of meeting his attorney."

"It would appear that Hendrickson's jealous streak had run its course." Hoskins said with resignation.

Chapter 8

The firing range was tucked between rolling hills of dairy farms scattered along the Orange and Riverside County lines. The smell of fertilizer overpowered the air, and the dust blown up by the winds hampered target acquisition and fouled the pistol lubricants. Hunter's forearms were sanded red from the block wall caps that he had aggressively scaled during the obstacle course, and his legs burned from muscle fatigue, but he felt surprisingly fresh for the next phase in his quest for the coveted SWAT eagle pin.

Two seasoned Team members posted eight silhouette targets on metal stands positioned 25 yards away reflecting to all that two applicants had failed to meet the qualifying time on the onerous obstacle course. Sergeant Hanniford barked directions for the courses of fire, emphasizing the need to keep track of the capacity of their magazines as well as the number of rounds required for each stage. The standard issue Sig Sauer .45 caliber pistols afforded the officer maximum knockdown power, reliability, and safety, but the magazine capacity was eight rounds, with one in the chamber. The stages of fire required rapid reloading to meet the time limit, and the accuracy needed for a passing score allowed only seven rounds outside the "center mass" kill-zone.

Hunter focused on every direction Hanniford announced as he stood at the 25 yard line facing his target. The whistle blew, his pistol cleared the holster smoothly, and within a split second he acquired his front sight. The rear sight aligned as his trigger moved the hammer into the cocked position. Twelve pounds of trigger pressure, was a safety characteristic of the Sig Sauer's first round fired, with subsequent six-pound flexing of the finger to empty the magazine.

The whistle sounded the end of firing. But at that distance it was difficult to see the location of every bullet hole in the ringed silhouette. Hunter fought the temptation to fixate on the "hits" and listened to Hanniford's articulation of rounds, time limits, and bullet placement – two to the body, one to the head. Realizing that he did not have his magazines loaded to capacity, he quickly drew round after round from the ammunition box, jamming them quickly against the springs of his "mags," while walking forward to the next station. Hunter glanced to his right, recognizing that a few on the firing line hadn't realized that their magazines weren't full, and he questioned for a moment if he was right or if they were wrong.

Hunter faced the final station at the three yard line, and quickly saw that all of his rounds were 10-ring hits and head-shots with the exception of one bullet hole touching the 8-ring, occurring when he had sneezed from the wind-blown dust that had activated his allergies. At this distance all he needed was to make the narrow time limit. The whistle sounded, and in his effort to anticipate the signal to fire, missed the thumb-strap on his holster. Hunter expended an additional second to engage his thumb against the leather restraining his pistol, and rapidly drove the barrel toward the silhouette while squeezing the trigger. He fought to control the barrel against the repetitive recoils. Then gunpowder smoke cleared, and Hunter's target displayed the remaining hits in the 10-ring – he and four other applicants would now advance to the next challenge.

~

Madam Manassarian was her commercial title, but her Romanian birth certificate stated her true name as Marianna Trovalesque. Her occupation was psychic, and her resume boasted clients that included a handful of significantly sized police departments, but more extensively, several law enforcement agencies whose names are rarely seen in headlines. Aside from predicting future events (for a nominal fee), she specialized in reconstructing past events in which no apparent witnesses had been located to corroborate the facts. This played well into her trained eye for sizing up police managers seeking to ingratiate their superiors when all leads had been exhausted on homicide cases.

Lieutenant Ben Sullivan was a veteran member of the police command staff, assigned to manage the Detective Bureau. His propensity toward neatness reached obsession levels, with every paperclip in its place on his desk, and an in-basket that was completely cleared by the end of each day. He stared intently as the 46 year old heavy set Romanian woman ceremoniously examined articles of evidence before rendering her assessment regarding the perpetrator of the Bethany Crutchfield homicide. Sergeant George Hoskins rolled his eyes over toward Detectives Phil Rasmussen and Nancy Ballesteros, non-verbally communicating his absolute distain for the entire spectacle.

"I am sensing that your suspect is drawn to commit crimes near railroad tracks, and may select a domicile in close proximity to such conveyances," Manassarian stated slowly, with pronounced accent for effect.

Hoskins pondered, "Great. We'll round up every hobo, along with the other usual suspects."

"Amazing!" Sullivan blurted out. "The Stoneridge Apartments are only a half mile away from the Santa Fe railroad tracks on Jeffrey Road!"

"Any fortuneteller worth her salt would have read the newspapers to gather that piece of enlightenment," Hoskins continued thinking to himself.

"The suspect likes fast cars, nightclubs, and lives near water," Manassarian continued, pulling a lock of her black hair away from her eyes as she gazed at the photographs.

Outstanding. That narrows it down to half the male population between Newport, Huntington, and Laguna Beach, Hoskins thought, barely able to contain himself.

"I sense that your suspect knew your victim and jealousy was the motive for his actions," Manassarian stated with conviction.

The expressions of Detectives Rasmussen and Ballesteros changed slowly from anticipation to cynicism as they came to the realization that their celebrated psychic was pontificating in generalities that could be applied to a variety of homicide cases gleaned from several media sources. However, it became apparent that the good lieutenant hadn't been struck by the same epiphany.

"My goodness, that seems to fit our victim's boyfriend!" Sullivan announced with excitement.

"Yes sir, a very close match except for the fact that his prints don't match the bloodied one left at the scene, and it would appear that his account for his whereabouts the evening of the crime are corroborated by video," Hoskins corrected respectfully.

~

The shoot house consisted of a four bedroom building constructed inside three tall, earthen mounds designed to contain stray bullets within the police firing range. Each room had three walls, with silhouette targets placed in the empty space created by the missing fourth wall. Clearly marked hostage targets were strategically placed in front of the suspect silhouettes, providing limited exposure of the suspect's head and center mass.

Rather than employing live fire scenarios with real bullets, the decision making portion of the SWAT test incorporated paintball, which marked targets, both living and inanimate, with paint contained in a tiny ball traveling at 300 feet per second. Although nobody dies from paintball, the thought of being struck by a projectile that bruises its recipient with two weeks of black and blue, is a stress multiplier. Participants, clad in fully enclosed headgear and groin protectors listened intently as Sergeant Hanniford provided directions regarding what was awaiting them once they crossed the threshold of the front door.

Suspect and hostage targets were clearly marked, with the suspect silhouettes requiring two hits to the head. One of the rooms would be occupied by live actors, and their actions would dictate whether lethal force would be appropriate. SWAT applicants would enter rooms in pairs, with a Team evaluator following and assessing their tactics while ensuring operational safety. Hunter's stress level began to rise as he mentally prepared for a challenging hostage rescue exercise. The eye protector shield on his headgear began to fog as he discovered that he would be paired with Officer Miles Cavenaugh, the weakest applicant left in a remaining field of five.

There was no doubting Cavenaugh's physical capabilities or his skills in striking a target where it needed to be struck, but his judgment under stress was questionable, and his motive for team membership was more a matter of resume building for the next sergeant's exam. Cavenaugh had discovered that there was a correlation between leadership and becoming a field supervisor. The last three sergeant promotions had come from the ranks of SWAT, so he figured that adding Team membership to his resume would ensure his advancement. His mistake was failing to recognize that the development of leaders was a by-product of the Special Ops group, and that his lack of fire in his belly to make critical decisions would soon lead to his downfall.

Although they had established that Hunter would stage on the hinge side and enter first, while Cavenaugh would position by the doorknob, when the whistle blew, Cavenaugh bounced into Hunter's shoulder and crossed the threshold ahead of him. Hunter followed, and stepped into a long hallway with multiple doors on each side. Cavenaugh pushed the door to his left and immediately fired two rounds from his paintball rifle into two targets, staggered with a hostage silhouette covering half of the suspect target directly behind it. Cavenaugh proudly focused upon the two hits on the suspect target's head, failing to realize that he had over-committed into the room, and missed the second target strategically placed in the blind corner behind the open door. Hunter, button-hooking behind him, took it out quickly, and then scanned the room for additional threats.

During the next two successive room entries, both officers exhibited better teamwork and eliminated threats effectively. However, upon entering the fourth bedroom, Cavenaugh entered first and was confronted by two actors walking toward him with hands in the surrender position. He stopped momentarily, partially blocking Hunter's vision into the room, and failing to learn from his previous error, neglected to check the blind corner. Rather than entering the room, Hunter had taken a kneeling position at the threshold and visually cleared the room using the gun barrel to "slice the pie" behind Cavenaugh's frozen stance. In doing so, Hunter picked up movement to the right, and took out the threat with two quick bursts.

Sgt. Hanniford stoically provided a sterile assessment of each participant's performance without any indication as to their status within the process. All five officers were assigned interview times for the next day, giving them 24 hours to prepare for a grilling the likes of which they would not soon forget.

~

"Detective Horvath?"

"Yes."

"This is James Bascomb. I don't know if you remember me, but I was the security guard that you interviewed regarding that girl who was murdered in the apartments that I was working at."

"Yes James, I remember you. How can I help you?"

"Well, I don't know if this has any significance, but I just remembered that the night that she was killed, I happened to see her boyfriend riding a motorcycle down Barranca Parkway by the apartments."

"How did you know it was him if he was wearing a helmet?"

"Well, I went to the Winchell's donuts for a coffee break shortly after seeing him, and I saw him walking out with a bag of donuts, and he had taken his helmet off."

"What time did you see him?"

"Around 10:00 pm."

"What kind of bike was he riding?"

"It was a stripped down Harley. I think it was blue or black."

"Did he recognize you?"

"No, I don't think so. He never made eye contact or acknowledged me."

"Thanks for the call. If you think of anything else, you know how to reach me."

"Interesting," Horvath thought. "The guy says he was home, but his new girl says he was with her, but Barney Fife places him in the area of the crime scene in Irvine."

Horvath walked over to Detective Rasmussen's work station. "Phil, when you ran Hendrickson for vehicles registered, did you find any motorcycles?"

"No, just the Porsche," Rasmussen replied, rummaging through his notes.

"How about running his brother through DMV for me?" Horvath requested.

Rasmussen entered Hendrickson's firefighter brother's name into his computer.

"Looks like his brother's got a Harley Davidson Sportster. What have you got?" Rasmussen inquired.

"Our security guard just called me to report having seen Hendrickson riding a motorcycle near the crime scene the night of the homicide."

"Do you believe the guy? Is he certain?"

"We need to meet with Hoskins, we've got some serious alibi issues with this Nimrod," Horvath responded with urgency.

66 Dave Freedland

Chapter 9

Sergeant George Hoskins and Detective Phil Rasmussen sat impatiently inside the detective interview room awaiting Paul Hendrickson and his attorney, Aaron Horowitz, to end their pre-interrogation meeting in the room next door. Hoskins and Rasmussen had collectively met with each investigator to piece together the witness interviews, which essentially identified three different locations for Hendrickson the evening of the murder.

Yellow legal notepads lay upon the table in front of Hoskins and Rasmussen along with two audio cassette recorders. Each notepad bore a vertical black line down the center, with questions scripted on the left column, and a blank right column awaiting responses from the interviewee. The door opened, and Hendrickson entered, glancing toward Hoskins before taking the seat in front of Rasmussen. Mr. Horowitz followed, seating himself across from Hoskins, as he retrieved his own cassette recorder from his briefcase. Following the exchange of business cards, Rasmussen advised Hendrickson of his Constitutional rights as he read them verbatim from his Miranda card. Hendrickson acknowledged his understanding, and agreed to answer questions subject to the advice of counsel.

"Mr. Hendrickson, during our first meeting you indicated that you spent the entire night at your apartment the evening that your former girlfriend was been killed. Since that time, we have received some conflicting information regarding your whereabouts that evening. Can you clarify for us where you were that Saturday night to Sunday morning?"

"Look, I never thought for one moment that I would be focused upon as being someone needing an alibi for my actions. When I told you guys that I stayed home, Bethany and I were having issues in our relationship, and things were falling apart. I had found someone else, but I didn't want that person to know that I had just left a relationship, and for her to think that I was on the rebound. The last thing I needed was for the police to tell her that I was recently the boyfriend of a murder victim."

"Let me be a little more direct. Where were you that night?" Hoskins interrupted impatiently.

"I spent the night at Tiffany Binghamton's apartment. You guys followed me and interviewed her!"

"Okay, you knew Bethany had been killed when we interviewed you. Why would you give a false account of your whereabouts to homicide detectives, when the possibility existed that you could be viewed as a suspect?"

"I told you I never thought that I would be viewed as a suspect in Bethany's death. Tiffany Binghamton is my boss' girlfriend, and if he found out that I had spent the night with her, I'd be out of a job. It was easier for me to just say I was home," Hendrickson responded with emotion, hoping to get some sympathy.

"You live rather dangerously. Is your resume up to date?"

"I got another job offer, and will be giving notice to my employer tomorrow," Hendrickson retorted.

"Well, we have a witness that saw you riding a motorcycle near Bethany's apartment complex the evening she was murdered. How do you account for that?"

Hendrickson's eyes widened, his forehead began beading with perspiration as he mentally re-traced his actions that night.

"Who told you that crock of shit?"

"The same person who saw you at the donut shop a little later."

"Okay, Tiffany had a craving for a maple bar. We were watching the movie *Grease*. It reminded her of high school, and she used to get maple donut bars during snack break. I offered to go get her one."

"That explains Winchell's. What about Bethany's apartment?"

"All right, I was curious. Both Bethany and Tiffany live in Irvine. I had ridden my brother's motorcycle that weekend, so I swung by Bethany's place just for a look. I never stopped."

"Can we take a break?" said Horowitz.

"Do you need a break?" Hoskins asked Hendrickson like a drill sergeant responding to a recruit's request for a potty break.

"I must insist that we take a break," Horowitz repeated with assertion.

"Okay," Hendrickson nodded in agreement.

As Hendrickson and his attorney left the interview room, Hoskins smiled at Rasmussen.

"He thinks he's got all the answers, but he can't control his temper, and he can't get ahead of us."

"Yeah, but we're not there yet. He's in the area of the crime scene, he's been caught in a lie, and he's got jealousy issues, but this circumstantial evidence won't deliver a conviction. It won't even support enough probable cause for arrest."

~

"Did you go to her apartment that night? If you did, we need to end this interview right now," Horowitz said.

"No, I was going to make it clear that I just drove by. It was simply a coincidence that someone murdered her that night," Henderson responded.

"Well do you have any idea who would want to kill her? It would certainly help your situation if you could demonstrate a willingness to assist the police in the suspect's capture."

"I have no idea. We were drifting apart, she said she wanted to date other people, but I don't know if she had actually started seeing others. That's kind of why I was cruising by her place."

"Well, they're going to ask you more questions regarding your proximity to her residence that evening. If all you did was drive by, they don't have anything for us to worry about. We're not going to discover that some witness exists that places you at her door that night, are we? I don't want any more surprises. We are here simply to demonstrate cooperation, and to clarify any inconsistencies that may cause them to focus upon you, in error."

"No, I never set foot on her complex that night."

~

Hendrickson and his attorney reentered the room, and the recorders were reactivated.

"When we last spoke, you had stated that you drove your brother's motorcycle by Bethany Crutchfield's apartment the evening that she was murdered. What was the purpose of your visit?" asked Rasmussen.

"I wasn't visiting her. I was simply curious as to what she was doing that night, since we hadn't talked for several days, and it was a Saturday night when we would normally go out."

"Without stopping and knocking on her door, how would you know whether she was home, or what she was doing for that matter?"

"I don't know. I suppose if her car wasn't there, it would indicate that she was probably out with a girlfriend, because a date would most likely pick her up at her apartment. If there was a light on in her second bedroom that would lead me to believe that she was out. That room was unoccupied, it could be seen from the street, and she would turn the light on to give the impression that someone was home."

"You seem to have quite an extensive knowledge of her habits," Hoskins interjected.

"Hey, we dated for six months. We got to know each other pretty well."

"Was your relationship sexual?"

"That's a bit personal isn't it?

"Well, it would be useful to the investigation to know how recently you had engaged in sexual intercourse with her."

"Was Bethany raped by this animal?"

70 Dave Freedland

"Whoa, we're simply asking a reasonable question regarding your relationship with your former girlfriend. Did you and she ever have sex, and if so, how often?"

"Only a couple of times. She got a case of the guilts and said that she should save it for marriage."

"What time did you drive by her apartment?"

"About 10:00 pm."

"What did you see?"

"Her car was not in the carport, and the light was on in the second bedroom."

"Did you stop, approach her door, or make contact with Bethany at any time that evening?"

"No. In retrospect, I wish I had. I may have missed an opportunity to have saved Bethany's life."

"Thanks Paul, appreciate your candor. For elimination purposes, may we call a blood tech to get a sample of your blood?"

Hendrickson glanced toward Horowitz and received a head nod.

~

Officer Miles Cavenaugh left the conference room shaking his head and looking at the floor, trying to second guess each answer he had given the SWAT examination panel. He knew he had blown the interview, but was not certain whether it had been the ethics question, or it had simply resulted from his academic-like demeanor that had turned off the sergeants. He knew Hanniford never liked him, so it was apparent that he was at a disadvantage before entering the room.

Scott Hunter stood in the hallway outside, waiting for his opportunity with apprehension, hoping that he could communicate his ability to think on his feet. Standing in his dress blues for approximately five minutes, his heart rate rose as the door opened, and Sgt. Hanniford extended his right hand for a firm grip handshake.

After giving his well-rehearsed opening and answering the anticipated questions regarding why he wanted to be a SWAT operator and why he would be a good candidate, Hunter braced for the stress inducing scenarios. He was confident that he had outlined sound courses of action for the two tactical scenarios, but felt his stomach tighten as Hanniford read an ethical dilemma from his question sheet. Hunter wasn't prepared for that.

"It is 11:00 pm, and you are assigned to a silent burglary alarm at a business in the industrial section of the city. You are familiar with the fact that the alarm has been activated several times in the past, and that in each instance, there has not been a break-in. Your follow-up officer is overweight, and in poor physical condition, and has already arrived at the location. Upon your arrival, he indicates to you that he has already checked the perimeter, and found it secure. You see that the front of the business has a main double door and several windows, but the back of the business has a material storage yard that is enclosed by a six foot block wall surrounding the entire rear perimeter. You ask your follow-up officer if he checked the back door, and he replies in the affirmative. However, you know that in order to accomplish this, he would have had to scale the wall. You also know that during your attendance at training the previous week, your follow up officer had been unable to scale a five foot wall and shoot a target on the other side. What actions, would you take, if any, to complete this call for service?"

Hunter tried to think fast. What are they looking for? Do you give up your partner? Is a partner like that someone to worry about giving up? How does one confront another cop who's obviously lying? Is there a SWAT answer that differs from that of a patrol response? Finally, he shook his head, smiled nervously, and then thought clearly to himself, just handle the call.

Looking directly at the panel he said, "I would turn to my follow-up officer and say, I'm gonna double check the back door. Keep your radio volume up in case I need help. I would then scale the fence, examine the back of the building for intrusions, and then return to the front of the business."

"Would you say anything to your follow-up officer?"

72 Dave Freedland

"I'm not really comfortable challenging a fellow officer by implying that he's a liar, but I would ask him whether I had misunderstood him when he had said he had checked the back of the business prior to my arrival."

"If he answered yes or no would it change any of your actions in resolving this call?"

Hunter thought, and then responded, "I guess not, but it would confirm the man's lack of integrity, and would have a definite impact as to how I would deal with him in the future."

"Are there any other actions you would take?"

"I would meet with my supervisor that evening, explain my observations and opinions, and hope that corrective measures would be taken."

"Thank you for participating. The list will be posted tomorrow."

Chapter 10

At 3:10 am the SWAT pagers rang, displaying a text directing the recipients to respond to the station for deployment to an armed barricaded suspect. The graveyard shift patrol sergeant had exhausted all his resources attempting to encourage the surrender of a bipolar University of California professor who had roamed his apartment complex with a shotgun, threatening residents as well as himself.

Sergeant Hanniford's Red Team members had all arrived at the station and were staged by their vehicles, awaiting the arrival of the snipers assigned to Sergeant Gaston's White Team. Sergeant Rob Gaston stood in front of the locker room full length mirror putting the last cloud of hairspray over his neatly coiffed pompadour. His ten years of law enforcement experience had given him an opportunity to work the Detective Bureau, only to be returned to Patrol upon his promotion to the rank of sergeant. Rob's perspective on SWAT was more social than operational. The executive men's club of Special Weapons and Tactics tended to focus more upon static displays of equipment at public events, and pistol contests with the Red Team to establish losers responsible for buying the beer.

Sergeant Rex Hanniford possessed less experience, but any lack of exposure to search warrants and surveillance was made up for by his sense of urgency and motivation toward operations efficiency. Hanniford pushed his men, and made them feel privileged to be members of an exclusive group of operators who were looked upon by their peers as warriors akin to the Samurai. Unfortunately, they comprised only ten members of a twenty officer Team, which was often judged by its weakest link. Hanniford knew that changes were needed, but at the rank of sergeant, he only controlled half of their complement, and Team Commander, Lieutenant Jim Bosworth, was awaiting reassignment of responsibilities following a "philosophical argument" with the chief of police.

Upon arrival at the Pacific West Apartments, perimeter, entry, and sniper assignments were given, and personnel deployed. Hanniford's team took up a position near the front door to the suspect's second story apartment, where the suspect had now hunkered down with his 12 gauge weapon of choice. However, due to vacation scheduling, Hanniford was short one operator to deploy chemical agents, so he borrowed Gaston's gas man, Officer Kenneth O'Shaunessy. O'Shaunessy had attended the basic chemical agent school with a hangover, five years prior, but failed to participate in the requisite updates. Gaston thought the Training Bureau had kept track of such administrative details.

Sergeant Gaston's team set up below the second story bedroom window, preventing the suspect from escaping into the neighborhood. Having been appointed to the Team only days prior, Officer Scott Hunter found himself in the stack of Gaston's perimeter team, fully equipped, but uncertified, possessing only a reservation to attend the basic SWAT academy in three weeks.

Telephone negotiations were going nowhere. As daylight began to approach, the suspect, a lanky associate professor with wavy black hair and thick framed glasses elected to crack his door partially open, and discuss his challenges with depression. Hanniford became greatly concerned that as these fruitless discussions continued, the time was rapidly arriving when the apartment complex would be teaming with workers, students, and children traveling to destinations requiring them to pass through the suspect's kill zones.

Hanniford directed O'Shaunessy to prepare a tear gas canister for deployment, and told Team members to don their gas masks. However, Gaston, assuming that his perimeter team's location on the ground level would separate them from a second story chemical discharge, coupled with a little attitude, signaled his men to disregard the gas mask admonition. Hanniford radioed a countdown as O'Shaunessy pulled the pin and held the "spoon" in preparation for deployment of the CS chemical agent. However, O'Shaunessy being the ever conscientious SWAT dog failed to recognize that he had procured a continuous burning riot and crowd control canister which would soon overwhelm the studio apartment with pulverized particles so dense that the point man on the entry element would be unable to see beyond the barrel of his carbine.

The signal was announced, the canister rolled through the door, and Hanniford's men crossed the threshold as the suspect leapt from the bedroom window. As the suspect's feet hit the grass below, Hunter drove his shoulder into the man's rib cage, and tackled him into the prone position. As Hunter struggled to close the clasp on his handcuffs, O'Shaunessy located the burning canister on the floor, and pitched it out the window to clear the air, and facilitate the search for the suspect. Hunter, still conducting a pat-down search of the associate professor, felt the impact of the smoking canister on the back of his ballistic vest, and felt his eyes swell with tears as the chemical agent continued to disperse onto his clothing.

Hunter would always remember his unceremonious introduction to Special Weapons and Tactics. The team needed transformation, and he resolved that it would begin with his own development into a superior tactical operator.

~

Sergeant Hoskins assembled the 3:00 pm investigative progress meeting in the Detective Conference Room. The time had come to again collate evidence and leads and to gather information about who was responsible for the murder of Bethany Crutchfield. Seated at the circular conference table next to Hoskins, moving clockwise, were Detective Nancy Ballesteros, Detective Phil Rasmussen, and Detective Russell Horvath. Sitting in a corner near the door, and poised to respond immediately to any beckoning from the chief, sat Lieutenant Ben Sullivan. Attached to each wall was a whiteboard covered with clues, photos, rap sheets, and diagonal lines connecting pieces of evidence in an attempt to create order out of conflicting fragments of information.

Hoskins opened with a recap of the victim's last day.

"Having experienced a falling out with her boyfriend of six months, Ms. Crutchfield had begun dating other guys, to the frustration of her ex, a Mr. Paul Hendrickson. To our knowledge, the last person, other than her murderer, to have seen her alive was her friend and co-worker, Kimberly Goodman. The evening of the homicide, they shared dinner together, visited a couple nightclubs, and then retired for the night. Russell interviewed her, and will now bring us up to date on the details pertaining to his investigative work conducted at her place of employment."

"Dinner at the Rusty Pelican at Newport Beach was followed by visits to Blackie's and The Ritz," said Horvath. "The waitresses at each location recalled seeing the victim with a girlfriend, however, although several male subjects were seen eyeing them, no one was observed at any of the three venues making contact with them. The tab at the Ritz, their final destination, was closed out at 10:47 pm."

Horvath continued, "The only person known by Ms. Goodman to have actually dated our victim since her separation from her boyfriend was her supervisor, Ken Smollar. However, the event was business related, and Mr. Smollar indicated a reluctance to pursue any further involvement with her due to the possessiveness and temper of her ex-boyfriend."

"Crutchfield's ex-boyfriend, Paul Hendrickson, said that he last saw the victim at dinner at McCormick and Schmick's in Irvine, the Friday night before the crime. Their waitress described their meeting as tense, and said their conversation degenerated into an argument over control issues. Her co-worker recalled an occasion at a bar during which Hendrickson yanked Crutchfield's arm when she spoke to a security guard she recognized as having worked her apartment complex. Smollar's contribution to Hendrickson's list of outbursts was an incident at Paragon Aerospace in which he was rude to the receptionist, after having been denied immediate access to the victim."

Detective Rasmussen acknowledged the head nod from Horvath, and took his cue to begin his account of the boyfriend interviews.

"Hendrickson was as big of a jerk as the witnesses had described him, but simply being a hot head doesn't necessarily make him a murderer."

Nancy Ballesteros rolled her eyes and thought to herself, *Oh please Phil, don't go soft on me.*

Rasmussen continued, "During our initial interview with him, he indicated that he had spent the evening of the murder at home in his apartment. For some time, we felt secure in this explanation, due to an apparent video corroboration from a construction site camera that placed his vehicle in his carport space all night. However, during a subsequent interview, a witness placed him in the area of the victim's apartment, and he admitted to having stayed at his new girlfriend's Irvine apartment. Hendrickson then amended his account by stating that he had borrowed his brother's motorcycle and had driven by the victim's apartment on the way to the donut shop. We think his two-fold purpose of purchasing donuts and "checking" his ex-girlfriend's apartment is suspect, and more reflective of stalking behavior."

Ballesteros thought, *Very clinical, Phil. Planning on taking the sergeant's test?*

Rasmussen elaborated, "Within weeks preceding the victim's death, Hendrickson had begun dating Tiffany Binghamton, who happens to be his boss' girlfriend. She corroborated his alibi, which he stated accounts for his motive for lying to keep the relationship secret from his boss, but seems risky in light of a homicide investigation. His admission of a prior drunk driving arrest, but exclusion of a record for battery is noteworthy, and we think he was consciously avoiding mention of a history of violence."

Ballesteros said, "I'd like to provide some additional context to the assumption that the victim's boyfriend should be considered a suspect.

Crutchfield's neighbor, Blake Gruden, a third year UC Irvine biology major, confirmed the observations of the security guards who saw several male visitors enter the victim's apartment. Gruden further related that his roommates viewed her ex-boyfriend as an asshole. Her parents were familiar with Hendrickson, and described him as Mr. Wrong. They encouraged her to see other more suitable men. Our victim would only share with them that she was casually dating others, but provided no details. We've seen this pattern in domestic violence cases over and over again. The boyfriend becomes possessive, jealous, and controlling until the girlfriend terminates the relationship. Frequently this scenario leads to stalking, assaultive behavior, and on occasion, the homicide of the female in the relationship."

Hoskins stood, pointed to a diagram of timeframes on the whiteboard, and added, "The security guard working the swing shift at the victim's apartment complex notified Horvath that he saw Hendrickson driving by the site at approximately 10:00 pm, which was one hour before the time-of-death range estimated by the coroner. Granted, these times are estimates, but they could be viewed as somewhat exculpatory by both the district attorney and whoever 'Mr. Wrong' may select as a defense attorney."

Lt. Sullivan interrupted, "However, our psychic was quite accurate in her description of the suspect, and his similarities to our victim's boyfriend, and his motives."

"Yes Lieutenant. However, her depiction of the crime was so generic that it could be applied to a broad spectrum of candidates, and really does not lead us to credible evidence," said Hoskins. "The coroner's forensic report identified two small semen stains on the bed sheets. With the consent of his attorney, Mr. Hendrickson provided a blood sample, which would be remarkable if his lawyer felt that there was a possibility of his guilt. Hendrickson's blood analysis indicated that he could be the donor of one of the stains. However, the second stain, below the victim's groin, was not a match to her boyfriend."

"What is most compelling is the fact that the suspect in this crime left his autograph in blood, and we don't know who he is. The bloody palm print on the doorjamb has been compared with every male known to have associated with the victim, and anyone in proximity to her apartment. Whether it is her evil boyfriend's, the nerdy neighboring college boys, or her supervisor's fingerprints and hand impressions, none of these standards of forensics match the suspect's palm print painted in blood within our victim's home. We have no other leads, and unless we find some information directing us toward the author of this ghoulish autograph, our case is cold." Hoskins concluded his statement in a voice filled with disappointment.

"The chief will not be happy with this development," Sullivan announced as he walked out of the conference room.

"Neither will Bethany," Hoskins said, shaking his head.

82 Dave Freedland

Chapter 11

Ten Years Later

The August humidity was intense that evening, and as it was appearing to be a rather large class for the night, the Jazzercize instructor propped open the back door leading to the alley for better ventilation. The North Meadow shopping center was filled with activity, as patrons were getting out of their vehicles and going to various popular local destinations including the market, yogurt shop, and Chinese take-out. Included in that mass of northern Irvine inhabitants were several soccer moms, co-eds, and secretaries clad only in leotards and leggings heading toward their exercise class, oblivious to whomever might be watching.

In the alley behind the center, he stared from the shadows hoping that the opening from the back door was wide enough to capture her image. As he'd hoped, she momentarily passed by the propped door, punctual as always, clad in a purple leotard and black leggings, with a United Airlines flight attendant carry-on bag slung over her shoulder. Excitement began to build as her familiar blonde pony-tail bounced into view followed by the remainder of her body backing into his picture, framed by the edges of the door and the doorjamb.

For the past two months he had followed this ritual after establishing the location, days of the week, and hour of her exercise regimen. He watched from the six minute warm-up stretching until the 50 minute synchronized dance movements ended with the traditional cool-down, lasting precisely four or five minutes. He knew that she was perfect. He had orchestrated the "chance" encounter at the yogurt shop last Wednesday following her class and was certain that her returned smile was an invitation to intimacy. During his most recent surveillance of her home the night before, he had followed her white Ford Expedition to the airport and watched her curbside embrace. The three silver bands on the sleeves of her lover's blazer caught the florescent lighting of the terminal, and announced to all that this first officer would be working the flight deck that night. But to her voyeur, his departure signified an to consummate their imagined relationship.

~

Sergeant Scott Hunter, call sign SAM 20, was in the shotgun position in the patrol car as it caravanned down Interstate 5 along with several other law enforcement vehicles heading toward the training site in Coronado. The destination for SWAT was a small, decommissioned submarine tender, which two members of the US Navy's elite SEAL Team 3 had converted into a venue for training sailors to repel unwelcomed boarders.

During the previous month's county-wide SWAT Commanders' meeting, the team leader from the Sheriff's SWAT complement had remarked that they had had their clocks cleaned by a small band of SEALs in a paintball exercise onboard a sub tender. Intrigued that four SEALs could take out a twenty-officer SWAT platoon, Hunter made contact with a Naval Special Warfare representative to schedule the training. Now a Detective Sergeant in charge of one of two SWAT squads, Hunter had been proactive in presenting challenging training exercises to the team. Sitting in the number one position on the lieutenant's promotional list, he needed the coveted gold bars on his collar in order to take command of the entire complement.

Upon arrival at the training vessel, Hunter met with Petty Officers Paul Reinhart and Jack Humphrey. Two additional Naval Special Warfare members attended to equipment on the deck in preparation for the day's activities. Reinhart, the square jawed leader of the training contingent explained how he and his partner had discovered a different approach to close quarters battle (CQB) tactics. During their assignment in training sailors to defend ships from being boarded, Reinhart and Humphrey had incorporated paintball rifles that fired projectiles traveling at 300 feet per second to visually and painfully confirm successful tactics. The standard scenario given was that the SWAT team's mission would be to retake the bridge of the submarine tender from four hostile adversaries played by four Navy SEALs. The SWAT team would stage from the galley below deck, then move topside, retaking territory until securing the bridge.

Hunter marked out assignments for his 18-officer team by first identifying a scout element to deploy onto the deck and sweep the stern to ensure that operators advancing toward the bridge were not taken out from behind. Upon commencement of the exercise, SWAT members exploded onto the deck, and were immediately pelted with paintballs raining from multiple directions. Both Hunter and his counterpart team leader, Sgt. Rob Gaston, moved their resources forward. Within seconds, their entire team was eliminated by one SEAL firing from the stern of the ship into the backs of eighteen stunned police officers.

As all weapons were placed on the deck and protective helmets were removed, Hunter assembled his team members to reconstruct just how this fiasco could have occurred. Petty Officer Reinhart approached their huddle with a smile, and pointed out his observations from the bridge to the assemblage of embarrassed faces whose bodies were still dripping with paint.

"My partner, Jack Humphrey, was hanging off the stern, and waited 'til your scouting party passed by to pull himself onto the deck and take you guys out," Reinhart stated without arrogance, but with a sense that the outcome was predictable.

Hunter thought through Reinhart's remarks. They had taken at least 15 minutes briefing in the galley, and Humphrey had the strength to hold himself and all his gear in the pull-up position. He had then pulled himself up to a shooting position and accurately hit 18 targets in rapid succession.

The team regrouped in the galley, and Hunter reassigned two new scouts for the stern sweeping mission. Again, they bolted onto the deck and were met with an unrelenting shower of projectiles. However, the scout element learned from their predecessors' mistakes and cleared the stern with certainty. Two squads of SWAT operators advanced toward the ladders leading to the bridge, but a familiar chorus of "I'm hit, I'm hit!" rang out in succession, as team members were struck by paintballs delivered by seemingly invisible adversaries.

Hunter's frustration quickly turned to fascination as to how these four mortals could deliver such punishment without being seen. He approached Reinhart and requested a brief tutorial on his secret to transforming sailors into true-to-life Lucas and Spielberg's Jedi Knights.

Reinhart prefaced his comments by stating that the SEAL teams, like any unit associated with a large organization are slow to change, and that these new tactics had not yet been adopted universally. During the course of his instruction to entry level seamen, Reinhart discovered common behaviors in shooting situations and sought to address them. Shooting while moving was essential, but accuracy was problematic. Reinhart studied old Marx Brothers movies, and found that Groucho Marx displayed a unique walk with his cigar that could translate into a "shooting platform" which kept a gun barrel level. Secondly, Reinhart's team members never shot twice from the same position. They shot from standing, kneeling, and prone interchangeably, giving their adversaries no way to predict where a target might be.

Finally, their most challenging tactic was to learn ambidextrous shooting techniques. This enabled this small band of SEALs to shoot around left and right hand corners, exposing only the barrel of the rifle and the sighting eyeball to an adversary. With several hours of practice, they could immediately recognize a right or left corner of a room, door, or object and instantly change the position of the weapon to minimally expose the shooter.

Hunter was further intrigued by Reinhart's use of light to aggressively enter rooms and identify adversaries. His team used the smallest, most brilliant flashlights to illuminate a threshold and its corners, then went dark during the critical passage from a hallway into a room. Hunter was impressed, but was skeptical about the time it would take to train the average police officer to master such skills. At the conclusion of the training day, he met with his two most motivated and talented team members, and they resolved to devote a day each weekend to assist Reinhart and Humphrey as actors in their training presentations, and learn the new CQB tactics for their own organization's adoption.

~

"Detective Tom Blackburn" the words on the nameplate read. Sitting at his desk, he pulled it from the box and slipped the clear plastic cover off. This assignment to detectives was, up to this point, only a dream whose reality required someone retiring, and him becoming lucky. But all the same, this was a unique opportunity for Officer Tom Blackburn to demonstrate in this newly created temporary nine-month position that he possessed the talent to solve crimes and arrest their perpetrators. As he placed the nameplate in the proper desk location so that others could see it, Blackburn wondered what he might have done to elevate his name on Sergeant Hunter's long list of applicants, many of whom were well known for their successes in capturing criminals.

"Nice job on those auto burg cases," said Detective Nancy Ballesteros, as she seated herself in the workstation next to his. He was relieved to hear his new partner just answer his question about the determining factor in their sergeant's choice. The auto burglary cases to which Ballesteros referred had reflected the resourcefulness that this new member of the detective-elite had employed, and which would eventually result in his permanent assignment to the coveted Robbery/Homicide detail.

A simple late night car-stop for a broken tail light last month had led to the discovery of twelve in-dashboard car radios strewn across the backseat of a Chevy Nova. The two Delhi District gang bangers from Santa Ana had sat silent and motionless in the front seat, as the heroin track marks on their arms and the property in the back said all that was necessary to indicate the elements of the crime of Possession of Stolen Property. What had made this case difficult was the fact that basically no one records the serial numbers of the stereos in their automobiles, and these street-wise home-boys weren't about to tell this tall, lanky and studious looking patrol officer where the vehicles were that they had just burglarized.

Blackburn had booked them into the Orange County Jail, then returned to the city and begun canvassing neighborhoods for victim vehicles with smashed windows, and alerted Dispatch to notify him when residents called to report that their cars had been victimized. He knew that he would somehow need to find a way to identify a specific radio to a specific automobile without any serial numbers in order for the district attorney to file charges against his suspects. His experience told him that victims recognizing identifiable "scratches" to the property wouldn't hold up in court.

As victim vehicles were located in the field, and as additional persons called the station to report their crimes, Blackburn had recorded the sequences from left to right that the victims had programmed their AM and FM radio channel buttons. No two channel sequences were alike, resulting in each radio found in the backseat of the suspect Nova matching each victim's automobile. Blackburn's linking of suspect, property, and victim had not been gratifying. not only because it solved a puzzle that resulted in a DA case filing, but also because it had rewarded him with a desk in Detectives.

He was now energized to learn from his new female partner and resolved to enhance the pace of his apprenticeship by studying cold cases on his weekends.

Lincoln 9 89

90 Dave Freedland

Chapter 12

Her home backed up to a small neighborhood park with huge maple trees bordering walkways leading to a tot lot with swings, slides, and a carousel. The street bordering the park was lined with an assortment of parked cars, enabling his Mustang to blend during his "visit" and planned departure across the finely manicured park lawns leading to the victim's backyard fence.

Anticipation filled the killer's mind as his imagination constructed a scenario in which the sleeping victim awakened to his pronouncement of her name and her subsequent surrender to his presence. Following his scaling of the five foot block wall, he hid behind a clump of junipers and donned the latex gloves secreted in his back pocket. Upon reaching the sliding glass door, he exhaled with relief at the discovery that the heat of the August night had prompted her to leave the glass slider ajar, generating a draft of cool air passing throughout the house.

The locked screen prevented access, but a silent slit with his folding Buck knife provided immediate entry. His heart pounded as excitement mounted with every step down the hallway leading from the kitchen to the master bedroom. No stairs to encounter, no yipping dogs, only a brief glance from an overweight cat curled on a pillow at the foot of the bed.

She lay motionless on the sheets as he gazed, fixated. For months he had crafted his fantasy toward this climax, when she would welcome him to her bed. He gently broke the silence by the whispering of "Kristen" in his unfamiliar voice. Startled, she threw the bedspread over her legs, and screamed with horror at the sight of the human shadow saying her name.

Lincoln 9 91

Panic filled him at the abrupt interruption of the culminating moments of his obsession. It wasn't supposed to happen this way. As she sprung from the bed toward the door, his fist slammed against her temple knocking her into the wall, dazed. Knowing that within seconds her screams would resume, he threw her across the bed, and shoved her face into the pillow. Still hearing the muffled sounds of her screams, he reached for the terry cloth belt from the robe lying at the foot of the bed, and maniacally double wrapped it around her neck. As he tightened the slack around her carotid arteries, she lost consciousness within seconds from the restricted blood flow to her brain.

Realizing his moment was slipping away, he clumsily mounted her, feverishly pumping, hoping for reciprocal pleasure from a fantasy whose life had already expired. A profusion of sweat filled his face, followed by a rush of nausea as the thought of escape became paramount.

He grabbed a small television set from the dresser and lumbered down the hallway, through the kitchen, and out onto the patio. With the TV in his right hand, he grasped a wrought iron patio chair with his left, and dragged it across the lawn to the back fence. Placing the television on the chair, he left enough room for his shoe to sufficiently boost him over the fence and into the park.

Quickly focusing his thoughts on his escape plan, which he had dry-run hundreds of times in his mind, he picked up the three-iron, along with a golf-size wiffle ball hidden behind the shrubs. He briskly walked across the park toward his Mustang, golf club and ball in hand, prepared to assume the identity of the eccentric golfer, in the event that he encountered one of Irvine's finest.

~

The summer sun had already raised the thermometer to 80 degrees at 8:30 am, as Sergeant Scott Hunter peered through the lens of the Eotech sight atop his refurbished M-4 carbine. Today was range day for SWAT, and Hunter, now in his second year as a detective sergeant, and fourth year as Red Team leader, had the comfort of knowing that his investigative in-basket was being covered by Sergeant Brig Maxwell during his firearms exercises. As he clicked the elevation screw on his sight, in an effort to zero-in his newly acquired variant of the M-16, he felt the vibration of his cell phone against his nylon web belt. He had hoped it was his secretary requesting clarification on a dictated report, but sensed an urgency that could spoil an entire day's opportunity to hone his shooting skills. He answered, hearing the stress in Lieutenant Billy Brisco's normally hyper demeanor, but skipped over the introductory narrative until it ended in the words, "apparent homicide."

Patrol units were rolling to the Village of North Meadow where a female flight attendant had been discovered deceased by her tennis partner. Lieutenant Brisco had directed Sergeant Maxwell to respond with a team of detectives, and he requested Hunter excuse himself from SWAT training and assist in the investigation. Hunter assigned his White Team counterpart to assume his range mastering responsibilities, and then entered the equipment van to slip out of his ballistic vest and fatigues, before donning his detective polo shirt and cargo pants.

Hunter thought to himself, "The good lieutenant could have at least waited until Patrol personnel arrived before assigning investigative resources to an unconfirmed crime." His Chevy Tahoe left the graveled range road onto Irvine Boulevard heading toward North Meadow.

~

Detective Tom Blackburn listened intently to the crackling transmissions on the police radio providing him with updates as he sat next to Detective Nancy Ballesteros, who drove their unmarked Ford northbound on Culver Drive toward the victim's residence. As he attempted to visualize the scene from the cryptic messages sent by the uniforms entering the home, he thought of the contrast that he and Ballesteros would present upon their arrival. Ballesteros was now a cranky, graying senior detective who dreaded attending any event requiring her uniform, as her ever expanding hips made buckling her Sam Browne gun belt a painful exercise. She hoped that this call was not as bad as it sounded. Work avoidance was a priority when retirement was within three months. In contrast, Blackburn, the tall, thin and quiet one hungered for the opportunity to get the "big case," and to not just arrest the perpetrator but to see the investigation through to conviction.

As the first officer on scene transmitted the confirmation that the North Meadow resident was deceased, Blackburn turned to Ballesteros and asked, "Do you know if there was a full moon last night? I think there was."

"What difference does it make? We're probably gonna get stuck with this can of worms," Ballesteros snapped back.

"Well, when I was a deputy working the central jail it was a common experience to have bookings increase exponentially when the moon was full. It may be attributed to lunar gravitational pull, but all the criminals and crazies came out from hiding at full moons," Blackburn answered studiously.

"Nonsense," Ballesteros retorted without explanation.

Blackburn thought to himself, *Maybe when she retires my new partner will at least have a sense of humor. A permanent assignment to the Bureau would be nice to have also.*

~

As investigative personnel began arriving on scene, patrol officers were already busily unraveling spools of yellow boundary tape around the front yard trees. Two officers walking the park along the perimeter fence were counting the number of houses from the street corner to the victim's residence, to establish where to begin cordoning off the rear of the victim's home.

Hunter arrived minutes behind Maxwell as Ballesteros turned onto the street. Upon meeting Maxwell on the sidewalk, he received a preliminary briefing that bore overtones of a case possessing similarities from his distant past.

"We have a thirty year old United Airlines flight attendant, Kristen Greer, who failed to answer the door when her tennis partner arrived to pick her up. She found the rear slider open, entered, and then discovered the victim face down on the bed in the master bedroom. The apparent cause of death is strangulation by her bathrobe belt, and it appears that the victim was sexually assaulted," Maxwell said, giving his normally sterile account.

"Where's her tennis partner now?" Hunter inquired.

"She's sitting in the front seat of a patrol car being consoled by one of our newer female officers."

"How do you want to split up responsibilities?"

"Since I've already started some things at the house, how about I handle the crime scene, and you set up a team to background the victim?"

"Sounds good. Hey, instead of having Ballesteros taking the lead, let's assign her and her partner, Blackburn, to start the background work since she's retiring soon."

"Good idea, I don't think she'll complain."

~

Phil Rasmussen, now a Patrol Sergeant, assigned a uniformed officer to initiate a crime scene log, then carefully walked the house to gather an overall perspective of the sequence of murder. As blood had pooled to the lower portions of the victim's prone body, her facial features had become unrecognizable from the framed photos on the wall depicting her athletic beauty. Maxwell entered the bedroom and joined Rasmussen scanning for clues, and focused on the ligature marks on her neck that matched the white belt made of the same fabric as the bathrobe strewn across the floor. The familiar plasma-like substance resembling semen soaked the sheet between her separated legs. Aside from the linen on the king size bed, there was no ransacking to the immaculately maintained room. Hunter saw that the only article apparently out of place was the missing earring from the victim's left ear. Her right earlobe was adorned with a single diamond stud, while the pierced hole in her left lobe was empty.

The sergeants walked down the hallway leading from the bedroom to the kitchen and stepped through the open screen door onto the patio. Maxwell and Rasmussen immediately fixated on the out of place television set sitting on the patio chair next to the back fence. Remembering the layout of the victim's bedroom, Hunter said to Maxwell, "The TV set obviously belongs on the dresser in the master bedroom. There was no dust to mark its place, but the arrangement of jewelry boxes and mirrored trays on the dresser left a space the size of the television screen. It is interesting that the jewelry boxes were not disturbed. Maybe the television was planted there to make this look like a property crime."

"What would be the motivation for doing that?" Maxwell inquired.

"I think the killer believes that it is somehow more acceptable to commit a murder during the course of a burglary, than to plan a sexual assault which results in the death of the victim."

"Warped dude," Maxwell concluded.

Chapter 13

Officer Rex Campbell started the lunch break discussion at the firing range while his fellow Team members sat in the shade opening their individual ice chests. The Department had for several years issued the Sig Sauer P220 .45 caliber pistol to all personnel, and the stopping power of the round could not be denied. But the P220 only held a capacity of nine bullets.

"If we switched to the Glock .40 caliber pistol we could have a fifteen round capacity before having to change magazines," Campbell said.

"But you're giving up the stopping power of the .45 round." White Team Leader, Sergeant Jim MacNeal responded.

"Yeah, but not much, and I would have six more bullets to keep me in the fight."

"The key to winning a gun battle is bullet placement. Make your rounds count. Besides, in the SWAT environment your primary weapon is your rifle, or carbine, which has a 30 round capacity. Your pistol is only for back-up."

The discussion continued for several more minutes before range exercises resumed. In actuality, the chief of police had no intention of earmarking funds he had designated for a motivational speaker for supervision and command staff, to another new "toy" for SWAT. The fact that the Team's marksmanship was stellar, and kept them competitive in the various competitions in which they had regularly participated, worked against any additional procurements. The issue for SWAT was moot. Firearms excellence was not as much of a priority for many who had sworn to protect and serve.

The victim's husband had been notified, and his return flight from the East Coast had two more hours until touchdown in Orange County. The coroner had already removed the body, after having estimated the time of death between 10:00 pm and 2:00 am. Crime scene investigation technicians had dusted for prints, swabbed for DNA, vacuumed for hair and fibers, and videotaped the scene prior to the victim's removal.

Ballesteros and Blackburn sat inside the Mobile Command Post Vehicle continuing their interview of Betsy Alarcon, the victim's best friend.

"What was Kristen's relationship with her husband?" Ballesteros inquired warmly.

"It was good. She and Rick had been married for three years and were hoping to start having a family when he got promoted to captain," Alarcon responded in a low voice that was now composed after the initial shock.

"Did she mention to you any contact from strangers or hang-up telephone calls?" Blackburn interjected focusing on clues.

"Kristen and I both noticed how there seemed to be an increase in male foot traffic in the shopping center that coincided with the evening hours of the Jazzercise class. However, she never brought up any particular individual. She relied primarily on her cell phone, but did ask me if I had gotten any hang-up calls recently. She said that her answering machine had a few messages with dial tones."

Ballesteros leaned over to Blackburn and whispered, "Maxwell gave me her cell phone and the cassette for her land-line answering machine."

"Betsy, was there anyone within her circle of co-workers with whom she was particularly close, or someone who showed an inordinate amount of interest in her?"

"No, she made it pretty clear that she was happily married, and Rick's presence in the workplace kept any ideas of extracurricular activity out of the question," Alarcon responded with conviction.

Outside the Command Post, detectives walked the neighborhood canvassing for witnesses who might have heard or seen unusual activity. Detectives Jack Pascall and Terry Nemeth happened upon a piece of information with potential for follow up. As with most neighborhoods, one individual stays home and serves as either an official or unofficial watch captain. In this case, the Greer's seventy-eight year old neighbor, Grace Coons, had noticed a van which she identified as "suspicious."

"What was unusual about this vehicle, or what drew your attention to it?" Recently promoted Detective Pascall asked.

"It was a box-type van, and it drove down the street on several occasions with the driver taking pictures."

"Okay, what led you to believe that it wasn't a realtor or appraiser working on a home being listed for sale?" Detective Nemeth asked.

"Oh, I hadn't thought of that. But I usually know when someone is planning on selling their house. And besides, I saw him taking photos on at least two occasions."

"What did the van look like?"

"It was, like I said, one of those square, box-type vans that was dark gray in color. I guess that by today's color schemes it would be called "graphite.""

"Can you describe the driver?"

"That would be difficult, with the windows having such a heavy tint. But I would say he was a male, white, in his late 30's, heavy-set, with dark, thinning hair."

Both detectives were surprised but pleased that Coons remembered details with remarkable precision for her age.

"Anything else that comes to mind?"

"The van had shiny wheels and a decal with some kind of a cartoon character on one of the back windows. I couldn't begin to describe it other than a circular sticker with a cartoon. Such a shame, that poor girl was such a sweetheart."

~

Detectives Ballesteros and Blackburn concluded their interview of Betsy Alarcon and then headed to John Wayne Airport to meet the victim's husband. Ballesteros prepared a list to conduct interviews of United Airlines flight attendants, pilots, and first officers on the victim's Orange County to Dallas route.

Detective Russell Horvath got out of his unmarked Ford and entered the Jazzercise studio located in the North Meadow shopping center. After explaining to the owner, Nancy Torres, the circumstances involving the victim, she shared with Horvath some complaints she had received in recent months about different men who were seen loitering around the open back door to the studio during hours of darkness.

"With the summer heat intensifying, the instructors and sometimes the students will prop open the back door to create cross ventilation," Torres elaborated.

"Did you report this to anyone?"

"I contacted Security for the center, and asked if they could step up patrols during our class times."

"What company furnishes services for this shopping center, and do you know if they identified anyone?"

"I think it is International Protection Service, and quite frankly, I have not seen any increased presence on their part, nor do I know whether they have made contact with anybody."

Horvath ended the interview and then walked the storefronts looking for potential additional witnesses. As he passed by the yogurt shop, he noticed a white compact car with the blue lettering and logo for International Protection Service parked in front of the Chinese restaurant located at the end of the row of shops. He entered the darkened lobby filled with the smell of fried rice, and acknowledged the Chinese hostess holding a stack of menus. He glanced around the curtain and saw a security guard seated in a chair waiting for a take-out order. James Bascomb made eye contact with the detective, and Horvath sat down next to him.

"I know you from one of my cases. I can't place which one. You were a witness weren't you?" Horvath began awkwardly.

"I think we met when I was working a construction site in the central part of the city."

" Okay, it's coming back to me. Do you work this shopping center now?"

"Actually, I'm field supervisor now for all centers north of Irvine Center Drive," Bascomb replied with pride.

"Congrats on your promotion. Say, I'm looking into some complaints regarding persons hanging out around the back door to the Jazzercise studio during the evening hours. Have you received any complaints about this, or have you observed any activity like that around here?"

"I'd have to check with the guards assigned to this venue, but I have independently observed and dispersed individuals on two occasions," Bascomb said with authority.

"Did you fill out field interview cards, or document anything identifying any of them?"

"Well no, but I can check our records to see if any of the personnel assigned here have submitted any documentation. If you could provide me with your business card, I can contact you regarding the results of my inquiry."

~

Sergeant Maxwell and his team of detectives closed down the scene after having concluded that there was no suspect immediately identified from the initial interviews and preliminary forensic evidence. While Sergeant Hunter's team continued to interview for clues, run computer searches on the victim's associates, and examine field interrogation cards for suspicious persons contacted, Hunter began to chart the homicide on the white board in the investigative conference room. As he printed the facts boldly with a black, dry erase pen, he paused momentarily thinking of the similarities to the Crutchfield murder ten years prior. He then walked out to the bullpen filled with detectives' work cubicles and scanned for Nancy Ballesteros' desk. Finding her with a phone to her ear, waiting on hold, he asked, "Did the victim or any of her associates have any relationship to Paul Hendrickson from the Crutchfield homicide?"

Ballesteros shook her head in the negative and answered, "Not yet."

Hunter looked across the partition separating Ballesteros' cubicle from Tom Blackburn's and saw a thick black three ring binder lying on Blackburn's desk.

"Is that the homicide book for the Crutchfield case?"

"Yeah, I've been reading cold cases after work," Blackburn said sheepishly.

"You're such a suck-up," Ballesteros announced condescendingly, before being taken off hold by a Records clerk.

"Have you found anything interesting?" Hunter followed.

"No, I just started looking at this one a few days ago, and I'm wading through the scores of interviews – some of these are as good as Sominex for putting me to sleep."

"Let me know if you dig anything up unusual."

Chapter 14

Within days of the Greer homicide, the rumors regarding the status of Detective Nancy Ballesteros were put to rest with the official announcement that her retirement within three months would be accelerated by the expenditure of vacation hours she had banked on the books. In two weeks she would take a 2 ½ month vacation leading up to her retirement date. Her husband had retired from the Sheriff's Department last year, and he was growing anxious for her to join him in a cross country trip in their motor home.

Ballesteros' departure left the Bureau light in experience in the Robbery/Homicide detail, and adjustments needed to be implemented. Lieutenant Briscoe had anticipated this possibility and tapped experienced Residential Burglary Detective Stephanie Winslow to fill the vacancy, and he would fill her opening from the existing detective applicant list. Winslow would be assigned as Blackburn's partner and would serve in a supportive role in the investigation of the young flight attendant's death. Blackburn welcomed Winslow's enthusiasm and resourcefulness in finding suspects, but was leery of her somewhat loud demeanor and mischievous sense of humor. Following the usual hallway discussions regarding the shuffling of positions, Blackburn engrossed himself in the answering machine evidence turned over to him by Ballesteros.

~

Hunter stepped onto the tatamis, bowed, and began stretching in the five minutes remaining before the commencement of class. The Japanese dojo had strict rules of etiquette that went into effect the moment a class participant set foot onto the mats. The building might be located in California, but once a person ventured inside, they were in Japan. The style was Shotokan karate, whose membership was the largest among the Japanese systems of self defense. However, having a strong connection to the mother country of Japan enabled the chief instructor, or Shihan, to invite guest instructors from other arts based in Tokyo to present Judo, Jujutsu, and Aikido as a complement to the explosive power of Shotokan.

Upon graduation from college, Hunter had spent a considerable portion of his time studying the myriad systems advertised as the perfect self defense. Working the city's concert venue had provided him with scores of opportunities to test each system's response to violence. Hunter found that he needed a solid stance, some grappling and control skills, and the ability to generate knockdown power with one strike. For him, Shotokan had answered the call, and Hunter had immersed himself in the system for the past fifteen years.

Wearing the black belt carried responsibilities, and as one moved up within the rank structure, the pressure rose to perform in accordance with expectations. Although there was no marking identifying the "Dan" or grade level of a black belt, everyone in class knew where to line up by rank at the beginning and ending of class for the ceremonial bows. Hunter's third Dan designated him technically capable of opening a studio and sufficiently dangerous to unleash hell. With the clap of the Shihan's hands, twenty individuals clad in crisp, white gi's quietly assembled with military precision, and all distractions departed.

~

Detective Blackburn was rapidly being seen by his peers as somewhat ritualistic, if not obsessive-compulsive in his mannerisms at work. He began each day at ten minutes to six arriving at his work station, and carefully removing his sport coat, revealing his badge, pistol, spare magazine, and handcuffs arrayed around his thick leather belt. On warm days, he sported a white, short-sleeve dress shirt and tie, which gave him an appearance similar to that of an aerospace engineer, if not for the weapon and shield announcing his membership in the elite fraternity of Robbery/Homicide detectives.

After placing his briefcase under his desk, he briskly left by the Detective Bureau's back door and headed down the stairs to the Patrol briefing room. Taking a seat in the back row, he listened intently to the sergeant's monotone reading of the daily log. Following the recitation of wanted vehicles and suspects, the sergeant opened the floor to any comments from detectives or members of the brass who happened to be in attendance at that early hour. Blackburn's contributions consisted of a precise accounting of investigative steps and resourceful interviewing that held the interest of the most inattentive one-year wonders that comprised the bulk of the Patrol division.

Upon leaving the briefing room, Blackburn headed directly up the stairs and grabbed a carton of milk from the refrigerator located next to the copy machine. He then returned to his desk, opened his briefcase, and retrieved a small, plastic cereal bowl featuring a well known Disney character. A single-portion of cornflakes was dumped into the bowl from a plastic baggie, followed by a proper soaking of milk. The bowl remained on Blackburn's desk until his departure for the day, which was the only variable in this ceremony of orderliness. All of this breakfast ritual was now observed by his partner, Detective Stephanie Winslow, who had arrived for work at a decent hour, and who was rapidly growing weary of his lack of variety. A competitive swimmer who possessed athletic obsessions of her own, Winslow seemed to display little patience for her partner's idiosyncrasies.

On Wednesdays, if there was not a "crisis of the day," Blackburn would stay late reading cold cases, looking for errors, missed clues, and gleaning tactics for asking the right questions. The Crutchfield case fascinated him, and in keeping with his obsessive tendencies, he scoured over every detail searching in hope of finding the one discrepancy that could lead to solving the puzzle. Thus far, the interviews of the victim's ex-boyfriend were intriguing but not convincing in terms of finding him guilty of getting away with murder. Blackburn pondered the similarities between the Crutchfield homicide and the case in which he was currently participating. A lone, attractive female in a residence strangled and sexually assaulted was a unique crime for this community. Generally, someone who commits such an act escalates to it from lesser crimes and has a record reflecting it. Blackburn sensed that forensic evidence coupled with investigative leg work held the answers, and that he would somehow pull the pieces together.

~

It started out as a typical early evening front desk incident. He was approximately 40 years of age, overweight and Persian. The desk officer listened courteously to his emotional ramblings, waiting for something to materialize into a report, or into a referral to some social service agency that could resolve what appeared to be a family issue.

The man was upset and worried that his brother was possibly suicidal. When asked what would prompt him to take his own life, this event was no longer an academic exercise in call classification, it was murder. His brother had suspected his wife of unfaithfulness, so he stabbed her to death along with her mother, and put them on ice in the downstairs bathtub. Never mind that his brother had committed a double homicide. The reporting party was most concerned over the welfare of his brother as a result of this psychological trauma.

At 7:35 pm, Hunter's SWAT pager alerted with the text, *"Poss. Barricade 54 Appleseed, homicide susp., 2 kids + deceased inside – resp. to scene."* The field command post was located at a nearby park where a Patrol sergeant had set up a dry erase board on the trunk of his car. Uniformed officers had established a perimeter around the two story tract home, and when the dispatcher had placed a call into the residence, the suspect had declined her invitation to exit.

Hunter arrived on the scene within twenty minutes of the page, clad in fatigues and had already mentally selected his React Team. Strategically placed near a structure's entrance, the React Team would be quickly assembled to respond to a crisis, as the inner perimeter was fortified with SWAT personnel, and snipers assumed the high ground.

While Hunter was briefed by the Patrol sergeant, arriving SWAT personnel donned load bearing level III ballistic vests along with M-4 carbines. Complicating an already horrific scenario was the fact that two children, aged 9 and 10, still occupied a house that contained their dead mother and grandmother. The crisis negotiator had succeeded in making contact with the suspect, but establishing rapport was another matter. Aside from the cultural challenges before him, the negotiator was attempting communication with an individual living in an alternative mental universe. No, he would not let the children exit. No, he would not come out, but he would consider further discussion when the police would put the President on the phone to discuss his Middle East policy.

A rear perimeter team had taken up a position behind the cinder block fence and near the springboard to the swimming pool. At the opposite end of the pool stood a small block wall enclosure for the filter and heating system. The team was fortunate to possess a panoramic view inside the back of the residence, which was enabled by the home developer's extensive use of tinted glass. The react team, headed by Hunter, was positioned by the number 4 corner. For accuracy and radio brevity, the structure's front door was assigned the number 1 side, and moving clockwise, each side of the residence was given a number, with number 4 completing the box. Corners were numbered by the meeting of structural sides, such as 1 / 2, 2 / 3, and so on. Hunter elected to place himself in the number 5 position in the "stack," which was the line of SWAT operators who would cross the first threshold of the residence. The first two officers would enter and encounter threats as a team, as would the second pair, and the Team Leader in the fifth position would direct additional resources stacked behind him. Poised an arm's length to his rear, Hunter's chemical agents operator held a battering ram.

Two-man sniper teams were positioned in high-ground locations in residences across the street and directly behind the suspect's home. The team facing the front door took a prone position on a pitched second story roof, while the rear team was fortunate to stage in an upstairs bedroom in a house on the street behind Appleseed. Night vision scopes and thermal binoculars gave the observer officers an excellent view through first and second story windows. Combining visual intelligence with audible information from the crisis negotiators, the Team Leaders could identify positions of occupants inside the structure.

Anticipating a possible entry, Hunter sent a scout to locate a house on Appleseed that possessed the same floor plan as the suspect's residence, to enable the react team to practice entries and room searches. Upon receiving permission from the resident to use his house, the scout brought temporary replacement officers to relieve the first four react team operators to practice at the duplicate residence.

Negotiations had deteriorated, and Hunter decided that the time had come for more pro-active measures to rescue the children. Information gleaned from snipers and negotiators indicated that the children were downstairs and that there were no firearms inside. Hunter radioed to the lieutenant in the command post his plan to create a diversion in front of the residence in an effort to drive the suspect towards the rear. Upon authorization, he signaled over the air that a flash-bang canister would be deployed by the front door, followed by an entry by the react team. The #3 man in the stack rolled the canister onto the porch, and within two seconds the front courtyard illuminated with white light, followed by a huge explosion of flash powder. The #5 man rolled out of the stack with the ram, and as his momentum carried him toward the door, the ram found its target at the deadbolt. The door flew open, and the react team poured into the living room like water.

The first pair of officers entered, hooking around the door jamb on each side of the front door, dividing responsibilities for threats like slices of a pie. The first officer took the larger slice, while the second's slice covered his partner's blind side. The next two in repeated the procedure, and Hunter followed by hooking around the hinge side of the heavy oak door. Scanning over the front sights of their M-4 carbines, the first team found the 9 year old girl and 10 year old boy huddled in a corner next to a sofa in the living room.

Simultaneous to the react team's dynamic entry, the rear perimeter team observed the rear sliding door swing open, and a silhouette resembling the suspect's description bolt out the back of the residence. The suspect ran to the pool heater enclosure, and crouched behind the block wall, brandishing what appeared to be a kitchen knife duct-taped to his right hand.

As officers yelled to the suspect to exit his position, the React Team scooped up the children and began a controlled departure from the living room, with officers #1 and #2 covering the rear. Hunter glanced to his left through an open door to a downstairs bedroom, and then with his left hand, pushed open the door to the adjacent bathroom. His peripheral vision picked up what appeared to be a human leg draped over the edge of the bathtub, with a shower curtain blocking all but the shin and foot. As Hunter and his team exited onto the porch, he could hear radio activity through his earpiece indicating that the team to the rear was in a verbal exchange with the suspect in the backyard. However, his immediate priority was moving the children to safety, so they continued their exit until reaching a patrol car where they were turned over to a uniformed Patrol officer.

In addition to the carbines aimed toward the figure frantically waving his arms behind the heater enclosure, there was a 40 millimeter less lethal projectile launcher guided by a holographic Eotech sight. Although accurate within 75 feet, a shot at that distance, in the night, against an erratically moving target would be a challenge. The young officer whose 40 millimeter launcher was trained on the suspect had just graduated from the SWAT academy and struggled to keep the sight centered on the occasionally visible torso. He made eye contact with his sergeant, Jim MacNeal, whose thumbs-up signaled he was clear to take a shot if a target was presented. He inched closer along the fence toward the block wall enclosure, closing the distance to approximately 50 feet.

Yelling obscenities in Farsi, the Persian rose from his crouched stance and momentarily brandished his right arm, his knife catching the light from the full moon, displaying that duct tape held the weapon firmly in place. The red dot in the SWAT rookie's sight held steady on the suspect's center mass, but as his index finger squeezed back on the trigger, his target suddenly dropped at the moment the hammer hit the ammunition primer. The bean bag round spun through the rifled barrel gaining a velocity in excess of 300 feet per second, and crashed into the suspect's jaw causing it to fracture. As he fell to the ground from the subsequent concussion, four officers effortlessly scaled the wall and rolled him into the prone position for cuffing.

After a second entry into the residence confirmed the presence of two deceased victims preserved on ice, Hunter's role changed to that of investigative supervisor, and the requisite assignments were given for the follow up interviews and crime scene evidence collection. The post-operation debrief would commence the following day, and aside from the usual nut cases in the neighborhood complaining about the overkill and militarization of the community, the incident will have been deemed a success. One murder suspect was now in custody, but two murderers were still outstanding. And the possibility existed that they were one, and a serial killer was planning his next move.

Chapter 15

The announcement was expected, and Lieutenant Billy Briscoe's retirement meant organizational movement up the promotional ladder into supervision and management. What the troops wanted was a lieutenant who had been a street cop and who would remain attentive to the rank-in-file rather than a self-promoter. Hunter, whose name had risen to the top of the list, was the leader who would wear the gold bars on his collar as a symbol of responsibility and trust. The Department needed leaders, not managers. The chief of police was old school, and he knew that the political winds were changing with a new majority in the city council. His time was short, and Hunter hoped that his promotion would not be delayed until the arrival of a new chief who might have different standards for his management team.

The notification came personally, and then officially on letterhead, that Sergeant Scott Hunter would be promoted to lieutenant in a ceremony in the Council Chambers the following week. The emotions were bittersweet, as Hunter was faced with the decision as to who would be pinning the new badge on his Class A uniform shirt. In most ceremonies the wife or significant other would assume that responsibility, but in Scott's case, he had the tragic misfortune of losing his spouse at the hands of a drunken driver.

Shortly following his academy graduation, his college sweetheart, Madison, and his sister, Cathy, had been driving home from a bachelorette party in San Diego. Their transition from Interstate 805 to Interstate 5 was abruptly halted by the wrong way driver whose two previous DUI convictions had not altered his destructive behavior. Cathy survived, but Madison lasted only long enough for the ER physician to pronounce her deceased. His plans for a family, perhaps a son to cheer through Little League, ended that evening on the interstate. It took over a year for Scott to even assent to the dates arranged by his sister. She went so far as to select friends and acquaintances whose tawny hair bore resemblance to Madison's flowing mane, not realizing that it made matters worse.

Sometimes badge pinning was a means of obtaining endorsement from someone already accepted in the organization as an authentic leader, or a political message announcing that the person promoted was supported by an individual possessing influence. In Hunter's mind the only candidate having the career credibility and integrity he sought to emulate was his father, the "Sage of 77th Division." The index card presented to the chief proudly bore his father's name for the announcement at the ceremony, and the issue was settled.

Hunter would be relinquishing a radio call sign to which both he and his entire organization had become accustomed. Out of the twenty sergeants within the Department's complement, he had risen to third in seniority, and his Sam 3 designation would now move to the next sergeant in the line of succession. Hunter would now assume the bottom position in the management ranks, and his new lieutenant call sign would be Lincoln 9.

~

Detective Blackburn meticulously examined each word of the reports documenting the DNA results from the Greer homicide which ultimately found no record to match to a suspect. He pondered the significance of this finding, and concluded that the CSI technician had either missed swabbing the article that held the crucial cells identifying a suspect, or the suspect's DNA had yet to be entered into the system. A backlog in data entry might explain this, or the suspect had been fortunate to have never been arrested for a crime that mandated DNA collection. Fingerprint analysis had been equally disappointing, so Blackburn turned to the investigative supplemental reports on witnesses, relatives, and friends to look for workable information.

Detective Winslow sat at her desk reading her own set of supplemental reports that she had split with Blackburn while she occasionally glanced at her computer screen to monitor responses to an e-mail she had sent seeking similar homicide cases from other law enforcement associates. She glanced over to Blackburn's desk, saw the ridiculous plastic cereal bowl, shook her head, and resumed reading.

~

Today was Monday, and it was, once again, time for semi-annual Block Training in the summer. Twice each year, the Department scheduled all sworn personnel to attend instruction in legal updates, state mandates, and perishable skills, such as firearms and defensive tactics. For some, it was an opportunity to take a break from the routine duties of answering Patrol calls for service, or emptying in-baskets. For others, it was misery to bake in 100 degree heat on a firearms range where Riverside and Orange Counties meet, and the smell of cows from the dairy farms of Chino is nearly overpowering. For Detective Russell Horvath, and several desk-riding members of the Detective Bureau, the latter description was more appropriate to their experience.

Horvath knew that he was overweight and out of shape, and his firearms skills could use some remediation. However, his sport coat and slacks fit him nicely when called to a crime scene, and the condition of his leather belt, holster, and magazine holders was admired by rookies and veterans alike. He used a particular brand of liquid shoe polish that provided his leather gear with the reflective qualities of patent leather shoes.

Upon completion of the morning classroom academics of law changes and procedural mandates related to domestic violence and the mentally ill, the training participants journeyed to the range where they were assigned to various stations for marksmanship exercises. Each station was staffed with firearms instructors primarily comprised of SWAT sergeants and assistant team leaders. To Horvath's horror, the first station presented a physical challenge potentially embarrassing due to the prospect of his inability to complete it. He had heard about the SWAT scenario given to applicants which involved scaling a wall, and shooting a target on the other side, but never personalized it to the realization that he was the example cited when it was formulated. The training committee never doubted his ethics, but believed that Detective Horvath and a small group of his peers had become lazy and failed to live by the Spartan standards of fitness for all officers.

Horvath knew that this would be a gut check, as he moved to the on-deck position on the range, and looked back at the younger generation of male and female Baker to Vegas cross country runners, triathletes, and surfers behind him. He saw the bill of the range master's ball cap nod up and down, signaling to start when ready and then sprinted to the five foot wooden portable wall approximately 25 yards away. The weight of his gun belt felt like a prisoner's ball and chain as he closed the distance to ten feet. Horvath reached for the 2 X 4 cap piece, and slammed his torso into the wooden slats. He tried to swing his leg up so that his toe could catch the edge, but his protruding stomach blocked its path. Horvath's arms were strong, and he tried to muscle it, but was only able to reach the top by running his legs in a circular motion resembling bicycle riding against the edges of a few boards. He straddled his body across the top, thinking he must look foolish, but swung his legs over by sheer determination.

He landed on both feet facing the wall, then turned and focused on the remaining ten yard sprint to the firing line where he would square off to a human silhouette target five yards beyond. His feet slid on the gravel and hard packed dirt, as he slowed to a stop at the chalked limit line. Horvath drew his Sig Sauer .45, and raised it to eye level as his left hand met it for support. His eyes strained to locate the front sight, and then found the rear dots, and aligned them only to discover his hands shaking with every beat of his pounding heart. His target was the ten-ring in the center of the silhouette's chest, and the course of fire required nine rounds: two to the ten-ring, and one to the head, performed three times, and then reload. The loaded magazine was then emptied into the center mass of the target as fast as the finger could pull the trigger.

Horvath fired two rounds, raised the barrel to the head, re-aligned the sights, fired, then dropped down to the ten-ring and repeated the procedure twice more. He fumbled the magazine from its pouch, found the empty magazine well, and then drove the ammunition home. His thumb caught the slide release. He chambered the next round and began firing until the pistol ran dry. Final score out of a possible 17: eleven hits – center mass, one head shot, and five misses. Not a stellar performance. He was fortunate to have cleared the wall and were the exercise an actual deadly encounter, his survival would be in question. Horvath pondered this first training evolution the remainder of the day.

That evening, Horvath's haunting memory of his lackluster performance became motivation for change. He began with cleaning his pistol at 10:00 pm, vowing to devote greater respect toward his weapon and its mission. He turned to his leather gear, and swabbed his holster, belt, and single magazine case with the jet-black liquid polish. He slid his 8-round back-up magazine into its case, and blew the bubbles from the polish before applying the last coat, not realizing that this simple act would lead to danger at a future date.

~

Detective Blackburn gathered his papers at the end of the day, organizing some on his desk, and placing others into his briefcase for further examination later that night. He and his fellow detectives had breathed a sigh of collective relief at the announcement that Hunter's promotion as a new lieutenant would not disrupt the Detective Bureau by re-assigning another manager to take his place. Although new managers normally went directly to Patrol, the chief felt that the Bureau needed to maintain continuity with the retirement of personnel, and the critical cases needed hands-on direction. Hunter, therefore, would remain in charge of criminal investigations, and oversee his replacement as sergeant. He would have to patiently wait for his coveted next prize, an appointment to command his team of meat eaters on SWAT.

Freshly promoted Sergeant Phil Brannigan would not be one to be characterized as a barn-burner when it came to the art of making arrests, however his reports were notorious for perfection. Elements of each crime were painstakingly articulated. Probable cause was clearly defined, so much so that even an editorial writer for the local newspaper had commented on his detail when one of his search warrants became public record.

Brannigan's elevation to the Big Boys arrived when he became a member of the Crocker Bank robbery apprehension team. In Irvine, there are no boiler plate crimes. A smoking gun homicide just doesn't happen, and every case rising to significance is characterized by epic brutality, diabolical craftiness, or unique methodology. The Crocker Bank, a landmark institution once marking Irvine's border with Newport Beach, stood several stories above the financial district's skyline. The call came across the radio waves in the form of three emergency tone alerts followed by a general broadcast for any units in the area of a robbery in progress at the bank.

The Irvine-esque characterization of the crime began with the announcement that the suspect was 60 years old, and he had taken the bank manager hostage. Brannigan worked that beat, and happened to be within a 30 second response. His follow-up officer however needed three minutes. As every unit within a five mile radius tried to get on the air, the radio transmission from a carload of detectives returning from lunch was never heard.

The dispatcher had the advantage of having an eyewitness within the bank whisper the suspect's every movement, which was directly relayed to the cavalry responding to the scene. The suspect, armed with a .45 semi-auto pistol, was leaving the bank and going into the second story parking structure, holding a bag of money and a balding bank manager in a headlock.

Brannigan arrived, bearing the Department's old .357 magnum revolver containing .38 special rounds and deployed himself behind a large circular cement pillar, only to discover an array of detectives displaying various forms of armaments ranging from Colt government .45's to .380 chrome pimp guns. As the suspect cleared the first set of columns in the parking structure, one detective yelled, "police, freeze," prompting the hostage to break loose from his captor and the suspect to raise the .45 in the direction of the commands. An eruption of gunfire ensued, with a total of fifteen rounds striking the suspect in various locations on his torso. He fell to the ground, but out of sheer orneriness began to rise, and was swarmed upon by uniforms and sport coats.

The rugged conditioning of this modern day Clyde Barrow kept him alive for three days before expiring. The autopsy revealed that Brannigan's .38 plus "P" rounds were some of the few munitions which had actually struck vital organs. It also announced to management the need for more effective ammunition, the standardization of firearms, and additional training in bullet placement.

Brannigan proved that he had the presence to keep his head while under duress, which Hunter saw as a resume requisite. Hunter was building a team for a mission whose members would come to realize it involved the apprehension of the most vicious of predators, the psychopath.

118 Dave Freedland

Chapter 16

James Bascomb sincerely believed that his promotion to regional security supervisor would somehow impress his dictatorial girlfriend, Anna Savoy. Her heritage may have been French, but her fondness for giving direction and orderliness led one to believe that there was some Prussian blood in her family tree. He spent his overtime money lavishing things on her in a vain attempt to stop her incessant complaining. In fact, he really had no emotional attachment to her at all, and merely saw her as a convenient opportunity for sex. She dressed in a manner commensurate with her responsibilities as a vice president for the county's credit union, which was a challenge with her continuing battle to control her weight. She refused to live with him, choosing to maintain her privacy in her Corona Del Mar condo, but compromised her standards to occasionally visit his place in Costa Mesa when convenience dictated. They met at a bar on the Balboa Peninsula, where Bascomb gave his best impression of a rugged individualist employed in the security business.

Savoy knew that he had some issues, but as is common in new relationships, she assumed she could fix him. Bascomb's lack of empathy for others and his shifting of blame for his errors would have been red flags to those clinically trained, but James had been adept at masking his more sinister personality traits. His bravado and confidence had been initially attractive, and it was too early for her to discern that his resume was fed more by ego than accomplishment.

Bascomb's two-year quest to achieve employment by a law enforcement agency had been plagued with continual rejection at the interview stage in the testing process. He could pass the written exams and had managed to survive the agility tests of two agencies that had placed them ahead of the oral boards as a screening eliminator. However, the seasoned veterans selected to sit on the interview panels had sized him up, and immediately recognized the personality disorder.

Bascomb viewed law enforcement's rejection of him as ludicrous and saw his new reason for living as a mission to demonstrate their utter incompetence. The fraternity of police was an exclusive club that selected on stereotype, which James believed weighted more on appearance than brain power. How could they not recognize his brilliance? He was constantly discovering the errors and omissions of his current employer, and displayed his absolute indispensability to them, but, he thought, also demonstrated how completely beneath his stature this organization stood in relation to his proper position in society.

Bascomb recognized that his younger brother, Nelson, was a simpleton but understood his role as somewhat of a guardian to him since their parents had died fifteen years prior. Although Nelson was a contented 35 year old self-employed gardener, James found his brother's occupation and pastimes of surfing, Angel baseball games, and beer totally pedestrian. However, it wasn't beneath him to occasionally share a brew. Ironically, it was James who introduced Nelson to their vice in common, strip bars. Anna was unaware of this particular interest, and James intended to keep it that way.

Nelson's van was large enough to hold his mowers and trimmers, as well as a bedroll for camp out nights at Doheny Beach for the purpose of catching the early morning wave sets. Surf racks and a set of Cragar mag rims were all the symbols of status that Nelson required. James, however, viewed Nelson's van as a necessary tool to borrow when trolling for hookers near the "resort motels" along Anaheim's Harbor Boulevard. In addition, the van provided a means of deflecting blame, should police focus upon him as a source of criminal conduct.

~

The call came in late Thursday morning on Sergeant Brannigan's cell phone from one of Newport Beach Police Department's detective supervisors, Sgt. Kevin McMullen.

"Phil?"

"Yeah, what's up Kevin?"

"Well, we're working this homicide in the Back Bay, and one of your cases came to mind, and I thought I'd give you a call."

"What are the circs?"

"We got a single female, late 20's, single family detached residence, and during the night a suspect forces entry, rapes victim, and then kills her."

"What's the cause of death?"

"Looks like trauma to the head from a lamp. You interested?"

"Absolutely, text me the address, I'm pulling a couple of my detectives right now. Thanks."

"No problem."

Brannigan grabbed Jack Pascall and Tom Blackburn, notified Hunter, and then headed southbound on Jamboree Road. Hunter left a meeting with the chief concerning prostitution reported in the area of the airport and walked into the back lot toward his staff car. As he tried to clear his mind of the scores of Asian massage parlors that needed to be worked, Hunter thought about the scene he was about to encounter.

Newport was considered one of the higher profile departments in terms of its culture regarding force. The residents included some of the wealthiest individuals in the country, living in multi-million dollar mansions on the water. Newport's pristine beaches, renowned for their body surfing shore break, drew inland dwelling riff raff, and the upper crust natives didn't take kindly to leniency toward drunken lawbreakers diminishing their property values. Newport Beach PD attempted to accommodate this philosophy of strict enforcement within the limits of the law. However, it was always prudent to recognize the locals, before making rash decisions.

Hunter approached the scene and flashed his badge to the rookie officer standing as a sentry at the first intersection before the victim's house. Normally, lieutenants rode their desks in order to finish their in-baskets before dinner time. However, Hunter was adept at prioritizing and sought to build time into each day for at least some field work. He located Brannigan, and received his briefing.

"Doesn't look like this is the work of our guy, but DNA will take a little time to confirm," Brannigan said. "Their victim was twenty-nine and worked as a department store clothing buyer. She had dinner at South Coast Plaza with girlfriends and retired early for the evening at home. When she didn't show up for her running club jog, her friend found the rear slider pried and the victim bludgeoned in the bedroom. Semen stains indicate intercourse, and there were ligature marks on her wrists. The unique piece of this puzzle is that the comforter on the bed was thrown over her head and body, and the metal lamp on the nightstand was slammed onto her head, causing death from blunt trauma."

Sergeant McMullen interjected, "Hey lieutenant, we videotaped the scene. Do you want to take a look?"

"Sure, thanks."

Hunter looked into the small viewing screen attached to the side of the camera. The CSI technician's lens captured the suspect's probable route of entry from backyard slider into the kitchen, down a short hallway, and into the bedroom. The haunting scene of a young woman lying motionless with matted hair covered with blood was more intense than any horror film Hunter had ever seen Hollywood produce.

"Sergeant, I appreciate you thinking of us in the middle of your mess, however, I think your guy is different from ours. Can you give us a heads-up if you develop any leads?" Hunter then left the scene.

~

Bascomb put the van in drive, started his brother's Grateful Dead cassette, and headed toward the 55 Freeway. His destination was Anaheim, and his goal was to find his preferred after-dinner dessert, a blonde street walker. His current female interest, Anna, described her hair coloring as strawberry blonde, but that was a stretch, and James didn't find it particularly appealing. She refused to respond to his suggestion of going "a little lighter," citing the fact that her skin tone required her natural hue.

As the van crept slowly down the boulevard, Bascomb's head began to ache from the unusually strong odor of gasoline that filled the vehicle's interior from his brother's mowers and trimmers. He scanned the storefronts, bus benches, and alcoves for mesh nylons, mini-skirts, and wigs to create the proper image of his fantasy. As they darted out between the parked cars, Bascomb one by one rejected each, while frequently checking his rearview mirror for blue and red light bars atop black and white patrol cars.

Seeing nothing that struck his fancy, he switched course, and headed for Irvine to hunt for an Asian alternative. He strolled into a Korean massage parlor on Skypark Circle, across from John Wayne Airport. Upon hearing his request, the young receptionist disappeared behind a dark curtain, and a small Korean waif adorned with an undetectable wig of straight blonde hair to her shoulders with bangs suddenly appeared. Bascomb and the girl then disappeared behind the curtain for a massage, which was not much more extensive than a TSA pat-down, and a brief experience of oral sex.

The following day a young waitress at a restaurant prominently located within the Irvine Spectrum Entertainment Center dropped a check at the table occupied by two business associates. Unknown to this 25 year old blonde, awaiting her discovery by the modeling industry, was that her every action was being mentally chronicled by a private security supervisor who sat at the counter waiting for his cheeseburger.

~

Lincoln 9 123

Tuesdays following a three-day weekend begin in catch up mode. This morning's backlog of cases was typical, but crimes against persons had unusually spiked, causing concerns that overall violence was rising. With such activity serving as a backdrop, Hunter listened more attentively to the radio traffic on his office scanner regarding a body found in the cab of a tow truck parked at the Exxon station at Sand Canyon and Interstate 5.

Hunter looked over the wall of Blackburn's cubicle and saw a handwritten sign affixed to his chair stating, "At Harbor Court with Winslow." He then stepped inside Brannigan's office and said, "Are you copying the call at the Exxon station? Winslow and Blackburn are tied up in court. Let's head out there and see what they're dealing with." The morning was brisk for spring, and Brannigan's staff car still had frost on the windshield that had not yet melted in the 7:00 am sun.

It's a long drive to Sand Canyon and the 5, but Irvine Center Drive was the quickest route in the morning. The Exxon station was earmarked for demolition, its remote location making the business unprofitable. Graveyard shifts were often staffed by military servicemen who moonlighted from Camp Pendleton after partaking in the city's nightclubs.

Upon pulling into the driveway, Brannigan parked next to Sergeant Austin's patrol unit and checked in with the uniformed officer who had started a crime scene log. Hunter and Brannigan walked through the office and turned right into the service bay where Sergeant Austin and the Area 5 Beat Officer stood by the parked tow truck that faced toward the gas pumps behind the roll up doors.

Seated in the driver's seat of the truck the body of a young man sporting a crew cut and wearing a heavy camouflage coat was slumped against the door. He appeared to be a Marine, but his head was leaned into the closed window, and his face pointed down in the space between the driver's door and the seat. A large amount of blood had flowed from the Marine's face, down the inside of the door, out the bottom edge, and onto the service bay floor.

Hunter looked at Sergeant Austin who was visibly tired from having spent the last hour of his graveyard shift trying to figure out why this Marine was dead and asked, "What do you think?"

Austin replied, "It looks like it might be a suicide, but I don't see a weapon that could have caused that amount of blood. I would suspect there might be a gun wedged between the driver's door and the seat."

Hunter studied the Chevy tow truck and noticed that the ignition key was in the "On" position, but the dashboard was not illuminated. Careful to avoid causing disruption to the body before crime scene photography, Hunter opened the passenger door that Austin had used to check the body for a pulse. He reached across the bench seat, slightly pulled back the Marine's coat, and lifted his tee shirt to examine his torso, which revealed skin that was bright pink.

Hunter turned to Austin and said, "Richard, I don't think you'll find a firearm in the truck. Last night, the temperature dipped below freezing and this Marine was cold. He got into the truck to get warm. He started the engine to fire up the heater, but didn't account for the carbon monoxide build up from the exhaust in the enclosed service bay. The pink skin is a classic indicator, and I would venture to say that the truck ran out of gas, the battery died, and this serviceman followed suit. The blood from his brain drained out his nose, and onto the service bay floor. Let me know if the coroner concurs when he arrives on scene."

Brannigan's staff car left the service station as the white van from the coroner's office slowed for the signal at the Interstate off-ramp. Hunter waived to the petite blonde with the ponytail awaiting her first dead body of the day, and whose analysis would soon validate his crime scene hypothesis.

126 Dave Freedland

Chapter 17

Hunter was carefully molding his homicide team into a cohesive unit capable of handling the daily crises while remaining focused upon the primary goal of cracking the two apparent serial crimes before discovery of a third. Sergeant Phil Brannigan was beginning to feel comfortable in his role as the supervisor but appeared to be more at home assigning cases, approving reports, and providing liaison with the district attorney's office to ensure that criminal charges were being filed. Similar to the Sergeant Major in the military, he made certain that assignments were completed, deadlines were met, and that things simply ran smoothly. This working arrangement suited Hunter well in that he was more action oriented and enjoyed getting his hands dirty in the field more than the traditional police manager. Brannigan's tactics were adequate, but he understood his strengths and gravitated toward them to the betterment of the team.

Detective Stephanie Winslow was clearly Type A personality, with enough energy and drive to mobilize the entire group. She complemented her partner, Detective Tom Blackburn, whose methodical approach to investigations often yielded hidden clues that were occasionally skipped by Winslow's endless enthusiasm. Detective Jack Pascall held much in common with his lieutenant, having an affinity toward athletic endeavors that enhanced his tactical skills. This attribute required discipline after having been paired with Detective Terry Nemeth whose continued fondness for empty carbohydrates still presented challenges to his Body Mass Index. However, there was no one more adept at finding information useful for law enforcement purposes by means of searching through various electronic media. Such was the line-up for Hunter's inner circle of investigators who bore the generic title of "detective," but through the power of Hunter's leadership and their own unique abilities, became the elite corps of respected professionals simply referred to as "Special Investigations."

~

The call was broadcast as a 914-S (Suicide), at the parking lot to the Marriott Hotel on Von Karman. Patrol was on-scene with three officers and a supervisor and had called for a detective to assist. At 8:30 pm, the odds of finding a detective were slim. But Detective Jack Pascall was finishing up a search warrant on a child molest suspect's computer that needed to arrive at the DA's office by 8:00 am. Hunter had finished his five mile run along the flood control channel and was drying off at his locker as his pack-set radio crackled with additional details from the call.

The victim had apparently scaled the 15 story condominium under construction overlooking the Marriott's northwest parking lot and either jumped, fell, or was pushed to his demise on the asphalt below. A rather untidy scene was on display for guests departing a wedding rehearsal dinner, but it could have been worse had the victim's coat not partially covered his face-down landing.

Pascall phoned Dispatch, notifying them of his departure from the station to the call, and Hunter simply keyed his mic to announce his request to be attached to the electronic call history. He grabbed the stenciled raid jacket from his locker before slamming the door shut and briskly walking out to the vehicle fleet.

Pascall was an accomplished triathlon competitor who consistently led the list of qualifying athletes for the annual Baker to Vegas run. The 120 mile relay through the desert, sponsored by the Los Angeles Police Department, was a celebrated event of law enforcement bragging rights, and a brutal test for participants braving the blistering heat. The department had been a long-time recipient of the coveted beer mug prizes, but as the organization grew in its sworn complement and correspondingly graduated to larger race divisions, the competition became more challenging.

Upon Pascall's arrival, he was surprised to see that the parking lot was devoid of the usual onlookers but glanced up to find several hotel rooms with guests sipping cocktails while watching from their balconies. His twelve years of experience gave him an edgy cynicism toward the public he served, but his sharp wit produced the usual ghoulish humor characteristic of cops and firefighters. He met briefly with the sergeant for a synopsis of the event, then walked over to the body as Hunter's Crown Victoria coasted on-scene behind the marked units. Pascall carefully raised the victim's left arm which displayed a Timex watch similar to the one adorning his own shock resistant Iron Man.

"Hmm, it's still ticking," Pascall announced as Hunter approached rolling his eyes in frustration. All Hunter needed was another complaint to resolve that resulted from a careless comment within earshot of some offended citizen.

It was apparent that head trauma was the proximate cause of his death, but Pascall and Hunter elected to journey up the stairwell to examine some papers left by the victim that a Patrol officer had discovered on the 15th floor. They met the unusually portly uniformed officer on the 15th floor balcony, where he was still perspiring from an elevated heart rate generated by the climb. He pointed out to them a small pile of cigarette butts and a booking slip from the Orange County Jail, listing indecent exposure, with priors, as the crime for which the now deceased Asian student from the University of California, Irvine had been charged.

"Usually see this result from bad grades," Pascall stated without emotion.

"It would appear that this confirms our initial hypothesis of suicide," Hunter stated mimicking Sherlock Holmes' British response to the obvious exclamation of Dr. Watson.

"Looks like he gave it a lot of thought," Pascall followed, pointing toward the Marlboro butts stamped out on the concrete deck.

"Does he have a record besides the indecent exposure?"

"Minor in possession two years ago."

"Call the coroner and see if they can handle the death notification to next of kin," Hunter directed before leaving the room and heading back to the stairwell.

Hunter drove the 2 ½ mile route back to the station listening to the radio activity picking up at the amphitheater as Iron Maiden took the stage. Hunter thought, *Those guys walking the parking lot must be working their asses off tonight*. Fights, narcotics, and ticket scalpers made the night go fast for the officers working the promoter-paid overtime at the Meadows. He was signed up to work Jimmy Buffet in a few weeks and although the crowds were generally mellow, the craziness led to some bizarre calls for service.

After parking his car in the secure lot, Hunter walked through the automatic doors into the station to notify the watch commander regarding the disposition of the suicide for official responses to the usual press inquiries. The command office was empty, and the public address system kept paging the watch commander to contact Dispatch. Hunter looked at the bank of television monitors displaying different angles of the custody facility and watched a lone jailer processing an obviously intoxicated male wearing a soiled tee shirt bearing the classic Iron Maiden logo.

Hunter thought, *The watch commander must be in the john*. He turned as the loud clank from the jail sally port door opened, and the jailer stepped into the room and made eye contact with Hunter.

"Lieutenant, can you help me a minute? I need to move a prisoner from one cell into another, and he's in here for fighting."

"Sure," Hunter replied, recognizing that the normal crew of custody officers were working at the amphitheater concert, and that the jailer making the request was a new employee.

Hunter, still holding his pack set radio in hand, followed the jailer through the heavy steel door and slammed it shut behind them. They walked past three empty single cells and arrived at the end of the hallway where two large cells stood on the left side, and a booking counter was mounted on the opposing wall. The jailer opened the large empty cell on the left as Hunter turned to place his radio on the booking counter to his right.

~

Ashley Horton sat at her dispatch console watching the activities in the custody facility on the overhead closed circuit television with a split screen providing pictures from two different cameras. One lens focused on the hallway leading from the watch commander's office, while the other provided coverage of the drunk tank and the safety cell, designated for combative inmates. She watched as Hunter laid his radio on the counter, and thought about him, wondering if he ever thought about her. She had met him once socially at a Patrol shift change party, and they had spoken for nearly an hour, sharing several interests in common. The chardonnay helped break the ice, but workplace relationships are awkward in paramilitary organizations. In many agencies, fraternization is frowned upon between supervision and line level personnel. It often creates harassment issues when break-ups occurred.

Ashley was a line level police dispatcher who had had several advances from officers seeking courtship. However, her preference for maturity had eliminated the 25 year old wonders whose academy buzz cuts had grown out long enough for generous usage of mousse. She was a 30 year old looker with reddish brown hair, wide blue eyes, athletic curves, and was on a mission to advance herself by attending night school in pursuit of her degree.

Although he exhibited a kinship to the street cop, Hunter occupied the stratosphere of management, who normally steered clear of in-house relationships for fear of potential litigation. But to Ashley,

Hunter seemed outside of such complications, and her hidden crush remained undeterred.

~

As Hunter turned from the counter toward the jailer he realized that the door to the drunk tank had already been opened, and he was immediately confronted with boxer-style fists advancing towards him. The jailer had stepped clear, allowing an inebriated Hispanic a direct line on Hunter, while this flummoxed custody officer froze as his brain attempted to process a course of action. Hunter blocked the first punch with his left arm while generating torque with his hips creating fluid shock through the aggressor, stopping him in place. Hunter's right hand found its target - the drunk's right wrist - grabbing it and swinging the arm in a half circle while twisting it into a wrist lock. Using momentum, Hunter walked him into the adjacent safety cell, then released him with a push, and immediately slammed the door behind him.

Hunter's pack set radio crackled with Ashley's startled voice, "Lincoln 9, are you Code 4?"

Hunter walked past the stupefied jailer, picked up his radio, and keyed the microphone stating, "Affirmative, please page the watch commander to meet me in his office."

Ashley acknowledged the request, and remembered one more reason why she thought so highly of the lieutenant smiling at her camera lens. Hunter had many skills in his toolbox and was decisive in applying them in a crisis situation.

Chapter 18

Blackburn sat fixated at his desk wearing a set of headphones and listening for any identifying signs a suspect left on the answering machine from the Greer homicide. A total of four immediate hang-ups and one message without an audible voice amounted to essentially no workable information. But was it?

Blackburn listened again to the one that had no voice but did have a few seconds or nearly imperceptible background sounds. It was breathing, but not the weighted sounds of the pervert waiting to climax. It was simply respiration. But there seemed to be faint music behind the sound of a vehicle engine which, after multiple reruns, Blackburn concluded was a song on either a radio or compact disc played during the idling of a vehicle engine. The person calling the victim was apparently using a cell phone inside a vehicle. By the sound of the idling engine, the vehicle was either stopped or parked. What was the music? Blackburn knew he had heard it before, but could not place it.

Then it came to him. The faint chorus had the word, 'Truckin'. It was a song from the Grateful Dead, and Blackburn's mind raced through visions of the band and images that their songs evoked. He then remembered Neighborhood Watch Captain, Grace Coons' statement regarding the van with shiny wheels and a cartoon decal. Blackburn wondered if what she had seen was a logo that some Grateful Dead fans place on their vehicles depicting a skeleton or skull character.

Blackburn remembered how skeptical he had become by relying upon decals as an indicator regarding a vehicle owner's interests or values. He had once responded to the report of drugs being sold out of a van in an apartment neighborhood. He located the vehicle, saw a Christian fish decal on its rear bumper and concluded that a Christian wouldn't be selling drugs. He let down his guard and assumed that he either had the wrong van or the reporting party was mistaken. Blackburn leisurely walked up on the passenger side only to discover the driver exiting the driver's side and running down the street as the pungent odor of marijuana wafted from inside the vehicle. The decal could have been placed on the van by a previous owner or even displayed as a diversion. Whatever the reason, he learned to refrain from conclusions until more evidence is gathered. He was fortunate to have escaped possibly walking up on a dope transaction and facing the wrong side of a Mac 10. However, the Grateful Dead decal information was worthy of putting out to the law enforcement community as a possibility for vans falling under suspicion.

Blackburn turned to the Field Interview cards generated by Patrol officers and now stacked on his desk by the Crime Analysis Unit. Under the search criteria of vans with shiny wheels, he began to examine approximately 50 cards issued over the past week. Tedious work, which Blackburn had often seen result in a dead end when it was discovered that the witness was mistaken. However, he knew that it had to be pursued. He remembered working the booking station at the Orange County Jail and having the laborious task of inventorying every tattoo on every prisoner booked during his shift. Upon asking his training officer why it was necessary to catalogue every sketch of ink permanently embedded within each inmate's skin, his response was, "The one you leave off is the only one the rape victim can remember." Detail was everything.

It became increasingly apparent to Blackburn that the suspect's actions exhibited profound psychopathology. If Crutchfield's and Greer's homicides were related, they would fit the classic pattern of being planned and purposeful. Their killer was narcissistic, lacking a moral compass, and displayed a complete failure to accept any responsibility for his actions. He would view his victims as pawns to satisfy his needs, and his lack of empathy would enable him to act in a cold-blooded manner, destroying his prey in order to achieve his goals. Images of Manson, Bundy, and Kraft gave Blackburn a chilling portrait of the kind of individual with which he was matching skills. This guy understood right from wrong, but he was willing to risk the consequences in order to pursue his sexual and/or homicidal interests. Whether it was caused by genetics, environment, or both presented only a passing thought to Blackburn. He recognized his urgency in identifying and locating this most dangerous of predators.

~

It was 10:15 pm and Officer Jim Janowitz drove his police cruiser eastbound on Irvine Center Drive approaching Culver when he heard the broadcast, "39-Delta-31 and Unit to follow, an attempt 261 (Rape) just occurred, Deerwood Apartments, suspect a male, black, 20's, 200 lbs., wearing a plaid long sleeve shirt, last seen running southbound through the complex." Janowitz, a recent grad from UCLA, a decorated track star, and freshly certified by his field training officer as qualified to ride solo, looked to his left, and made eye contact with a male, black, in his 20's, weighing approximately 200 lbs., wearing a plaid shirt, who promptly crossed southbound over Irvine Center Drive.

The suspect passed in front of Janowitz' patrol car and began sprinting across Culver Drive towards the Stoneridge residential village. Janowitz hit the accelerator and the cruiser lurched across Culver where he parked it as smoke from his burning tires caught up with him. He jumped out of the car, scanned over the flashing light bar on his roof, and caught a glimpse of the suspect traversing the sidewalk into the greenbelt. Janowitz keyed his mic, gave his location, and announced he was in foot pursuit of the rape suspect as he kicked in the after-burner.

The suspect collapsed onto the ground as Janowitz' shoulder crashed into his kidneys in a manner reminiscent of the Dick Butkus days with the Chicago Bears. Although the suspect outweighed him by 30 pounds, Janowitz gained control in time to hear the sirens of back-up officers from the four corners of the city. Within minutes, the victim, a 22 year old blonde, grad student from UC Irvine was transported to the scene of the detention and promptly identified the suspect as the man who had followed her into her apartment, and had attempted to disrobe her.

At 10:45 pm, Hunter received the phone call from the watch commander advising him of the arrest made by Janowitz, and Hunter was on his way to the station to meet with Blackburn for an interview of the suspect. He hadn't considered the suspect in the Greer and Crutchfield cases to be black, but witness accounts can be prone to errors. Grace Coons' description of the subject casing in the van was a male, White, but although his actions were suspicious to her, a real estate appraiser's work could result in criminal assumptions.

Hunter felt guilt about his theories regarding black suspects, but he knew that the demographics of the city ruled against a black serial killer. The actions of these perpetrators required planning and preparation, which necessitated blending in with the populace and remaining un-noticed. Although Irvine is a multi-cultural city, African-Americans represent a small percentage of the population. Residents are conscientious, generally trust their police services, and call when conditions appear suspicious. Unfortunately, a small minority of residents have viewed being black as being suspicious. For this reason, Hunter knew that the prejudices of a few created a situation in which the casing activities of a black suspect for a serial murder would generate phone calls. Neither the Crutchfield nor the Greer homicide case had been preceded by reports of suspicious black males in the area of their homes, businesses, or recreational venues.

~

Upon arrival at the station, Blackburn notified Hunter that Detective Winslow was on her way and would like to participate in the suspect's interview. It was a bit of a risk having a female investigator interviewing a male rape suspect. The detective had to be a special individual who would not personalize the crime to her own circumstances and would not interrogate with a judgmental attitude.

When Winslow arrived, Hunter advised her that she would assist Janowitz with the interview and that Blackburn and Hunter would observe in an adjacent room on a closed circuit television screen. For Janowitz, this was a unique opportunity to learn, and for Winslow, it was her chance to show the boss her chops as an accomplished interrogator.

Janowitz led Andre Moore into the room and removed his handcuffs. Winslow was seated furthest from the door and introduced herself to Moore then opened her notebook revealing notes she had taken from Janowitz' briefing along with a rap sheet for grand theft, burglary, and assault. Janowitz began the interview by reading Moore his constitutional rights from his Miranda card. Moore waived his right to an attorney but asked if he could change his mind later and was advised of his ability to stop at any time.

Janowitz stated, "The victim said that she had just finished walking her dog and that she entered her apartment, turned, and found that you had followed her in."

Moore interrupted, "Yes, but I thought I was in another apartment, and I got lost."

"You live in Santa Ana. What were you doing in Irvine tonight?"

"I was visiting a friend. I thought I knew where he lived."

"What's his name?" Winslow asked.

"Jerome Jackson."

"The victim said you grabbed her breast and tried to take her clothes off," Janowitz stated argumentatively jumping to the thermonuclear option immediately.

"That's a lie. She's accusing me of being black in Irvine."

"You had mentioned that you were visiting a Mr. Jackson. What was your business there at 10:00 this evening?" Winslow jumped in, toning down the conversation.

"He owed me some money, and I was coming over to collect it."

What's his apartment number?"

"I don't remember. I'd been there before in the daytime, and thought I remembered where it was."

"What's his phone number?"

"It's on a piece of paper, but I left it at home."

"We found your car, that Monte Carlo, up the block. Do you drive any other vehicles?" asked Winslow, probing to see if he would mention the van.

"No, that's my only ride."

"Nice car, do you always carry lubricant in the glove box?" Janowitz inquired sarcastically.

"Well, I never know when my lady's gonna be riding with me, and you never know what might happen. You know what I'm saying?"

"Did you know the girl in the apartment?"

"I never seen her before tonight."

"How'd you get those scratches on your bicep?"

"Playin' basketball."

"Her blouse was torn and she had scratches on her arm. Maybe she saw you while walking her dog, you connected with conversation, she might have led you on, and you got the wrong impression. Do you think that that might have gone down that way?"

"I ain't goin' down that road. I want my lawyer."

Winslow closed her notebook dispassionately and stated, "Mr. Moore, remember that technician who swabbed beneath your fingernails in the holding cell before we interviewed you? He's going to find our victim's DNA, and you're going down that road."

Moore was escorted out the door to the sally port where a patrol car awaited his transport to the Orange County Jail. Winslow and Janowitz entered the adjacent holding room and met with Hunter and Blackburn.

"Nice try soliciting an admission from him with that hypothetical scenario," Hunter said with a smile.

"Clearly he's institutionalized and has already been exposed to that line of questioning, and he's obviously too young for the Crutchfield case. He's too disorganized with his story to have planned Greer, but with the physical evidence and his lame answers to your interview questions, he's a lock for his third strike on this one."

Chapter 19

At 5:30 am, Hunter's Crown Victoria drove northbound on Jamboree crossing MacArthur, leaving the Newport Beach city limits and entering Irvine territory. Hunter's plans were to catch the dayshift Patrol briefing and get some in-basket work done before an exciting training day on legal updates. His condo overlooking Newport's Back Bay nature preserve was the perfect location for seclusion and rapid access to work for the frequent calls to respond to the station. The second story three-bedroom was well-suited for entertaining, an endeavor for which Hunter held great distain, but the realtor convinced him of the value for re-sale. Generally, water views yielded land developers exorbitant premiums for their products, but Newport Beach's price tags were stratospheric. Early on in Hunter's childhood, his father had invested generously in stocks of a famous cartoon filmmaker's company that had also begun construction on Anaheim's most famous theme park. The venture proved profitable, and provided Hunter with a down payment sufficient in size to produce an affordable mortgage for his public servant salary. It still chaffed him that bloggers would whine that he and his peers were overpaid, despite the hazards and the master's degree from night school he now possessed as a requisite for the gold bars on his uniform collar.

One half mile ahead, Sergeant Rob Gaston, in his last hour on the graveyard shift, initiated a car stop on an older model gold Mercedes driven by a tall, thin male, and his dishwater blonde female passenger. Gaston called immediately for a back-up, which was unusual for the experienced SWAT team leader. Hunter radioed his arrival at Campus Drive, and rolled to a stop behind the flashing red, blue, and amber lights of Gaston's patrol car. Gaston stood on the sidewalk next to the driver, who was pacing back and forth as his passenger remained seated in the front seat.

Hunter approached and saw that Gaston looked concerned that the driver's manic actions were rapidly becoming a problem. Gaston's uniformed back-up was three minutes out, responding from the area of Turtle Rock, and Hunter felt that it might take all three of them to control this apparent poster child for methamphetamine addiction. The driver rattled words out of his mouth in staccato, but stopped long enough to hear Gaston ask for his vehicle registration. As he reached through the open passenger window toward the glove box, the passenger now identified as his wife, grabbed his hand pulling it away from the handle.

Upon observing her intervening actions, Hunter wrapped his arms around the driver, and pulled him clear of the vehicle. Gaston reached inside the window, opened the glove box, and retrieved a large .357 magnum revolver. Hunter placed the subject in handcuffs, and commenced a pat-down search for additional weapons. Gaston began interviewing the wife, who was now standing on the sidewalk shivering from the cold early morning air. Finding no other apparent weapons, Hunter moved the subject next to the hood of his staff car, and leaned him against the quarter panel with his handcuffed hands behind his back. Noticing that the air was sufficiently cold to produce visible vapor from his breath, Hunter stood next to his car and placed his hands on the hood and warmed them as the engine idled rhythmically. He re-searched the driver and discovered a large Buck knife hidden in his blue jeans near the small of his back. Hunter exhaled deeply relieving his sudden rush of tension and astonishment that the cold had numbed his hands so significantly. The driver turned to Hunter and stated, "I was going to cut you, man."

Gaston's back-up officer arrived, and emptied the suspect's pistol of ammunition, while Gaston continued interviewing the wife. Hunter looked at the trunk of Gaston's patrol car where his back-up partner had stacked the six rounds in an upright position on their primers. He saw that the first two bullets were actually snake shot, standard shell casings with plastic tips containing tiny ball bearings. The remainder, were standard wad cutters. Hunter looked at the meth-crazed driver as he opened the patrol unit's prisoner cage and inquired,

"What's with the snake shot?"

Through the narcotic haze his mind searched for an answer, but was interrupted by the static-laden voice of a female dispatcher transmitting over the air waves, "Lincoln 9, you Code 4?" (All right)

The addict's words then congealed into a sentence in response to Hunter's inquiry,

"I like to hurt 'em before I kill 'em."

Hunter seat-belted the man into the patrol unit's cage, shut the door, and keyed the mic on the dashboard to answer Ashley Horton's transmission.

"Lincoln 9, we're Code 4, 39-Alpha-11 will be transporting one for 11550 [under the influence of narcotics] and CCW [carrying a concealed weapon without permit}.

"10-4, please 10-21." Horton cheerfully answered.

Hunter thought to himself that Horton knew that she could find all the information that she needed from Sergeant Gaston, since it was his arrest but suspected that she was simply looking for a reason to talk. For a moment, he felt excitement that she would be interested in sharing a conversation with him, and then dismissed the thought as fantasy. Still, she might need to give him a message from the chief, but it was 6:00 am, and he wouldn't be awake.

Hunter stopped the mind games and dialed his cell phone.

"Dispatch, this is Ashley."

"This is Hunter. You called?"

"Yeah. You're up early. So Gaston found another doper. You guys are magnets for trouble. That's the second time this month that you've followed him up, and ended up in a felony arrest. You miss working Patrol?" Horton rattled off a series of statements/questions, which

Hunter recognized were energized with caffeine, the rocket fuel for graveyard dispatchers.

"Well, this guy was unique. He had all the classic symptoms of meth, but was quite prepared to inflict violence on us and tell us how he was going to do it. We stopped him before he could reach his .357 magnum." Hunter recounted in narrative, hoping that she would reciprocate with small talk.

"Wow, that's intense. Are you guys any closer to solving the Greer homicide?" Horton responded, looking for some way to make a connection with him.

Hunter pondered, I actually think she likes me. How do I build on this? These are recorded phone lines."

"We're still digging for clues and need a break. She was such a pretty gal – petite blonde, flight attendant," Hunter continued, showing he was human, and capable of noticing attractiveness in the opposite sex.

"Partial to blondes, are you," Horton countered playfully.

"Well no, girls with an auburn tone can be just as attractive," Hunter responded with embarrassment, remembering that his words were being recorded and subject to review.

"Please hold, I've got a 9-1-1 call," Horton interjected, and the phone went silent.

Hunter recognized that that was the end of their moment. As he listened to the injury traffic accident being dispatched, he knew that Horton would be tied up answering calls from citizens reporting the accident, and complaining about the traffic back-up. The early morning sun had crested over Santiago Peak and as Hunter opened the door to his Crown Vic he looked up, saw the reflection on the full moon and knew that the night would be as crazy as the day was beginning.

Chapter 20

Dinner at the Spectrum Entertainment Center would normally be a romantic event which Anna Savoy had hoped would light some fire in James Bascomb's flickering candle. His inattention gave cause for her eyes to wander, but she decided to provide him an opportunity to demonstrate his continuing interest in her. At her behest, he made the reservation, and went so far as to pick her up at home after they had both finished work.

However, trouble was afoot when James mistook the waiter's courtesies toward Anna as a flirtatious prelude toward intimacy. James' radar was so off target that he failed to recognize that "Jeremy, your server tonight," was more than a co-waiter to "Bentley" working the adjacent set of tables.

James held his tongue until they reached his car and Anna insisted that she be taken home. He vented his displeasure with her behavior, but she was much more adept at the art of debate, which only further enraged him. He walked Anna to her door, but when her key disengaged the deadbolt, he pushed her inside, causing her to slam into three bar stools before falling to the floor. Lying on the floor, gazing at the ceiling Anna watched as James locked the door.

Bascomb continued the argument and paid little attention to Anna's pleading to "Just leave." He dropped down, straddling her and grabbed both ends of the lavender scarf draped around her neck pulling it tight in an "X". The scarf became a garrote, applying pressure on both sides of her carotid arteries causing her face to change from red to blue. As she bordered on lucidity, he released his grip to facilitate the removal of her pantyhose from beneath her dress. Upon mounting her, his climax arrived with a passion she had not witnessed before, and brought her to the edge of unconsciousness. She felt like she was a victim, but trembled in excitement from the explosion of emotions that had just enveloped her. As he left the condominium, she couldn't decide whether she should call the police or try to fix him. After all, his anger was fueled by his jealousy for her. The fact that the question even arose, revealed that her mental pathologies were significant. She failed to recognize that his were far more profoundly savage than she had just witnessed.

~

Hunter finished the day at the range having had a rare opportunity to take his team of detectives through firearms exercises at the FBI range hidden within the city limits. The former pistol range had been appropriated by the Bureau when the El Toro Marine Corps Air Station was closed, and the Marines moved to Miramar.

Tucked behind the hills north of the runways, there were no road markings to indicate anything existed beyond the rows of strawberry plants tended by the Irvine Ranch. Ironically, the Federal Bureau of Investigation made no effort to conceal its existence. In fact, they had posted an official sign at the turnoff road behind the steep hill supporting the homing beacon guiding civilian and military aircraft. However, two sets of chain link gates across the dirt roads leading to the training facility limited access to all but federal agents and SWAT operators. Normally booked for SWAT teams and platoons from SEAL Teams 3 and 5, Hunter was fortunate to find an opening on the calendar to reserve the facility for his detective team to hone their perishable skills.

Hunter swabbed the last remnant of Hoppe's solvent from the barrel of his Sig Sauer, and now focused upon what he would pick up for dinner. He knew he needed a market run for Sierra Nevadas, a favorite ale acquired during a recent Tahoe ski adventure. However, it was settled that he would first make a stop at Harvard and Main where a tiny restaurant produced a variety of delights he had grown to crave during his martial arts visits to Japan.

As the grocery cart lumbered past the check out stations loaded with a case of Nevada's finest brew, Hunter made a last minute turn down the ice cream aisle to grab a quart, and hurry home before the tempura waiting in his car got cold. Upon placing the dessert in the cart, he looked up and saw that the evening's agenda could just have changed. Traveling down the aisle in his direction, a distracted Ashley Horton, clad in sweats, pushed her own cart while intently checking a grocery list, oblivious to the fact that Hunter was awaiting her arrival.

"Hello Ashley."

"Lieutenant!" a startled Horton responded, dropping her list into her cart.

"Please, call me Scott. We're off duty."

"Maybe I am, but you're always on-call."

"Well, that may be, but we don't need to be so formal," Hunter responded softly, surprising Horton at his approachability.

"Do you live around here?"

"Yeah, I have a condo in the area of the Back Bay. How about you?"

"I just moved to an apartment in Corona del Mar."

Hunter picked up the carton of coffee flavored ice cream and placed it back into the freezer. Horton looked at him.

"Change your mind on the ice cream?"

"No, we're having a conversation and I'd like to continue, but I don't want it to melt."

"Partial to coffee flavored ice cream?" She questioned him with curiosity, but did so flirtatiously.

"Actually I like mud pie, and I have a quick homemade recipe that's outstanding," Hunter said hoping for an invitation to expound.

"Really?" Horton inquired, impressed that he had another dimension besides gun oil.

"I take the filling out of Oreo cookies, crumble up the halves and place them in a bowl. I take a scoop of coffee ice cream, place it on top of the cookie crumbs, and shoot some whip cream. Sprinkle some crushed peanuts on top – and you're in business."

"Wow, sounds wonderful!"

"I'll have to make you some soon!" Hunter declared with anticipation.

"I would like that very much." .

"Are you coming or going to your workout?" Hunter inquired, also impressed that she had an exercise regimen.

"I'm heading to my yoga class."

"You'll have to try a class at my karate studio some time. The flexibility from your yoga would give you an advantage." Hunter hoped he wasn't being too pushy as he retrieved the coffee ice cream.

"I just might take you up on that, take care."

"You too." Hunter was thinking what a sweetheart she seemed to be, and pondered the complications with workplace romances.

~

It was 10:15 pm, and Detective Tom Blackburn sat at his desk transfixed upon each page of the giant three-ring binder referred to as the Crutchfield homicide book. The grotesque photos, the scores of witness interviews, the medical examiner report, and the evidence booking sheets all wove a tapestry of clues that held a mountain of information which Blackburn felt was within his power to solve. He gazed at a picture of the bloody doorjamb propped against a paper bag for support for the photograph. The palm print painted with blood had been determined by the Sheriff's Crime Lab to be a "no match" when sent for comparison within the state's database. It possessed the answer to the crime, but it wasn't talking.

It didn't make sense that the person responsible for this crime had never been arrested for any offense for which his prints had been taken. Blackburn suddenly realized that in 1979 DNA evidence was in developmental stages, and that sending swabs for analysis was not yet in practice within the law enforcement community. He decided that he would check with Hunter the next day to see what his thoughts were

148 Dave Freedland

on swabbing some blood from the evidence and sending it off to the lab.

Blackburn turned to the witness interviews and searched for the statement of a security guard that had caught his attention regarding timelines. He found the interview of James Bascomb, one of two International Protection guards who had worked the evening of the crime. During Detective Horvath's interview of Bascomb, he told the detective that the hours that he worked the victim's apartment complex were from 8:00 pm to midnight. Yet, when he flipped over to Ballestero's interview of the other guard, Jorge Quintanar, Quintanar indicated that he worked from 1:00 am to 6:00 am, and that Bascomb was relieved by him at 1:00 am, when his shift ended.

The hour difference between Bascomb's end-of-watch could have been a memory error by either guard, but their timecards weren't time stamped that night. They were written longhand. Timecards for other dates were time stamped, but not that night. Bascomb and Quintanar had written across their cards that the clock was inoperative. However, the time stamps on their cards for the month displayed Bascomb working 8:00 pm – 1:00 am, and Quintanar working 1:00 am – 6:00 am. Why on that night was there a one hour lapse between shifts; and why on that night did the lapse fall in the middle of the range of hours for the victim's time of death? Some of the questions could have been answered had both guards been interviewed by the same person. But, for some reason Ballesteros conducted the interview of the second guard instead of Horvath. Blackburn wrote a note to himself to contact Horvath to see if he could remember the discrepancies.

Blackburn mentally constructed a scenario in which the murder took place between midnight and 1:00 am. If one of the guards had some involvement or knowledge of the crime, he would want to place himself away from the crime scene no later than midnight. Bascomb misquoted his hours, and was observed by Quintanar sweating at 1:00 am at shift change.

As Blackburn turned the pages to close the binder, an inventory page of the coroner's autopsy report caught his attention. The victim was wearing a pierced earring on her right ear, but her left earlobe was unadorned. Bethany Crutchfield wore a tiny, gold cross pierced earring on her right ear at her time of death, but her left ear bore no jewelry. Both Crutchfield and Greer were missing earrings, and it was now apparent that their homicides displayed similarities, in that their murderers collected souvenirs.

~

Upon emptying the revolver's six rounds into the target, Nelson Bascomb turned the barrel sideways and pushed the lever opening the cylinder to extract the shell casings onto the counter. Realizing his half-wit brother had not only sprayed several "misses" into the silhouette target, but he had violated the range safety rules by pointing the barrel toward shooters next to them. James Bascomb admonished his brother before the range master noticed his infraction.

The fact that the Full Magazine firing range was the only indoor civilian shooting facility in South Orange County weighed heavily on James Bascomb, who was hoping that their privileges would not be revoked for his sibling's indiscretion. Nelson stood all of 5'6", 180 lbs., with his week-old growth of beard and matted hair, and resembled a character in a 1930's gothic horror film. He looked toward his brother, flummoxed that he had been scolded, but was used to making errors and receiving James' wrath.

James was a good marksman and practiced whenever possible to hone his skills and prove to himself that the police agencies that had rejected him were seriously mistaken. He had become quite familiar with his Glock semi-auto pistol and prided himself on his firearms capabilities which, in his estimation, exceeded the skill-sets of the average street cop. He watched to ensure that his brother reloaded without taking out the five shooters to his left, then slammed a fresh magazine into his .40 caliber, and commenced blowing the head off the caricature hanging on the target holder fifteen yards away.

~

Hunter's day began with Blackburn's discoveries regarding the Crutchfield homicide book. Upon hearing Blackburn's account of the time discrepancies involving the security guards' shifts, and the issues related to the bloody doorjamb, Hunter inquired,

"Have you spoken to Horvath?"

"Not yet. I wanted to hear what your thoughts were."

"Have CSI swab the doorjamb for DNA and send it off to the lab. Then get hold of Horvath when he comes in, and find out why he didn't conduct the interview of the second security guard. Do we know if this Bascomb guy is still around?" Hunter directed with a sense of urgency.

"Not sure."

"Ask Horvath if he knows his whereabouts also." Hunter couldn't help looking inside the evidence bag containing the bloodstained wooden doorjamb.

152 Dave Freedland

Chapter 21

The night was unusually clear after the Santa Ana winds had wiped the skies clean of any clouds, and the full moon glowed with the brilliance of a finely cut diamond. Ambrose struck a statuesque pose on the Anaheim street corner hoping that the next John would be her last trick for the evening. Of course, Ambrose was her street name but nobody really knew her by any other. Hoping for a new beginning from her native Haiti, she had not expected to revert back to a life of prostitution so quickly, but her heavy accent created limitations in the career market.

She looked like a slender African American model, standing close to six feet tall with spiked heels, mini-skirt, and large ruby colored lips. Although she was far from the stereotype of the typical illegal alien, Ambrose was just that, an undocumented refugee from an island which had no future beyond tomorrow.

~

James Bascomb found the night appealing to his baser instincts and suddenly felt an urge to venture out from his comfort zone of fair skinned ladies. Rather than risking the dangers of intimacy posed by a victim's home, he would appropriate his brother's van and maybe even allow him to share in the plunders of his conquest. As it turned out, Nelson and his vehicle were available and they commenced trolling the streets of Anaheim for that perfect combination of looks and talent. Oddly, James tossed Nelson an old Polaroid camera and told him to snap a few pictures of some of the ladies of the night for later perusal. Nelson, unfamiliar with the device, struggled with the controls.

As their van crept along Harbor Boulevard, James directed Nelson to wait in the back of the van so as not to frighten any prospective candidate with his Igor-like characteristics worthy of screen consideration by Central Casting. It did not take long before James' perfect fantasy entered his sight-picture, and it became apparent he could stop shopping. He needed to activate his Bascomb charm, which in James' world would be irresistible to this obvious bottom-dweller in the lowest caste of society.

James' eyes locked with Ambrose's as the van came to a stop curbside.

She inquired through the open passenger window, "Are you looking for a date?"

"That depends on what it would take," James answered smugly in code.

"You look like police," Ambrose responded in her thick Haitian accent.

"Military," James responded, attempting to explain his close cropped haircut.

"I love you a long time for C note," Ambrose struggled to articulate, mistaking Bascomb's knock-off Rolex for real.

"Come on in," Bascomb invited, as Ambrose grasped the passenger door handle.

As the young prostitute's head and shoulders leaned in over the passenger seat, she looked left, making eye contact with Nelson, then screamed. James grabbed her bicep, and pulled her torso across the seat. She clawed his arm with her long arching nails, struggling to break free. But as Bascomb's foot pushed the accelerator to the floor, Ambrose tumbled between the seats into the back of the van where Nelson waited, pillow in hand. As the van gained speed, the volume of her screams rose exponentially, and Nelson struggled to silence them with his pillow. In his zeal, the pressure he applied not only baffled her noise but restricted her airway. With legs flailing violently as panic overcame her, Ambrose exited this life and entered the next.

154 Dave Freedland

"I think she's dead!" Nelson bellowed.

"You idiot, you were supposed to get lucky tonight, but your luck just ran out," Bascomb shouted back.

He drove the van to a public park, pulled into a parking stall, and crawled over Nelson's bedroll and gardening tools to reach the prostitute's body. He placed his index and middle fingers across her carotid artery to check for a pulse and found none. Shooting a dirty glare at his brother, he climbed back into the driver's seat and headed toward Irvine.

Bascomb remained on surface streets, driving cautiously, and entered Irvine's West Industrial Complex. Although it was after 10:00 pm, the full moon illuminated the landscape, and Bascom was afraid the van's license plates would be identifiable. So he drove down Langley Street, which was short in distance, and fronted by business offices for several small manufacturing companies, most of which he knew would be empty at this time of night and many of which had parking in the rear for employees. He found one building, obviously vacant, with tall weeds shooting through the asphalt driveway and a large leasing sign from a commercial realtor prominently posted by the double glass doors leading to the front offices.

He turned down the driveway leading to the rear, all the time checking his mirrors for headlights and light bars atop cruising patrol cars. Now sweating profusely, he ordered his brother to help him lift the body out the back doors of the van. Although Ambrose was light, her dead weight made maneuvering her torso through the mowers and weed whackers challenging. They laid her on the cracked asphalt, face up. Bascomb spotted the large hooped, pierced earrings framing her neck. He grabbed the right hoop, pulled the ring through the cartilage of her earlobe, then stuffed the jewelry piece in his pocket

He then reached back into the van to retrieve a metal can of gasoline and some matches. After dousing the body from head to toe with the accelerant, he grabbed a rag and carefully wrapped it around the rear license plate.

Lincoln 9 155

He moved the van to the driveway, left the engine running, and then directed Nelson to sit in the passenger seat. He took another gas can, gave the body one more soaking, and then continued to pour gasoline along the parking lot leading from the body to the van, creating a rudimentary fuse. He lit a match, dropped it onto the gasoline soaked ground, and jumped into the driver's seat. He watched the bluish flame quickly travel toward the body, and upon seeing the motionless figure explode into a blaze, he moved the gearshift into Drive. Not wanting to draw attention, he left the business at a moderate rate of speed, even though his heart raced in fear of an imminent discovery by a patrol officer.

~

Within minutes, Orange County Fire Authority Station Number 28, located about a half mile away on Gillette Street, received the alarm from a graveyard shift employee on Reynolds Street reporting the flames. Patrol officers working Area Two rolled to the scene along with a supervisor who was having dinner at the Atrium Hotel on MacArthur. Unknown to Bascomb, the gasoline had flashed spectacularly, but the body had not been sufficiently soaked to sustain consumption beyond clothing and some second degree and third degree burns.

Sergeant Phil Brannigan received the first phone call from the supervisor on the scene who had locked down access from both entrances on Langley. Fortunately, the hour was approaching midnight so there was a strong likelihood there would be no media infiltrating the crime scene. Although the police frequency was encrypted, which prevented monitoring through scanners, the Fire Authority's frequencies were not. However, nightshift news crews were understaffed and often missed fire dispatch transmissions generating only single alarms.

Hunter was awakened by Brannigan's call and discovered that the movie he had rented was now displaying the credits. Worried that his neighbors might complain about the increase in volume, he turned off the TV and answered the phone. Brannigan was already on his way in, and Hunter directed that Detectives Blackburn, Winslow, Nemeth, and Pascall be contacted through Dispatch to respond as he strapped on his .45 and grabbed a windbreaker.

Hunter listened to the primary Green Channel radio frequency as his Crown Victoria accelerated northbound on Jamboree. Brannigan had begun making requests that Dispatch contact CSI personnel and that the coroner be notified. Hunter jumped on the air and added a request that a call for Sheriff's Department crime scene technicians be made for the collection of laboratory samples. He added a suggestion that radio traffic for the homicide be switched to a tactical channel so that normal radio activity for the city would not be stepped on by detectives running records checks and making notifications.

Hunter arrived to a scene of firefighters in turn-outs rolling up hoses and uniformed officers unrolling spools of yellow police tape. He walked over to the Patrol sergeant's Tahoe, which was parked on the street with supervisory personnel huddled around a pull-out table in the back with checklists and diagrams spread over the plastic sheet covering a map. Next to the Tahoe was a huge Fire Authority ladder truck, with the ladder fully extended over the building, and a large floodlight attached to the end, shining down onto the crime scene in the rear parking lot. As Hunter looked toward the top of the ladder, a fire captain advised him that an additional generator truck with floodlights was on the way from headquarters near the Tustin Marketplace.

Hunter met with Brannigan and Winslow to receive a briefing on the most current information as Blackburn, Nemeth, and Pascall arrived shortly thereafter.

"The call came in on the 911 line about 10:20. An employee working the graveyard shift over on Reynolds saw the flames and called, stating that she saw a bright flash that died down before she could call on her cell phone. The first person on the scene was Officer Jenkins who saw some weeds and grass still smoldering behind the vacant building. He threw some dry chemical fire extinguisher on the embers and checked the victim for a pulse," Brannigan explained methodically.

"Did he find one?" Hunter inquired.

"No, he said that the skin on her neck was surprisingly cold," Winslow interjected.

"Engine Company 28 arrived and doused the vegetation with water along with some fabric that was still burning, but for the most part, left the body intact for evidence," Brannigan continued.

"Any identification?" Hunter questioned hopefully.

"She had a purse, but no I.D. whatsoever."

"I suppose no witnesses?"

"It was after hours for all of these businesses except for the one on the end, and they have a swing shift ending at midnight. We've got a couple blue suits interviewing employees, but so far, nothing seen."

"Let's have a look," Hunter said as they started down the driveway to the back lot.

Rounding the corner of the building, Hunter was surprised at the amount of light generated by the combination of the full moon and the overhead floodlight. The victim lay on her back, some remnants of a skirt, blouse, and spiked heels remaining despite the fire. Her small purse and several cosmetic articles were strewn around the area, but no wallet was to be found. Her body reflected health, the absence of tattoos or narcotic track marks and displayed good muscle tone. Winslow rolled her ankle inward, and noted to Hunter that rigor mortis had not yet set in, but the calf showed that her body had been lying face up long enough for blood to pool in the lower extremities. Surprisingly, her face showed minimal signs of burn damage.

Hunter looked up and said to Brannigan, "Have the guys look around to see if any of these businesses are running video cameras on their sites. Make sure that before the coroner moves the body that either our CSI people or theirs scrape under her nails."

"What do you think, boss?" Brannigan asked, wondering if Hunter, infamous for his predictions, would venture another guess.

"Well, she looks like an expensive call girl who probably said, no to something. But I would be very interested in what the autopsy has to say, and who it is that eventually reports her missing. Hey, I just noticed. She's had the earring on her right ear ripped through her earlobe," Hunter announced to his team, who were well aware of the souvenirs linking the previous homicides. "There's a good possibility that the vehicle that brought her here was passed by or even stopped by one of our patrol officers working this beat. Let's get the patrol shift roster and look at the activity logs for all officers working this evening."

Hunter thought to himself, *Curious, this victim is black, but if the autopsy shows her cause of death as asphyxiation, this would probably be number three for our killer, who apparently does not discriminate by race. He likes this city for some reason, and if we don't find him soon, this community will be in a panic.*

160 Dave Freedland

Chapter 22

The next morning Hunter met his long-time friend, Lieutenant Luke Barnes, for breakfast at the Strawberry Farms Golf Course coffee shop. Barnes was the son of Irish-Catholic immigrants, but spoke with an elegant New England accent and was built like an NFL running back. As an officer, his articulate method of communicating with people ultimately landed him the command position in Professional Standards, commonly referred to as Internal Affairs. Additionally, the fact that he had just passed the California State Bar Exam weighed heavily in the chief's decision to place him where his law degree could be maximized to the Department's benefit. Having previously worked Narcotics and Vice, Barnes possessed some technical knowledge that Hunter sought in coordinating the previous evening's homicide.

"Sounds like you had a pretty ugly scene last night," Barnes said as the waitress poured his coffee.

"Yeah, body dumps are bad enough, but when they torch them it's a horror movie made real," Hunter replied, still groggy from five hours sleep. "The victim was an attractive black gal who might be a prostitute. Do you know where the areas are that someone like that would work?"

"In this city or in the county?" Barnes responded, narrowing the search criteria.

"Well, let's start with Irvine."

"When we started this business, the hotels were the hot spots, but they've pretty much cleaned up their bars. Now it's the Asian massage establishments around the airport that are generating the action."

"She's not Asian, so where might a street walker operate the most profitably outside the city?"

Lincoln 9 161

"You might hit Santa Ana, but they're predominantly Hispanic. So I would start by checking Anaheim along the motels in the area of Harbor Boulevard and Katella and radiate out. But keep in mind our team primarily worked this city, and we never had hookers walking the streets. However, our counterparts in other cities within the county did say they were experiencing an influx of women from Caribbean countries. I would contact Anaheim P.D.'s Vice Unit and run it by them for some advice. I can give you a business card when we get back to the station," Barnes suggested, fully aware that Irvine's prostitution issues were generally minimal in comparison to their narcotics operations.

"Thanks, I think it's reasonable to believe that our victim was picked up elsewhere, but our suspect knows this city and probably works or lives here. So, is police corruption keeping you busy in your new assignment?

"Right, I'm a regular Serpico. Actually, I just unfounded a personnel complaint involving an elderly man who claimed an officer issued him a citation and when the complainant dropped his copy, the officer threatened to arrest him for littering."

"Really? Sounds a little Draconian," Hunter remarked skeptically.

"Well, the old guy was behind a motorist who was making a left turn, and didn't realize that the car in front of him was yielding to a pedestrian in the crosswalk. The old man impatiently laid into his horn to hurry him up, and the cop stopped him for unnecessary use of a horn. What the complainant didn't know was that the officer's video camera was rolling, and the video captured the man's profanity at the officer, as well as his wadding up the citation and throwing it on the sidewalk."

"Did you show him the video?"

"Yeah, he got up and walked out in a huff without saying a word."

~

Upon arrival at the station, Hunter was met by Sergeant Phil Brannigan who had attended Ambrose's autopsy with Detective Jack Pascall and seemed eager to share with his lieutenant the preliminary results.

"Boss, the coroner gave an initial finding of death by asphyxiation for our Langley victim."

"I was hoping for a different outcome. Anyone report her missing?"

"Not yet, but we sent Blackburn and Winslow to Anaheim to check with their vice unit on possible locations where she might have been hanging out. CSI was able to get a decent photo of her from the neck up with some Photo Shop work on the burns, and Pascall and Nemeth are hitting our hotels to see if anyone had seen her."

"Were any F.I. cards completed on anyone suspicious in that area within an hour of the 911 call?"

"No, the closest contact was at MacArthur and Main, and it was a homeless person on foot," Brannigan responded, looking at his notes.

"I'd like Crime Analysis to send a teletype out to Orange County, L.A., Riverside, San Bernardino, and San Diego Counties for similar crimes, and have CAU conduct a records search for citations issued within a two mile radius of our crime scene."

Hunter thought, *maybe I'd better spend some time looking at that homicide book on Blackburn's desk.*

Bascomb sat in his security supervisor's car turning pages of the Orange County Register's morning edition, searching for any word on his "event." He stopped on page three of the Local section where the only mention was a paragraph on the discovery of a woman's body that had been torched behind a building. His anger raged at the disrespect of being on the third page, but rationalized that it could be attributed to his brilliance in destroying the evidence. The whole incident was not his fault. His ugly brother had spoiled a perfect opportunity for them to score a piece of ass, but he had taken the necessary steps to remedy the situation.

Blackburn and Winslow finished their meeting with Anaheim Vice and sat in the Mexican cantina in Heritage Center mapping out locations where they would check motels that evening looking for streetwalkers. While awaiting Detective Russell Horvath's arrival to join them for lunch, they discussed strategies for finding a suspect.

Horvath arrived with a printout of citations issued the evening of the Langley homicide, with the majority of activity occurring in the areas of MacArthur and Redhill, and Redhill and Barranca. Within one hour before and after the 911 call, a total of twelve citations were issued between two officers.

"Have you checked any of the cites yet?" Winslow asked, following the placement of their food order.

"Not yet, it won't take long to see who we stopped and run them for criminal histories," Horvath responded, wiping the sweat off his brow with a handkerchief.

"Hey Russell, I've been reading the Crutchfield homicide book in my spare time, and I noticed that there were two security guards that worked the apartments that evening. You interviewed the one guy who worked the first part of the evening, but Ballesteros interviewed the other one later. Do you remember why you weren't able to interview the other guy?"

"That was over ten years ago, Tom. Do you know how many interviews I've done over the past ten years? Quite frankly, I don't remember."

"So then you probably wouldn't remember if you checked with Nancy Ballesteros as to whether the statements of the two guards matched, correct?" Blackburn shot back with a hint of sarcasm.

"Look Tom, that was a long time ago, and we all put in a lot of hours trying to gather enough evidence on that poor girl's boyfriend to put him away."

"That's kind of my point. In reading that case, it looked like you guys were so focused on her boyfriend Hendrickson that you weren't open to other possibilities," Blackburn continued with increasing passion.

"It's a whole lot easier to sit down after the fact and throw stones at an investigation when you're not caught up in the heat of following leads and chasing down suspects," Horvath threw into the conversation in an attempt to place the facts in context.

"We've got Crutchfield, Greer, and now this Jane Doe case on Langley that we have yet to solve, and we don't know what clues we've missed that could solve these crimes," Blackburn stated, now clearly implying Horvath's mishandling of his interviews.

"Well, what we do know is that lunch is served," Winslow interjected as the waitress arrived with her arms stacked with plates. She hadn't before seen her partner so animated. For the remainder of lunch, she carried the conversation away from the topic, as tension hovered over the table until the check was paid.

~

Since Bascomb's "missed opportunity" for sex with a black prostitute, his mind had been continually fixated on satisfying his testosterone charged urge for relief. It didn't help that a new women's yoga studio had recently opened on Skypark Circle, and young ladies attired in outfits ranging from sweats to color coordinated leotards paraded from their cars to the studio. He needed an outlet, but after his last encounter with Anna Savoy, he wasn't sure where he stood with her, and he was reluctant to risk another venture into the world of working girls. He decided that he had nothing to lose with an overture to Savoy, and maybe she might have actually enjoyed her introduction to rough sex with James.

"Hello Anna? I know that when we last met, I lost my temper and may have behaved poorly, but I am truly sorry. And please don't hang up, but my passion for you has been burning since that evening, and really, my actions were solely motivated by jealousy. I would like to make things up to you. Would you be open to going out with me Saturday?"

Lincoln 9 165

"James, you really need to control your jealous emotions, but your apology is accepted. I do have a question, where did you come up with those, well, unusually rough bedroom...ah, techniques? I felt that..."

Bascomb interrupted, further apologizing, "I'm sorry, I don't know where that came from. I just..."

"No James, I'm not exactly condemning your actions. I just had never well, been exposed to sex that scared me." Anna was awkwardly trying to ask the question without sounding overly interested.

"Anna, I don't know if it was your perfume, your dress, the combination of emotions related to that waiter flirting with you that unleashed something in me that I had not experienced before. Your skin, your lips, I don't know..."

"Okay James, maybe we can discuss this further over dinner Saturday."

"Great. Thanks Anna, I'll pick you up at 7:00." Bascomb ended the conversation, excited that his possibilities were improving.

Chapter 23

The evening karate class started promptly at 6:30 pm, and Hunter was relieved that traffic had been sufficiently light to enable him to hit the mats at 6:20 to warm up. The traditional protocols were strict, but the discipline minimized injuries. As Hunter looked up from his stretch, his mouth opened in surprise as a petite female figure with auburn hair, dressed in a shiny white gi, joined the other twenty class members warming up on the tatamis. The chief instructor grabbed a female brown belt and directed her to instruct the new member regarding the bowing-in procedures.

Hunter made quick eye contact with Ashley and smiled nervously. His heart leapt at the thought of her taking him up on his invitation to attend a class, but felt a sense of anxiety, knowing that his status as an upper ranking black belt required his performance to be especially stellar tonight.

A clap of the hands followed by the command, "Line up!" commenced the opening of class. From highest rank to lowest, the participants came to order for the ceremonial bows, and then the action began. Drills in basic stances, punches, blocks, strikes, and kicks up and down the mats were challenging enough, but for newcomers, the commands in Japanese were particularly difficult. Ashley's yoga experience gave her an advantage in conditioning, but the emphasis on generating power was a foreign experience and surprisingly fatiguing.

Hunter was primarily paired with black belts, but occasionally rotated into a 30 second training evolution with Ashley. During a drill requiring one partner to punch the face, while the other performed a basic overhead block, Ashley punched awkwardly, but as Hunter blocked with precision, the motion from her karate jacket wafted her perfume across his nostrils. For the remainder of the class, he struggled to disregard her scent and concentrate.

Class ended with the requisite bows and the usual rush to the drinking fountain, while lower belts solicited help from their seniors in correcting their stances and timing. Hunter again locked eyes with Ashley and tipped his head indicating his invitation to walk out to the parking lot with him.

They stopped near her Chevy Camaro which was highlighted by two pole-mounted floodlights illuminating the parking lot. Hunter's theory on automobiles and their owners postulated that their selection was a direct reflection of their personality and wondered what implications that held for Ashley.

"Where did you get this?" Hunter inquired, admiring the British racing green paint finish.

"Oh, my dad helped me find this through the Chevy dealership at the auto center. When I was growing up, I always admired his 1968 Z28 Camaro, so he encouraged me to buy one when Chevy re-issued the model."

"I never thought that you would accept my invitation to take a class."

"Well, it sounded like a challenge, and I thought that it might be interesting. You guys are intense; I could barely keep up," Ashley replied with spirit.

"Actually, I was pretty impressed. You've got stamina and coordination. If you stick with it, you could become quite accomplished."

"Thanks, I might consider it. I really enjoy yoga, though. It's obvious that this is a part of your life. Your focus and intensity show it, and it's clear that it plays a role in the respect that others feel toward you."

"Thanks, I..." Hunter smiled with embarrassment and was stopped mid-sentence as Ashley grabbed his sleeve and pulled her lips up to his cheek and planted a kiss on it.

"See you at work," Ashley said, as she jumped into her car and revved the engine.

Hunter stood, rubbing his hand over the spot on his cheek where she had kissed him. He waived toward her rearview mirror thinking *This could get complicated, but she's so damned pretty.*

~

The doorbell rang at Anna Savoy's condo, and James Bascomb awaited final adjustments to Anna's hair before she granted him access to her living room. He was dressed neatly in designer jeans and Hawaiian shirt. Anna greeted him in black stretch pants and a white long sleeved blouse with pleats, displaying her ample cleavage.

"What's the plan?" Anna inquired with energy.

"I thought we'd eat at the Rusty Pelican in Newport and then check out the band playing at Neptune's in Sunset Beach," Bascomb replied, awaiting approval.

"Sounds great, let's go."

Small talk during the drive was uncomfortable, but after the first round of drinks at dinner, both Anna and James loosened, and conversation regarding each other's work became more tolerable. By the time he had finished his second Greyhound, Anna found him extremely charming.

Following an expensive meal of surf and turf, they headed north toward Sunset Beach. At Neptune's, the atmosphere was dark, but the smell of the restaurant's famous clam chowder was inviting. The band, recommended by one of James' co-workers, was just setting up. He generally favored Stones and Aerosmith, but Anna preferred Earth, Wind, and Fire. James' co-worker liked U-2, but failed to mention to him that the band played U-2 on specific nights, and tonight was the band's evening set aside for covering Led Zeppelin. As the lead guitarist launched into "Heartbreaker" from Zeppelin's second album, James started powering down Margarita's on the rocks.

As Bascomb's sobriety began to deteriorate and he started to heckle the band to play songs from U-2's Joshua Tree album, the partisan Zeppelin crowd started shooting looks of disgust at him. Becoming increasingly uncomfortable, Anna began to urge James that it was time to leave. When one of the bouncers whispered for him to quiet down, Anna stood and walked to the parking lot. Bascomb followed slurring profuse apologies, so Anna told him to get into the car, but demanded that she drive them home.

Bascomb slept until their arrival at Anna's condo. When he awoke and she offered to call him a cab to take him home, Bascomb begged for permission to sleep off his intoxicated state on her sofa, and she eventually relented. After entering her home, Anna poured herself a glass of wine, and James asked to join her with one more before retiring.

As the wine began to affect her own discretion, Anna again brought up the subject of James' behavior that evening. Now away from public scrutiny, Bascomb exploded in a rage, yelling obscenities that quickly escalated to physical abuse. He grabbed Anna's wrists and shoved her into a china cabinet causing several plates to fall forward into the doors and crash to the floor in multiple shards. The noise reverberated to adjoining condo units, resulting in numerous calls to Newport Beach's Police Dispatch Center.

Arriving at Anna's condo, Officers Roberts and Mulcasey could clearly hear the continuing drama through closed windows and began their intervention with heavy knocks upon the front door. A disheveled Anna answered, breaking into tears upon seeing crisp blue uniforms and chiseled jaws.

After separating the parties, the red marks around Anna's wrists made it apparent to the officers that Bascomb was the dominant aggressor. He soon found himself handcuffed and seated in the backseat of Roberts' patrol car.

Rather than driving to the county jail in Santa Ana, Roberts checked Bascomb into Newport's city jail where the custody officer took the usual set of prints and mug shots, which would be shipped to the Sheriff's Department the following morning. Bail was set at $5,000 for the misdemeanor charge. Bascomb posted the $500 bail before being released on his written promise to appear in court for arraignment next month.

Anna was through with James, and was thoroughly disgusted with herself for having set her standards so low. Bascomb held Savoy responsible for picking a fight with him, but felt the anxiety building regarding the possibility that his employer might learn of this episode.

Chapter 24

Seeking clarification about the time discrepancies he had discovered in the timecards for the security guards on a ten-year-old homicide, Tom Blackburn tracked down retired Detective Nancy Ballesteros' cell phone number and discovered that she was vacationing in the great state of Texas. "Hello Nancy?"

"Yes."

"This is Tom Blackburn."

"Hi Tom, you solve that Crutchfield case yet?" Ballesteros replied sarcastically.

"As a matter of fact, I'm kind of still working it on the side, and I had a quick question for you."

"I'm retired, fishing in the state of Texas, and you really think my mind is in a place where it could remember some remote detail that you have discovered needs correcting?" Ballesteros continued in her usual caustic style.

"Well, it's a long shot, but I was hoping you would remember an interview you conducted on a guy named Jorge Quintanar, a security guard working the apartment complex where Bethany Crutchfield was murdered."

"Yes, surprisingly I do remember him. Russell Horvath was supposed to interview him since he had already spoken to the other guard, but Horvath called in sick. I interviewed Quintanar for him, and found him quite credible."

"Good. Did you notice that the time that he stated that he relieved the other guard, James Bascomb, was 1:00 am, but that Bascomb's statement to Horvath was that he ended his shift at midnight that evening? There was a one hour discrepancy."

"Whoa! I just interviewed the second guard as a favor, and left it to Russell to match up their statements. I was never directed to conduct any analysis or comparisons," Ballesteros responded defensively.

"Well, I was just hoping that you might remember looking at the statements and comparing the timecards. It could be just memory error by the guard or Horvath in writing the statement down, but it's just a loose piece of information that doesn't match up."

"I'm assuming Russell can't remember anything. You think this Bascomb guy is a suspect?"

"Not enough information yet. I ran a records check on him a couple weeks ago, and there's no record other than his applications for security guard. The guy still works for International Protection Service and lives in Costa Mesa. He drives a Mustang, which isn't exactly the van that we're currently looking for, and as of today, there are no DNA hits. Horvath can't recall the details. It sure would have been better to have had Horvath handle both interviews. Do you think I ought to re-interview Bascomb?"

"You've got nothing to lose, but his memory could be as bad as ours, or he could use the lapse in time to excuse his inability to recall whether it's true or not," Ballesteros responded, demonstrating she still possessed interviewing skills.

"I'll bounce this off the boss and see what he thinks."

"Who's running the Bureau now?" Ballesteros inquired, starting to miss the action.

"Lieutenant Hunter."

"Hmm, young guy. How's that working out?"

"He's a taskmaster, but he's got his shit together, and he's not one to ride the desk."

"Well, hopefully he won't get in the way."

"Actually, he's been leading the charge. Thanks for your help Nancy."

~

At 1:00 am, Hunter received the dreaded "middle of the night call" advising him that a homicide had occurred at a 7-Eleven store and uniformed officers were working an active scene with suspects still on foot in the neighborhood. Two male, white subjects had attempted to rob the convenience store and had stabbed the clerk to death before fleeing into the Deerfield condominium complex.

Clearing the proverbial cobwebs from his head, Hunter knew that he would need to arrive on scene alert, looking sharp, and in control. Moments like these reminded him of morning inspections at the Sheriff's Academy. Drill instructors yelled incessantly and he and his fellow recruits would recite memorized elements of crimes, or memorable quotes from the father of professional law enforcement, Sir Robert Peel. Famous for his namesake, the British Bobbies, one of Peel's policing reforms asserted that "Good appearance commands respect."

At the time that Hunter memorized it, he assumed that the concept pertained to the relationship between the officer and the public. However, as he gained experience in the ranks of supervision, he realized its significance to successful leadership.

In his closet, Hunter always maintained a pressed pair of slacks, dress shirt, sport coat, and tie. In addition, a fresh police-logo polo shirt, cargo pants, and windbreaker hung nearby, awaiting selection based upon the nature of the call. Judging the late hour and the possibility of working from a field command post all night, the polo and cargo pants became the attire of choice.

The display of firearms, holsters, and additional magazines by detectives was always interesting entertainment for those assigned to uniformed patrol. In Patrol, such equipment was generally regulated by the procedures manual, but in many departments investigative personnel were given greater latitude as to how they might harmonize the tools in support of lethal force with their civilian wardrobe.

Sexy shoulder holsters, switchblade knives, and multiple back-up weapons could be categorized as apparel for either rookie detectives or those possibly being candidates for psychoanalysis. Hunter elected to carry his standard .45 caliber pistol in a retention holster on his strong side, two extra magazines, handcuffs, a high-intensity micro-flashlight, and a 5-shot .38 revolver strapped in an ankle holster.

Hunter drove northbound on Jamboree and called Phil Brannigan to ensure that his homicide team was rolling out. He concluded that the Dispatch Center was inundated with phone calls from worried residents by the fact that even Ashley Horton's supervisor was transmitting information over the air. As the suspects fled over fences and through greenbelts, awakened homeowners called in to the station, sensing a hot pursuit by the chopping sound of the police helicopter overhead.

As Hunter closed to within a mile of the parking lot command post, he could see the bright beacon from the helicopter shooting into backyards like a cannon-sized laser. Upon arrival, he watched the K-9 handler guide his barking bloodhound to clothing articles that had been strewn across a grassy mound by the suspects during their escape. He saw that Sergeant Phil Brannigan was already on scene and was standing next to the Incident Commander, who was marking a perimeter on a dry erase board that had been laid on the hood of a patrol sergeant's Crown Victoria.

"Are you ready for briefing, Phil?" Hunter inquired.

"Sure. About 12:30 am, two white male suspects were seen by a parking lot vacuum truck operator fleeing from the 7-Eleven. He goes inside to check on the East Indian clerk, finds him stabbed to death behind the counter, and dials 911." Brannigan paused, waiting for the first question.

"Have either of the suspects been located?"

"Not yet, the bloodhound has just picked up the scent trail. The suspects were described as being in their early 20's, wearing heavy coats, and one of them had a shaved head. Patrol has set up a perimeter, search teams are working northbound through the complex from Irvine Center Drive, and the store manager is on the way in to retrieve the video from the camera," Brannigan continued, rapidly checking off what he'd written in his notepad.

The conversation between Hunter and Brannigan was suddenly interrupted by a transmission by the K-9 officer that the bloodhound had located one suspect in the laundry room of a building housing several condominium units. The suspect had been taken down by an arrest team following the dog, but was reported to have refused to divulge any information regarding his partner or his whereabouts.

"Get his name, and run him for arrests, field contacts, and vehicles registered as soon as possible. Guarantee you that he's been connected with his crime partner by the cops at some time, and either his or his partner's vehicle will be parked somewhere around here," Hunter announced after keying his pack-set radio.

Eric Simonson sat in the backseat of the patrol car listening to his name being run for records over the radio, as he traveled the short distance to the station for interrogation. He was a known hoodlum who had grown up in the city and graduated from truancy to methamphetamine and now murder.

Within minutes, a dispatcher in the Communications Bureau had located a recent field contact entry in which officers had stopped Mr. Simonson in the company of a Mr. Tim Barnhart. The manager of a Denny's restaurant had called police regarding the charge of defrauding an innkeeper. A third party, who was a friend of Simonson and Barnhart, had charged up a tab and fled the restaurant, leaving the other two to deal with management. Simonson's DMV records showed that he had a 1990 Toyota Pickup registered to him, and a citation for a faulty brake light indicated that the truck was a Tacoma and the color was green.

Very shortly following the broadcast concerning Simonson's vehicle, a perimeter officer located the suspect's pickup truck parked on Deerfield Street 50 yards from the 7-Eleven. Both doors were found unlocked for rapid escape, Simonson's wallet was in the glove box, and Barnhart's driver's license was located under the passenger seat. Circumstantial evidence now placed Barnhart at the crime scene.

As dispatchers began searching computer records for Barnhart's residence, a second bloodhound was brought into the neighborhood search, and the 7-Eleven manager arrived to retrieve the videotape linked to the camera directed toward the cash register. During the gruesome playback, it was discovered that Barnhart jumped the counter and immediately stabbed the clerk in the torso while Simonson walked behind the counter and attempted to open the cash register. As Simonson struggled with the register, Barnhart moved to the safe and began demanding that the clerk, gurgling on the floor, give him the combination. Simonson then turned toward Barnhart and said, "You fucking idiot. You killed him before we got the money!" Both suspects then ran out the door empty-handed.

Hunter assigned Sgt. Brannigan and Detectives Blackburn and Nemeth to go to the station to conduct the interrogation of Simonson. Field personnel continued to methodically search grids established over the residential tract bordered by Irvine Center Drive, Deerfield, Harvard, and Culver. Hunter glanced around the command post assessing his resources in the event that Barnhart was possibly located off-site, and made mental selections of personnel to take with him to apprehend the suspect.

At approximately 5:15 am, Dispatcher Ashley Horton's voice broadcast over the radio frequency that they had located a traffic citation for Barnhart listing his address on Fashion Street in Anaheim. Simultaneous to this announcement, Simonson's girlfriend, who had been notified by Simonson via cell phone of his impending arrest while he hid in the laundry room, called the police station. She believed in her heart that Barnhart had pressured her boyfriend to participate in this property crime turned homicide. She confirmed that Barnhart stayed with his girlfriend at the Fashion Street residence in Anaheim and shared with dispatchers that Simonson believed

178 Dave Freedland

Barnhart had escaped the neighborhood prior to the establishment of a police perimeter.

Hunter quickly mobilized a team consisting of Detectives Pascall, Winslow, and Horvath. Recognizing Horvath's deficiencies, Hunter scanned the parking lot and recognized Officer Jim Janowitz standing by the yellow police tape holding a clipboard to log personnel in and out of the crime scene. Janowitz had gained distinction with his arrest of the attempted rapist, possessed sound tactical skills, and could provide his marked patrol unit to transport the suspect in the backseat cage. Hunter directed Dispatch to request that Anaheim Police Department assign two officers to meet them at a nearby school to assist in containing the suspect's house.

Upon arrival at the school, Hunter's team met with two uniformed officers from Anaheim PD along with two narcotics officers who had already driven by the residence and determined that Barnhart's car was parked on the street. Hunter assigned the two uniformed Anaheim officers to the alley behind the house, the two narcs in their van behind the suspect's car next door to the suspect's house, and Janowitz behind the detective team which would line up on the hinge side of the front door.

Hunter considered the possible options in his mind regarding the team's approach to achieving access to the house. It was reasonable to believe that Barnhart was inside. It was 6:30 am, his car was parked on the street near his residence, and there was a light on inside the master bedroom. They had not yet obtained a warrant for the premises, but they were within the outermost parameters of fresh pursuit. Barnhart could be alone, or his girlfriend or others could be present inside. If she answered the door, what would be their response?

Not wanting to jeopardize the case on a technicality, Hunter left the Anaheim officers in their positions, and had Janowitz cover the front of the residence in his patrol car parked a few houses down, and directed Horvath to prepare a telephonic search warrant while the detectives waited in their cars. If Barnhart left the house, he would be subject to immediate arrest on sight.

The minutes ticked into two hours as Horvath read the warrant to the judge over the phone. Back at the crime scene, the perimeter had been broken down, the coroner had removed the body, and CSI personnel were still dusting for prints and collecting DNA samples. Upon Judge Alexander Ruiz's authorization to search, Hunter assembled his team on the hinge side of the front door, hidden from view through the bay window on the other side. The three bedroom stucco home, built in the 1940's, was a rental in disrepair, and a crash pad which was loathed by the mostly retired homeowners residing in the neighborhood.

Pascall took the point position, with Hunter directly behind, and Winslow, Horvath, and Janowitz completing the stack prepared for entry. Pascall knocked and waited, while Horvath held a small battering ram, awaiting Hunter's signal. The door opened, and a thin female with long straggly blonde hair wearing a tee shirt and jean shorts answered. She gazed at Pascall's badge hanging on a chain around his neck, acknowledged when asked her name, and answered affirmatively when Pascall inquired as to whether Barnhart was inside. The team poured into the front room, with Pascall, Hunter, and Janowitz continuing on toward a back bedroom, while Winslow and Horvath remained with the suspect's girlfriend.

Pascall crossed the threshold of the now darkened master bedroom and saw a human form springing from the bed toward him swinging arms and fists. The methamphetamine coursing through Barnhart's veins kicked in, and his heavy frame advanced toward the three .45 caliber gun barrels now arrayed against him. Within a microsecond, Hunter's support hand left the side of the pistol grip and formed a left hook which solidly caught Barnhart's right jaw, knocking him out instantly. Barnhart's body collapsed to the floor with his legs twisted up in the blankets, and his head planted face down into the carpet. Janowitz affixed a set of handcuffs to Barnhart's wrists behind his back and seated him upright on the floor as he slowly regained consciousness.

Following Blackburn and Nemeth's grueling interrogations at the station, both Simonson and Barnhart were soon booked for murder at the Orange County Jail while the convenience store video procured by the media, played incessantly across the evening news stations for several days. An attorney representing Barnhart's family held a press conference alleging brutality in the incarceration of his clients' son. However, given the savagery of the crime and the victim's family's pleas for justice, the story never found legs. Hunter was elated that his team had functioned with the efficiency of an artillery battery, and that there was minimal investigative follow-up with no suspects outstanding. It was now time to redirect their energies toward the apprehension of a killer who may have already struck again.

182 Dave Freedland

Chapter 25

Stephanie Winslow crouched outside the back door to the police station tightening her running shoes while awaiting Hunter's arrival for their weekly five-mile run down the flood control channel leading to Newport's Back Bay. They had a regularly scheduled Wednesday run along the bike path at noon, which began at the station and traveled southbound under several streets, but above the sandy marshlands occupied by various forms of wildlife. The 2.5 miles out was the more challenging leg due to the off shore breeze, but the wind kept one's body temperature cooler. The run back was characterized by winds gently pushing, but legs burned from the constant up-hills and down-hills from the ramps beneath the thoroughfares.

Stephanie possessed the classic runner's frame and dressed appropriately for the role, clad in shorts and matching tank top that would be fitting for a camera shoot for any athletic magazine displayed at the racks adorning supermarket check-out stands. As she waited, she pondered a conversation she had had one day prior in which she and her sergeant, Phil Brannigan, had discussed the status of the Langley homicide. It so troubled her that both she and her roommate, Officer Natalie Grisinger had brainstormed until midnight as to how they might proceed. They found it heartbreaking that no one had reported the victim missing, and her horrific demise demanded that they devote every resource and employ everyone's imagination toward finding a lead to solve this crime.

Hunter went out the automatic doors and greeted Winslow with a warm smile. As they walked past the gasoline pumps, across the service road to the bike path, Winslow said, "I thought we might slow the pace today so that we could discuss some points related to the Langley Street homicide. Sound okay with you?"

"Sure, let's drop it down to an 8.5 to 9 minute mile pace."

They were both athletes, well in tune with their capabilities. Those unfamiliar with the personalities of the two investigative colleagues would possibly raise an eyebrow to the apparent workplace relationship. It had been long assumed that officers Winslow and Grisinger were more than roommates sharing housing expenses, but their lives were so private that no one probed further. Upon reaching the spray painted start marker, they began their run.

"Brannigan says the autopsy results show that our Jane Doe died from asphyxiation," Winslow said.

"Looks like she represents our third in the series," Hunter responded, already breaking a sweat.

"What's an absolute shame is the fact that no one has reported her missing."

"Well, it happens. We get the bulletins all the time - photos of dead women, detective bureaus searching for a name."

"But this is Irvine, and we do things differently."

"We're not immune from the crimes experienced by other agencies."

"But we have the talent to solve these challenges. I guess I'm not comfortable with the concept of an unsolved crime."

"We take each lead as far as humanly possible, but at some point, you need a break."

"Well, let's create a break. We have no matches on prints or DNA, and no hookers have recognized anyone close to her description. Let's get the photographer in CSI to touch up her face, and solicit the public's assistance."

"Sure, we could try that. Any other detail of significance that you think would be useful to share?" Hunter inquired, now in a full sweat, as the pace gradually increased.

"You know, her spiked heels are unique. We might want to include a photo of one of them in the flyer."

Hunter's was trying his best to remember the woman's shoes.

"O.K., when we get back, let's see what wizardry Andrew Norbett can do for you in his photo lab."

~

Bascomb walked from his International Protection car across the parking lot, carefully remaining in the evening shadows between the box-like structures of the Skypark Business Complex. The new women's yoga club that had recently opened deserved another look. No harm in venturing slightly out of one's assigned territory to check out the "talent," in the event that the temperature inside necessitated opening the back door for better ventilation. This brief departure from the numbing routine of security supervision would serve as a diversion from his obsessive thoughts concerning the pending court date resulting from the accusations of that wicked Anna Savoy.

As he rounded the corner of the building leading to the rear doors, he felt excitement at the discovery of light projecting brightly through a door revealing a spacious room lined with mirrors, hardwood floors, and leotard-clad beauties. Then, Bascomb's glance to his left brought terror as he recognized the familiar silhouette of a patrol car light bar backlit by building floodlights. Could it be the officer occupying that patrol car was there for the same reason as Bascomb? Was he just parked there for the view? Was he watching him? Had he been discovered? Bascomb decided he couldn't risk it. He needed to be proactive and approach him.

"Good evening officer. James Bascomb, International Protection Services, at your service. I see you have also discovered this new establishment in your beat," Bascomb rambled on, hoping to distract a surprised officer who had buried his head into a report on a clipboard resting against the steering wheel.

"Actually, I'm waiting for a tow truck to pick up that Porsche over there which is a stolen I'm recovering. Glad you're on top of things in

Skypark," the officer responded, chastising himself for letting his guard down, but counting it fortunate that the guy seemed like a harmless geek." Bascomb bid him a good evening and went directly back to his vehicle, shaken.

~

The calls to the Dispatch Center began to light up the consoles at approximately 2310 hours (11:10 pm) as Turtle Rock residents alarmed by the loud crash reported hearing a possible traffic collision in the area of Turtle Rock Drive and Starcrest. The fog prevented visual confirmation from the comfort of their upscale homes, but some ventured out. They wished they had not.

The driver of the Porsche had never traveled this route and therefore never experienced the degree of the curve nor the level of downgrade. Add alcohol and a velocity of 80 miles per hour, and a relationship argument to the equation, and you have four barrel rolls and nine points of impact.

Officer Jim Janowitz drew the lucky straw when he signed up to work the overtime shift to help save for a new jet ski. "Alpha Eleven with Alpha Twelve to Follow, a 901 Turtle Rock and Starcrest, handle Code 3, 91 [Orange County Fire Authority] en-route."

Janowitz was hoping for a quiet evening, but instead it looked like he would be investigating a mess. As his patrol unit cut through the fog, Janowitz saw a single vehicle on its side with significant structural damage to the body, a tall male wandering the scene, bleeding from a gash on his forehead, and firefighters pulling a blonde female through the open passenger window.

Judging from the condition of the female passenger, who had now been placed upon a gurney, Janowitz determined that in all likelihood this collision would become a fatality. He transmitted his request for the Major Accident Investigation Team to respond as additional uniformed personnel arrived to lay out flare patterns and record witness statements. As Janowitz walked toward the driver, he glanced at the passenger window from which the blonde had been extricated, and recognized what appeared to be brain matter along the edge of the window frame.

The driver paced by the curb holding a handkerchief to his forehead. As Janowitz requested the man's driver's license, a fellow officer also handed him the license for the passenger, whose ambulance by now had departed for the trauma center. He momentarily illuminated the name with his flashlight. It read Tiffany Binghamton-Hendrickson.

The driver fumbled his license out of the sleeve of his wallet and asked, "Is she going to be all right?" As was routine in a situation like this, Janowitz replied that he couldn't comment on the quality of her medical care. At the same time, he carefully examined the physical condition of what appeared to be the classic drunk driver. Paul Hendrickson stood swaying side to side with bloodshot eyes, flushed face, and wreaked from the multiple Greyhounds he had consumed over the past few hours. As his wife was dying in the ambulance while a trauma team struggled to establish a pulse, Hendrickson answered the standard list of questions posed by Janowitz regarding the source and extent of his alcoholic beverage consumption.

"How fast would you estimate you were driving when you lost control?"

"Probably 40 miles per hour, I'm not completely sure, we were arguing. She accused me of cheating, and I told her she was being irrational."

"How many drinks have you consumed?"

"Just a couple, I was having Greyhounds and she was drinking Margaritas."

"If you would, please place your hands behind your back. You're under arrest for suspicion of felony drunk driving."

Neither Hendrickson nor Janowitz knew at this time that the charges had now elevated to vehicular manslaughter as Tiffany Binghamton-Hendrickson's death had just resulted from the negligent actions of her husband. With the arrival of the watch commander,

Lieutenant Keith Miller, the former narcotics sergeant who had overseen the surveillance of Mr. Hendrickson ten years prior, Janowitz was about to find out a lot more about the arrestee's colorful background.

"You know anything about the background of your of 10-15?" Miller asked.

"He's got a prior DUI. You have something else on this guy?" Janowitz replied curiously.

"Yeah, he was the boyfriend of the victim in the Crutchfield homicide ten years ago. We thought he might have been responsible, but couldn't prove it. He was a complete jerk."

"Well, he may be spending quite a bit of time locked up if his wife doesn't make it. Did you check out the window frame? I think there's brain matter sticking to it."

"Just got word from the hospital – she's 10-7. By the way, the accident reconstruction guys say the formula measuring the centrifugal skids indicates around 80 miles per hour.

Chapter 26

Saturday morning Hunter awakened after sleeping in until 8:00 am. He checked his cell phone for messages and discovered that Lieutenant Keith Miller had left a text indicating that Hendrickson had been booked into Orange County Jail for vehicular manslaughter. He phoned the station to get a more detailed report from the day watch desk sergeant and then dressed in workout clothes before heading in to the gym. He had signed up to work an overtime shift that evening at the amphitheater which had scheduled a lively concert of heavy metal bands for hard core head bangers. Lieutenants generally didn't receive overtime, but concerts at the amphitheater required a command officer whose salary was paid by the promoter and passed on to the consumer through the price of the tickets.

By the time he had finished working out and eating lunch, Hunter was getting ready for the afternoon concert briefing prior to the front gates opening. He hadn't put on his uniform for some time, so he factored in sufficient time to make sure shoes and metal accessories were shined and communications gear functioned properly. He had checked the weather report to determine that rain gear was not needed. It was a full moon, and the crazies would be off their meds.

~

James Bascomb was looking forward to the metal concert at the Meadows Amphitheater and made certain that there was plenty of beer, vodka, grapefruit juice, and ice to load into Nelson's van for parking lot festivities. Bascomb was not at all a fan of the music but had a fetish for the kind of women who attended such events wearing black leather, metal studs, heavy makeup and tattoos. The action was the parking lot, and Bascomb was anxious for the frenzy that awaited him.

After loading the van and telling Nelson to stay alert and say nothing unless it served to warn him of any problems, they headed southbound on the 405 freeway, exiting on Irvine Center Drive. Upon reaching the entrance, they parked by the portable toilets near the former wild animal park. Bascomb and Nelson began their evening's entertainment by consuming beer and liquor in the front seats while lustfully gazing at the ladies on display lining up to use the restroom facilities.

~

After presenting a locker room half-time speech on safety protocols and rules for handling violent incidents, Hunter left the briefing room and joined the caravan of patrol units and traffic vans heading down the freeway to the amphitheater. Upon arrival, he stationed himself with the officers working the front gates to assess the crowd as they submitted to searches by security personnel. He watched the bikers with jackets emblazoned with their colors, the wannabe rockers displaying tee shirts in support of their favorite bands and artists, and the lady-metal goddesses with their tight pants, leather jackets, and massive cleavage, occasionally flirting with the blue suits standing at the ready for intervention.

After thirty minutes of gate duty, Hunter checked back at the command post vehicle where a temporary jail had been established and two large pole cameras in the parking lot provided a live feed to officers monitoring closed circuit TVs. Roving patrols of officers in vans worked the parking lot for fights, narcotics, and ticket scalping. Motorcycle officers controlled access, while foot patrols in concession areas scooped up the drunks ejected from general seating by private security personnel. Overall, it was an efficient operation until the concert ended. The limited egress had not been expanded by the cost conscious property owner. Exit times from large concerts and festivals could reach sixty minutes, and tempers often exploded from impatient motorists with drunken passengers.

~

Darkness now covered the lot, and most of the ticket holders had made their entrance while a remainder of party animals continued their parking lot debauchery. One Chevy Malibu that had previously contained four thirty-something female rockers who had powered down several vodka tonics with a little cocaine was now occupied by only one. She had passed out in the backseat with her head hanging out the door and vomit soaking the pavement below. Her friends had left her there to sleep it off while they scurried into the venue so as not to miss a moment of their favorite stars. Bascomb was on the prowl, and his radar had homed in on a potential target.

~

The camera officer pushed the joystick left and caught a glimpse of activity near the fence separating the VIP lot from general parking. Two males stood next to a pickup truck whose hood was covered with plastic cups filled with what appeared to be beer, and women were approaching the truck and lifting their blouses. Hunter signaled him to activate the zoom function, which revealed a sign posted on the windshield stating, "Show Us Your Boobs for a Free Beer." He keyed his radio and directed a roving van to make contact, while he kept the camera focused on their continued solicitations of indecent exposure, and pushed the record button.

~

Bascomb was not aware that there were cameras covering the parking lot nor the fact that none were currently directed toward the Malibu he was approaching. He was prepared for this opportunity, however, and was armed with condoms, lubricant, and a 9mm pistol. He gazed at her unconscious body and saw the up and down motion of her respiration. The bottom of her blouse had ridden above her belt line, revealing an ornate tattoo across the small of her back. The hem of her black mini-skirt had worked its way up to below the buttocks, displaying pink panties above black mesh nylons.

Bascomb signaled to Nelson to position himself against the trunk of the Chevy, to serve as a lookout while he crawled into the back seat and retrieved a condom. After pulling down her undergarments, Bascomb entered her, feverishly pumping while his victim remained oblivious to her violation.

As the lights of the police van illuminated the parking aisle, Bascomb quickly got out of the backseat, jettisoned the condom onto the ground, and pulled his blue jeans up as he walked between the cars to the next aisle with Nelson dutifully following.

What Bascomb didn't know was that a young lady leaving the portable toilets had seen the woman passed out in the parking lot and had walked to the front gate where she notified an officer of about what she saw. His subsequent radio broadcast had sent a parking lot patrol van to investigate while Bascomb was making his hasty escape. Officers on scene notified paramedics of their discovery of the used condom and requested a rape kit exam be administered by hospital staff in the event that the woman had been a victim of a sexual assault.

Hunter monitored the call over the radio and shook his head in frustration at the fact that the incident had occurred on his watch. He assigned an officer to follow the ambulance to the hospital to attend to the victim and make sure that whatever evidence was collected was properly booked.

Bascomb had evaded apprehension again, but he had left his mark behind as his successes continued to lead toward increasing acts of carelessness.

Chapter 27

Blackburn arrived at work and followed his normal check-in routine, attending 6:00 am briefing, eating his cereal bowl filled with cornflakes, and responding to phone messages and e-mail. However, something seemed out of place or missing, and he couldn't figure out what was wrong until Hunter arrived at his cubicle, and handed him the murder book from the Crutchfield homicide.

"I hope you won't mind, but I borrowed your binder and read through the Crutchfield case over the weekend, looking for similarities to our other homicides."

"No, another perspective would be helpful. Any ideas?" Blackburn responded, surprised that the boss had the time to pay attention to his old case.

"It would be helpful if there was physical evidence, but the commonality is strangulation and souvenirs."

"I hear we had a possible sexual assault at the amphitheater Saturday night. Any updates on that?"

"Yeah, the victim remembered nothing. She was passed out from too much alcohol and coke, but is certain she was assaulted. The suspect discarded a used condom which was sent this morning for DNA. Patrol took the report. Here's the face page. When the narrative comes in from dictation, I want you to take the case for follow up. Oh, and here's the flyer with the retouched photo of our victim from the Langley Street homicide. The picture makes the victim look like a teenager. When your partner comes in, show it to her and see what she thinks."

~

Hunter returned to his office in time to answer the phone before voice mail kicked in. He wished he had not been so conscientious in catching the call, when he heard the voice.

"Lieutenant Hunter! How good to hear from you."

"Knock off the bullshit Hannigan, what is it you would like to misquote me on today?" Hunter hated having to deal with Roger Hannigan, the newspaper reporter who fancied himself as Orange County's answer to investigative journalism, and who was notorious for creating his own news.

"I thought that it might be interesting for the public if we examined the unsolved murders that have occurred in America's safest city. I would like to know if the following cases are currently listed as being actively investigated by your Bureau."

"Go ahead, ask."

"The Bethany Crutchfield case, the Kristen Greer homicide, and that young lady set on fire on Langley Street not too long ago."

"The Crutchfield case was closed in-active by my predecessors, the Greer case is still open and active, and the Langley homicide still has lab work and investigative follow-up to be performed," Hunter responded, choosing his words carefully.

"Do you think that these cases are related?"

"Don't know, we don't have enough information at this time to reach a conclusion."

"Is there enough to show similarities?"

"Very little."

"Well, is their cause of death similar? How did they die?"

"Asphyxiation."

"See, they are linked together!"

"Hold on Roger, you can't make that conclusion. That's like saying Presidents Kennedy, Lincoln, and McKinley homicides were linked because all three were shot to death."

"Stop generalizing, there's a story here, and you guys are always stonewalling us in our pursuit of truth."

"You wouldn't print it if it didn't match your preconceptions. We're done Roger. Goodbye."

~

Sgt. Brannigan was driving out the back lot to meet Blackburn for lunch when the phone message hit his answering machine. Winslow and Hunter were on their way back from Superior Court in Santa Ana, where they had testified on a robbery case. It was a message that they needed to hear, but would have to wait.

"Hello Sergeant Brannigan, this is Criminalist Johnson with the Orange County Crime Lab, and we have some DNA results on the samples you submitted on homicide cases ending in the last four digits: 1084, 2569, 3110, and 2571. I have sent you a report with our findings. Please call me at your earliest convenience if you would like your results over the phone." The message ended with Brannnigan's phone number.

~

Hunter drove his staff car through the drive-up window at Carl's Jr. located on Barranca Parkway as the call came over the air: "Any unit in the area, a 211 Bank in progress, Wells Fargo, 4850 Barranca, male Persian suspect in his late 30's wearing a backpack, holding a knife – more to follow." After Hunter paid for his order, he and Winslow drove two blocks westbound toward the bank.

Hunter keyed the mic: "Lincoln 9 and 621 are 10-97 the bank, setting up in the parking lot east of the main doors."

"Lincoln 9 and 621, 10-97."

"I need the next unit to park on the south side of the bank, facing the ATM machines," Hunter continued.

"Bravo 31, I'll handle."

"Bravo 31, Copy. The bank manager states that the suspect is apparently a customer and is demanding $10,000. He has a knife of some type, and is stabbing it in the air. He is yelling in broken English that he demands the money immediately, and is now counting down to ten. Suspect is possibly 5150 [Mentally Disturbed]."

Lincoln 9 195

As Hunter and Winslow sat in the staff car awaiting the next unit, the suspect suddenly ran out the front doors heading southbound through the parking lot. He wore a tan backpack on his back, held a white bank bag in his left hand, and clutched a shiny object in his right hand. Hunter zeroed in on the object and determined it to be a potato peeler, but Winslow, seeing the thumb over the end of the handle and the suspect holding the object over his head with his right hand, thought it might be a detonator for a bomb.

The dispatcher resumed broadcasting, "The suspect was given a bag of money, and he just exited the front doors and turned right heading southbound."

Hunter and Winslow jumped from their seats and moved to a cover position behind the car parked next to them. Hunter drew his Sig Sauer and began yelling the suspect to stop. Winslow, however, drew her .45 and began firing rounds across the lot, striking several parked vehicles while trying to track the suspect with her front sight.

Hunter thought, *Is she seeing something I'm not?*

The suspect continued running but turned eastbound heading past a large medical building. Winslow's eighth round struck the suspect's hand, but her ninth and final round struck the A-post of a Honda traveling westbound, causing the bullet to rick-o-shay into the tire of an eastbound Prius, which subsequently crashed into the lobby of the medical building. The suspect, now wounded, rounded the building and hobbled down a bike trail, holding his left hand that continued to bleed profusely.

Winslow slammed another magazine into her pistol and began her sprint after the suspect, while Hunter grabbed his portable radio and followed after her, calling in the collision and their direction of travel. The first marked unit on scene responded to the collision, and the next officer diverted to Creek Road to head off the suspect. However, the suspect had already passed there with Hunter and Winslow in pursuit. So the officer parked and joined the foot pursuit which ended on a grassy embankment where the suspect had fallen.

Winslow and Hunter held the suspect at gunpoint as he lay against the embankment still holding his potato peeler while stabbing into the air. Upon arrival at the scene, the patrol officer drew a Taser from his Sam Browne utility belt. He then launched two barbed darts into the suspect along with 50,000 volts of electricity which ultimately resulted in the suspect dropping the cooking implement as his body contorted with rigidity.

The suspect was later determined to be a mental patient who had neglected to take his medication. The backpack was filled with nothing more than a sack lunch and a notepad containing the ramblings of a deeply disturbed individual. He was transported to the mental ward of the county jail following treatment of his hand and Taser wounds.

The Prius was removed from the lobby, which had fortunately been empty during the lunch hour.

Hunter stood by the embankment lecturing Winslow on what the Department faced regarding restitution for seven bullet riddled automobiles, and the need to take his detective team through more realistic shooting scenarios similar to those he had implemented for the Department's SWAT Team. This live-fire lesson on the effects of stress on accuracy, beyond the customary range courses of fire, could well be a precursor to what awaited them, when the encounter with a psychopathic serial killer could possibly become a reality.

~

No sooner had Hunter reached the station than Brannigan confronted him with the DNA findings from the crime lab. It confirmed suspicions but brought them no closer to the suspect.

"The DNA taken from the crime scenes at the Crutchfield and Greer homicides, as well as the DNA found under the fingernails of our Langley victim, matches the same suspect," Brannigan announced enthusiastically. "However, our Langley victim's fingernail scrapings contained DNA from an additional male for whom we have no record."

"What about the DNA that matches all three? Do we have any hits?"

"No, the suspect responsible for these crimes has no DNA entered into the system."

"Well, we may not know who he is, but we now know what he is. Our suspect is a serial killer."

Chapter 28

Hunter sat at his desk fixated on the laboratory report on the DNA findings from the three homicides. His office was a study in orderliness. Diplomas and certificates adorned the walls, law books and manuals filled the shelves, and in/out sat on the desk next to the comuter. What differentiated his desk from those of his counterparts was the lack of open projects awaiting additional work. Hunter's habit of closing folders and filing them disciplined him to completely focus on one mission before moving to the next. He reasoned that detective work presented enough distractions without having to search through documents strewn across the expanse of a desktop. As the afternoon sun illuminating the open lab report, his concentration was interrupted by ring of his desk phone.

"Lieutenant Hunter."

"Do you know that you're $10,000 over your overtime budget, and we've got nearly five months left in the fiscal year?"

"No Chief, I was not aware of that. However, we knew that money would be tight if we exceeded our average of four homicides per year. We're at three now, with an extensive amount of follow-up on a 10-year old murder case that we've just linked to two of this year's cases."

Chief Daniel Steinhoffer was the current occupant of the corner office reserved for the Chief of Police. He had just passed the first anniversary of his short tenure with the Department, and for many of his subordinates it seemed like a decade. Originally from the New England area, his Bostonian accent rubbed like sandpaper on the nerves of his command staff. He had risen to the rank of first line supervisor in a medium sized Massachusetts police department, and then discovered that he had had enough work in the snow, and decided to take his law degree to a climate more suitable to his liking.

Steinhoffer landed a chief's job in a tiny Arizona town, and then worked his way into a slightly larger California hamlet needing a hatchet man to excise the deadwood. He struck gold when he attended a government seminar and met the city manager of "America's Safest City," and convinced him that he was the embodiment of the next generation of policing. Upon being appointed Chief, he declared everything prior to his reign as being old school, and proceeded to immediately change every departmental program, despite admonishments by his consultants to ease into his transition.

"I'm catching hell from the City Manager, the Council, and the Finance Commission for these continual overruns in our overtime accounts. You need to control your budget."

"Understand sir, did you happen to explain to them that it is difficult to forecast the number of murders, and even more difficult to prevent them? The timing as to when these events occur does not necessarily coincide with a detective's hours on the clock, and the Fair Labor Standards Act requires that we pay them overtime if they investigate these crimes beyond their ten-hour shifts."

"Don't lecture me on the law. I'm an attorney. Did you forget?"

"No. By the way, did you see my request to assign Detective Blackburn to a permanent position in the Detective Bureau? We have an opening, and it does not impact the overtime budget."

"You detective lieutenants are just like the SWAT commanders. They always ask me for bazookas and other crap they don't need."

"Sir, Blackburn is performing exceptionally well and deserves to be rewarded for his efforts."

"Let me talk to my budget guy. What's his name?"

"Monahan, sir."

"That's it, to make sure I don't need the money for something else. I'll get back to you later."

Hunter listened for the click on the receiver indicating that his first exercise of the day in the development of patience had ended. In his youth, the priests had encouraged his study of the Book of Job in an effort to build patience in a young parishioner who was quick with his temper. The only Biblical character this chief seemed to resemble was Emperor Nero, minus the lions and the Coliseum. Hunter reflected, *Interesting that he had no concern for the fact that we had just linked three homicides.*

~

"Interested in coffee? I'm O.D. at 2:00."

The text from Ashley Horton could not have had better timing. Emperor Nero could motivate anyone to imbibe some afternoon caffeine.

"Sure. What 10-20?"

"Starbucks – Culver/Alton."

"See U there."

As Hunter eagerly headed to the parking lot, he could hear radio chatter on the portable radios of officers passing him in the hallway. The transmissions had urgency, but he elected to wait until he arrived at his staff car and listen to the unit radio while driving to Starbucks.

Two sheriff's deputies serving an eviction notice in the University District had neglected to check with the local jurisdiction to determine if there was any history at the residence. Had they taken the time, they would have discovered that the person residing there had a long record of police responses for mental commitments. That information would have also alerted them to the possibility of violence, as evidenced by the gunshot from the interior of the townhome.

The deputies called their station for assistance, which resulted in Code 3 runs with red lights and sirens from both sheriff and Irvine police units traveling at Mach 3 to get a piece of the action. Hunter waited to hear a radio transmission from any command officer who would take responsibility for providing assistance to the two sergeants on scene who were in the process of establishing a perimeter. As

Hunter grabbed his microphone and waited for the radio traffic to clear, a sergeant at the scene reported that the assistant sheriff was asking for a landing zone at an adjacent park so that his pilot could land his helicopter.

Realizing that the Sheriff's Department response was taking on a life of its own, Hunter keyed his microphone and announced that he was responding and further initiated a call-out of on-duty SWAT personnel. He then called Ashley to communicate his disappointment in having to reschedule, hoping that the next opportunity to see her would be soon.

"Ashley?"

"Yes Scott, I heard. I hadn't left my console yet, and when the helicopter landing zone business came over the air, I figured I'd be hearing your voice."

"Look, I'm so sorry —"

"Scott, I understand. I'm in this business too, and we'll just have to schedule another day."

"I was really glad to see your text. I'll call you when this event is over."

"I'm looking forward to it."

Hunter had now reached the field command post located in the parking lot that bordered a small neighborhood park, which was a block away from the townhome. Assistant Sheriff John Hargrove's copter had just landed, and he walked to the Chevy Tahoe command vehicle and greeted Hunter as he arrived to take charge of the event. Hunter scanned the scene, and noticing that a Sheriff's sergeant and five additional deputies had already arrived, recognized that he had sufficient resources to evacuate, but needed to delay the dismissal time of nearby Irvine High School to avoid crowd control issues caused by students coming home from their classes.

Hunter knew Hargrove from the courses the assistant sheriff taught at the SWAT academy, and held him in high regard for his ethical leadership, and broad base of experience in tactical operations.

However, he knew that the helicopter landing would generate problems within the city's sensitive political environment. Hunter understood Hargrove's motives to quickly arrive on scene to support his deputies, and to return the neighborhood to normalcy.

It was pretty cool for a command officer to have the ability to land in the middle of a situation and immediately get to the business of fixing a problem. But Hunter also realized that his chief, the city manager, the mayor and the city council would view Hargrove's grand entrance as a violation of their sovereignty, and the chief would somehow be held responsible for failing to prevent the entire event in the first place. Hunter put these issues aside for the moment and directed his attention toward extricating the resident from the townhome without causing injury.

"Afternoon Scott, how can we help you guys in resolving this mess that we left you?"

"Chief Hargrove, we appreciate the rapid response of your personnel on scene. Let me check with my sergeants to see how we plan to proceed."

This was a Sheriff's operation that went bad, but had occurred within city jurisdiction. Sheriff's personnel would be more than happy to take over the problem and solve it, but if it wasn't handled well, the Irvine command officer in charge would have to answer as to why he let someone else do the job. Hunter's position was clear - he would use deputies to control the inner perimeter, while local SWAT officers would be responsible for entering the residence in the event that negotiators could not convince the occupant to come out peacefully.

Assistant Sheriff Hargrove offered the Sheriff's SWAT team and bomb squad's robot for camera surveillance, but was content to have his personnel wait until summoned for assistance. By now, Irvine's SWAT commander had arrived, and his REACT team was poised for entry. However, continued calls into the residence resulted in non-responses.

A collective decision to move toward a more pro-active approach resulted in a battering ram to the front door, and a robot bearing Sheriff Department stars venturing across the threshold. A 180 degree camera scan revealed a body. This discovery was followed by a methodical entry of SWAT operators who cleared the residence in seconds and determined that the deputies' service of the eviction process had been the proximate cause of the resident's self-inflicted gunshot wound to the head.

~

"Hi, this is Ashley, sorry I can't come to the phone right now, but if you leave your name and number, I will get back to you as soon as possible. Thanks."

Hunter left his message as promised, and for the next several hours couldn't take his mind off his last contact with her, and continued to wonder as to where this was heading.

Chapter 29

The following morning Hunter drove through the electronic gate into the station parking lot which was filled with all but the twelve units deployed on a Tuesday day shift. His mind was occupied by doing the right thing for his star detective by taking steps to change Blackburn's classification to permanent status. He would meet with Management Analyst Charles Monahan, manipulate the authorized complement to make space for the additional position, create an authorization document, and figure out how to secure the chief's signature.

As he strode across the expanse of concrete, Hunter noticed Councilwoman Betsy Moscowitz standing in awe next to the huge armored truck assigned to SWAT. Designated the B.E.A.R., (Ballistic Emergency Armed Response vehicle), it stood poised to rescue citizens from terrorist attacks and deliver tactical officers to in-progress events involving firearms, explosive devices, or chemical agents.

Hunter approached the liberal leaning councilwoman. "Good morning Councilwoman Moscowitz, can I answer any questions for you regarding this piece of equipment?"

"Has it gotten so bad that we need one of these in our fleet?"

"Unfortunately yes. Since 9-11, the world changed and we need assets that will adequately protect our citizens from new threats. Our city has been designated as one of five government agencies to possess these vehicles as part of one of this country's first counter-terrorist teams that serves a county-wide jurisdiction."

"How much did this cost our budget?"

"The funding came from a Homeland Security grant ma'am."

"How often do things like that really occur, that we would need such expenditures?"

"Only once, ma'am."

Ms. Moscowitz departed shaking her head. Her thoughts drifted to the complaints anticipated from her constituents upon witnessing another militaristic monstrosity procured by the police to further intimidate those for whom they serve.

Hunter passed through the automatic doors and scaled the stairs to the second floor where the detectives and administrative types resided, separated from the backbone of the organization, the Patrol Bureau. The physical separation served to reinforce the mental divide between uniforms and suits.

He stepped into Monahan's office, closed the door, and sat across from a diminutive fifty-something pocket-protector who was generally intimidated by members of the sworn complement, but relished his control over their purse strings. Hunter sought to build bridges by communicating to him his recognition of Monahan's ability to make things happen through his financial skills.

"Chuck, I know you can make this work without pissing off the guy occupying the office next to yours, and believe me, I know it will take your wizardry. Tom Blackburn has been in a temporary detective position for approximately nine months, and I would like to change his status to permanent. What can you do with salary savings from positions that have yet to be filled?"

"Well, we have three officer positions that were funded for the full year but have been vacant for six months since they dropped out of the academy. Our background investigator moved out of state, and Human Resources has been slow to set up a purchase order for the new guy running backgrounds. If the chief buys off on it, we could move Blackburn's position into the Investigations budget, fund it with the salaries not spent on the academy drop outs, and request the new position in the next fiscal budget. The chief only needs to justify the additional position in writing for the city manager."

"Great, I'll write the justification. Just write up the authorization for the chief's signature for me, and I'll walk it into his office."

"No problem."

"Thanks Chuck."

~

Upon Hunter's return to his office he was met by an unusually enthusiastic Detective Stephanie Winslow who proudly displayed a flyer that she had jointly prepared with the photographic computer skills of Crime Scene Investigator Andrew Norbett. The full-face photo of Ambrose had been cropped to conceal most of her second degree burns, and depicted, instead a state of peaceful slumber. Adjacent to her picture, a pair of women's shoes resembling spike heeled sandals were included for their unique design. The flyer bore the normal heading alerting readers to the identity request of a homicide victim and was accompanied by a brief narrative of the crime along with the name and phone number of the lead investigator.

"Her face looks almost child-like."

"Yes, Norbett's attempt to minimize the burns removed some of the aging lines to her face, but I think the photo and the age range in the narrative are enough to identify her to someone familiar with this victim."

"Okay, let's send it out to the usual homicide bureaus and have you and your partner take a stack of them out with a sanitized version of the narrative to the prostitution hot spots in Anaheim and Santa Ana."

~

"Are you trying to sandbag me?"

"What are you talking about?" Hunter felt his stomach tighten as he recognized the chief's voice on the phone.

"This Personnel Action Form for Blackburn that Monahan dropped on my desk."

"When you didn't get back to me, Chief, I thought I would expedite things by preparing the paperwork for Blackburn's permanent assignment. Actually, I had requested that Monahan give me the document so that I could walk it into your office for further discussion."

"I can just hear the union board members complaining to me. We're losing another Patrol position to Detectives. If it isn't wages, it's officer safety in the field."

"Sir, the union won't be knocking at your door. I already spoke to the president, and he's fine with it. They all think Blackburn deserves the permanent status, and the move would create another opportunity for advancement."

"So now you're negotiating on my behalf with the police union? You've got a lot of nerve."

"Chief, it's called being an advocate for one's staff, and I thought that I was being proactive in preparing the work for your signature."

"More like presumptive if you ask me. I'll sign the PAF, but you need to be careful with your incursions into my responsibilities or you'll be working graveyards on the weekends."

"Sir, if you feel the organization would be better served by my assignment to that shift, then that is certainly your prerogative."

Hunter listened for a response, but heard the click and accompanying dial tone. He knew that this chief was a bully, and would soon be moving on to his next resume entry.

Chapter 30

It was late Saturday morning when Hunter's cell phone rang during his last minute on the treadmill at the gym. The sergeant from the University of California, Irvine Police Department was requesting a detective to assist his investigators in an arson that had just occurred in the library. A Middle Eastern male subject wearing a backpack had entered the library, doused a bookshelf with a flammable material, and then set it ablaze before fleeing the building on foot. Ordinarily, UCIPD handles its own investigations, but on major cases Irvine PD detectives provided technical support. Investigators weren't certain as to whether they were dealing with a mentally disturbed individual, a radical protestor, or possibly terrorism. However, there was significant pressure to have the issue resolved or at least stabilized quickly, as the university would be hosting a medical school graduation on campus that afternoon.

Hunter assigned Sergeant Phil Brannigan and Detective Terry Nemeth to respond and provide guidance and support to the UCI team of investigators who normally handled burglary cases. The Fire Authority's arson investigator would be delayed in his response due to a large structure fire in the northern section of the county near Brea, but the fire captain assigned to the engine company on-scene had prior arson experience and was helpful in his initial assessment.

The preliminary findings indicated that gasoline was the accelerant. Library staff had successfully neutralized the flames with chemical fire extinguishers. There were no video cameras to capture the suspect's image, but several witnesses provided consistent descriptions of a Middle Eastern man approximately twenty-five years of age, 5'10", 200 lbs., unshaven, and wearing baggy clothes. It was unusual that the suspect made no statements, and that no one recognized him. Engine, Truck, and Haz Mat Companies from Fire Station 4 across Campus Drive responded and assisted in collecting evidence and began cleanup operations.

Brannigan and Nemeth's interviews of the librarian and clerical staff provided no information regarding suspicious persons loitering around the library, nor did they receive any threatening or hang-up phone calls. The investigation continued into the afternoon and was about to wrap up when a disturbance was reported during the commencement proceedings for the medical school graduation.

Since the graduating class numbered less than 100 students, the ceremonies were held at a smaller venue located on campus at Aldrich Park. A male, Middle Eastern subject, approximately twenty-five years of age, 5'10", 200 lbs., unshaven, and wearing cap and gown was seated among the graduating doctors but was not recognized by his fellow graduates. The graduating class was so small that everyone was familiar with each other, and a confrontation occurred with the suspected intruder. UC Irvine uniformed officers intervened and arrested the subject on suspicion of arson, and Brannigan and Nemeth were summoned to conduct the interrogation of Amir Fayed.

"Mr. Fayed, may I call you Amir?"

"Yes."

"I'm Detective Nemeth with the Irvine Police Department, and I'm assisting campus police with their investigation involving an arson occurring at the library. However, first I would like to ask you what happened at the commencement ceremonies. Do you know why those doctors were claiming that you were not a student?"

"I have no idea."

"Well, they say that none of them recognize you as having attended a single class in the medical school. Your father has said that your family came here to see you graduate from a course of study for which they have paid your tuition."

"I am a student, and a graduating doctor. It is a large campus, how would they know if I was registered or not?"

"Well it is a large campus, but they don't make a lot of doctors here, and it's reasonable for them to question your legitimacy if no one has seen you in a class."

"They're prejudiced against me because I am Middle Eastern."

"Don't change the subject. I've been provided with this printout showing the graduating class from the medical school and your name is missing. Can you explain why?"

"That must be a clerical error."

"Okay, then how do you explain this document that shows that you registered for first year medical school classes four years ago, but that each class is incomplete, and there is no record of you having registered again? And by the way, we have four witnesses that have identified you as having set fire to the library earlier today."

After approximately 20 seconds of silence, Fayed looked to the floor, shook his head and remained quiet.

"Okay, Amir, here's what I think happened. You tell me if I am wrong. Four years ago you registered for classes, and you either couldn't do the work, or you decided that being a doctor wasn't your passion anymore. But you couldn't tell your parents because they wouldn't understand. So you put off telling them and acted as if you were continuing your studies while you tried to figure out a solution to your dilemma. You continued this charade, cashing the tuition checks sent to you by your father and hoping that you'd be able to fix your situation before your parents found out. But the day came, and you needed to make commencement go away, so you made a distraction by setting fire to the library. Am I right so far, Amir?"

"Yes."

"Okay, so I'm going to ask you some more questions about the fire, but would you like me to explain your situation to your parents, or do you want to tell them yourself when we're through?"

"I would appreciate it if you would explain it to them. I will tell you whatever you need me to say."

Amir Fayed completed Nemeth's interrogation and provided sufficient information to clear the case and ensure conviction and restitution. UCIPD detectives marveled at Nemeth's ease in his folksy interviewing techniques which productively resulted in a confession in a matter of minutes.

UCIPD Detective Paul Abramson commented, "Nice work, Terry. This could have taken a ton of work for us to unravel."

"Thanks Paul. Happy I could help. We haven't heard much from you guys lately. Anything exciting happening here that we might be interested in?"

"Not really, just the usual auto burgs and domestic violence in the married housing dorms. Although we have had some peeping Tom incidents reported at the yoga classes recently."

"Really, like how?"

"Oh, some troll-like guy, possibly a gardener, watches the co-eds through an open door. You might check the fitness center across Campus Drive to see if he's been seen hanging around in your jurisdiction."

"Will do. Can you send me your reports and let me know if he hits again?"

"No problem, I'll fax 'em over in the morning."

Chapter 31

Working a Sunday day watch for Patrol was normally easy overtime money. When Detective Jack Pascall had checked the overtime book, he was surprised to see that the Sunday shift had not been snatched by one of the blue suits, so he quickly signed his name in the book to complete the minimum staffing requirements for the weekend complement. His expectation was minimal radio traffic until about noontime when the domestic disputes began during the pro football games. His intent was to maintain his perishable skills in the field while reinforcing strong relationships with his fellow officers working the backbone of policing.

Following a typical 30 minute briefing, Pascall headed out to the back lot to check out marked Unit #26. It had been a couple of months since he had last worked a Patrol shift, and he had already forgotten how heavy and cumbersome the equipment felt arrayed about his waist. His pistol and radio sat on opposite hips and counterbalanced each other with similar poundage. His two extra pistol magazines loaded with sixteen 230 grain .45 caliber bullets held sufficient girth to stop aggressive advancement, but carrying them for twelve hours posed a detrimental cumulative effect on his spine. Handcuffs, Taser, flashlight, and pepper spray rounded out the assortment of tools at his disposal but significantly hindered any notions of setting any records on foot pursuits.

Upon arrival at #26, he found the driver's door unlocked and fast food wrappings on the passenger side floorboard. *Not a good start. The previous officer using this equipment was a slob*, Pascall thought to himself. This vehicle was to serve as his office for the next several hours, and he knew that his checklist for this unit would need to be thorough based upon its first impressions.

The Remington 870 shotgun held the requisite six rounds of rifled slugs, and the 30 round magazine for the AR-15 held 28 Federal 55 grain .223 bullets, which was an appropriate number for spring tension and proper feeding. He booted up the computer, logged on, checked the emergency lighting and siren, and then radioed to Dispatch he was in-service and headed north to his assigned beat in the Portola District.

~

At the 10:00 hour, the North Meadow Food Emporium supermarket had been open for two hours, and the Sunday shopping crowd was just beginning to develop as early church services ended and East Coast ball games got underway. The market's management had a long established practice of hiring handicapped bagging personnel as well as those suffering from mental disabilities. Unfortunately, William (Bill) Tomlinson, a member of that special group, had not reported for work for the past three days. Bill suffered from schizophrenia, and unbeknownst to his employers was experiencing severe episodes of intermittent voices taunting him and encouraging aggressive behavior.

Tomlinson was currently staying at the residence of an elderly female friend for whom he had provided assistance in the form of gardening and handiwork on her single story tract home in the City of Orange. She had noticed Bill's signs of withdrawal, but never recognized the depths of his pathology. She rationalized his fixation with the Highlander movies as simply a hobby, not realizing that his persona had become an actual character from the series. She also failed to discover the samurai sword he had purchased and hidden under the sofa where he slept.

This morning, the harassing voices had reached crescendos of unbearable volume, and Tomlinson sought relief by acting out his fantasies. He put on a full-length trench coat, placed a black beret on his head, grabbed his samurai katana, and drove to the market of his employ. Upon arrival, Tomlinson met the market manager, Joe Palmer, just inside the automatic front doors on the southern side of the business. Palmer gave him a friendly greeting, and asked Tomlinson why he had not reported for work. Tomlinson replied that he had been ill, and he was also mourning the death of a friend. Palmer requested that Tomlinson call him in the future if he would not be responding to work, and told him that he would see him the following day, when his next shift was scheduled. Tomlinson left but remained outside the market as he lit a cigarette and began pacing back and forth.

As the voices of schizophrenia increased, Tomlinson re-entered the market and withdrew his sword from beneath his coat. Having practiced well his passion for swordsmanship, Tomlinson sliced the air with vengeance, catching customers with his down strokes. As security cameras captured glimpses of the rampage, customers fled like bison stampeding to escape the hunt, some bearing bloody wounds while others departed missing limbs.

911 calls flooded the Communications Center as dispatchers scanned the tracking screen for the closest unit in the area. "Bravo 51, Bravo 61, and Sam 10 to follow, a 245 in progress at the Food Emporium, Culver and Bryan. Weapon is a sword. Bravo 51 and 61 handle Code 3."

Pascall acknowledged his call sign, Bravo 51 and activated his Unitrol controls, spinning his red and blue overheads while sounding the wail of his siren. He was three miles from the Marketplace, and his back up was approximately five miles from Walnut and Jeffrey. Pascall thought to himself, *Was the call genuine? Would the suspect still be there when he arrived? What kind of sword? What kind of casualties will I encounter? Stop thinking and just drive.*

Deli manager Jim Scarletti recognized Tomlinson and approached him with his hands outstretched, waiving side to side, yelling, "Bill, Bill, put the sword down!"

Tomlinson advanced, eyes fixed, staring through him, mouth slightly parted,sword pointed horizontally with the hilt rested on his hip. He thrust the katana through Scarletti's mid-section forcing him to drop, gasping for air as red and yellow fluid drained from his gut.

Tomlinson turned and proceeded toward the back of the market, where Joe Palmer had just left the storeroom and was dialing his cell phone feverishly trying to reach the police while keeping track of Tomlinson's movements. The would-be "Highlander" reached the island freezer containing poultry and began to chase Palmer in a fast walk around the perimeter of the rectangular appliance, as Palmer yelled into his speaker phone. Palmer broke toward aisle 9 then ran to the north automatic doors and out of the building.

Pascall arrived to a parking lot scene of fleeing patrons, blood and screams. Some ran toward his patrol unit while others fled to their cars. Distant sirens of Fire Authority engine companies, paramedics, and his back up officer grew louder as help screamed up Culver Drive. Pascall considered waiting for backup, but his "active shooter" training kicked in.

Since the Columbine High School shootings the term "active shooter" had changed the protocols for responses to criminals actively killing victims when police arrive on scene. Police no longer had to contain and wait for the arrival of SWAT or specialized units. Officers were now trained to immediately neutralize suspects.

Pascall grabbed his Colt AR-15 from the rack and waded through the stream of victims fleeing the market. He reached the automatic doors of the south entrance, charged the carbine, and then button hooked to the right inside, next to produce. As Pascall scanned the store for movement, he glanced to his left and saw Scarletti's body lying face up, motionless, eyes wide open and obviously dead from the massive wound soaking his apron.

Suddenly Tomlinson bolted from the freezers toward the milk refrigerators, catching Pascall's attention. Pascall raised the barrel of his gun to a level slightly depressed below sight alignment. Quietly, he moved forward of the registers then laterally to his left taking quick peeks around each aisle. As he looked around aisle 11, Pascall inhaled sharply as the figure in a trench coat with a samurai sword protruding toward the floor darted across the opening from aisle 12 toward aisle 11, then disappeared.

Pascall entered aisle 11 and crept toward the refrigeration units in the rear where he found Tomlinson right in front of him.

"Drop the Sword!" Pascall yelled at Tomlinson. But Tomlinson simply stared at Pascall, turned to his left and began to move toward the shelter of the end display.

Pascall quickly aligned the front and rear sights, squeezed the trigger, and launched a burst of three rounds cutting through a shelf of mayonnaise. The bullets missed Tomlinson, with one round striking a circuit breaker, cancelling power to all refrigeration.

Pascall moved deeper past the halfway point in the aisle, and was suddenly confronted by the trench coat clad monster clutching the sword raised over his head, and advancing toward him.

He quickly re-aligned the sights and squeezed off three more rounds. This time they struck the center of Tomlinson's chest, and he dropped instantly. Pascall kicked the sword two aisles away and then turned to his right to see his backup officer, Bob Ramirez, holding his Sig Sauer pistol on a rapidly fading Tomlinson. Pascall presented his carbine to Ramirez.

"Hold this, I'm starting CPR!"

Ramirez holstered his pistol while Pascall pulled on his latex gloves and started chest compressions.

Two additional officers escorted paramedics to the end of aisle 11, while Paschall and Ramirez searched the remaining aisles for additional victims. On aisle 20 they found grocery clerk Alice Huntington, a 52-year-old woman partially decapitated by the deranged schizophrenic whom she had once trained in the art of grocery bagging.

~

Hunter sat in the pew and glanced toward the text message on his cell phone that had just vibrated during the morning church offering:

"Multiple homicides @ mkt .@ Culver / Bryan. Suspect with sword enroute hospital with gunshot wound from Det. Pascall. Need assist with OIS (officer involved shooting) invest."

Hunter recognized that the new internal affairs lieutenant would need to conduct an investigation separate from the District Attorney's inquiry which would focus on any policies that might have been violated during the shooting event. She had not yet been assigned cases of any magnitude, and this event would clearly be challenging.

Hunter quickly left the church and headed north on the toll road, listening to the radio transmissions crowding the airwaves with calls for resources. The DA's shooting team was summoned, along with Sheriff's Department C.S.I. and teams of detectives to interview the scores of witnesses being bused to the station and victims being attended to at various trauma centers.

Hunter arrived at the command post vehicle and met with Internal Affairs Lieutenant Luke Barnes. Only two of the ten assigned members of the district attorney's shooting team had reported to the scene, and relatives of the deceased victims were becoming increasingly upset with the delay. The market was in crime scene lockdown, so Irvine detectives commenced their interviews of victims and witnesses for the homicide portion of the crime report.

Hunter and Barnes approached the supervising investigator from the DA's office, Roger Calabrese, to notify him that they would need access to the scene. However, Calabrese had other plans.

"We want to limit contamination of the scene, so you guys can get what you need from our report," Calabrese announced.

"Well, this is our city, our officer shot the suspect, and we need to take our own measurements rather than wait five months for the completion of your report for us to determine if corrections need to be made in our shooting procedures."

"The DA's shooting report takes precedence over all others, since it determines if the officer's actions involved criminality."

"Okay, but our officer involved shooting policy is in harmony with yours and states that we will work jointly in this investigation. If you have a problem with your own policy, I'll just call my chief and have him call the district attorney."

After a few more tense moments of chest pumping, Hunter and Barnes entered the market and began diagramming floor plans, shell casings and body placement. Although there were no signs of life, simply two dead bodies, samurai sword and bullet damage, the public address system eerily broadcasted the Beatles song from their *Sergeant Pepper* album, "A Day in the Life."

Chapter 32

When Nelson Bascom wasn't camping out in his van at Doheny State Beach, he would crash in his temporary residence, a detached garage behind a single story Irvine Ranch house located at Sand Canyon and Burt. The house was occupied by a Hispanic family whose head of the household was a foreman for the ranch who accepted the home rent-free from his employer as a benefit for his many years of devoted service.

Situated between the Irvine Country Store and the old Irvine Hotel, the small house was the last of the occupied structures left on the block. The Country Store, which once housed a working post office, had long been abandoned with the advent of a modern postal center a quarter mile south. The hotel had not been in service for over fifty years, and although boarded up, transients would occasionally take up residence in the basement until ranch deputies would conduct their raids and evictions.

Nelson had been befriended by the foreman during harder times when Nelson's landscape clients had dwindled, and he had been hired to work the fields with the Mexican nationals tending the strawberry crops. Nelson had rigged the garage with electricity to provide him with lighting, heat, and power to his small Panasonic 23 inch TV. He shared this abode with his most prized possession, after his seven-foot Harbour surfboard – his fully restored, graphite colored, Ford Econoline van.

To save gasoline, Nelson traveled locally on a second hand Vespa he had procured several years prior at a Santa Ana garage sale. Not cool by U.S. standards, Vespas tended to be favored by British "Mods" who were fans of the rock group, The Who, a band for whom Nelson held a great affinity.

Although both Nelson and his older brother James had a shared fetish for strip bars, James was unaware of his younger sibling's criminality in the form of exposing himself publicly to the opposite sex for the sheer exhilaration from the shock effect. Nelson found the beach cities to be a target rich environment. However, during winter months, he found health spas and fitness centers more plentifully stocked with beauties attired in tight fitting apparel, a prerequisite for his perfect victim.

This evening he had discovered that the martial arts studio in the strip mall located at Jeffrey and Alton served as a yoga studio on Tuesday and Thursday nights, following the kids' intermediate karate class. The proprietor who had purchased one of the commercial self defense franchises had sought to supplement his income by renting space to an enterprising university phys-ed instructor who was financing her doctoral studies by providing instruction in the art of yoga. Her students were all women, most of whom were either soccer moms living nearby, or young co-eds staying toned for weekend adventures in clubbing. Rounding out the profile of class participants were two police dispatchers from Costa Mesa and Irvine, with the latter being a Miss Ashley Horton.

Nelson had scouted the venue carefully, making certain that when yoga classes ended, there were no martial arts staff on-scene to interrupt or intervene. He checked the parking lot to ensure that lighting was sufficient to illuminate the necessary part of his anatomy, but that it was not so bright as to provide victims with a clear description of both him and his vehicle. Most important, however, was access to escape routes. Nelson would have the ability to exit the shopping center and either enter the maze of cul-de-sacs and greenbelts of Stoneridge or hop the 405 freeway heading either north or south to evade any pursuit by citizens or police.

Excitement grew as he watched tonight's class wind down to the last stretch, and the usual departing waves and hugs were followed by leisurely strolls to parked SUV's and compacts. Nelson had positioned his Vespa in the parking space facing Jeffrey Road with a small maple tree to his left and a 1968 green Camaro in the space to his right.

As the tawny brunette approached, he checked her reflection in his rearview mirror as she removed the band holding her ponytail in place, shook her hair free, and retrieved her keys from the side pocket of her gym bag. Her blue sweatshirt had the neckline cut deep, revealing portions of her white sports bra. Her black stretch pants clung tightly, displaying curving hips leading to sculpted legs ending in white running shoes.

As she reached the driver's door, she glanced to her left peripherally catching the silhouette of the male figure sitting side saddle on a motor scooter normally ridden by nerds and geeks. She opened the door, and then heard the male's voice beckon, "Hey!"

She looked toward his smiling face then realized that his erect penis was fully protruding through his unzipped blue jeans. The brunette retorted, "Fuck off little dick," and then dropped into the driver's seat, turned the ignition, and rammed the shift selector into reverse. The Camaro screeched backwards with its headlights illuminating the Vespa as well as the flasher who was now straddling the scooter, which had jumped the curb onto Jeffrey Road.

Ashley's classmates sprinted to their car doors, alarmed by the burnout noise, smoking tires, and erratic driving of the odd looking man on the motor scooter.

Ashley shouted, "That jerk just flashed me," as she dialed 911 on her cell phone.

"911 what is your emergency?"

"Hello this is Ashley Horton. I just left my yoga class and was flashed by a 314 suspect!"

"Ashley, this is Nancy. What's his description, vehicle, and direction of travel?"

"Male, white, 5'6", 175 lbs., dark long sleeve shirt, dark Levi's, white motorcycle helmet, riding a black motor scooter with a trash bag covering his license plate. Direction of travel was southbound on Jeffrey past Alton."

Officer Jim Janowitz heard the call broadcast and drove into the area. At this time, Nelson had already entered the southbound 405 freeway and was now approaching Irvine Center Drive. He left the off ramp and backtracked toward Sand Canyon heading for the sanctuary of his garage. Janowitz drove the surface streets, and then patrolled the shopping center where he ultimately met Horton who was still standing next to her Camaro along with two other classmates.

"Hi Ashley."

"Hi Jim."

"Well, I checked the neighborhood, but I would bet that he jumped on the freeway. Let me get my clipboard to take the report. Newport had one of these at the end of last summer with a guy matching that description."

"Thanks Jim. I've never been flashed before. Always been on the receiving end of these 911 calls. It's a little weird being the victim calling in." Ashley presented an unflappable front, showing no signs of emotional trauma. However, she was clearly aware of how rattled the event had left her, and the impact was more damaging than she would choose to let on.

~

Hunter read the log for the previous evening's crime activity and locked onto the entry for an indecent exposure with the reporting party listed as an Ashley Horton. He pulled the face page of Janowitz's report onto his computer, read the summary of the crime, and then speed dialed his cell phone to her phone number.

"Hi Scott!"

"Hi Ashley. I was reading the log and saw that you were listed as the reporting party on a 314. Are you okay?"

"Yes, I was actually the victim. I had just finished my yoga class and some gnome-like character on a motor scooter flashed me."

"We'll see if we can get any matches in the county; the description was pretty distinctive."

"Janowitz said that Newport had a similar incident reported a few months ago."

"Right, I didn't know that you trained in a martial arts studio. You ever watch their classes? How do they compare to the class you attended?"

"Oh, it's one of those chain or franchise places that appeal to the masses. Your studio is pretty hardcore, and I'll have to do some more cardio before I take my next class."

"You did fine Ashley, just like you handled that knot-head last night. I read some of the narrative. You took evasive action, and provided good witness information. Say, when are we going to redeem that rain check on coffee?"

"I would like that very much. I work tomorrow until 2:00 pm again. You want to try the Starbucks again?"

"Sounds great, Ashley."

"Okay, we'll see you then. Bye."

Chapter 33

James Bascomb stood with his attorney before the judge's bench at Harbor Justice Center. The plea bargaining arrangements had already been hashed out, and he would plead guilty to the misdemeanor assault of his former girlfriend, Anna Savoy.

"Mr. Bascomb, how do you plead?"

"Guilty your honor."

"You understand that you will be convicted of the crime of assault?"

"Yes your honor."

"I hereby sentence you to three years informal probation, $1,000 fine, and completion of a court approved anger management course of instruction. You must also submit a DNA sample for entry into the state automated system. Failure to complete all portions of this sentence will result in revocation of your probation and incarceration. Do you understand?"

"Yes your honor."

"Very well, see my clerk for necessary documentation. Case closed."

~

James Bascomb felt apprehension at the prospect of his employer discovering his conviction and vowed to refrain from any mention of his legal issues or that dreadful "ex" Anna Savoy. He had been directed to report to a police station for submission of his DNA sample as soon as practicable, but wondered how long he could prolong compliance. He was certain that avoidance of Irvine's station was paramount, lest someone piece together a trail leading to his culpability.

Upon arrival at his corporate headquarters in Newport Beach, he discovered that a regional manager had announced his retirement, and the possibility existed that James could be in contention for the position. He recognized that his chances were remote, having only an associate's degree with no actual law enforcement or military experience, leaving him under-qualified to ascend into the ranks of management. It was rumored that the regional supervisor for Newport was being groomed for the job, but his inexperience worked against him. Bascomb's advantage was bolstered by the fact that the person who had originally hired him was his uncle. He would apply for the vacancy and place a call to his now favorite relative.

~

Detective Jack Pascall returned to work after having taken his mandatory three days off following an officer-involved shooting. The death toll at the market remained two employees, with injuries to five patrons. The suspect died from his wounds at Western Medical Center two hours following his being on the receiving end of a 55 grain, .223 caliber round that tumbled through his internal organs at 3200 feet per second. Although Lt. Barnes would present his internal affairs report to the chief in two weeks, the average return on a DA report on criminal culpability would be five months. Pascall's advantage in having Barnes preparing the internal report's findings was that his boss, Lt. Hunter, had assisted him in the report's preparation. He knew that the document would be straightforward, devoid of agendas, and had already been assured informally by his lieutenant that based on his observations, his actions would be viewed quite positively.

Pascall checked the teletypes for homicides indicating similarities to the department's "Serial 3" and found no modus operandi bearing any resemblance. He noticed that his in-bin had a fresh stack of reports with the top face page displaying the indecent exposure one from the yoga studio. Pascall phoned his counterpart at Newport Beach PD and requested a fax of the report documenting a similar event and suspect occurring the previous summer.

As the fax machine pushed out the pages, Pascall noticed that the location of the crime was the infamous "wedge," where the most experienced body surfers braved the hazards of the treacherous shore break. The victim was an 18-year-old senior from Corona Del Mar high school who, while entering her car, was flashed by a subject on a Vespa. The victim had described as looking peculiar or ghoulish.

Pascall then searched the wanted flyers on sex crimes for the past year, looking for motor scooters and for suspects with any unique descriptors such as ghoulish. One Irvine flyer bore a suspect description as "troll-like," but the suspect vehicle was a gray van. He read on, finding it interesting that it was an indecent exposure occurring behind a Jazzercise studio in Skypark. Near the end of class, the 40 year old victim had walked toward the back door to push it further open for greater ventilation, only to be confronted by a suspect masturbating. The perpetrator was described as approximately 5'6", 175-185 pounds, and "troll-like" in appearance.

Pascall pulled the original report for the Skypark exposure and searched the narrative to see if the uniformed officer taking the report had asked the victim if she could elaborate as to what her "troll-like" description meant. The report stated, "He looked like one of those characters in an old black and white horror film who assists the mad scientist, and is small and stocky with monster features." Pascall chuckled to himself, *Today they parody those characters in music videos, but when I was a kid, those movies scared the piss out of me.*

~

It was 2:15 pm, and Hunter sat at the back of the Starbuck's sipping his blended mocha while awaiting the arrival of Ashley Horton. His eyes elevated from his glass toward the front door as it swung closed to frame the outline of a tawny brunette drawing closer to his table. Every male in the room took a second look. It was customary for dispatchers to arrive at work dressed comfortably and then change into their less than flattering uniforms. However, Ashley's attire indicated to Hunter that this meeting's goal was more than a rendezvous for coffee; her purpose was clearly to impress. Her classic white blouse had a plunging but tasteful neckline, and the tight black skirt displayed legs combining elegance and athleticism.

She smiled warmly as Hunter rose to his feet. As their eyes met, Ashley looked deeply into his, and his return gaze into her blue sapphires brought butterflies as she cleared auburn strands away from her face. She reached with both arms to embrace him, and he reciprocated, pulling her close, taking her breath away.

"Ashley, you look gorgeous. I'm speechless."

"Thank you. I was beginning to think that this coffee break wouldn't happen."

"Well, I would make certain that we wouldn't let this slip away. So how was work today?"

"Oh, we had the usual crazy people and officers not paying attention to their radios."

"Sorry, I suppose it keeps things interesting. So, where were you raised?"

"Lakewood, California, I went to Lakewood High School, was a cheerleader, and competed on the women's swim team."

"Interesting, I attended SC on a water polo scholarship and participated in some triathlons following college. You went to college also, didn't you?"

"Yes, I graduated from Cal State Long Beach, got my teaching credential, but couldn't get a full-time teaching position, so I applied for the dispatcher job."

"Do you think you'll switch to teaching when the job market in education opens up?"

"Probably not. I make more money dispatching, and the adrenaline and action of dispatching would be hard to come down from to the slower pace of a classroom. I think I would like to eventually put in for the supervisor position in Communications. Maybe then I could get closer to catching up with you."

"Ha-ha, trust me, the personnel issues take more time than the more interesting challenges in supervising operations. But I think that you would excel in whatever you decide to do."

"Thanks, well I've got your resume to serve as a model."

"You looked at my resume?"

"Sure, I checked Linked In, and the public portion of your Facebook."

"Why?"

"You're interesting."

"Well, um, I have to confess, I checked your public Facebook too."

"Did you find me interesting?"

"Oh, more than that. From your photos, you look like you're really happy, and I think you're really pretty.

"Really? Thank you!"

"You remember when we talked in the parking lot at my karate studio following class and you kissed my cheek before you left? That was really special for me."

"That was special for me also. That's why I kissed you – you're special to me. I know you've got to be heading back to work now, but I'm glad we had this chance to meet and share."

"Ashley, I can't tell you how much this meeting means to me."

Ashley rose and stretched out her arms as Hunter met her next to the table. She moved her lips forward, and as her eyes began to close, his lips met hers as they embraced. The kiss continued for a few seconds, stopped, and she whispered, "Call me tonight."

As she turned and started toward the door, Hunter grabbed her hand and they both headed to the parking lot. She opened the door to her Camaro, spun around, planted another kiss, then left.

Hunter knew his life had just changed.

Chapter 34

The results were posted, and James Bascomb became International Protection Service's new regional manager, serving the Newport – Irvine service area. Patronage won the day. James knew that some people would question his suitability for the position, but that was how things were done in corporate America. At least that was how James viewed it. And besides, he had worked the streets all these years, and it was owed him.

James would now have an office; he would attend meetings, and would have a voice in how the organization operated. He realized he would need to clean up his life commensurate with his position, starting with his brother, Nelson, who would be an embarrassment should his co-workers in corporate find him in his company. On the other hand, his opportunities for relationships with women would most likely improve now that he had a new title to impress them with. The more he thought about it, the more it became apparent to James that his situation was definitely improving.

~

Ashley recognized the phone number as having a prefix matching the police department's detective bureau, but thought it odd that Hunter would not use his cell phone. To her surprise, it was Jack Pascall calling on official business.

"Ashley?"

"Yes."

"This is Detective Jack Pascall."

"Hi Jack."

"I'm calling regarding the recent 314."

"Oh yeah."

"Well, I've looked at another report from Newport that appears to involve the same suspect. The guy's description is so distinctive that I think it might be helpful if we have a police artist make a sketch based on your recollection of his appearance. Would you be willing to give it a try?"

"Sure, I'll give it a go."

"Okay, when do you work next? I'll try to arrange for the artist from Huntington Beach PD to come to our station."

"My next shift will be on Monday from 6:00 am to 6:00 pm."

"Great, I'll call you back to see if she can meet us during that time."

" Okay thanks, bye."

~

Dennis Billingsly, Senior Vice President for West Coast Operations, strode into James Bascomb's office congratulating him on his recent promotion. Bascomb was familiar with his name, but found his first meeting with him intimidating.

"James, you've been given a tremendous responsibility in protecting the interests of our Harbor-area clients. Your uncle speaks highly of you, and word from our larger Irvine accounts is that you have been extremely attentive to their security concerns."

"Thank you, sir, I hope to make you proud of me."

"I'm sure you will. Listen, I'm told that the Irvine Police Department hosts a quarterly Police and Private Security Partners Meeting that covers crime trends in your territory. Their next meeting is scheduled this coming Thursday. I would like you to attend to introduce yourself, and use it as an opportunity to network."

"I'll put it on my calendar and will be there, sir."

"Great, please let me know if you need anything James."

The tall, overbearing executive exited the office as Bascomb's mind raced in a panic over the prospect of rubbing elbows with the very detectives who were undoubtedly methodically tracking him down. He paused momentarily, then gathered his thoughts and realized that for over ten years he had evaded discovery through his brilliance, and that it would actually be exhilarating to sit under the noses of those fools. However, lest he push his luck, he would provide his DNA sample at the Newport Beach Police Department.

~

Hunter looked into Luke Barnes' office, checking on the progress on the investigation into Pascall's shooting of the Samurai sword suspect and saw he was on the phone. Barnes signaled with his right hand for Hunter to come in as he wrapped up his phone call with the chief.

"How's the report coming?"

"Which one? I've got a boat load of crap delaying and distracting my ability to get anything done."

"Welcome to Internal Affairs my friend. Just checking on the Samurai caper."

"It's almost done. I'm waiting to see if I have to subpoena the suspect's medical records. I have the coroner's report, but need his psych documents."

"Okay, Pascall says he's fine, but I can tell he's a little edgy."

"Say Scott, while you're here, I've got a question for you. I've got a memo from a female officer claiming that a certain sergeant is harassing female officers and wants the department to have him knock it off."

"What kind of harassment, sexual?"

"No, she claims he's condescending, picks on them, you know, treats them with distain, differently than their male counterparts. When she brings things to him, it's like, 'talk to the hand'."

"Are you going to start an IA?"

"No, the chief doesn't want an internal affairs investigation. He told me to write the sergeant up on a Supervisor's Observation form telling him to cease what he's doing. I'm worried that from a legal standpoint, if we don't conduct a formal investigation to determine the validity of the charges, we have some liability exposure. What do you think I should do?"

"Well, you're an attorney, why don't you call the chief's Special Counsel and ask him what he thinks?"

"Okay, good idea, I'll try that."

Chapter 35

It was the perfect location for his first residential purchase, and he was thrilled that the escrow period was short and that the time had come to consummate the transaction. James Bascomb's new responsibilities had brought greater income. His new salary certainly couldn't give him an ocean view. However, the Riverwalk condos gave him a water-themed environment with loud rushing streams, boulders, and small wooden foot bridges connecting a community of condominiums near the intersection of Irvine Boulevard and Yale.

The escrow officer's blouse was coral, and clung almost as tightly as the white skirt which gave Bascomb a full view of the outline of her ample curves. Her jet black hair reflecting light like the waxed finish on a hearse would almost put her in the category of Gothic were it not for the dark rimmed glasses resting on the tip of her nose.

Her striking appearance provided sufficient distraction for Bascomb to miss any typographical errors which might have been committed in her careless effort to expedite the transaction. His excitement at the realization that he was now a homeowner hastened his signing of the myriad papers declaring that he would be responsible for repayment of the loan. In three days he would move from Costa Mesa to Irvine and his residential status would rise along with his inflated sense of self importance. He wondered if his new neighbors would be targets for romance.

~

Hunter and Barnes returned from lunch and stopped by Barnes' office long enough for the phone to ring. Hunter reached in his pocket for the peppermint gum, sensing pending indigestion from the look on Barnes' face.

"Have you seen Hunter?"

"Yes, Chief, he's in my office."

"I want you both to come to my office now."

Following the click and the dial tone, Barnes relayed the information to his partner and commented, "I think I know what's pissed him off." Although Barnes was always the consummate professional, he was also known to possess a quick wit and the ability to do a wide assortment of character impersonations. As Hunter turned to walk toward the hallway leading to the chief's office, Barnes picked up his classic lawyer's leather briefcase while saying to Hunter, "Watch this."

They walked down the hallway with Barnes now leading as they crossed the threshold into the dreaded corner office. Barnes stretched out the arm holding his leather briefcase and slid it under the meeting table adjacent to the chief's desk. In a perfect German accent, Barnes opened the conversation by stating, "Mein Fuhrer, may I place my satchel under your table?" Hoping their nemesis would recognize the failed Valkyrie plot to assassinate Hitler with explosives, Barnes with Germanic precision then snapped to attention.

"I know history, and that's not funny! You guys talked to my attorney over this bogus harassment claim," he continued.

"Sir, the reason ..." Barnes interrupted.

"Let me finish. I had told you there would be no internal affairs investigation, and I directed that you issue that sergeant a Supervisor's Observation memo."

"Sir, it was my fault. I thought I had an obligation to protect your interests and the Department's by seeking the advice of your Special Counsel so that we would not be vulnerable to litigation."

"When I need additional advice, I will ask for it. I ought to write the both of you up right now. Are you going to write the Sergeant's log or not?"

"Yes Chief, I will take care of it."

"Hunter, when are your detectives going to give me an arrest on that Langley homicide with the burning body?" the chief said, changing the subject. "I'm starting to get questions from members of the City Council."

"Sir, as I had mentioned, it's linked by DNA to two other homicides, and we do not have the suspect's DNA identified in the state system. We are hoping for a break while we continue to follow up leads."

"I don't recall being advised of that information."

"Sir, I brought it to your attention the last time we spoke."

"Next time send me an e-mail or something in writing."

"Yes sir," Hunter responded wondering if Lieutenant Colonel Von Stauffenberg had felt like he did at the moment he discovered that the Fuhrer had survived.

240 Dave Freedland

Chapter 36

The squad of SWAT officers stood in a line, side by side, M-4 carbines at port arms with the bolts locked in the open position. The sergeant walked down the column inspecting each breech, then wrapped blue tape around the fore-grip, signaling that the weapon was devoid of ammunition. A second sergeant followed, inspecting each magazine holder to ensure that no officer carried any ammo. The squad then moved forward of the yellow police tape into the sterile zone cordoned off to signify that all bullets had been cleared.

Today's venue for training was the abandoned F-18 flight simulator building. The Marines vacating the El Toro Base for Mira Mar was a rare opportunity to utilize vacant buildings now under the control of governmental staff charged with developing a county-wide regional park. Well-meaning folks, many of whom were intimidated by such militarization, often required hand holding and safety assurances when the base's deteriorating structures were used for training.

Across the runways, in the officers' housing, Huntington Beach SWAT was practicing explosive entry on residences soon earmarked for the bulldozers. Aside from the Orange County Sheriff's Department, Huntington Beach was the only other municipal agency in the county that possessed explosive capabilities, and Irvine's team practiced with both.

Hunter viewed this as a good time to elevate his homicide team's tactical skills by tagging on to the SWAT team's scenarios. Sgt. Brannigan and Detectives Winslow, Blackburn, Nemeth, and Pascall stood in line after the last SWAT operator, holding their Sig Sauer pistols at port arms, with slides retracted, awaiting the sergeant's inspection. A handful of civilian actors were standing by for the final training that would involve suspects and hostages. Hunter decided to drive around the runways to watch Huntington Beach practice their detonations while his detective team practiced their first entry and search of the main floor.

Huntington Beach operators had finished their first series of breaches on front doors and were now testing charges on walls to create their own doors through the blasting of stucco and wood. The technician, methodically fabricating a package containing water, C-4 plastic explosive, and det-cord, announced to Hunter that it might be prudent to notify park staff that the next explosion would be loud. Hunter agreed and phoned in the alert.

The blast reverberated through Hunter's chest and despite wearing earplugs, the vibration radiated across his jaw. When the smoke cleared, the living room wall had a gaping hole, but the chicken wire that stretched across the wooden frame remained intact. A larger charge could jeopardize hostages, and wire cutters could delay entry. While Hunter listened to the discussion analyzing their options, Hunter's radio broadcast an odd conversation between Brannigan and the Team Leader leading the exercise at the flight simulator building.

"I thought there were no actors on this evolution," Brannigan's was heard transmitting.

"The actors are outside the building," the Team Leader replied.

"Detectives Blackburn and Winslow just took off running after a subject."

"You sure it's not one of the SWAT operators?"

"Negative. The guy was dressed in blue jeans and a sweatshirt."

The Team Leader then radioed for all units to exit the building. He directed next squad of SWAT operators to charge their weapons with ammunition and establish a perimeter around the entire structure. Two operators radioed that they had located Blackburn and Winslow outside a back door where they were detaining a white male subject.

A second SWAT group of six officers plus a K-9 with his handler had already charged their weapons gone through the front door to search for additional suspects. The K-9, Axel, was a German Shepherd who had amassed ten bites in his first year of service, a stellar record for a rookie.

The building was without power, and with the absence of windows, officers relied entirely on their weapon mounted lights. Axel was barking, whining, and pacing at the foot of a staircase. The team encircled the location with some covering the point of contact while others faced outward, protecting their backsides. The point officer removed the slack from his M-4's sling, un-holstered his pistol, and illuminated a rectangular metal grate covering a channel running the length of the room. Inside the channel, tangled within the twisted wires, a man was crawling toward portions covered by metal plates.

The officer ordered the man to exit or risk deployment of the dog, but he continued to wriggle further down the channel. The grate was lifted, giving Axel access. He grabbed the man's leg, sinking his teeth through the pant leg and puncturing his calf. The suspect yelled as the dog pulled him back toward his handler. When he started striking the K-9's nose, the shepherd ripped into his forearm tearing ribbons of skin toward his fingers. Realizing he was rapidly being overwhelmed, the man screamed his surrender. The dog ended his relentless assault at the handler's command of "Out!"

The search of the second suspect produced a pair of wire cutters and a wad of copper wire matching some of the material winding through the floors and walls of the aviation simulator. Following a Miranda warning, Blackburn began his questioning.

"We just found one of your partners inside. Who else was in there with you?"

"It was just the two of us; there was nobody else."

"What's your name?"

"Nelson Bascomb."

"What's the other guy's name?"

"Gary Collier."

"Okay, you guys were stealing copper wire. Where's your car?"

"Gary's Volvo is parked on Irvine Boulevard."

"Where do you live?"

"Sand Canyon and Burt. There's a garage behind a house there where I stay."

"Where do you work?"

"I do landscaping; I'm self-employed."

"Where do you guys fence this stuff?"

"There's a recycle yard in Santa Ana."

"What have you been arrested for before?"

"Possession of alcohol when I was sixteen."

As the bleeding suspect was carried outside to await the arrival of an ambulance, the remaining members of the interior team continued their search for additional suspects. Finding no one else in the building, the sergeant broke down the perimeter.

Pascall went to the location where Blackburn's interrogation was continuing. Upon arriving, he stared the man seated on the ground with Blackburn, Winslow, and a SWAT officer standing over him. Having met with a police artist and Ashley Horton the previous day, the sketch of the suspect in her indecent exposure case was fresh in Pascall's memory. The man's features were distinctive, bearing a strong resemblance to the drawing on the flyers presently being printed by a detective aide at the station.

Pascall called Blackburn aside. "Tom, this guy resembles the suspect in our composite sketch for Ashley Horton's 314 case."

"Really? This cretin does look like a pervert. Why don't you ask him about it? He's already been Mirandized."

"All right."

Blackburn and Winslow stepped a few yards away while Pascall began to question Bascomb regarding the sex crime.

"Nelson, I'm Detective Pascall and I've got a few questions to ask you regarding a different incident that you might have knowledge of."

" Okay."

"What do you drive?"

"I have a Ford van."

"Do you also own a motor scooter?"

"Yes."

"What kind?"

"A Vespa."

"A few weeks ago, you were parked by the martial arts studio in the shopping center at Jeffrey and Alton. Do you recall what day that was?"

"I don't remember being there."

"Did you know that they teach yoga classes there at night?"

"No, didn't know that."

"Do you body surf?"

"I use a surfboard."

"You ever go to the Wedge in Newport Beach?"

"I've seen it before, but it's not for boards."

"So you've been there. Do you remember going there last summer?"

"I don't remember; it's not a place where you can surf with a board."

"But you've been there before. Wouldn't it stand out in your mind when you had been there, if it was not some place you would normally go?"

"I don't know. I can't remember."

"When you last went there do you recall seeing a lot of girls there? Isn't that some place where the chicks hang out?"

"I've heard that they do."

"Look Nelson, I've tried to ask you some simple questions, but you seem to be evading me. I think you drove your Vespa to the strip mall at Alton and Jeffrey and parked it next to a gal's car. You waited until her yoga class ended. When she arrived at her car, you exposed your private parts to her, and then drove off. I also believe that you exposed yourself last summer to a girl at the Wedge in Newport Beach. I've got witnesses to these crimes, but there are always two sides to the story. So, this is your opportunity to come clean and tell me your version of what happened."

"I never did those things that you said, and I'm not going to talk to you anymore."

Pascall took a few steps away from Bascomb, and signaled for Blackburn, Winslow, and Brannigan to come over to discuss his next course of action. Hunter had now arrived on scene. He checked on the status of the injured burglar before meeting with Brannigan regarding the sex crime interview.

"He's not willing to admit to anything, but his appearance is a dead ringer for the flyer that's coming out today. I'm going to prepare a six-pack photo line-up and show it to Ashley Horton Then I'll meet with the detective handling the Newport case to see if we can show the photos to his victim."

"Okay, let's have a patrol unit transport him to the station, get booking prints and photos, then transfer him to County on the burglary charge. Before they take him to Santa Ana, try one more time to get him to talk before you send it to the DA with a warrant request."

"Sounds good. Of all the places for a crook to hit, he picks a police training venue. Brilliant."

Chapter 37

After posting bond for his embarrassment of a sibling, James Bascomb lectured Nelson during the entire ride back to his garage/apartment. Clearly, James would need to take a stronger hand in controlling Nelson's finances to avoid any careless criminal ventures in the future that could expose both of them to the legal system.

James headed back to his Costa Mesa apartment to begin the packing process as the escrow closure date was rapidly approaching. His mind wandered to fantasies of bondage and experimentation. His new condominium would need to be an example of normalcy, but perhaps an off-site venue, removed from scrutiny, could serve as shelter for his debauchery.

~

Lieutenant Alan Bixby's selection as SWAT commander seemed to be a logical choice throughout the department. The square jawed, flat topped Major in the Marine Corps Reserve served his two-week military commitment at the Pentagon planning troop reductions in combat zones in the Middle East. His annually absences would require on-call coverage for command of the team, and Hunter willingly accepted Bixby's request that he mind the SWAT dogs while he was gone.

It was this most recent of Bixby's departures to the East Coast that gave Hunter his first opportunity to demonstrate his leadership skills at the command level for SWAT. Lieutenant Ron Claypool's phone call to Hunter presented the staffing dilemma that was certain to be second guessed at higher levels. As the Special Weapons and Tactics Team commander for the Costa Mesa Police Department, Claypool was faced that Saturday morning with a suspect barricaded with firearms in his home following a violent domestic disturbance with his wife.

Claypool had one sniper team to cover the front door, but needed two additional personnel to protect ground-level officers dispersed around the residence's odd shaped perimeter. The flu had taken its toll on his tactical complement, so Claypool asked Hunter for two additional sniper teams from Irvine to ensure a better outcome.

Hunter was flattered that Costa Mesa felt confident in his team's capabilities but remembered that the deployment protocols prohibited cannibalizing the team by sending partial numbers of operators. His response to Claypool was that the on-call Red Team would send a team leader/sergeant, scout, chemical agent grenadier, breacher, sniper, and observer. Hunter would join him in the command post to assist in the decision making. Claypool welcomed the additional resources.

Once on-scene, it became apparent that Costa Mesa faced a serious and complex problem. The husband had a record of abuse of his wife, and neighbors reported hearing loud shouting and objects being thrown. Arriving patrol officers observing him walking the yard carrying a bolt-action rifle at port arms. No sound from the wife had been heard during the past hour, and their six-year-old son had answered the phone stating that his father was too busy to speak to police.

Upon seeing officers in fatigues taking up positions around his house, the suspect phoned the crisis negotiators, telling them to keep their distance. A React Team staged at a corner of the front side of the house as sniper teams provided coverage for front and rear doors.

Unknown to the tactical personnel tightening their containment, a certain James Bascomb was at the window of his second story apartment watching and learning every tactic being implemented. SWAT officers had assumed that Costa Mesa's patrol complement had locked down an inner perimeter. However, the apartment located one building north on the street behind the suspect's house had been evacuated with the exception of Bascomb's unit. He had failed to answer his door. His mental cataloging of responses by police to the suspect's maneuvering was instructive, and he memorized it for possible future application.

As night fell on the small wooden house was dark, and contact with the suspect was intermittent. Hunter suggested switching negotiators and staging fire department floodlights near the front door to be illuminated should the suspect ultimately indicate he would surrender. With the change in personnel, the suspect agreed to release his son but refused to answer any questions related to his wife.

Without warning, the suspect announced to negotiators that he would exit and surrender. The team leader signaled to his React officers to switch on the lights and prepare for a suspect takedown. However, the fifty-year-old, gray haired, slovenly abuser suddenly walked out the front door holding the bolt-action rifle pointed toward the lawn. Blinded by the beams of floodlights painting his face, the suspect raised the barrel stating, "shoot me, shoot me" as he walked the small perimeter of his yard.

Hunter had left Costa Mesa's command post vehicle and positioned himself behind an armored truck to obtain an elevated view of the scene. The suspect continued to raise and lower the rifle, demanding that officers shoot him and end the stand-off. Hunter's heart-rate rose as his mind anticipated the visual of a man's head exploding from the impact of two or more .308 Hornady TAP rounds piercing his skull from the snipers. Yet nothing was happening, and the suspect was still in control.

Hunter could not reconcile the mental disconnect between what was occurring and the manner in which this crisis should be immediately ending. The suspect wasn't pointing directly at anyone. With the floodlights in his eyes, he was not able to acquire a target. However, at any moment this guy was capable of taking out one of his men the second he discharged a round into a floodlight. Were both his sniper and observer unable to drop the hammer when the circumstances demanded it? Was it the fact that the teams were mixed? Were they waiting for some green light from command personnel? Was he so off-base as to have completely misjudged what was a "shoot" and what was a "don't shoot?"

In frustration, the suspect threw the rifle to the ground, turned around, and ran back into the house with the React team following behind. Within seconds, a sergeant broadcasted "Code 4, suspect in custody" and tensions ratcheted down while the team continued to sweep through the house searching for the man's wife.

The absence of radio traffic did not bode well for a positive outcome. The team moved to the detached garage which was wrapped tightly around an early model Cadillac sedan. One SWAT operator quickly exited and entered the kitchen, returning with a ring of keys. With gun barrels pointed toward the trunk, the upward spring of the trunk lid revealed that the six-year-old would not be raised by his parents. His mom had been bludgeoned to death, and his dad would be imprisoned for the remainder of his miserable life.

Hunter turned to Claypool, who had now advanced to Hunter's position. "Ron, can you get us a DNA sample from this asshole? I know he probably has DNA in the system from his prior domestic arrest, but I just want to make sure he's not our serial suspect."

"No problem, Scott. Are you going to be talking to your snipers? I can't believe that my guys didn't take him out."

"I was going to ask you, but I see that you and I are of the same mind on this. I don't know what went wrong. Are we sending them to the wrong sniper schools? Is this how they're training them, or is it the type of people we're selecting for the position?"

"Maybe we're not asking the right questions when we test these guys. I'll let you know what I find out from our end. Thanks man for the help. We really needed you guys on this one. I'll have our chief send over some attaboys."

"You're welcome Ron. We'll be in touch."

~

Officer Jeff Page, the senior most Irvine sniper, was walking toward the equipment van when he saw Hunter wave him over to his staff car. He hoped that the encounter would not be over some error he had made, but he knew from Hunter's expression that the lieutenant was troubled.

"Jeff, I wanted to hear your thoughts on the call-out, and any areas you felt needed shoring up."

"Sure, I thought things went well. I still think that we need new night vision scopes for our sniper rifles, but overall, I felt the operation ran smoothly."

"Well, in this event you really didn't need your night vision scopes. The suspect was illuminated by floodlights, which brings me to a question regarding the shooting of an armed suspect. At what point do you think you would have been justified in taking out that homicide suspect?"

"Good question, we came pretty close to dropping the hammer on him. I guess I felt that he had not crossed that mental line where he posed a threat to anyone by pointing his rifle."

"Isn't it too late if he is able to point the weapon at a specific target?"

"We can't just shoot him if he's not an immediate threat, like pointing the rifle with his sights."

"What makes you certain that he intends or needs to use his sights, when the closest operator was within twenty feet of him?"

"Sorry sir, are you angry with us since we exercised restraint?"

"I'm not angry. I'm concerned that maybe the schools we're using to train our snipers are sending the wrong message. Restraint should not be confused with hyper-caution that places people at risk. I'll be having a conversation with Lt. Bixby when he returns regarding sniper protocols. Maybe you and the other members of your sniper team could discuss scenarios similar to today's, that challenge your judgment on the legal and moral decisions regarding neutralizing threats."

James Bascomb continued to watch the operation with interest through his binoculars. He thought about the apparent boundaries restricting the ability of police to act. He adjusted the focus and saw that the fellow with the longest barrel was having a discussion with what appeared to be one of his superiors. He thought to himself that if the gist of their conversation was to give him a pat on the back, then the possibilities of James getting shot when confronted were pretty slim.

Chapter 38

"Why am I paying overtime for six SWAT officers when Costa Mesa only needed four?"

"Chief, they requested two sniper teams consisting of one sniper and one observer each. However, our procedures manual directs that any responses to assist outside agencies will require that the on-call team respond."

"Who wrote that policy, a union shop steward?"

"No sir, that's industry standard. It ensures that we provide a minimum amount of resources that may be needed, and that those human assets are properly supervised."

"You sound like you're reciting from a military manual. That's the problem with SWAT teams, there's too much militarization."

"Sir, with all due respect, that statement comes from a think tank study that has since been discredited."

"I'll be the judge as to what serves as a valid law enforcement study and what does not."

"Chief, there are sufficient funds in the Patrol Overtime Account to cover this expenditure, and Costa Mesa used every one of our guys."

"I've got this e-mail from a resident complaining that he saw our armored vehicle outside the city, and that it was driving over the speed limit. Do you know anything about this?"

"Sir, that guy makes a hobby out of clocking the speed of police vehicles and complaining. Just last week I received a call from the LA Sheriff's Department SWAT commander asking about whether I had heard about him. He was pacing one of their black and whites."

"Well, were we speeding?"

"I don't believe so, but we were trying to get to Costa Mesa's call-out as quickly as possible. I don't think that any normal person would begrudge us that. But I will look into it."

Once again the infamous click and dial tone was the next sound that Hunter heard. Rumors were flying that he was applying elsewhere, and many hoped that his departure would be soon.

~

It was moving day, and Bascomb could hardly contain himself. Being homeowner carried a certain amount of status, well-deserved from his standpoint. As Nelson carried boxes across the second story threshold, James waived to the neighbor sitting on a lounge, sunning herself on a balcony facing the sun. The attractive blonde was wearing a red blouse and blue jean shorts and reading a romance novel. She returned his wave with a becoming smile. James made a mental note that to research the relationship status of this potential conquest.

Bascomb gazed at the rapids rushing over rocks and marveled at the noise created by the man-made streams. He wondered if the loud splashing baffled noises from the units sharing common walls. This feature could present some obvious benefits.

~

Hunter stood at the doorstep of Ashley's apartment clutching a bouquet of pink roses in his right hand and grocery bag with dessert in his left. She had promised him a home cooked meal which she hoped would provide a good start for a romantic evening. His promise was his own custom mud pie, and he had procured premium ingredients: coffee ice cream, whipped cream, Oreo cookies, and Hershey's syrup.

She opened the door and his eyes widened. She gave a new twist to the term 'casual attire' – designer jeans, clinging white sweater, and spiked heels.

"Ashley, you look stunningly beautiful."

Stunningly beautiful? He thought to himself, *You idiot, get hold of yourself, take a deep breath and try to relax.*

"Thank you, Scott, those roses are gorgeous. I love roses. I'm assuming you have your special fixings for your famous mud pie?"

"Well, yes, I had told you about it at the market. Now I will have to rise to the occasion. By the way, your spaghetti smells wonderful."

She gracefully moved across the room with the roses, placed them in the sink and filled it with water in preparation for trimming the stems. He opened the freezer to store the ice cream and placed the whipped cream in the refrigerator. As he turned to put the cookies on the counter, she wrapped her arms around his waist and hugged him whispering, "Thanks for making this evening so special. I'm so glad that you're here."

He kissed her softly, whispering back, "You're quite special yourself. He thought, *I haven't seriously dated for a while, this is awkward, she's making me as nervous as a teenager.*

They sipped her Chianti and then sat for the salad course. She felt uncomfortable asking the question, but Ashley needed to determine his emotional place with regard to his deceased wife.

"Do you think about your wife often?"

"Yes, fondly, and I miss her, but I've resolved that God had a reason for her passing. I don't blame Him, but I no longer ask why. I know that he has a plan for me, and that it does not require that I be lonely."

Ashley thought this was an encouraging answer, and she was impressed that he had so carefully thought it out. She was reassured that he had moved to a point of resolution and was now open to a new relationship.

"I'm so sorry for your loss. I can't imagine losing a spouse. I'm glad you have so thoughtfully resolved losing Madison, and that, well, there is a possibility for you and me.

"It's comforting to me that you feel the same way. There are going to be difficulties having a workplace relationship, but I'm willing to see where this leads."

Ashley smiled as she refilled his wine glass. She knew she had landed a good one and was now determined to present herself to him as the perfect partner.

Chapter 39

Bascomb climbed the steep set of steps leading to the glass doors of the Newport Beach Police Department. He dreaded the moment, but knew that any additional procrastination could lead to the danger of another arrest. Giving them his DNA would place him in the position of constantly worrying about how thorough he had been in removing physical evidence from his crime scenes. He had evaded capture for so long, but had technology caught up with him?

The technician led him down a hallway to the custody facility and directed him to be seated while she prepared the fingerprinting materials. "I thought I was only giving a DNA sample," Bascomb said with alarm. "You are, but we're directed to take a set of prints also, just to ensure that any previous sets taken don't have any smudges or missing deltas."

Under normal circumstances he would have paid more attention to the slender blonde in the white lab coat, but he scarcely gave her his accustomed once-over. "Deltas?"

"Yes, they're little triangles in your prints we use in counting the ridges."

He could sense that she seemed irritated with him and decided his best strategy was to stop talking. She rolled each finger, cuticle to cuticle, and then swabbed his palms with ink from the roller. After pressing them flat on the cards, she handed him some damp handi-wipes and then grabbed a test tube containing cotton swabs.

She had Bascomb rub the buccal swabs against the inside lining of his mouth, then placed them into the thin glass tube. She sealed the tubes in an envelope, removed her latex gloves, and directed Bascomb to the lobby. The envelope was carefully placed in a banker's box marked "CODIS" where it awaited submission into the Combined DNA Index System.

Bascomb slowly walked across the parking lot, perspiring profusely, overcome with stress at the prospect of his DNA setting off alarms and the prospect that his world could be ending.

~

Hunter scanned the stack of Monday morning crime reports awaiting assignment to the three detective sergeants responsible for the city's geographic policing districts. Mondays were the heaviest day of the week, with cases being held over the weekend, but today's stack rose particularly high above his in-basket. He had hoped his responsibility for covering Bixby's absence from SWAT would end before any more tactical assignments arose, but that wish ended with his first phone call of the day.

Lieutenant Klaus Hanover had been recently promoted and assigned as the Sheriff's Department's SWAT commander, but had held various positions on the team over the past ten years. The son of German immigrants and a former Marine Corps sergeant, Klaus was a man of few words, and discipline was his favorite noun.

"Hello Scott, this is Klaus."

"Hey Klaus, what's up?"

"I understand you're covering for Alan while he's on reserve duty, and we have a warrant service that will require two, possibly three teams."

"Wow, big job. How can we help?"

"We've got a major dope dealer we've been working for over a year. He's living in a 20,000 square foot home in Laguna Canyon, and every Valentine's Day he throws a big party. He charges a $100 entry fee for males and the chicks have free admission. Our informant tells us that last year he brought four or five high priced call girls, and that this year he's rumored to have hired Hell's Angels for security."

"What narcotic is he dealing in?"

"Cocaine."

"What makes your informant think that there'll be large quantities of dope that night?"

"Our Narc Bureau has a court ordered wiretap on his land-line, and a court order for his cell phone text messages. He's getting delivery at noon that day and unloading it that night."

"How much?"

"Only a couple of kilos. He normally does his transactions at multiple locations in Santa Ana but the party at a multi-level house serves as a cover with legitimate foot traffic coming in and out."

"That's a huge house to contain, how many levels?"

"Three levels. It's built into the side of the canyon. Street level is the main entrance, there's an upstairs, and a downstairs below the main entrance, with bedrooms on every floor."

"Logistical nightmare; can you get high ground on the place?"

"Nope, we believe some neighbors are sympathetic with him. They have no idea about his clandestine life and could tip him off or possibly be attending his party themselves. We would have to bring our own high ground using the turrets of the BEARS."

"Just talking with you over the phone without diagrams, it sounds a definite on the third team. We only have twenty guys. Do you have anybody in mind?"

"Huntington Beach. The plan is to have your team take down the street level floor and have my team split responsibilities for the upper and lower levels. The third team would cover the perimeter."

"I'll need authorization from the chief and might need your boss to provide some encouragement."

"No problem. Can you and your sergeants meet here today at 3:00? We're getting aerial photos right now. Oh, one more thing, our suspect is actually advertising this event on the internet."

"Wonderful, we'll see you then."

~

During his usual internet search for porn, James Bascomb discovered the Laguna Canyon Valentine's Day party. He decided that the $100 cover charge was well worth the cost for the opportunity to meet girls as hot as those pictured on the website. This was not some back page of the Sports Section of the newspaper, displaying pictures of Asian women offering massages. The model-quality vixens splashed across his screen aroused passions.

Chapter 40

The Police and Private Security Officers meeting was scheduled to begin early. For a 7:00 am start time, attendance was heavy, and Bascomb was still groggy from a rough night with little sleep. Jittery nerves subsided as he recognized some faces in the security industry walking across the piazza leading to the entrance to city hall. Check-in at the Conference and Training Center went smoothly, after which Bascomb found a seat and began perusing the written materials handed out at the registration table.

Bascomb's blood pressure rose as a line of uniformed police command staff entered the room, followed by two obvious detectives clad in blue blazers. He felt panic rising as he wondered whether they had put the pieces together. What a perfect way to affect an arrest, have the suspect willingly respond to the station, and then spring the trap.

Bascomb looked down at the presentation outline, saw that the topic was identity theft, and decided he would take some notes, collect some business cards, and ride it out. His boss wants him here, so be it. He listened to the introductions of speakers, and then for the next hour and a half, was riveted to his seat, vigilantly watching for any law enforcement officer making eye contact with him.

~

The evening forecast was rain, and Sergeant Phil Brannigan had hoped to work an overtime shift in Patrol with minimal drama, but rainy nights tend to generate bizarre events. Aside from the potential for traffic collisions, burglars recognize that some cops don't like getting wet and generally refrain from even getting out of their patrol cars. This creates opportunities for all manner of mischief. Brannigan had planned to work a shift before Valentine's Day to pay for a memorable evening with his wife, but the choices for the prime shifts were normally scooped up by Patrol officers hovering around the overtime book. Graveyard on a weekday was obviously a last pick among shifts to be filled.

Corporals John Oswald and Juan Melendez had had too many margaritas at TJ's Cantina in Heritage Center, and they both knew it. They loved their blessed Corps and recognized that driving to Camp Pendleton in San Diego County was not an option. However, Oswald's brother lived in the Riverwalk condominiums one mile away. They could walk to his condo, sleep the night, and then have John's brother drive them back to the cantina to pick up his car in the morning. They began their short journey heading northbound on Culver Drive, and then turned eastbound on Trabuco Road.

Following James Bascomb's dramatic exit from Anna Savoy's life, Anna's life compass lost its direction. It wasn't so much that she had been on the receiving end of a beating, but that she had allowed her standards to have fallen so far. She sought solace in the company of female friends, but unfortunately her comfort was more often attained in the form of fermented refreshment. Tonight was a particularly low point for melancholy reflection, and Anna and friends gave patronage to the Spectrum Entertainment Center's most popular sites for libations. Anna's consumption had reached a personal record, but assurances of her sobriety were convincing, so she ventured into the parking lot and located her prized Beemer.

Somehow her directional awareness became flawed, and her Corona Del Mar destination was detoured onto eastbound Trabuco Road. Anna struggled to stay awake, but her intermittent moments of unconsciousness resulted in an occasional carom into the south curb-line. The two corporals' sudden encounter with Anna's bumper severed Oswald's leg at the calf, and launched Melendez first into Savoy's windshield, and then ultimately into the trunk of a eucalyptus tree.

Anna realized that something bad had happened, but panic brought sobriety sufficient to determine that home was in the opposite direction. She located the freeway and managed to reach the garage of her Newport Beach condo, failing to recognize that she had left her front license plate at the scene along with two Marines struggling to survive. It was there that Anna's blood alcohol level reached its peak, causing her to again lose consciousness in the driver's seat, until the arrival of Officer Jeff Janowitz thirty minutes later.

Corporal Melendez stared at his partner's body resting in the earthen drainage ditch running parallel to Trabuco Road. His alcohol induced stupor only allowed him the cognitive ability to recognize that he needed help. He flagged down a motorist driving westbound, who drove him to Western Medical Center for treatment. Meanwhile, the driver of an eastbound SUV dialed 911 to report seeing a body lying in a drainage ditch along Trabuco Road, between Culver Drive and Jeffrey Road.

Sgt. Brannigan was dispatched as the closest unit and idled his Crown Victoria eastbound along Trabuco with both spotlights canted to the right. The beams soon illuminated the severed leg with attached boot protruding upward from the ditch. Brannigan got out, approached the body, and reached for the carotid artery to check for a pulse. Finding none, he looked toward the severed limb and discovered a huge amount of pooled blood, indicating that Corporal Oswald had bled out.

Brannigan's crime scene was littered with automobile parts and clothing, and the full moon shining overhead was rapidly being obliterated by a bank of storm clouds blowing in from the west. He radioed for road closures at Culver and Jeffrey as K-9 Officer Russell McCloud and Axel arrived on scene to assist. As raindrops began to strike the asphalt, Brannigan sent Officer Janowitz to the address of the registered owner associated with the bent license plate he recovered from the number two lane.

Lincoln 9 263

The rain began to beat heavily onto the highway, prompting Officer McCloud to grab a stack of orange traffic cones from the trunk of his unit and place them over pieces of evidence to protect them from the driving sheets of water. Brannigan sent an officer to the hospital to check on Melendez' condition and to get any statements he could provide. As Brannigan finished his radio transmission, his eyes widened upon the discovery that the cloud burst was now filling the drainage ditch with so much rainwater that Oswald's body was beginning to rise. Within minutes the body would float downstream into the storm drains. He signaled to McCloud, who ran back to his trunk and retrieved six wooden stakes resembling croquet posts. Ever the resourceful K-9 officer, McCloud used the stakes to train his canine partner to slalom during his open field searches. He quickly planted them in a line on the downstream side of the body, temporarily preventing it from floating away from its place of rest.

Brannigan radioed a request that Dispatch summon an on-call Public Works employee to bring a skip-loader to the scene. His plan called for the tractor's shovel implement to dig a channel upstream through the drainage ditch to divert the rain flow into an orange grove. Time was critical, and success was dependent upon the sense of urgency aroused within an awakened blue collar government employee and the amount of runoff generated by the driving rain.

Officer Janowitz's follow-up officer soon arrived with both struggling to communicate with a marginally coherent Ms. Savoy. Field balance tests would be ill advised; she could hardly remain upright while leaning against her fender. The cracked windshield, dented hood, and flesh-mixed denim hanging on the bumper provided stark contrast to Anna's white lace blouse, black pencil skirt, and red patent leather heels. Janowitz called for a Crime Scene Investigator to respond for photos and evidence collection under the shelter of Anna's garage. Brannigan directed that a second CSI tech be summoned to the Trabuco accident scene while he and McCloud stood clad in yellow rain slickers fixated on Oswald's water soaked body precariously positioned against the wooden stakes.

The pounding rain baffled the sound of diesel heavy equipment lumbering down Trabuco road, but as the headlights grew closer, Brannigan's hope soared at the possibility that his crime scene could be saved. He directed the driver to a strategic point fifty yards upstream where the drainage ditch needed to be diverted. The skip-loader ran its shovel into the earthen wall shaping the street side of the ditch, and dug southbound, creating a new ditch running directly toward the orange grove. Brannigan and McCloud watched and waited as Axel paced anxiously in his backseat kennel. In less than a minute, the water receded and Oswald's body lowered into the mud where it would now be awaited the crime scene investigator's camera.

Melendez's statement was a disjointed recollection of walking from the cantina and then finding himself in the emergency room. His introduction to Anna's windshield was the most likely proximate cause of his concussion induced amnesia. Anna's restoration to sobriety arrived slowly while handcuffed and seated in the back of Janowitz's patrol unit.

266 Dave Freedland

Chapter 41

Rebecca "Becca" Lyons had not yet realized her status of victim in waiting as a result of becoming the new neighbor of Mr. James Bascomb. The thirty-year-old blonde, whose travel agency in Orange had turned a profit for the past year, had also recently found her financial situation sufficiently stable to afford her new condominium. The moonlighting aspiring actress had also successfully landed two commercials for cosmetic cleansers based upon her nearly flawless creamy complexion.

The two sources of income rendered her schedule too busy to todate, and she seldom ventured home other than to sleep or memorize lines for theater productions recommended by her actors' workshop. If auditions in Los Angeles grew any more in number, she seriously considered renting an apartment there and hiring someone to cover the travel agency during her absences. She barely noticed Mr. Bascomb and would have believed that her striking appearance placed her in a category beyond his imagination.

Bascomb had methodically plotted out Becca's hectic schedule, and had also determined that their shared neighbors all worked weekdays. His recent obsession with her prompted him to plan gaining access to her condo to explore her most personal and intimate possessions. Tuesdays at noon provided the lowest probability of discovery. Becca frequently parked her silver Kia on the street. Her rear courtyard gate was never locked, and she occasionally failed to place the dowel in the rear slider's track, which was intended to allow sufficient clearance for access by her Himalayan cat, Lester.

This Tuesday was fortuitous; James had no luncheon appointments, and he had overheard Becca mentioning to their neighbor that she had an audition in Burbank. Bascomb arrived home, parked his Mustang in the carport, checked Becca's parking stall, confirmed her Kia's absence, and entered his condominium. He climbed the stairs to his master bedroom and monitored Becca's condo. Ten minutes passed with no activity.

Bascomb went down the stairs and headed out to the carport as if leaving, but instead walked over to Becca's courtyard gate, unlatched the hasp, and entered. He was relieved to see the slider ajar and the dowel carelessly left on the carpet next to it. Bascomb pulled a handkerchief from his pocket, pushed the sliding glass door to the left with the cloth, and stepped across the threshold. He was greeted by the Himalayan cat stretching on the carpet and yelled up the staircase, "Hello Becca, your cat was in the carport, I put him in your living room."

When he heard no response, Bascomb slowly ascended the stairs and entered her master bedroom. The California king size bed was unmade and clothing was strewn across it. Bras, panties, sweaters, and blouses were tossed atop a cedar chest stationed at the foot of the bed.

Bascomb studied the family photographs mounted on each side of the mirrored dresser, and then carefully wrapped the handkerchief around the knob on the nightstand's drawer. He pulled it open searching for articles of sexual activity or trophies he might appropriate. A small vibrator, sterile lubricant, and an unopened box of condoms were neatly placed next to the open box of tissues. Upon discovering her clothes hamper inside the open wardrobe closet, Bascomb closed the nightstand drawer and walked toward the laundry container.

On the carpet, adjacent to the hamper was a pair of white lace panties positioned as if it had missed the edge after being tossed from the area of the bathroom sink. Bascomb slowly reached down, lifted them from the floor, and then ran them under his nostrils before placing them into his pants pocket. His excitement peeked at having found treasure, and he quickly descended the stairs and advanced toward the kitchen slider.

Looking across the courtyard, Bascomb stopped in panic at the sight of Becca's silver Kia pulling into her space in the carport. He spun around and sprinted to the front door. Turning the handle, Bascomb pushed in the lock on the knob, and then walked out, while quietly closing the door behind him. He went around the row of condos, re-entered the carport, and then casually slid into the seat of his Mustang. He concluded that Becca's absence from the carport indicated her entry into her residence. Bascomb left Riverwalk heading southbound back to work, tapping the trophy in his pocket while fantasizing the enjoyment he could plan with it that evening.

~

Something wasn't right. Could it be the faint odor of men's cologne? Becca knew that she had smelled the fragrance but couldn't place it. Lester was also acting strangely. He was uncharacteristically crouched under an end table, instead of curled up in his usual domain, his cat pillow by the TV set.

Becca scaled the stairs, quickly scanning her bedrooms and bathrooms. It was difficult to assess if anything in her bedroom was disturbed, since its normal state was disarray. She lurched toward her jewelry box, flung it open, and found similar clutter among her jewelry pieces, but could not identify anything missing. She stared out her window momentarily, then quickly went down the stairs and ran out to the carport. When she arrived at her car, she looked to the right and realized that Bascomb's Mustang which was parked there upon her arrival was now missing from its parking stall. Then she remembered who wore the scent she had detected.

270 Dave Freedland

Chapter 42

The 10:00 pm warrant service briefing concluded at Irvine's University High School. SWAT officers from the Orange County Sheriff's Department, Irvine, Tustin, and Huntington Beach Police Departments left the gymnasium and went to the parking lot where their armored BEARS and Suburbans were staged for deployment. It would be difficult to explain to the typically inquisitive resident that this enormous gathering of testosterone was assembled for a dope deal at a Valentine's party. The sergeants were instructed to uniformly respond to questions by stating that it was a "high risk operation outside the city."

Upon command, all vehicles were caravanned to a secluded parking lot off Laguna Canyon Road near Laguna Beach's Sawdust Festival grounds. The Sheriff's narcotics unit provided real time intelligence through undercover officers stationed around the neighborhood, and from the information being relayed it appeared that turnout was greater than anticipated. This was not altogether a deal breaker, since an informant had reported that the drug supplier was delayed in his departure from San Diego. Sheriff's Lt. Hanover reasoned that the partygoers' numbers would thin out as the hour grew later, and officers could better control the venue with fewer revelers.

The entire operation was nearly burned when a disgruntled neighbor complained to Laguna Beach Police that the music noise was excessive, and two officers were dispatched to the residence to notify the host. Upon contact at the front door, the property owner suspect assured the officers that the music would be turned down, and they left without incident. However, the Sheriff's narcotics sergeant then discovered that the Laguna Beach watch commander had neglected to notify the next shift that the sheriffs were conducting an operation in their jurisdiction. He scrambled to send a detective to track down the officers to debrief them on their observations. Were Hell's Angels actually serving as security providers?

~

Clearly, Bascomb was experiencing sensory overload. Loud music, crowds of people, and gorgeous girls provocatively dressed. As he sipped his Margarita on the rocks, Bascomb carefully watched the action near the bar. Two to three of the most striking beauties would hover nearby, men would engage in brief conversation, and then the newly formed couple would retreat down the hallway to one of the bedrooms. Bascomb moved closer to hear what the formula was for scoring this bedroom gig, but the music was overpowering.

He inched closer and strained at the conversation, but to no avail. It couldn't be that easy, but it looked like a simple solicitation, negotiated price, and a transaction. He watched a few minutes longer, and then took his chances. The blonde was his type, or so he thought. He introduced himself, remarked on her beauty, and asked if his observations were correct, hoping that he wouldn't get slapped. She told him $500, and he followed her to the bedroom.

Upon arrival, she locked the door, and assuming he was inexperienced, gently told him that they needed to get business out of the way first. Bascomb stammered that he had $300 in cash, and asked if they could make some sort of arrangement. The impeccably dressed blonde smiled, rose from her seated position at the edge of the bed, unlocked the door, and then pushed the speed-dial on her cell phone.

Within seconds, a weightlifter appeared, and directed Bascomb to leave the room or risk bodily injury. Bascomb met him in the hallway, and felt the man's left hand grip his tricep and tighten like a vice. They walked to the main entrance, where the weightlifter whispered into his ear, "Leave now, and do not return." Bascomb trudged down the driveway, hands in pockets, and continued down the narrow road past the long line of parked cars. As he reached a fork, he broke to the right and arrived at his Mustang, three vehicles down.

Bascomb heard the rumble of a powerful diesel, uncharacteristic to the hour or the neighborhood. He froze, keys in hand, and mouth gaping open as three armored BEARS lumbered up to the fork followed by two black Chevy Suburbans with platform runners holding six SWAT operators on each side, clad in full load outs. Several dark Crown Victorias pulled in behind, with four operators alighting from each. The BEARS idled forward as two lines of officers formed behind them on each side of the armored behemoths.

The BEARS approached the mansion's driveway and fanned out, creating a wall of armor with snipers perched in each turret, while the operators on foot formed a perimeter containment. From the backs of the BEARS, three entry teams left the 800 pound doors and took up a position to the left of the mansion's cathedral-size oaken planks protecting the entrance.

Intelligence gleaned from the Laguna Beach patrol officers revealed that one front door was left partially open with a muscular bouncer inside protecting a petite brunette collecting admission. Security personnel were described as football linemen or weightlifters, but with no tattoos, colors, or insignias displayed that would indicate any presence of outlaw motorcycle gang members. However, a bouncer located next to the bar was observed by the informant to have a handgun in his back waistband.

The informant had signaled that the primary courier had arrived, and that the transaction would occur on the third floor master bedroom. The SWAT mission was to secure the residence, control all movement, and provide protection for the narcotics officers' search, seizure of contraband, and arrest of participants in criminal activity.

The first wave of Irvine SWAT officers swept in through the open door, ordering all within view to hit the deck, while the second wave of sheriff's operators followed and stormed up the stairs. The third element of Huntington Beach officers sped past the first floor, and plunged down the staircase leading to the lower levels of the mansion.

~

Lieutenants Hunter and Hanover stood by the Suburbans, along with Huntington Beach's SWAT commander, listening to the radio traffic. Partygoers who hadn't yet made it to the front door to pay their entrance fees scurried to their cars, fleeing from whatever it was that awaited those inside facing the business end of an M-4 carbine. Bascomb made momentary eye contact with Hunter immediately after his headlights illuminated the three command officers standing in the roadway. He broke into a sweat wondering what crime he had been exposed to that would warrant such a police response.

~

Hunter's team moved methodically through the main floor, clearing each room with precision. A two-man element hitting a back bedroom interrupted a naked couple under the sheets. The awkward moment was tempered by the soft but authoritative commands directed by the point man. The operational plans directed that all occupants of the residence to be herded into the great room at the entrance. However, this team allowed the young man and woman to put on their clothes before leaving the bedroom. It became apparent that other pairs of operators were not as sympathetic, as some couples seated near the entrance were covered with blankets or bedspreads. One of the blondes, clearly a call girl, berated the deputies incessantly for their lack of decency.

The team hitting the master bedroom on the third floor benefitted greatly from the volume of music. The primary suspect/homeowner and his drug courier were caught flat footed with cash in hand and kilo on the bed when the deadbolt blew across the room from the impact of the Avon shotgun round. The deputies zip-tied the two, then radioed their discovery to Hanover.

Hanover was relieved to be vindicated for having deployed so many resources resulting in the retrieval of contraband, and finally, the apprehension of a major player. Hunter joined Hanover in decompressing at the sound of "Code 4, Secure," over the radio waves, signaling that all threats had been rendered safe.

Chapter 43

Hunter sat at his desk listening over and over again to the voice mail left by Ashley thanking him profusely for the beautiful pink roses he had sent her. Unable to present them in person due to the narcotics operation, they had decided to wait until the weekend to celebrate the romantic holiday. His concentration was interrupted as Blackburn entered and sat in one of two chairs facing Hunter's desk.

"I've been busy with some computer checking on the name of the security guard on the Crutchfield homicide, and found two Bascombs of interest."

"Okay, and the significance?"

"Well, the security guard, James Bascomb, has a brother named, Nelson Bascomb. He has a prior arrest for commercial burglary, pending a trial beginning this week."

"Are you saying that the security guard had help? And by the way, have you had an opportunity to re-interview him?"

"I have not yet re-interviewed him; I'm preparing a list of questions. But what I find interesting is that the vehicle registered to Nelson Bascomb is a Ford van. If you recall in the Greer homicide, the neighborhood witness, Grace Coons, remembered seeing a gray colored van with shiny wheels possibly casing the victim's neighborhood. Nelson Bascomb's arrest report listed his residential address as being the same as his brother, who lives in Costa Mesa. I'm gonna take Stephanie with me to start checking James Bascomb's residence for Nelson's van. He's a self employed gardener, so he doesn't have a place of employment for us to check."

"All right, you might also touch base with Costa Mesa and Newport Beach records bureaus to see if Nelson has been cited in either city, and offered a different address to any officer that issued him a citation."

~

Blackburn and Winslow left the parking lot and headed down Jamboree toward the 405 freeway. Unable to locate any recent traffic citations for Nelson Bascomb that listed a different address from his brother's, they set out to check James' neighborhood.

"James Bascomb gave incorrect information on his work hours on the night of the Crutchfield homicide. I think he lied, but it may be too easy to wiggle out of the discrepancy in court by stating that he got the days mixed up," Blackburn theorized to Winslow.

"Well, if that's all you got, that's reaching."

"I'm waiting for DNA to come back on the bloody palm print left on the bathroom doorjamb. At the time of the crime, DNA was not operational yet for crime scene investigation. I looked at Bascomb's palm print and the print left on the doorjamb, and they look similar, but clearly weren't the same, and anyway that's not my area of expertise."

"Who compared it at the time of the murder?" Winslow opined.

"The Sheriff's Department. CSI report found no matches."

"You ever consider having Norbet taking a look at it?"

"Yeah, I thought about it once I found the discrepancy in Bascomb's statement, but he's been so busy lately I was waiting for an opening. You know how cranky he can get."

"This is no time for courtesies, Tom. This is a fucking homicide! Somebody died and you're worried about getting your head bit by someone long overdue for retirement? That guy should be sipping Mai Tais on Maui, so we can get someone in there with a little more energy and a lot less bark."

"You're right; I need to suck it up. Who knows, maybe he'll actually find something, and he'll be all happy when they start throwing him accolades."

After transitioning from the 405 freeway to the 55, they exited at Fair Drive and turned right. They drove up to Fordham, and then crept slowly up and down streets in the neighborhood looking for gray vans, on the outside chance one of the Bascombs might be around. Winslow pointed out the irony of them living between the Costa Mesa Police station and Fairview Mental Hospital.

Blackburn stopped a half block down from their apartment building, and they sat for a minute observing the character of the street and the level of activity. They got out of the car and walked toward the building, with Blackburn holding his legal size leather notebook containing case questions in the event that they encountered one of the brothers for an interview. First, they made contact at the manager's apartment, hoping to glean something useful regarding their habits or behavior as tenants.

Rachel Cohen met Blackburn and Winslow and spoke through the closed screen door, suspicious that the police would be interested in anything concerning her. The mezuzah stationed on the upper right doorpost announced that this seventy-year-old Jewish transplant from Brooklyn was proud of her heritage.

"Good afternoon, Ma'am. I'm Detective Blackburn and this is Detective Winslow with the Irvine Police Department. We'd like to ask you some questions regarding one of your tenants. Can we talk?"

"Please, come in. Which of my tenants are you interested in?"

She led them to the sofa and offered them iced tea, as she began to recount her journey from Brooklyn to California. Her deceased husband had been an engineer responsible for the construction of many of the now famous buildings shaping the Manhattan skyline.

"It was the cold, you know. He never liked shoveling snow, so we saved until we could buy this small apartment building where it never snows."

It soon became apparent to Blackburn and Winslow that Mrs. Cohen was the perfect neighbor for their purposes. She was inquisitive and observant. Both detectives opened their notebooks as the elderly chronicler poured them iced tea.

"We're interested in some information concerning James Bascomb and his brother, Nelson."

"Well, you're a little late, James moved out a few weeks ago."

"Do you know where he moved? Did he leave a forwarding address?"

"He said that he had purchased a condominium in Irvine, and he boasted it was near water. He didn't leave a forwarding address, but did say he would call me once he got settled."

"Did his brother Nelson live here also?"

"No, but he would frequently stay the night. Oye, was he ever a pain in the *toucas*. Played his rock and roll music too loud. He was ghoulish. I think he was *mishuggah*. He looked like a character out of a 1930's horror picture, like Frankenstein. He didn't say much, but he would often stare at you."

"Do you remember what kind of car he drove?"

"It was a van he used to shlepp his gardening tools around with."

"What color?"

"It was gray."

"Anything else stand out about the van?"

"It had silver wheels."

"Do you know if he had any business or gardening clients in the neighborhood?"

"He said that most of his work was in Irvine, but he made it sound like he was proud of it, like he wouldn't lower his standards by working around here."

"Do you have any idea where Nelson lives?"

"I don't, but I sense from their conversations that he may be staying somewhere in Irvine."

"Did James ever bring girls by the apartment?"

"He would occasionally bring one girl, professional looking. A couple of times she stayed the night, but they were not living together in sin. I would have said something. I didn't see much of her lately, though."

"Did you have occasion to enter his apartment?"

"Yes, once in a while I would let a repairman in for leaky faucets, stuck disposal, and the like. It was a typical bachelor apartment, messy. But I've seen worse."

"Did you see anything unusual?"

"He had a bulletin board in the kitchen with Polaroid pictures of young women. I wondered if he left them up when his lady friend came over."

"Were they scantily clad? Were they just women, or were there any men with them?"

"They were mostly candid, in various forms of dress, but nothing risqué. If there were men pictured, they were in the background."

"Did you ever see any firearms in the apartment?"

"Well, one time he set off the smoke detector. I think he burned something on the stove, and I could hear it in my apartment. Before I called the fire department, I ran upstairs to check, and the door was unlocked. I rushed in, and saw him putting a smoking pan in the sink. I helped by opening windows to air the smoke out. He apologized and thanked me. As I was walking out, I saw that he had a gun dismantled on his kitchen table. It was in pieces, lying on newspaper, and there was a coffee can with some type of solvent. We were fortunate that the fumes from the coffee can weren't ignited by the gas burner on the stove, and I told him that."

"Could you tell if it was a pistol or a rifle?"

"It looked like a pistol, but I could be wrong. It didn't have a long barrel."

"Did he pay on time?"

"Yes, he would write a check, put it in an envelope, and drop it through the mail slot in my front door. He would frequently wear his security guard uniform home, but he said that he got promoted recently. I think that's why he moved."

"Do you have his original rental application and references?"

"Yes, I have them in a file in my office. If you can wait a minute, I will go get them."

Blackburn turned to Winslow and smiled, knowing that they had scored a winner with Rachel Cohen. Circumstantial background information that produced as many questions as it had answered. Mrs. Cohen then returned with the requested documents.

"I made you copies on my computer printer. My son installed it for me. He's taught me so much regarding computers. I even have a Facebook account. You know, all this time we have been chatting, I forgot to ask you why the police are interested in the Bascomb brothers."

"We think they might be witnesses to a crime," Winslow said.

"Oh, I think there's something more that you're not sharing."

"Well, Mrs. Cohen, there is, but we can't say at this time. I promise you that we will let you know when we have more information, but right now it would be premature to share any more than we are investigating a significant case that may or may not involve them. We do know that you have helped us immensely in determining if they are involved, and we are thankful."

"You're quite welcome. I am happy to help. My grandson is an officer with the New York Police Department. He's patrolling the Bronx, and I always worry about him."

"They're a fine police department and you have every reason to be proud. I would ask, however, that if either of the Bascombs contact you, that you please call me; here is my card."

Chapter 44

Having just scored their dope for the night, Alex Flynn and Alyssa Jorgenson resumed their normal regimen following ingestion of methamphetamine – they argued. Their six month romantic relationship was really not much more than narcotic fueled lust. Tonight was unusual in that they were forced to select Plan B to supply their habit, leave his Lancaster house, and travel to Lake Forest for a secondary supply source when their primary dealer was hospitalized with appendicitis.

Somewhere in the area of Interstate 5 and Barranca Parkway. the argument escalated, causing Alex to get lost and exit the freeway. Trying to regain his bearing, he turned left on Banting, and then right on Alton Parkway as he struggled to find a freeway on-ramp. As his Ford Taurus stopped for the red light at Alton and Sand Canyon, both meth freaks reached critical mass, and shouting exploded into violence with fists, slaps, and scratches. Alyssa reached into the glove box, retrieved Alex's Ruger .357 magnum revolver, and shot him in the right foot, causing motorists stopped on each side of them to dial 911 and speed away from danger.

As Alex struggled to control the weapon, the Taurus drifted diagonally across the intersection, jumped the curb, and coasted to a stop in a field located on the southwest corner. Alex jerked the revolver from Alyssa's grasp and responded with two bursts, one striking Alyssa's head causing death instantly.

Sergeant Richard Austin had just cleared the graveyard shift 9:00 PM briefing and was heading out to the Spectrum Entertainment Center to check on the two officers working a foot beat until midnight. The call came out over the radio as a possible disturbance in a vehicle involving a firearm, and Austin was the closest unit at Alton and Jeffrey. With red lights and siren, his Crown Victoria sprinted one mile eastbound to Sand Canyon as Dispatch sent him two additional units plus a helicopter from the Sheriff's Department. He could feel his blood pressure begin to rise, but tried to reassure himself that this city was notorious for calls sounding horrific, only to be downgraded from genocide to road rage.

Upon arrival, Austin saw Flynn standing next to the open driver's door to his Taurus, revolver in hand, limping around the car with a wound in his foot, likely a bullet hole. Austin drew his pistol and yelled to Flynn to drop his weapon, but the suspect was unresponsive. Austin grabbed his pack-set radio and advised responding units the conditions at the scene. He directed one officer to park on Alton facing eastbound and another to park on Sand Canyon south of Alton facing southbound. As Officer Victor Nishimura assumed the Alton position and Officer Nancy Valenzuela set up at the Sand Canyon position, the Sheriff's helicopter hovered overhead and ordered Flynn through their PA system to drop his pistol. Austin remained at the intersection corner between the other two units, coordinating the scene as Flynn elected to re-enter the vehicle and sit in the driver's seat.

Austin could see a woman in the passenger seat slumped against the window but was unable to ascertain her condition. Nishimura held his Remington 870 shotgun trained on Flynn from a southbound angle. Valenzuela held her Colt AR-15 pointed toward Flynn from a westbound direction. As the deputy in the helicopter continued to broadcast orders to Flynn to surrender, Flynn, still operating in a manic state from the speed, got out of the vehicle and resumed limping while brandishing his pistol.

Complicating an already chaotic scene, Chief Steinhoffer, listening to the event unfolding on the radio, left a late adjourning council meeting, and decided to drop by and render assistance. Once on scene, he immediately lashed out at Austin for failing to assign one of his officers to control traffic. He then questioned the deployment and placement of the AR-15, alleging that the patrol rifle and shotgun were in a position of crossfire.

As Steinhoffer continued to animate his displeasure with the tactics employed, Austin, who normally supervised in a calming, understated manner, turned toward Steinhoffer and assertively declared, "The trajectory angles of the weaponry are appropriate. The next unit that arrives can perform traffic control. I need to contain an armed suspect. Do you want to take over this scene?"

Steinhoffer, not accustomed to challenges, declined, stating, "No." He remained disengaged until the event was stabilized. However, Austin experienced even greater anxiety upon hearing that his third responding officer had been T-boned in a traffic collision at Alton and Jeffrey when a motorist failed to yield to his red lights and siren.

As the methamphetamine's potency degraded with time, Flynn's powers of reasoning increased exponentially. He threw down his Ruger, and lay prone in the weeds adjacent to his car. A team of officers approached, handcuffed him, and then had him transported via ambulance to the hospital for treatment and later booking. Jorgenson was pronounced dead at the scene, and Hunter received the requisite phone call in the middle of the night for a detective call-out.

The following day, SWAT commenced their training day in the Patrol briefing room outlining the day's schedule of firearms exercises. Chief Steinhoffer interrupted the meeting seeking vindication of his previous night's criticism of the sergeant's and officers' tactics. He recounted the officers' positions and articulated his issues with the deployment of the patrol rifle, the potential for crossfire, and the lack of traffic control.

Every officer, sergeant, and lieutenant in the room sat silently weighing the risks of speaking freely and being targeted, agreeing with the chief and selling out, or simply remaining silent, hoping the nightmare would pass. Finally, a crusty, seasoned sergeant, spoke what every experienced tactician in the room knew was correct, even based upon Steinhoffer's own account.

"Chief, the sergeant was correct in his placement of his resources, the patrol rifle was an appropriate tool due to the distance involved, which exceeded 25 yards, and traffic control, though important, was secondary to containing the armed suspect."

The chief responded, "I disagree," and then left the room without further comment. Within months of this event, Steinhoffer departed to greener pastures and ultimately left the state. A newer, brighter direction awaited the department, and Hunter no longer faced an adversarial relationship to impede his pursuit of a killer.

~

In consultation with his attorney, Nelson Bascomb elected to plead guilty to the burglary of the FA-18 flight simulator building, and in exchange for his plea, he would serve four weekends in the county jail, would be placed on formal probation for two years, and submit a DNA sample. The combination of jail overcrowding and Nelson's lack of a criminal record enabled him to escape a three month sentence.

Nelson left the Harbor Justice Center courthouse and drove southbound on Jamboree Road to the Newport Beach Police station to submit a DNA sample. Despite the fact that he lived in a garage near the intersection of Sand Canyon and Burt, he listed his current address as that of his brother's previous address in Costa Mesa. He could not remember the number for his brother's new condo, thus leaving his whereabouts as unaccounted for with respect to law enforcement purposes.

Chapter 45

James Bascomb began the weekend struggling under a box spring mattress as he and Nelson carried it from Nelson's garage to his van. It wasn't so much the weight of it as it was bulky and difficult to grip. James needed to transfer some of his belongings to the storage unit he had just rented a few blocks from his condo. Moving from a two bedroom apartment to a smaller condominium left him with extra furniture which he was forced to temporarily store with Nelson. The limited storage space at Riverwalk gave him no room for his snow ski equipment, and he eventually planned the purchase of a dirt bike, which would need the additional space.

They drove to the intersection of Jeffrey and Bryan where the storage facility was located across the street from a former packing plant earmarked for eventual replacement by a new housing tract. James read Nelson the combination code for the key pad, and the gate lurched as the motor engaged.

Once at his unit, James unlocked the padlock, lifted the door, and the two of them unloaded the mattresses and night stands. The dresser was already at the back with the mirror on top with skis, poles, boots, and racks leaning against it. As James returned to retrieve the two lamps for the night stands, he glanced in Nelson's open tool chest and discovered a small metal container marked 'ether'.

After placing the last pieces of furniture in the unit and locking the door, James met Nelson at the van, and they left the facility heading westbound toward James' condo. As Nelson's van lumbered down Bryan Road, James asked about the unusual substance in Nelson's tool chest.

"What's with the ether in your toolbox?"

"Huh?"

"I noticed you had a container of ether in your toolbox, and wondered what you use it for?"

"Oh, you can spray it into the carburetor of the van on cold days when it has trouble starting. I also use it sometimes on the mowers and edgers to get them started."

"Is that the same ether that they used as anesthesia in the olden days?"

"I don't know. It's got a pretty strong smell, and if I get too close, I get a headache. I learned to use it in auto shop in high school."

James' mind wandered as the conversation ended, and he began to think of warped applications for the substance. If the drug was what he thought it was, it could be introduced to incapacitate. Date rape drugs were dependent on the female ingesting them, but ether could be controlled by the male. Of course she would immediately know who was drugging her, but if she wouldn't survive to be a witness, then it wouldn't matter. He would more closely examine the label of the container he had surreptitiously appropriated from his brother's tool chest and research the matter further on the internet. Bascomb continued to descend into the depths of depravity, encouraged by the police department's inability to stop him, as well as his new found hobby of cocaine supplied through his brother's surf buddies via Santa Ana.

~

Blackburn looked intently over the shoulder of Crime Scene Investigator Andrew Norbet as he placed James Bascomb's palm print card next to the wooden piece of bloody doorjamb stained with the imprint of the killer's bloodied palm. He hovered a magnifying glass over the card, and then held it over the wood, and then back again. He rubbed his eyes and repeated the procedure. "They look similar," he said, "but they don't match, yet they look like they should."

Norbet then stood and looked at both imprints from a distance of two feet above them. He then pulled the 35 mm 1 to 1 photograph and negative of the doorjamb that had been sent to the Sheriff's Department CSI lab for processing and compared them with Bascomb's print card.

Norbet then said, "I think I know what happened. It appears that the Sheriff's technician compared Bascomb's print card with the negative of the doorjamb, rather than simply using the photograph. In essence, they compared a positive, the print card, with the photographic negative. It was an error."

"You mean that's actually Bascomb's bloody palm print on that doorjamb?" By this time Blackburn was shouting.

"I think so."

"You think? How do we confirm?"

"Well, to be absolutely sure, you could take the print card and the doorjamb to the FBI Crime Lab in Quantico and subject them to a laser."

"Come with me, we've got to get the lieutenant to weigh in on this."

Blackburn led Norbet out of the CSI lab and up the stairs leading to the Detective Bureau. He glowed from vindication, having persevered in scrutinizing the cold case and now being supported by direct evidence.

Hunter sat behind his desk conversing on the phone, but paused momentarily, seeing the look of urgency on the faces of his two subordinates. "I'll call you back," he said into the receiver, then signaled for Blackburn to close the door.

Blackburn summarized the Crutchfield case, and then explained Norbet's hypothesis. Hunter listened with interest, feeling a sense of exhilaration building.

"We need to move on this now, but we have to be sure. Andrew, we need to send you and this evidence to Quantico, and Tom, you need to track Bascomb down without alerting him. We need to find where he lives and works, and hope that he doesn't bolt. If Andrew calls from Virginia with good news, we'll scoop him up."

"Do you want anyone to go with Andrew?"

"No Tom, he's a big boy. I'll need you to get the Crutchfield case dusted off and start lining up Greer and the Kettering homicides. The DNA on these three cases is linked, but apparently we don't have Bascomb's DNA in the system."

"Andrew, I want you to contact Karen in the Training Bureau to set up your air travel and hotel reservations. See if you can catch the next flight out in the morning. We will contact the FBI's Los Angeles office to make arrangements with bureau headquarters in Washington, D.C."

Hunter pondered the significance of possibly solving a case that had been cold for over ten years. It would certainly elevate the prestige of the Department's detective bureau, but what harm would it cause to their partners at the Sheriff's Department?

Hunter thought about the details of the Crutchfield homicide, and how it was the first case of murder for which he had intimate knowledge as a new officer. It shocked him to see the viciousness depicted in the crime report, and the terror the victim must have experienced being strangled by a monster fully enraged.

He then visualized Kristen Greer's horror, and the absolute terror of the young woman torched on Langley Street.

Chapter 46

Bascomb signed out from his office in Newport Beach, writing on the status board, "Checking contracts in North Irvine." His planned meeting with Nelson was more than just lunch. James would bring the burgers, but Nelson had scored the dope. Nelson texted that he had procured the "dessert," but added that he was running a little late.

James arrived at his condo, pulling into his parking space in the carport at the moment his new neighbor and current fantasy, Becca Lyons, got out of the driver's seat of her Kia. He could smell her Oscar de la Renta cologne as it caught the afternoon breeze and traveled through his open passenger window. He waived to her, and she waived back, giving him a tepid smile, knowing that he had violated the sanctity of her home, but unable to establish any proof.

Bascom carried in the burgers, fixated on his last vision of Becca, as she disappeared behind the gate leading to her rear courtyard. Her response to his greeting was problematic. She should have come over to his car and engaged him in conversation, the narcissist fantasized. Instead, she gave him a weak smile and left. *Stuck-up, arrogant, bitch.* His mind kept labeling her with condescending descriptions, but he couldn't get past his warped desire to mount her.

After placing the burgers in the oven and setting the temperature to low, he returned to his Mustang, fired up the engine and left the carport. He drove to the street leading into the condo complex and parked at the cul de sac, which placed his vehicle directly next to the block wall separating the street from his carport.

His escalating use of cocaine was beginning to manifest itself with obsessive compulsive behaviors and paranoia. Bascomb had begun sensing anxiety about being caught while being paradoxical engaging

Lincoln 9 291

in more risky conduct. The placement of his Mustang provided him with a more direct escape route in the event that he was forced to make a hasty retreat from his condo through the carport, and over the fence. He was determined to avoid apprehension at all costs.

Bascomb returned to his condo and decided to check e-mail while he awaited the arrival of his brother. After finishing his in-box, he jumped to his search engine and checked the various forms of ether as an anesthesia. After reviewing the factors contributing to its discontinuance for use on humans, he determined that brief exposure to women that he wished to exploit would produce the desired effect. He retrieved Nelson's container, applied a few drops on a cloth napkin, and placed the napkin in a clear plastic baggie. He stuffed the baggie into his pants pocket and tested whether the fumes would pass through the plastic container and the wool in his trousers.

Bascomb suddenly realizing that it was Thursday noon. His obsessive monitoring of the schedule and habits of his lovely neighbor with the aid of a video camera directed at her condo had revealed that she had recently developed the practice of running at noon on Thursdays for approximately 45 minutes. His prized souvenir panties had lost their allure, and he hoped that she would soon depart and enable him to retrieve a fresh pair for his perverted enjoyment. His train of thought was interrupted by the familiar sound of the front door deadbolt being thrown, announcing the arrival of his brother.

Nelson produced the cocaine, and James placed the rectangular mirror on the coffee table, before walking over to the living room window and drawing the curtains. Nelson tapped out several lines of the white powder, and James handed him a red and white straw from a small, black nylon zippered camping bag lying on the table. He withdrew his own straw from the bag and waited for Nelson to finish the ingestion of his last line of powder into his nostrils. Nelson sat back into the leather sofa and gazed at the ceiling, while James began the ritual of making the snowy substance disappear into each side of his septum. James breathed deeply, and then walked over to the oven to retrieve their lunch.

Bascomb stopped suddenly in the kitchen, alerted by the image of Becca appearing partially through cracks in the slats of his wooden fence. She was wearing a pink tank top, white jogging shorts, running shoes and a ponytail. She was going for a run, and he had 45 minutes.

He handed Nelson a burger, told him to wait for him upstairs in the master bedroom, and directed him to call his cell phone if he saw his female neighbor who was wearing a jogging outfit return to her gate leading from the carport. He then walked briskly out his courtyard gate, opened Becca's gate and then checked her sliding glass door. Finding it unlocked, he entered and went up the stairs to her bedroom. His heart raced from the combination of excitement and the cocaine coursing through his central nervous system. It peaked at the discovery of a pair of black lace panties lying atop her hamper, which he lifted slowly toward his nostrils.

Nelson's cocaine elevated metabolism necessitated an immediate bathroom call as his bladder filled with urine. This unfortunate timing caused him to miss Becca's return to the carport due to a sudden attack of leg cramps. She opened the gate, walked through the open slider, and then stopped in her tracks remembering that the glass door had been left closed, but unlocked. The familiar faint odor of men's cologne alerted her to danger, but she was frozen in place from both fear and the tightening of the cramps in both calves. She watched in terror as Bascomb leapt from the stairs to the kitchen floor striking her left jaw with the fist of his right hand, knocking her to the floor, unconscious. He reached in his pocket, retrieved the napkin from the baggie, and held the ether soaked cloth tightly around her nose and mouth with his hand. Assured that she was unresponsive, Bascomb grabbed his cell phone and called his brother.

"Why the fuck didn't you call me?"

"What are you talking about? I just took a leak."

"You idiot, I told you to call me if she returned, and she came back early. Go get in your van and drive it around to my carport space, back it in, and come in the back door of my neighbor's condo."

Nelson scurried out the front door of James' condo, jumped into the driver's seat of his van and drove it around to the carport. He walked through Becca's rear gate, and entered her kitchen. James stood facing him, while Becca lay sprawled on her back with a white cloth napkin covering half of her face.

"Come, help me roll her up in this Oriental rug and put her in the back of your van."

"Where are we taking her?"

"To the storage unit, we can't leave her here. We'll take her there and deal with her tonight."

They lifted her onto the Oriental rug and rolled t around her torso. They then carried her out to the van, closed the doors, and put her condo back to the condition in which she had left it.

Bascomb handed Nelson a storage unit business card with the entry code written on it and told him to drive the van to the unit at Bryan and Jeffrey. He said he would meet him there with his Mustang shortly. James walked back to his condo and took several more lines of cocaine before heading up to his bedroom closet where he grabbed his handgun safe and laid it on the bed. He opened the lid and extracted his loaded Beretta 92F 9mm pistol, two extra magazines and a holster. He changed from his slacks and tie to a pair of Levi's and a long-sleeved Pendleton shirt. He holstered the pistol, threw the magazines into his pocket, and buttoned the shirt outside his pants, to cover the holster that he had strung to his belt. He picked up a pair of handcuffs in the safe, placed them in his left rear pocket, and grabbed the Polaroid camera and ether bottle from the top of his dresser.

He closed and locked the door to his condo and, with some effort, managed to walk naturally along the sidewalk leading to his Mustang. He got in the car and left the cul de sac heading down Yale Avenue to the storage yard. Arriving at his unit, he found Nelson waiting there in the van. He took the padlock key and opened the door. Nelson opened the back doors to his van, and they pulled the rolled up rug out and walked it into the unit. James turned on a lantern, and then pulled down the roll-up door. He unrolled the rug, and saw that Becca was slowly regaining consciousness. He re-applied ether to the napkin, and then handcuffed her hands around the vertical water pipe leading to the overhead sprinkler system.

James then held his camera and took a photo of the unconscious Becca, before placing a small towel in her mouth and taping over it with duct tape. He then bent down, kissed her neck, caressed her hair, and turned to Nelson.

"I'll need you back here with your van and a shovel around 6:30 pm. I will call you first, before you come. Do you remember the gate combination?"

"Yes. I'm late for some lawns in College Park. Do you need me for anything else?"

"Not right now."

Nelson handed James the storage unit business card and left for College Park. James returned to his condo, where he paced the floor in between a few more lines of coke. He posted the photo of Becca next to the Polaroid of Ambrose on the bulletin board. Now arrayed with photos of Crutchfield, Greer, Ambrose, and the new addition of Becca, the board was a tribute to Bascomb's conquests. Displayed below three newspaper clippings of the three homicides were earrings for each victim. Bascomb took the business card for the storage facility with the gate combination and unit number written across it, pinned it to the board, and hung the key on the plastic head of the pin. He thought to himself, "It'd be just my luck for Nelson to lose this. I've got to remember to get one of Becca's studs when I go back to the storage unit."

Chapter 47

As Blackburn rushed into the lieutenant's office, Hunter quickly closed his phone conversation. Sgt. Phil Brannigan followed Blackburn, having already been apprised by Norbet of the break in the case, and Blackburn's face said it all.

"Norbet just called, and the FBI Crime Lab confirmed that James Bascomb's palm print matches the bloody palm print on Bethany Crutchfield's bathroom doorjamb!" Blackburn announced, barely able to contain his enthusiasm.

"How did Norbet get them to process the evidence so quickly?" Hunter replied somewhat skeptically.

"Well, he held the blood caked doorjamb next to Bascomb's print card, and told them it was a capital crime, and challenged them to prove him wrong. When they told him it would take a few weeks, he stated that he would not leave Virginia without their confirmation. Within twelve hours he had an official letter confirming the match."

"So the Sheriff's Department error has let a murderer go free for ten years."

"Yes, and I think he continued to commit homicides unabated."

"Well, we've got to go out now and bring him in. Have you located his place of employment and residence?"

"Yes, he still works at International Protection Services in Newport Beach. I searched the County records and discovered that he just bought a condo in the Riverwalk complex in the north end of our city."

Hunter's secretary stepped into the doorway and politely interrupted.

"Lieutenant, I've got the Sheriff's Crime Lab on line 1."

Hunter rolled his eyes at Blackburn, placed his hand on the receiver and thought to himself, *I should blast this guy for their incompetence. But there'll be time for that later; we've got to get moving.* He picked up the phone.

"Lieutenant Hunter."

"Lieutenant Hunter, this is Rhonda Cunningham, Assistant Coroner. The DNA samples that you submitted for entry into CODIS have returned with hits on your three homicide cases, and the one rape case you submitted. James Bascomb's DNA was found at each of the homicide cases, DR numbers: 1084, 2569, and 3110, and was present in the condom in the rape case number: 2571. In 1084, the blood forming the palm print was primarily the victim's, Bethany Crutchfield. However, there were traces of James Bascomb's DNA also present. James Bascomb's brother, Nelson Bascomb, left DNA which was found in the cells under the victim's fingernails in homicide case number 3110. I will fax you this information immediately."

"I'd forgotten the rape. We'll need to have a discussion regarding some fingerprint issues, Rhonda. But right now, we've got a murderer to apprehend. Thanks for the personal contact on this information. Take care."

Hunter assembled his team in his office and briefed them on the forensic findings from the coroner's office. He then made assignments for the apprehension of the elusive serial killers.

"Tom, you deserve the collar on this one. It's 3:00 and I would suspect that he can be found at his place of employment. Take Stephanie. Phil, you go with them to the security company and take him into custody. I'll take Nemeth and Horvath with me, and we'll check his residence just in case he called in sick. When you scoop up James, see if he'll tell you where his brother is, and we'll try to find him while you're dealing with James."

~

Detectives Tom Blackburn and Stephanie Winslow left the secure parking lot. Sergeant Phil Brannigan followed. Both detective units were well-equipped, containing the requisite firepower as marked units - AR-15 carbine, 12-gauge shotgun, less lethal launcher, and a search warrant box filled with every document necessary to search for and collect evidence.

International Protection Services was a short drive down Jamboree Road into Newport Beach. The company conducted a very aggressive marketing campaign which resulted in the procurement of several contracts with businesses in the Newport Beach/Irvine corporate community. Many of its business values coincided with those of the top organizations in the country. Unlike the stereotype security company that hires minimum wage workers who sit in their cars sleeping at new home construction sites, IPS had evolved into a corporation focused on a professional image.

James Bascomb was a throw-back to earlier days when security guards were primarily rejected applicants to police positions, much like Hillside Strangler Kenneth Bianchi. Bascomb's promotion from line-level to corporate was an anomaly, an unexpected retirement created his opportunity, when the one being groomed was not quite ready. Plus, a little patronage was certainly helpful in his case. The fallout from this arrest would obviously be damaging. Having a member of one's management staff arrested for being a serial killer would do little to enhance the organization's professional resume.

Sgt. Phil Brannigan, the systems guy, was genuinely excited to see the forensic evidence, the witness statements, and the detective legwork come together to create a positive result. Detective Stephanie Winslow, however, was still fixated on Ambrose. The unnamed, unclaimed black prostitute for whom no one seemed to display an interest would now receive justice, and Stephanie would be an integral part of that.

Detective Tom Blackburn was having difficulty concentrating on driving the short distance to Newport while trying to fathom the magnitude of the pending arrest. He knew that the answer to this on-going puzzle was within reach, but just needed a case breaker. He could not have been prouder to be a member of this elite team assembled by Hunter.

Blackburn pulled into the parking lot of International Protection Services corporate, a high-rise building jointly shared with a number of insurance companies, brokerage firms, and a real estate franchise. Brannigan and Blackburn entered the lobby and waited at the elevator while Winslow remained in the parking lot driving through each aisle looking for James' Mustang and the Ford van registered to Nelson. Finding neither vehicle, she then met with two uniformed patrol officers dispatched to the location to assist the detectives. Hunter had increased their staffing in the event that problems developed if Bascomb resisted or attempted to escape.

Winslow briefed the officers with a general summary of the cases and handed each , James' and Nelson's mug shot photos. Ashley Horton, who was working her Dispatch shift that day, had also sent the mug shots electronically to each officer's mobile data terminal when she learned that detectives were attempting to locate the Bascombs to affect their arrest. Winslow sat in the driver's seat of their staff car, parked near the middle of the lot, with the driver's door open, and her left foot planted on the ground, ready to spring into action should one of the Bascombs come flying into the parking lot.

Blackburn had parked near the building's front entrance to facilitate a quick exit with the prisoner. The marked units were stationed out of sight. There was no rear parking area or alleyway leading to the building, which made the establishment of a loose perimeter easier. Sgt. Richard Austin, who was working a dayshift overtime slot, read the service call on his computer terminal, responded to the scene, and parked behind the unit stationed at the northern parking lot entrance. Upon assessing the deployment, he tightened it up by sending the officer at the north position on foot to the building's back service doors, while he assumed his place in the position at the north entrance to the parking lot.

Brannigan and Blackburn got out of the elevator on the fifth floor and walked through the two glass doors leading into suite 500 and the receptionist for International Protection Services. Brannigan scanned the lobby, reception area, and hallways with offices leading from each side of the reception counter. He made a quick decision as to what would be the safest and most discreet way to gain access to the suspect and then spoke to the receptionist.

302 Dave Freedland

Chapter 48

"Good afternoon, I'm Sergeant Phil Brannigan with the Irvine Police Department," Brannigan announced softly as he placed his badge case on the counter and slowly raised the badge side up from the ID card, while blocking it from the lobby with his body."Who is the highest ranking official in your organization that is currently in his office?"

"That would be Mr. Billings," a neatly dressed redhead answered with a look of alarm.

"We would like to meet with him privately concerning a law enforcement matter."

"Certainly, one moment please," she responded politely and then disappeared down the hallway to the right. She returned momentarily and said, "He will be right with you." In less than a minute, a balding, 5'10",portly gentleman greeted them at the counter.

"Good afternoon gentlemen, I'm John Billings. Let's meet in my office." They walked three doors down and entered an expansive executive suite with a shoreline view extending from Newport to Catalina. Brannigan glanced across the walls adorned with diplomas and certificates, looking for a credible document. His eyes stopped on a P.O.S.T. (Peace Officer Standards and Training) management certificate, indicating that he had attained the rank of lieutenant or higher with a California law enforcement agency, which announced to Brannigan that he would be talking to another cop.

"We're here to speak with one of your managers, James Bascomb. We would prefer to keep the purpose of our visit confidential."

"Can you at least tell me if he is wanted as a suspect or a witness?"

"We'd rather not at this point. Is he working today?"

"Let me check the status board." Billings excused himself, and left his office momentarily, knowing that Brannigan's non-answer told him that his employee was suspected of something big.

"He marked out on the status board that he was checking contracts in North Irvine," said Billings. "That was a little before noon; he should be returning before the end of the day. We have several clients in Irvine shopping centers so there is a multitude of locations he could be visiting. Would you like me to phone him and request that he return?"

"Sure, if you could, please ask him where he is responding from."

"Certainly."

~

After several rings on his cell phone, James Bascomb looked at his caller I.D. and recognized that his boss was trying to reach him. In his current cocaine induced paranoid state, and having just kidnapped his neighbor, he feared imminent discovery at any moment.

"Hi John, what's up?"

"James, are you anywhere near the office?"

"No, I'm up in North Irvine, why?"

"I'm having an impromptu meeting to discuss a complaint regarding one of our guards, and I wanted to know if you could join us to provide your input."

"I've got some appointments scheduled up here. Who's the guard?"

"Well, I'd rather not say over the phone right now, we can discuss this when you come in."

"Okay. I guess I'll have to wait until I come in tomorrow morning."

"All right then James, we'll see you then."

Bascomb paced the room, wondering if he should respond, or if he was walking into a trap. He knew he had ingested too much coke, and he was in no frame of mind to discuss personnel issues. He continued pacing, and mentally reviewed options for the disposal of Becca.

~

"He says that he has scheduled some appointments in northern Irvine, and won't be coming in until tomorrow. He usually arrives around 8:30 – 9:00 am. I don't think I alerted him. Is there someone that I can speak with at some point to find out what Mr. Bascomb is wanted for? Will you be here again tomorrow?"

"He's probably not coming back, but if he arrives here in the morning, please call me at this number. I will most likely be able to explain the purpose of our visit tomorrow." Brannigan handed Billings his business card, and Billings, upon request, provided Brannigan with a list of IPS clients in the northern portions of Irvine. The two detectives left, and prior to their entering the elevator, Blackburn radioed the officers outside that the suspect was not on-scene. The perimeter was broken down, and the detectives headed up to Hunter's location to provide assistance in the search for the Bascomb brothers.

Blackburn located James Bascomb's cell phone carrier and placed a call to their law enforcement back line, requesting an emergency ping of his phone to determine its location relative to the nearest cell site. Upon receipt of this information, he radioed Hunter.

"Lieutenant, Bascomb's cell phone company places him in the area of his home near Yale and Irvine Boulevard."

"Thanks Tom, we're checking the residence now."

306 Dave Freedland

Chapter 49

Hunter sent Horvath to the rear of unit #1056, relying upon Blackburn's meticulous chronicling of Bascomb's personal information. However, the reliance on the competency of the lowliest of bureaucrats cannot be overstated. In this instance, the simple act of changing a nearly empty toner cartridge would soon result in tragic consequences. The clerk at the County Recorder's office misreading the number 1058, as number 1056, provided Blackburn with the wrong address, placing Hunter, Nemeth, and Horvath at the unit adjacent to Bascomb's.

Bascomb was now in a perfect high ground position to take out all three of them. His disadvantage, however, rested upon the fact that the cocaine level in his bloodstream agitated his aim, and all his practice at the firing range would fail to come into play. Hunter and Nemeth stood on each side of the front door, as Nemeth radioed their location to Dispatch.

"Unit 39-611, 615, and Lincoln 9, Code 6 [Out for investigation], 1 Riverwalk, unit # 1056."

Since no record of a phone number could be located that was associated with Bascomb's residence, Nemeth then requested Dispatch to place a call to Bascomb's cell phone, directing him to exit the front door of the condo unit. Bascomb, alerted by the phone's vibrate mode, looked out his second story window at the two athletic detectives stationed at his neighbor's front door, with pistols in hand, tucked behind their right legs. He then walked over to the window facing the carport and rear courtyards, and observed the overweight Horvath leaning against his neighbor's back gate.

As Bascomb's phone continued to vibrate, he returned to the front window, partially open for ventilation, and considered his options. He drew his Beretta, attempted to aim with his shaking hand, and fired two rounds each towards Nemeth and Hunter. Both officers hit the ground, with Hunter being struck in his left shoulder by one 9mm round, and Nemeth sustaining a gunshot wound in his right femur. Lying on his back, Hunter fired two quick rounds toward the second story window behind him, and heard Horvath radioing the dreaded, "998," radio code for officers involved in a gun battle.

Horvath heard the exchange of gunfire at the front of the condo complex, but soon found that he was also under assault as Bascomb sent a hail of rounds in his direction. Hunter grabbed his radio and transmitted, as he struggled to his feet, that the suspect was actually in unit #1058.

Now crouched behind a parked car in the carport, Horvath raised his Sig Sauer and fired three rounds in rapid succession as Bascomb pushed open the wooden gate leading to the carport. As he turned left toward the block wall separating the carport from the cul de sac, Bascomb looked back in Horvath's direction with his right arm pointing backwards, and fired two rounds, keeping Horvath's head down.

Hunter turned toward an immobile Nemeth, who heard Horvath's plea for help, and said, "Go ahead, Boss, help Russell, I'll call for an ambulance." Nemeth's decline of assistance, however, was problematic, in that neither officer knew that Bascomb's 9mm round had severed Nemeth's femoral artery, and time was becoming a critical commodity.

Hunter ran around the row of condos with his mind racing with thoughts of survival fighting against his warrior instincts. "How bad am I wounded? Is this going to affect my shooting skills? What are his skills? He shot my partner, he will need to pay. Is Horvath going to still be alive when I round the corner? If he is, will he be able to assist? Control your breathing, you need energy, you're losing blood."

Horvath was terrified and exhausted, and he had not moved more than ten feet since the first shots had been expended. He sprawled over the trunk of a parked Camry, braced his pistol with his hands supported by the vehicle's sheet metal, and returned three more rounds in Bascomb's direction. By this time, however, Bascomb had reached the block wall, grabbed the top cap of bricks, and began clumsily pulling his torso up, as Horvath's .45 caliber slugs gouged the wall on Bascomb's right, sending chips of brick into his shirt.

Bascomb reached the top cap, and dropped to the ground on the other side of the wall as Horvath's next three rounds sailed over. Horvath stepped out from behind cover and ran toward the wall with labored breathing. As his right shoulder struck the bricks, he looked down at his pistol and discovered the slide fully retracted and realized to his horror that the liquid polish had dried his magazine into place within its leather pouch. No matter how ferociously he tugged, the metal magazine containing the eight more rounds that would keep him in the gun battle would not budge.

Bascomb's momentum slammed him into his Mustang's left rear quarter panel as he reached for the driver's side door handle. Hunter sprinted past the assortment of cars scattered throughout the carport. He caught a glimpse of Horvath struggling against the wall and yelled, "Where is he?" Horvath's response was, "Over the wall!"

Hunter's right foot hit the wall as his left elbow slapped the top row of bricks. His right hand held the Sig Sauer in master grip as his torso sailed over the top. On his way down, he saw Bascomb's Mustang parked on the far side of the cul de sac with Bascomb standing next to the driver's door, feverishly struggling to pull the key fob from his pants pocket. Hunter's shoulder screamed from the brick wall's impact, but he was resolute in his focus upon target acquisition.

As Bascomb swung the door open, Hunter's judged the distance of the shot to be 10 – 15 yards. He raised the front sight of the Sig and covered Bascomb's center mass. As he lifted his left hand in support, and aligned the two Tritium rear sights, a pain from his wounded left shoulder shot like electric current, causing the front sight to rise, and the sympathetic reflex of his trigger finger to snap toward his palm. The 230 grain hydra shock hollow point round exploded out the barrel striking Bascomb's temple at 900 feet per second. Shards of skull bone littered the air with a crimson background as Bascomb's body dropped like a canvas bag filled with cement.

Hunter depressed the barrel and advanced toward the suspect's limp corpse sprawled face-down on the asphalt slurry seal. Half of Bascomb's skull was missing, but his right hand still clutched the Beretta that had caused Hunter's rapidly increasing lightheadedness from blood loss. Hunter dropped to a knee onto Bascomb's right arm, holstered his Sig Sauer, and then removed the Beretta from the suspect's death grip. Seeing that he was already dead, Hunter elected to forgo the handcuffing protocol for suspects, wounded or not.

Hunter withdrew his radio from its holder and began transmitting inquiries to his two unaccounted for subordinates.

"Unit 39-615 (Detective Horvath), Lincoln 9, Code 4? [O.K.]"

"615 affirmative, I'll 10-87 with you in a minute."

"Unit 39-611 (Detective Nemeth), Lincoln 9, Code 4?"

No response was rendered.

"Unit 39-611, Lincoln 9, Code 4?"

"Lincoln 9, Dispatch, Suspect is down and deceased on the Riverwalk cul de sac. What is the ETA of Station 91 [OC Fire]?"

"Lincoln 9, Dispatch received no request for Station 91; we will send them now. Are you reporting injuries?"

"Affirmative; 611 has a gunshot wound to the leg, and I sustained a gunshot wound to the shoulder. Unit 39-615, respond to the front of the condo, 611 needs medical attention."

"615, copy, en-route."

A crowd began to gather as Hunter continued to kneel next to Bascomb's body, fighting to stay conscious until help arrived. Within two minutes the first uniformed patrol officers and supervisors were on-scene, in time for Horvath's sobering radio transmission.

"I need back-up! I'm starting CPR on Nemeth; I'm in front of Unit #1056!"

Two patrol officers ran to Horvath's location, finding Nemeth pale and near death, while Horvath was sweating profusely with his chest compressions. The two young rookies took over CPR, while a third wrapped a tourniquet around Nemeth's thigh. Horvath rolled to the side and lay on his back struggling to regain his breath.

Paramedics arrived with oxygen, and fought to stabilize a failing Nemeth. An engine company paramedic jumped from his cab and took command of Hunter's injury as he lay in the street, now weak and fighting shock. Sergeant Phil Brannigan and his team rolled into the cul de sac and took over responsibilities for the two crime scenes. Brannigan directed closure of the street, adjacent condos, and carport, and then summoned CSI and additional detectives from the Bureau.

Detectives Blackburn and Winslow staged at the correct address for Bascomb's unit and requested the three uniformed officers, now freed from first aid duties, to assist them in clearing the condo of additional suspects. Nemeth was now on his way via ambulance to the nearest trauma center, Western Medical Center in Santa Ana.

Blackburn thought, "Could Nelson Bascomb still be around after all of this blood and bullets? What kind of horrors will we find in this killer's lair?" Blackburn spelled out his entry plan to Winslow and the three patrol officers, and they then moved into position on each side of the front door. Winslow checked the doorknob and found it locked. She signaled the closest patrol officer, now holding a ram retrieved from the sergeant's unit, and he swung the business end into the deadbolt. The door burst inward, and they poured into the room covering all immediate fields of fire. After checking every room, closet, and cabinet capable of containing a person, Blackburn determined that the condo was empty.

The three patrol officers returned to crowd and traffic control duties on the street where Hunter was now being loaded into an ambulance as he called on his cell phone to the officers accompanying

Nemeth to the hospital to check on his condition. Blackburn sent Winslow back to the car to retrieve her search warrant kit while he stood looking around the first floor from the kitchen, hoping to pick up anything in plain view that he could legally see before preparing the search warrant. He turned slowly around and discovered a bulletin board that caused him to freeze in place, mouth open.

Chapter 50

The bulletin board was neatly organized with newspaper clippings displaying a killer's accomplishments. Blackburn marveled at the resemblance it bore to the white board of clues he had himself constructed in the investigative conference room.

At the top left, a photo of Bethany Crutchfield and an Orange County Register news article directly beneath. Next to Crutchfield, Bascomb had posted a candid photograph of Kristen Greer leaving a fitness center and the newspaper clipping that had headlined the front page of the Local section of the Register. The nameless victim of murder #3, investigated under the pseudonym of Ambrose, was in the third position along with the newspaper article of her murder. However, the photograph atop the heading was a blurry, unrecognizable profile shot of what appeared to be a black street walker with short hair. Beneath each article was mounted an earring with its post inserted into the cork-like material of the bulletin board, displayed as trophies of his homicidal/sexual conquests. Blackburn then recalled Bascomb's former landlady, Rachel Cohen having mentioned it.

Blackburn's eyes moved to a grainy Polaroid photo of what appeared to be an unconscious blonde leaning against a vertical water pipe in a storage unit stacked with furniture and boxes. Her condition looked unnatural, disheveled, and her arms were awkwardly pulled behind her back. There was no newspaper article, nor any display of an earring or jewelry associated with the photograph. Blackburn thought for a moment, *This board is telling me this woman has not yet been murdered. My God, she's still alive!*

He quickly scanned the board for additional clues. The bottom border was lined with business cards, and Blackburn's eyes stopped at the card posted on the far right with a key hanging on the plastic tack. Hand printed across the North Meadow Storage business card was a series of numbers resembling a gate combination, followed by *Unit C25*. Blackburn pulled out his cell phone, activated the push-to-talk mode, and summoned Winslow, "Stephanie, come up here now, we've got a problem!"

Within seconds, Winslow appeared and Blackburn pointed out the urgency of his discovery.

"We need to secure this scene, respond to that storage unit, and send an ambulance, now!" Winslow exclaimed upon hearing Blackburn's summary of the clues displayed before them.

Brannigan needed to be involved, but his plate was full dealing with the coroner and the District Attorney's Officer Involved Shooting Team at Bascomb's homicide scene. Blackburn elected to radio him while they were on their way to the storage yard.

Blackburn pulled two patrol officers to stand guard at Bascomb's condo, and requested two additional officers and an ambulance to meet them at the storage yard. On the way, Winslow phoned Hunter's cell phone, and was surprised that he answered.

"Hunter."

"Lieutenant, this is Stephanie. How are you doing?"

"Pretty weak. They stopped the bleeding, but the ER doctor and surgeon are discussing whether or not to remove the bullet now or to wait."

"Blackburn and I are driving to a nearby storage facility where we think that Bascomb may have taken a girl that he kidnapped. We're not sure if she is still alive, but we're going on the assumption she's still breathing."

"How'd you find that out? Excuse my speech; they shot me full of opiates."

"Bascomb kept a trophy board with photos and clippings, but had one photo of a girl in a storage unit that had no newspaper clippings, and no jewelry yet posted. The board was in plain sight in the kitchen, and we left two patrol officers to stand guard until we can get a search warrant."

"Has Brannigan been apprised of this?"

"Yes, Blackburn just radioed him with this information. He's supervising the shooting scene, though, and can't leave."

"Okay, get a patrol supervisor to meet you at the storage yard. I think Sgt. Austin is working the field today."

"He is. He's assisting on traffic control at Riverwalk, but we can break him loose."

316 Dave Freedland

Chapter 51

Ashley Horton was the first person Hunter called from the emergency room once his condition had stabilized and the doctors could deliberate as to how to proceed with the 9mm bullet. She arrived at Western Med within minutes and was granted access to his bed in the emergency room. She had received the call at home while preparing for her night shift and was dressed in a crisp, new uniform. Hearing the news, she made certain that her make-up was impeccable, with an ample dose of perfume to provide Hunter with a memorable presentation, regardless of the painkillers dulling his senses.

"Scott, thank God you're alive! What happened?"

"We took down the serial killer we'd been chasing; he'd been operating for decades. Any word on Terry Nemeth? No one's giving me any information. They either don't know, or don't want to tell me."

"Sweetheart, Terry has passed away."

Hunter looked stoically straight ahead at the white curtain encircling his bed. Controlling his emotions, his mind drifted back to the memory of their lining up on the wrong porch, and Terry's last act of placing the mission ahead of his own well-being.

"Terry was a warrior; one of the toughest guys I've ever known. We'll talk more about this later…" Hunter's train of thought was interrupted by the metal hooks holding the privacy curtain screeching against the pipe encircling his bed.

The orthopedic and vascular surgeons entered and provided Hunter with their recommendation – surgery to remove the bullet and repair his fractured clavicle. In just two to three hours he would be out of the operating room and on the road to recovery.

~

Blackburn and Winslow arrived at the storage yard gate where Sergeant Austin and two patrol officers were waiting. As Blackburn punched in the combination code, they could hear the wail of the sirens from Engine Company 26 in the distance. The gate jerked upon activation of the electric motor, and then moved like molasses as it retracted. The marked patrol cars led the way to unit C25 where Sergeant Austin pulled a large set of bolt cutters from his trunk. Blackburn yelled that he had a key, but Austin didn't hear, and the tool cut through the hasp with ease.

The patrol officers' flashlights illuminated the interior, and focused on the female torso with eyes wide with terror as the horde of blue suits swarmed over her. She screamed as they pulled the duct tape from her mouth. The handcuffs were removed, and Becca burst into tears as Stephanie Winslow cradled her head. As she sobbed uncontrollably, the detective attempted to assuage her pain by whispering in her ear, "It's okay now; he's been shot and killed."

Paramedics checked her vitals and carefully placed her on the gurney. Detective Winslow accompanied Becca in the ambulance to Western Medical Center while Blackburn stayed as he scanned the unit's contents to assist in preparation of his second search warrant. He handed the storage lot manager, who had been waiting outside, a $5 bill for the purchase of a new lock to secure the unit until he could return with a warrant. Blackburn then left to meet with his partner, interview the victim, and update Hunter on the case developments.

~

Hunter was out of recovery, sans the 9mm hollow point round, and headed for his hospital room. Ashley rode the elevator from the waiting room to meet him. She arrived first, and impatiently paced until the orderly pushed the gurney into the room. The anesthesia had worn off, but the morphine was in full force, yet Hunter was sufficiently cogent to realize that the most important person in his life was waiting for him.

"Scott, the doctor said you tolerated the surgery well and you'll be out of the hospital in a couple days." Ashley paused for a moment, and then softly exclaimed, "I love you, Scott."

"I love you too, Ashley." Hunter hoped he didn't sound sappy. He recognized the seriousness of the day, but understood that neither of their expressions of affection was solely motivated by the emotions of the moment.

~

Blackburn alighted from his staff car in the hospital parking lot and paused momentarily to look up at the full moon illuminating the evening sky. He then walked briskly into the Western Medical Center lobby elevator.

Detective Stephanie Winslow had finished her interview of Rebecca Lyons before her sedation had kicked in and was now headed toward Hunter's floor, notepad in hand. Blackburn got off the elevator as the doors opened to an expansive waiting room occupied by a few families awaiting word on the status of their wounded loved ones. As he turned right toward the hallway leading to Hunter's room, he heard Winslow's voice behind him as she approached from the opposite end of the corridor.

"Hey Tom, hold up, just finished interviewing Bascomb's neighbor."

"Great, I was just going to brief Hunter on the case. We can update him together."

"Any word on Nelson Bascomb's whereabouts?" Winslow inquired, having been off the air during her interview, while the radio had been crackling for the past hour with information regarding the hunt for Bascomb's monstrous brother.

"Nothing yet, but I'm sure he's running scared."

They approached the door to Hunter's room and acknowledged the uniformed officer that had been stationed there by the new chief to ensure security as well as privacy from any media representatives seeking an exclusive for the 11:00 pm news. As Blackburn and

Winslow entered the room, Ashley awakened from her nap, now suffering jet lag from the odd hours created by mixing her graveyard shift with the excitement of Hunter's shooting. Hunter, awake now from his evening blood draw, was ready to hear the detectives' account about how the evidence puzzle came together and what remained to be accomplished.

Winslow began with the most critical development in the serial killings, Becca Lyons' status as the potential fourth victim. Stephanie combed the loose strands of hair away from her eyes with her fingers, cleared her throat, and put her game face on.

"Lieutenant, Bascomb's neighbor is alive and in this hospital recovering from having been drugged and kidnapped by James Bascomb and his brother, Nelson. Becca Lyons doesn't believe that she was sexually assaulted, but they're processing the rape kit right now. We think that Bascomb used ether, and we're running labs on the soaked rags or cloths we picked up in the storage unit where she had been left handcuffed around a water pipe. She thinks that he had previously burglarized her condo and had been stalking her since he moved in. Lyons says that James Bascomb sucker punched her, causing her to black out when she interrupted his break-in. Her doctor indicated that she has a hairline fracture on her jaw and she'll be admitted for a couple days to get her stabilized from dehydration."

"What about this bulletin board you mentioned?"

"Tom can brief you on that now since he found it and figured out that we had another victim."

"Thanks, Stephanie."

"Lieutenant, I've gotta say, nice shot. We can only imagine how many lives were saved by that one bullet, ending this nightmare."

"Thanks Tom, I was operating on adrenalin, and completely spent by the time Bascomb hit the ground."

"This case has been my obsession, and he's been right below our noses. When Stephanie and I went back to his condo to check to see if Nelson was still there, I found James' trophy board hanging on a kitchen wall. It bore a remarkable resemblance to the clues I posted on the white board in the Investigative Conference Room. He pinned Bethany Crutchfield's photo on the left, with news clippings of her homicide, and her earring at the bottom. Pamela Greer's photo, clippings, and earring were next, and the black gal that was torched on Langley was posted third. What was alarming was the presence of a fourth photo of a female that had no newspaper article or earring displayed. The photo looked like she was in a storage unit, and a key attached to a business card for a storage facility was hanging on a plastic tack that was stuck into the cork board on the right."

"Good job, Tom; you put it together and saved her life," Hunter interjected.

"Thanks boss. Phil Brannigan has assigned the Narcotics Bureau to prepare the search warrants for Bascomb's condo and storage unit. They write search warrants so often, we figured they could get it done quickly without any rewrites."

"Well, hopefully we can find something in the searches that will give us more on Nelson. We'll also need to research where the breakdown occurred in our lining up on the wrong address," Hunter reasoned, already planning his return.

Blackburn continued, "Essentially, the evidence points to a handful of key elements, linking the Bascombs to sex crimes and murders spanning over a decade. James Bascomb's palm print was left in blood on the doorjamb of Bethany Crutchfield's apartment bathroom. Analysis of the semen stain on Pamela Greer's sheets matched James Bascomb's DNA. Both James and Nelson Bascomb's DNA was found under the fingernails of the black girl they torched on Langley Street. James' DNA was found in the condom discarded at the rape scene in the parking lot for the amphitheater."

"Their DNA didn't enter the system until they were convicted of lesser crimes and were required to submit samples as a condition of their sentencing. The palm print was always there, pointing to Bascomb, but an error at the Sheriff's Department incorrectly compared the positive print to a photo negative. Ashley's identification of Nelson's photo as being the suspect in her indecent exposure case also cleared a series of Newport's previously unsolved exposure cases." Blackburn ticked off clues like a grocery list for Easter dinner.

Neither of the men in the room had noticed the change in Ashley Horton's demeanor as Blackburn's list revealed the extent of Nelson Bascomb's involvement in assisting his brother's and his own victimization of Ashley. Stephanie Winslow watched the building of anger and frustration on Ashley's face, and wondered when her emotions would boil over.

Ashley turned her attention from Blackburn, and focused on Hunter with her piercing blue eyes and announced in a voice never previously heard, "Can you please take out that cretin for me with the same efficiency you used on his brother?"

The room fell silent for a few uncomfortable seconds, as each participant to the conversation processed the emotion and suddenly recognized the pain she had been harboring. Hunter smiled warmly and stated with confidence, "I'll be glad too."

Chapter 52

Nelson's distinctive facial features enabled the public to quickly identify him as their gardening contractor, surf buddy or neighbor when his mug photo hit the newspapers and evening news. It was the category of "neighbor" that proved most useful in locating his whereabouts. Enrique Contreras, the ranch foreman who had so graciously offered his garage to Bascomb, was appalled to discover that he had exposed his family to this serial killer tenant.

Upon receipt of his morning paper, Contreras turned to his wife and asked her to take his two boys to her sister's house in Fountain Valley before he contacted the police. He packed a suitcase for the evening and vacated his house with an extra set of keys. While driving to the police station, he called the number posted in the news article for investigative leads and requested to meet with a detective at the front desk of the police station.

Detective Blackburn met with Contreras, was briefed on Nelson's habits, and given floor plans to the house and garage, along with the second set of keys. Contreras indicated to Blackburn that on the evening of James Bascomb's death, he saw Nelson's van parked briefly by his garage, but had not seen him since.

~

The very fiber of Sergeant Jack Huerta's being was destined for tactical operations. He was a problem solver who could quickly put the puzzle together and act decisively in the implementation of an operational plan. Serving high risk search warrants was routine, but he fought any tendency toward complacency. The service on this small framed house and detached garage was basic, and would normally take less than a minute to clear every room. However, the simpleton residing in the garage had a brother whose diabolical crimes had eluded police for over ten years. Huerta could not rule out Nelson's brother's assistance in providing technical support to affect his escape. His Marine Corps sniper training had prepared him to think from the enemy's perspective.

Huerta's counterpart on the second team hitting the house was Sergeant Pete Hernandez, an athlete whose obsession for thoroughness in weapons training made him a perfect complement to Wilder. Hernandez kept his Tahoe equipped with his call-out gear loaded and ready, and made certain that each operator on the team was equally prepared when the pager called. His Red Team would be responsible for the house, while Huerta's Blue Team would take down Bascomb's rented garage. The two team leaders represented the new era of SWAT supervision leading the department into the 21st century.

The detonation of the flash-bang diversionary devices signaled the commencement of the coordinated entry that lit up the intersection of Sand Canyon and Burt. A phone call into the residence had gone unanswered, and the absence of any vehicles on the premises indicated that it was most likely unoccupied at the moment. However, nothing was taken for granted.

The Red Team advanced on the house, while the Blue Team simultaneously took the garage. Huerta's seven-operator element breached the service door using a one-man ram. He held up the scout from crossing the threshold, when the setting sun illuminated the trip wire stretched across the door frame. They carefully stepped over the obstacle and cleared the cluttered interior within seconds. A mattress, television set, and small dresser were surrounded by an assortment of gardening tools, surfboards, and clothing. A small table, mini-refrigerator, and microwave oven were in a corner farthest from the door. A small toilet and sink had been plumbed into the opposite corner, and the now infamous Vespa rested against the large pull-up door.

Hernandez's team swept through the house causing minimal disruption after using the key furnished by Contreras to facilitate entry. No sign of the younger Bascomb was discovered in the immaculately maintained rental, nor within the detached garage.

During Blackburn's debriefing of Contreras, he learned that Bascomb's surfing lifestyle necessitated five boards to address different wave conditions. Huerta's team counted three in the garage, and noticed the absence of any power mowing equipment, causing both team leaders to surmise that Bascomb might have permanently fled the location. Upon arrival of the bomb squad, the trip wire leading to det-cord attached to a small brick of C4 plastic explosive was disassembled. The sophisticated device was capable of eliminating the first four operators, and was clearly beyond the technical capability of Nelson Bascomb. For now, the surfer/landscaper would be presumed to be a fugitive included in the thousands of surfers inhabiting the scores of beach communities providing campgrounds.

Chapter 53

Lieutenant Scott Hunter was halfway through his Wednesday evening physical therapy session and was making progress on the rehabilitation of his shoulder, wounded only three months prior. He would normally finish at 6:00 pm, but the blast of an underground Edison transformer wiped out power to the entire strip mall at Jamboree and Bristol. This common occurrence in the Newport/Irvine metropolitan area often took one to two hours to resolve, so Hunter ended the session at 5:00, left the therapy facility, and entered his staff car to head home.

Hunter stored his .45 in a gym bag since the elastic on his sweat pants was insufficiently rigid to support the weight of the weapon. He elected to strap his backup pistol, a 5-shot, .38 Chief's Special, around his ankle in a leather holster covered by his left pant leg. If he needed to stop by a grocery or liquor store for a last minute pickup, he afforded himself a minimum level of personal protection with this potent revolver, given to him by his father upon graduation from the police academy.

Wednesday evenings had become a regularly scheduled event in which Ashley prepared Hunter a much anticipated home cooked meal. At this point in their relationship she had been given a key to Hunter's condominium to allow her access to the residence to prepare dinner. Despite this milestone, each maintained separate addresses, but clearly the gun battle had brought them closer.

Hunter's injury resulted in his placement in a "light duty" status, which limited his participation in field activities. A byproduct of these restrictions was the standardization of his work hours. Good for relationships, but the regularity of schedules can leave an individual vulnerable to tracking by those harboring bad motives.

And Hunter was well aware of the fact that Nelson Bascomb was still at large and might well be planning to avenge his brother's death.

Ashley's failure to lock Hunter's front door after kicking it shut upon carrying in groceries to the kitchen, made Nelson's use of a pry bar unnecessary. Clad in a maintenance man's overalls, he had blended into the fabric of the complex unnoticed. His discovery of Ashley inattentively fumbling with the pre-heat controls of the oven, afforded him a moment to consider the prospect of sampling her sexual pleasures before finishing them both off with a Beretta he had secreted in his toolbox.

Holding the 9mm in his right hand, he grabbed her shoulder with his left, and slammed her to the kitchen floor. The travertine tiles knocked the air from her lungs as her shoulder blades struck the hard surface. She gasped, trying to breathe and began to scream as she beheld the hideous creature standing over her holding a pistol in one hand, and stretching his other hand out to cover her mouth. He dropped to his knees, straddling her waist, as she struggled to break free. Placing the pistol on the floor above her head, he freed his right hand to remove her clothing while his left hand stayed clasped around her mouth.

Nelson's plan to throw the deadbolt to announce Hunter's entry was sound, but he had not counted on the ferocity with which Ashley fought to resist his efforts, so Hunter's entry was silent. Hearing a struggle in the kitchen, he suddenly remembered that his .45 was buried in his gym bag under his street clothes, so he gently placed the bag on the throw rug, and drew his snub nose revolver.

Hunter took a pie angle on the doorway leading to the kitchen, and momentarily glanced from the darkness into the lighted kitchen. Seeing only one adversary, he darted across the threshold and planted a round kick with his left instep across Nelson's ribcage, knocking the monster onto his back. Hunter followed with a double-tap from his

.38, striking Nelson's center mass, and then a single shot, hollow-point into his forehead ending all movement.

Hunter exhaled, relieving the stress, and then focused on the face of the night creature that had entered his domain and nearly violated Ashley. It suddenly registered with him as blood filled the grout lines in the tile, that the image gazing in horror at the ceiling was that of Nelson Bascomb. He quickly turned toward Ashley, who still labored to breathe, but forced a partial smile, recognizing that her ordeal had ended.

Hunter then looked back to Bascomb with satisfaction, and returned a reassuring smile toward Ashley. "Wish fulfilled."

Acknowledgements:

I would like to acknowledge Deputy Chief (retired) Michael Hillmann, Los Angeles Police Department, a pioneer in law enforcement operations who consistently demonstrated exemplary leadership through numerous challenging tactical and political storms, and Investigator Larry Montgomery, Orange County District Attorney's Office, (Irvine Police Department, retired) whose work ethic has been reflective of the highest example of investigative tenacity and thoroughness. These two law enforcement professionals represent outstanding models of excellence whose qualities were applied in the development of the story and characters
.

Other Aakenbaaken & Kent books you might enjoy:

Mariachi Meddler
Andy Veracruz Mystery Book 1
by
D.R. Ransdell

Andy Veracruz is the leader of a mariachi band in Southern California, but when his boss goes out of town, the restaurant where Andy performs turns to chaos. Andy tries to avoid the boss's flirtatious wife, but when Yiolanda is accused of murder, Andy isn't sure whether to help her or to run the other way. The more Andy learns, the more trouble he gets himself into. He's a sleuth only by accident! He would much rather spend afternoons working on new songs instead of following leads or trying to decipher Yiolanda. He goes to his lookalike brother for advice, but why is he too stubborn to listen?

Island Casualty
Andy Veracruz Mystery Book 2
by
D.R. Ransdell

An island paradise, a lost engagement ring, and a midnight chase add up to Island Casualty. When Andy Veracruz flies to Greece for a holiday, the California native expects to spend afternoons swimming and nights making love. After all his troubles in *Mariachi Meddler*, he deserves a break! But at an outdoor cafe, he meets a fellow traveler who accidentally leaves behind a package. Before Andy can return it, the man disappears. Andy tries to enjoy the rest of his vacation, but after he and Rachel are run off the road by a determined motorist, the musician starts doing undercover work by playing in a bouzouki band. Soon he realizes that he's not safe anywhere on the island. While he's around, his friends aren't safe either! He vows not to take any more vacations, but he has to uncover the truth before he can make his escape.

Dizzy in Durango
Andy Veracruz Mystery Book 3
by
D.R. Ransdell

Andy Veracruz travels to Durango, Mexico, to catch up with Rachel, but he's puzzled by a fellow traveler en route to visit her girlfriend. The woman entrusts Andy with her bag but doesn't board the plane. When he tries to locate the woman's friend in Durango, she has disappeared as well. Before he can discover more about the women's connection, he's saddled with two children who aren't his, an angry would-be lover, and a self-appointed younger brother who is more reckless than he is. No wonder he's dizzy! But what will he do with two crying children?

Substitute Soloist
Andy Veracruz Mystery Book 4
by
D.R. Ransdell

Andy Veracruz regrets his new job with the Tucson orchestra. He would rather play mariachi songs than classical symphonies. He doesn't have the same experience as the other players or an expensive violin. But when the concertmaster exits mid-concert and a man is found dead backstage, Andy takes over. Impressed, the conductor recruits Andy for a European tour to help him track down the concertmaster, a brilliant and passionate woman. Andy throws himself into the musical challenge, but how can he find a woman who's determined to hide? And how will the orchestra members react when they realize Andy is a fraud?

In God's Trailer Park
by
Susan Lang

In God's Trailer Park is an unforgettable novel that, with tenderness and humor, depicts the nitty-gritty lives of residents of a small Mojave Desert town. The story is bursting with indelible characters: Social worker Charlotte Sall does her best to plug up holes in the dam holding back the flood of miseries threatening to inundate her clients' lives–all the while dealing with issues that arise with her own children. Recently widowed with a seven-day-old baby, Linda Farley, stubbornly persists in finding work, determined not to let a flood of bad fortune drown her and her young children. Waitress Alice Landers tries her best to protect her schizophrenic son from himself. All of these and other quietly heroic characters find themselves entangled in the mysterious disappearance of a newborn belonging to one of the residents. The diverse ways the characters face down their hardscrabble lives gives a vision of hope to us all.

The Forever Child
by
Janie Hopwood

Gene, a most enterprising young man, flees security toward the unknown — dependent only upon his own ingenuity. He lands in the middle of the red-light district of Albany, Georgia and becomes an integral part of Madame Valdimer's household. Meanwhile, Sarah, snatched from this very house only a short time before, is separated from family, handed into servitude, used, and abused. Fate helps her to escape and she rushes back to the house where she meets Gene. Amid the backdrop of a great depression, in a changing nation that moves rapidly from horse power to "horsepower," to air power, and war, two children, lost to those they were born to, torn from those they lived with, find refuge in a most ludicrous place where they create family. A struggle to survive becomes a struggle to succeed supported by the most unlikely cast. Here they learn from those with no past how to forge a future.

Waltzing with an Echo
by
Dale Lovin

Native American artifacts become items of barter for sex trafficking, forcing former FBI Agent Brad Walker into a dark world where the sacredness of history and dignity of human life are not recognized. Only by listening to the echo of voices within ancient Native American cliff dwellings is he able to see a way out.

Riddled with Clues
by
J. L. Greger

Xave Zack receives a mysterious note shortly before he is seriously injured while working undercover to investigate the movement of drugs into the U.S. from Cuba. The note is signed "Red from Udon Thani." However, he doesn't know anyone called Red, and the last time he was in Udon Thani was during the Vietnam War. After his friend, Sara Almquist, listens to his rambling tales of all possibilities, both she and Xave are attacked. He is left comatose. As she struggles to survive, she questions who to trust: the local cops, her absent boyfriend, the FBI, or a homeless veteran, who leaves puzzling riddles as clues.

A Summer to Remember
by
Amy M. Bennett

Bonney Police detective J.D. is trying to focus on his budding relationship with Corrie Black, owner of the Black Horse Campground. But when a serial killer case he thought he solved is reopened, he fears killer is poised to strike again. Who held a grudge against the three cold-case victims? And who is the next target? With the help of Bonney County Sheriff Rick Sutton, J.D. probes the memories of several Bonney residents who knew the victims and begins to make connections. Then another death occurs. Corrie is attacked and loses her memory, including the identity of her attacker. Will she remember what happened? Or will she end up as a memory?

Unresolved
by
F. M. Meredith

The mayor of Rocky Bluff is the first body discovered. The second is a woman who died in a bizarre method. Because neither his estranged wife nor the city council members liked the major, the suspects are many. Are the cases connected? Can the small Rocky Bluff Police Department solve the murders?

Yom Killer
A Rabbi Aviva Cohen Mystery
by
Ilene Schneider

No time is ever good for a family emergency, but for a rabbi the period just before Yom Kippur is especially difficult. Yet even though the Holy Day is approaching, Rabbi Aviva Cohen rushes off to Boston to be at the bedside of her mother, who was found unconscious in her apartment at an assisted living facility. The big question is: was it an accident or an attack? The search for the truth uncovers everything from old grudges to family secrets to fraud—and possibly murder.

The Easter Egg Murder
Harrie McKinsey Mystery 1
by
Patricia Smith Wood

The Easter Egg Murder is loosely based on the real-life murder of Cricket Coogler in 1949 in southern New Mexico. The murderer was never brought to justice, although several men went to Federal prison for violating the civil rights of a suspect. Patricia Smith Wood's fictional account of this event and her equally fictional ending create a captivating mystery that spans more than fifty years and winds in and out of the lives of a diverse cast of New Mexicans.

Murder on Sagebrush Lane
Harrie McKinsey Mystery 2
by
Patricia Smith Wood

Harrie goes out for her morning paper and finds instead a small child sitting in the flower bed, her pajamas smeared with blood. Harrie's search for the child's parents involves her in a grisly murder investigation, a second murder, an attempted kidnapping, stolen top secret data, and a killer who intends to make her his final victim.

Murder on Frequency

Harrie McKinsey Mystery 3
by
Patricia Smith Wood

There's nothing unusual about a ham operator contacting other radio enthusiasts. Unless he's been dead for five years. When Harrie McKinsey and Ginger Vaughn decide to study for their ham radio licenses, they get pulled into this mystery and find a trail leading to a long-lost treasure somewhere in New Mexico. Before it's over, there's another murder, an abduction, and a showdown with an aging Mafia don who values treasure more than human life. Harrie, Ginger, and their merry band of FBI, APD, and private detectives have to be on their toes to prevent another murder and save a family.

Touched by the Moon
by
Lisa M. Airey

The timber wolves of South Dakota fall prey to an international ring of fur trappers. Unfortunately, timber wolves are not all they capture. Taken by a savage group of criminals, two young boys must set aside their sibling rivalry to survive the violence that surrounds them. Julie Walker is haunted by the loss of her sons and by the reappearance of the one man she never wanted to see again in her lifetime. He has an agenda and a surprising ally, forcing Julie to confront a side of herself that she has fought long and hard to deny. As victim becomes victor and hunter hunted, there is a world of gray. And Gray Walker is out for blood.

Making Story
edited by
Timothy Hallinan

It's often said that everyone has a book inside him or her, but how do you plot it? In Making Story, twenty-one novelists—who have written more than 100 books among them and sold more than a million copies—talk about how they go about turning an idea into a plot, and a plot into a book. This is an indispensable book for aspiring authors and the first in a series, each focusing on a different writing challenge.

Although all Aakenbaaken & Kent books are available online from all booksellers, we recommend you buy or order them from your local independent bookstore. If you do not have an indie bookstore, you can order them from Book & Table, an independent bookstore in Valdosta, Georgia where all Aakenbaaken & Kent books are discounted 10% and shipping is free. Ordering is easy. Just email the store at bookandtablevaldosta@gmail.com.